She watched Chase come around the front of the truck. His dark jeans were slightly worn, faded around the knees, and outlining the generous haunches of his behind. A real cowboy in black boots, a white tee was molded to the muscles of his chest. Over the tee he wore a dark blue button down shirt. The edges flapped open when he walked, and she could see the outline of his erect nipples. The beaten cowboy hat had fallen to the ground when he kissed her hello. She gripped the brim as she remembered the way her lips sizzled when he'd kissed her. He climbed into the truck, every muscle clearly defined as he hoisted himself up. He was a walking *Playgirl* poster—the southern hunk special edition, of course.

CONQUERING DR. WEXLER'S HEART

KIMBERLEY WHITE

Genesis Press Inc.

Indigo Love Stories

An imprint of Genesis Press Inc.
Publishing Company

Genesis Press, Inc.
P.O. Box 101
Columbus, MS 39703

All characters in this book have no existence outside the imagination of the author and have no relation whatsoever to anyone bearing the same name or names. They are not even distantly inspired by any individual known or unknown to the author and all incidents are pure invention.

ISBN: 1-58571-126-8
Manufactured in the United States of America

First Edition

Visit us at www.genesis-press.com
or call at 1-888-Indigo-1

CHAPTER ONE

Frozen, Dr. Sheridan Wexler stood in the clinic lobby of Duck River Family Medicine watching a little boy's blood form a pool at her feet.

"My son is bleeding! Look at him! Do something, Doctor!"

Ted moved to take the boy from his mother's arms, but the child shrank back, refusing to let the nurse touch him.

"He doesn't want to go with you!" the woman yelled, as she pulled the child from Ted's reaching hands.

Ted looked to Sheridan for leadership. "Doctor Wexler?"

The office manager rounded her desk and joined the chaos. Carolyn tried to reason with the woman. "If you won't let us take him in the back, why don't you carry him yourself?"

The boy yelled his protest and clung tighter to his mother.

"At least tell us what happened," Ted said. "Where is all the blood coming from?"

The boy shifted his body, shielding his injury from the medical crew.

"He's losing a lot of blood. We're going to have to take him." Ted struggled to pull the young boy from the screaming woman's arms. "Just let him go. It's okay if he yells." The boy shrieked, refusing to be separated from his mother.

"I can't make him go when he's like this," the mother sobbed. "Oh God, somebody help us!"

The mother's cries pierced Sheridan's heart, cutting through her fears. First and foremost she was a doctor, sworn to help and heal. She couldn't let past mistakes keep her from saving *this* little boy. She looked into the eyes of the hysterical woman. Pain and fear were reflected back at her, forcing her to dismiss the agonizing memories of all that had been stolen from her. She stepped into the middle of the chaos. "I'm Dr. Wexler, ma'am." She gently, but firmly grasped the woman's chin, compelling her to focus. "You have to let the nurse take your son so we can help him."

The woman shook her head, holding her child as tightly as he gripped her around the neck. She needed someone to take control of the situation. Signs of emotional shock were already evident in her refusal to let the medical staff treat the boy; her cries had turned to hiccups, and she blinked slowly to cover pupils that were widely dilated.

"What's his name?" Sheridan asked.

The woman looked down at the puddle of blood and trembled. Sheridan's adrenalin began to pump, reminding her she had been well-trained to handle emergency situations. Her mind raced, knowing she needed to see to the child, but she understood his mother would never release him if she didn't feel comfortable with the town's new doctor.

"What's his name, ma'am?"

"Reggie."

The boy continued to scream.

"Reggie," the woman repeated. "His father is on the way here. He works in Nashville."

Sheridan nodded, assessing the growing puddle of blood. The metallic smell filled the air.

"He's only six."

She rubbed the woman's arm, soothingly, encouraging her to calm down. "Tell me what happened."

"He was outside playing with fireworks with his brothers. One of them exploded in his hand." She looked at her son and yelled, "I told you boys not to play with those things!"

"Okay, here's what we're going to do. Ted will take him out of your arms so I can examine him." As Sheridan spoke, she helped pry the woman's cold fingers from the clinging boy.

Dr. Chase Larson burst through the entrance, filling the clinic with his massive presence. Whenever he entered a room, with the lofty height of a basketball player and the muscular body of a linebacker, he usurped everyone's attention. "I received an emergency page, Carolyn. What's going on?" He stopped abruptly, stepping in the blood trail.

The woman swung around to face him. "Everything's going to be okay now, Reggie. You remember Dr. Larson."

Chase surveyed the room, taking in the tense atmosphere. At once he was alert, and in command. His composure had an instant calming effect. Despite the continued emergency, everyone seemed to sense things would be fine now that he had arrived. A palpable concern beating off him confirmed he genuinely cared for this patient. Sheridan remembered a time when she had cared more about her patients than the perceptions of lawyers.

Chase smiled, stepping forward to rustle the boy's tight curls. "Of course I remember Reggie. Looks like you hurt your hand." The smooth timbre of his voice helped to quiet the child's shrieking cries. Within seconds, he had calmed both the patient and his hysterical mother. Things Sheridan had been too afraid to do because of past failings.

"Mom," Chase said, "Reggie needs to come in the back with me so I can take care of him."

The woman's eyes grew wide.

"You want me to help you, don't you, Reggie?"

The boy nodded, his grip slipping from around his mother's neck.

Chase glanced at Ted, giving him a silent signal to go ahead and prepare the exam room. His eyes swung to the frightened mother, and then to Sheridan. She stepped forward, reading him as well as Ted had. "Ma'am," she touched the woman's shoulder, "we need to see to him quickly." The woman's eyes met hers and Chase used the distraction to whisk Reggie away, rushing him to the examination room. Sheridan turned the sobbing woman over to Carolyn before joining them.

"What do we have?" Chase donned surgical gloves as Ted settled the young boy on the stretcher.

Sheridan answered, "Reggie was playing with fireworks and one exploded in his hand."

"How bad is it?"

"I haven't examined him yet."

Reggie writhed on the stretcher, howling from pain and fear. Ted moved around the exam room, anticipating the doctors' needs and gathering supplies.

Chase approached the stretcher slowly, speaking in low tones. "Reggie, Dr. Wexler and I are going to take care of you." Sheridan slipped on gloves, preparing to take action, as she watched him work the magic of his bedside manner. His charm worked on little boys as well as it did on her. His voice hypnotized, and his smile demanded compliance. Very quickly, he had Reggie talking about baseball while he removed the makeshift bandage his mother had applied.

"How are his vital signs?" Sheridan asked.

Ted rattled off the numbers. "Stable, but he's lost a lot of blood." He directed her attention to the basin he was using to collect the saturated bits of towel Chase had cut away from the wound. He lowered his voice. "There are three missing fingers."

Sheridan's adrenalin surged again. She had seen the danger of fireworks many times while she completed her emergency room residency. Although the boy seemed stable at this moment, he could crash quickly depending on how much blood had been lost. There were many factors to consider. How many minutes had passed, consuming the golden hour of trauma intervention? How much blood was lost at the scene and during transport to the clinic? She scanned Reggie's medical record. The boy had no significant medical history, which would work in his favor. No allergies and no past surgeries.

"How do you usually handle an emergency like this?" Sheridan asked Ted, watching Chase occupy the boy's attention while he removed the last of the bandage.

"Dr. Larson stabilizes the patient and then we transport to Nashville by ambulance for emergent care."

She continued to read the boy's history. "He'll need a tetanus shot."

"I'm on it." Ted held up the syringe he'd been preparing.

"And antibiotics." Sheridan scribbled the order. "Bet you anticipated that, too."

Ted smiled. "I'll draw the lab work when I start the IV. Just tell me what tests you want to run."

Sheridan wrote more orders then handed the chart back to Ted. He had proved his competence when she joined the clinic two months ago, but his ability to anticipate the patient's needs in a crisis was priceless. She stepped to the stretcher just as Chase pulled away the last of the wrap covering the boy's wound. A geyser of blood shot from the area where Reggie's third finger should have been, hitting Sheridan mid-chest.

Arterial bleed.

Chase jumped to apply pressure to the area, temporarily stopping the bleeding.

Sheridan rushed to his side. "Needle and sutures, Ted."

"We need those fluids, Ted." Chase's calm tone contradicted the panic in her voice.

Ted hurried to deliver the suture kit Sheridan would need to repair the artery. "Pain medicine?"

She gave the order for a low dose analgesic. "He's getting sleepy from the blood loss. We don't want to put him under too deeply." She opened the sterile kit as Chase moved onto the stretcher, cradling Reggie to keep him still while continuing to hold pressure on the bleeding artery. Ted had the IV started before she placed the sterile field.

The increased activity upset Reggie, and he struggled against Chase's hold on him. "Get that pain medicine on board before we get started."

Ted administered the pain medicine through Reggie's IV. It had an immediate effect, and the boy became limp in Chase's arms.

"Ready?" Chase eased off the stretcher, careful not to release the pressure on Reggie's hand. Sheridan grabbed a pair of sterile gloves and moved in close. He held his left hand up and she covered it with the sterile one needed for the complicated procedure they were about to perform. His hands were large; too big to be the hands of a surgeon.

"We need to reverse positions. You're the surgeon," Sheridan pointed out.

He nodded, making contact with her eyes as they silently counted, finding synchronism. He nodded once more, released Reggie's hand, and blood shot in the air from the damaged artery. Sheridan quickly replaced the pressure.

Ted moved around the stretcher, monitoring Reggie's status while the doctors worked together to stop the bleeding geyser. Chase's eyes narrowed, concentrating on the task. He held the needle and suture between thick fingers that moved with surprising agility. The doctors functioned as a team, instinctively learning each other's strengths, communicating without words, and anticipating the other's next move. They worked as if they had been in many emergency situations together.

Chase looked up for the first time, smiling with relief when the spurting arterial bleed diminished to a small ooze. With that one gesture, he renewed her belief in the importance of helping others, despite the possibility of negative consequences.

"Good job, doctors," Ted complimented. "Repairing the artery of a scared, six year old with three missing fingers is no easy task. I'll make sure Carolyn called for the ambulance."

Sheridan moved in to clean and bandage Reggie's hand.

"Thanks for your help," Chase said, removing his soiled gloves.

"It's my job, Dr. Larson."

"Let's go to talk to his parents."

"I'll stay with the patient."

"Ted can handle Reggie while we speak with his parents."

She searched for a way to avoid Reggie's parents. "Yes, but we need to complete the paperwork before the ambulance gets here."

"I'm sure they'll want to thank you for everything you did."

"No thanks is needed." Before he could protest, she turned her back, concentrating on bandaging Reggie's hand. She glanced up at Ted as he turned away from the scene.

During the past year, Sheridan had perfected the art of avoidance. She'd adopted the behavior of breezing into the room, completing her exam with as few words as possible, and disappearing as quickly as she had appeared. She left the comforting of patients and families to the nurses in the clinic. She missed not being able to invite her patients into her office for a private consultation after their exam, but she had learned that being too honest and open could place her medical license in danger. Chase hesitated behind her, offering her one last opportunity to change her mind. If she wanted to join the practice, she needed to impress the medical director of the clinic. On the other hand, if she wasn't very careful, she would find herself in front of a medical board reviewing her techniques again. Or justifying her bedside manner to her malpractice insurance carrier.

After the ambulance transported Reggie to the hospital in Nashville, Sheridan found sanctuary in her office. She had almost blown it—freezing up the way she had. No one in Duck River knew about the malpractice suit that had driven her out of Nashville, but if she didn't pull it together now, she would never be asked to join the clinic as a permanent partner. She'd left her family and friends to move to the small town, hoping to practice medicine again. She had to complete her six month trial without incident or she would be forced to find another way to continue her career.

But when she followed Reggie's cries to the lobby and saw his blood soaking the carpet, her past flashed before her. The woman had stood on the side of the road, her car a mangled mess. The truck that had T-boned her sizzled as steam shot up from the hood. Sheridan could still hear the woman's screams. "Save my baby! Save my baby!" As a physician, and a human being, she had no choice but to pull to the side of the road and offer her services.

She had performed CPR until the ambulance arrived, but an EMS vehicle was sent instead of a paramedic unit. The woman was hysterical. She didn't want Sheridan to leave her; the doctor had been the first responder and a bond had formed. Sheridan agreed to drive the woman in her car, following the ambulance closely.

The baby boy was pronounced dead after the woman's husband arrived. The scene was so emotional Sheridan broke a cardinal rule of medicine: show empathy, not sympathy. Living a patient's emotions could impair a physician, rendering one useless. The young parents had clung to her, grieving openly. Never having been a mother, but wanting children, Sheridan could not imagine the weight of their loss. In a moment of emotional intensity, she tried to comfort the parents by saying, "I wish I could have done more. If only I had had the right equipment with me, I might have been able to save him."

She would live to regret those words.

When the couple stopped grieving, they became angry. Angry with everyone: the hospital, emergency services, God—but most of all, the doctor at the scene who didn't do all she could have done to save their new baby.

"You were great when treating Reggie, but you shied away from the family. Why?"

She whipped around and found Chase standing in the doorway. "I guess I'm the stereotypical doctor. Can't deal with the emotional side of medicine."

"I thought that stereotype referred to my specialty's cold nature."

Two months of working with him had not revealed anything but warmth and caring for his patients.

"Besides," Chase continued, "there are no sides. Practicing medicine is a continuous, circular event. Skill and knowledge are a necessity, but the ability to comfort patients and their families is paramount to being a good doctor. Especially in this setting."

She watched him, wanting to share the experience that made her so guarded in her practice. She liked being the recipient of his unconditional kindness and thought to test his limits. But she remembered her career options were limited right now, and taking a chance on destroying this opportunity wasn't wise.

If Lester could have spared one drop of tenderness or understanding for her, she wouldn't be divorced from her husband *and* the clinic she had worked so hard to build.

"Was there a problem before I arrived?"

Sheridan turned away, sitting behind her desk. She knew she would have to explain why she froze when the young mother rushed into the clinic, desperately seeking help for her son. This much she could be truthful about. "I was caught off guard by the woman—and Reggie's—screaming. I froze." She shook her head. "My lack of action is unacceptable. I won't make excuses."

"Don't be so hard on yourself. I've seen the best trauma doctors freeze up under certain circumstances. What's important is that you jumped right in when it mattered."

"Reggie lost a lot of blood."

"Yes, he did. It could have turned out a lot differently. But everything worked out."

"Carolyn had to page you."

"She did."

"I wouldn't be surprised if this incident made you rethink considering me for a partner."

"I'm talking to you about what happened because we should discuss any issues that arise when treating patients. You froze for a minute or two. It happens." Chase watched her, reading her with his dark eyes. "You'll work on it."

Her lashes dropped, relieved she hadn't ruined everything. When she looked up his gaze softened. He pointed to her chest. "You should change."

The front of her shirt was soaked in Reggie's blood. "In all the excitement I didn't notice."

"We keep a few pair of scrubs here." She'd noticed his confident strut on their first meeting, and it mesmerized her as she watched him walk over to the closet. He retrieved a green surgical uniform and handed her the shirt. "The pants are probably too long. Ask Carolyn to order your size."

She let her fingers graze his when she took the shirt. Now that the emotional high of the emergency with Reggie was over, the desolation she felt over being alone in a new town hit her hard. Chase could easily wrap her in the protection of his towering height, broad shoulders, and rippling muscles. His strength of character never would have allowed him to abandon her while defending her skills and her devotion to practicing medicine. She watched him, searching for evidence that he would have stood beside her, offering encouragement, showing her he believed in her.

"Are you okay?" he asked.

She nodded.

"What were you doing here so late?"

"I was dictating my notes."

"Have you had dinner?"

She shook her head. "I'll grab something at home."

"Do you need a ride?"

"I'll change and then head home."

"I could drive you."

"No. Really. I want to walk."

He angled his head, concerned. "Are you sure you're okay?"

She offered a smile. His lips parted to question her further, but she interrupted. "It's been a long day."

He watched her for a moment before stuffing his hands in the pockets of his lab coat. "Good night."

Sheridan stared at the door after Chase had left her office. She wished she'd had the courage to take him up on his offer for a ride home. Being alone after reliving the mistake that started the downward spiral of her life was the last thing she really wanted to do.

CHAPTER 2

Sheridan sat across from Chase in the small diner, wondering if she would drown in his country charm. He'd insisted on dinner when he found her working late at the clinic and learned she'd skipped lunch. His laid back, easy going relationships with his patients had been evident the first time she'd seen him comfort a crying child, but she'd thought she could suppress their effects on her.

She watched him, her elbows on the table, as he prattled on. He liked to talk, a real turn-on for her. She'd had her share of men who were intimidated by her career and stuttered and stammered all through their dates. He moved easily from subject to subject, pausing to introduce her to the many people who came by their table to say hello.

His dark eyes and bright smile were distractively sexy. His eyebrows lifted subtly when he became intense. When he laughed, his full lips curved in a tempting smile that made her feel like she was on the beach of a tropical island under the warming sun.

"The people in Duck River really like you," Sheridan observed.

"Thank you." He sipped from his after-dinner coffee. "It's really an honor for me to serve this community; the town where I grew up." He folded his elbows on the table and leaned toward her. "I thought I might have given you the wrong idea."

"How so?"

"I don't want you to think I'm unhappy practicing here. Or that I'm ungrateful because I want to put in more time in Nashville."

"I understand. You want to keep your surgical skills current. Stay up on the latest in research."

He nodded, relaxing back. "You do understand."

"Perfectly." It had been a hard, but necessary decision for her to move to a small town like Duck River. She'd had a choice: move there or face the possibility of never practicing medicine again.

"Your background is very impressive. Duck River Family Medicine doesn't see patients with the severity of illness you're used to treating at a clinic affiliated with a teaching hospital. Why does working at a small clinic appeal to you?"

"I'm tired of the HMO's dictating what I can do for my patients."

He watched her behind a thicket of dark lashes, scrutinizing her response. His eyes were serious, but soft at the same time. Eyes that could probe deep into the depths of her soul and uncover everything she was hiding. Or he could use the intensity of his heated gaze to touch a part of her heart that hadn't been caressed in a long time, prompting her to confess all her secrets and seek shelter in his arms.

"You gave that answer on your application. I'd like to know the real reason you left Nashville to practice in a town one-tenth the size when you're at the top of your game." His tone matched his eyes. A deep, low sound she'd only expect to hear in a darkened bedroom.

"Are you having second thoughts about relocating here permanently? About leaving your family to move to Duck River?" He leaned forward and whispered, "I must tell you, I like having a colleague as beautiful as you around." He sat back in his seat, his body leaning to the left. He smiled, but not boldly. The right corner of his lips went up an imperceptible degree. "I'm looking forward to exploring your mind, Dr. Wexler. Dissecting your intensity." He sat forward again, maintaining the warmth of his gaze. "I see a lot of myself in you. Especially your love for family medicine."

She studied the uplifted corner of his mouth, trying to decide if he was toying with her. His words, innocent enough, blazed with flirtation when combined with his seductive expression. "I answered your ad for a partner because I want to practice family medicine the way it's supposed to be practiced. I want to give my patients what they need without the other doctors in the office having a collective 'vote' in my treatment plan. I want to work with someone who values what I do. Not see it as a second rate area of specialty."

"You're making an ethical stand about how you'll conduct your career." He looked pleased.

"I'm trying."

He ran a long, slender finger around the rim of his coffee cup. "I'll admit I wonder if you'll make a long term commitment to the clinic. Medicine here is about family practice, bumps and bruises, and an occasional machinery accident. You saw the worst of what we get with Reggie." He paused, reflecting while slowly stirring his coffee. "What we provide at the clinic is much more than medical care. We give the residents of Duck River a safe haven. They trust us. They know they can come just to talk if they're lonely. They can speak candidly about anything, and we don't judge them. People need that. They need to know someone who doesn't have to, cares. Make sense?"

"It does." She folded her arms on the tabletop and leaned forward. "Now tell we why you really wanted a partner."

He smiled bashfully at her reversal of the discussion. "Like I said, I'm honored to become the physician for the town I grew up in. I love what I do here, but I miss surgery. It's what I went to medical school for. I want to free up some time to work at the hospital in Nashville, so I can see patients with higher acuities and perform surgery again. A good doctor has to keep his skills sharp."

"Why did you stop operating?" she asked.

His piercing eyes swept over her face, returning to hers as he answered. "The doctor running the clinic before me passed away. When no one else stepped up to reopen it, I took over. At the time I was ready for a change. Much like what you experienced, surgery became a commercialized business venture, instead of being about helping the patient. I needed to step away to maintain my ethical standards."

She and Chase were operating from the same moral point of view. Just like earlier at Reggie's bedside, they were in sync, each understanding and identifying with the other's love of practicing medicine—miles apart, they'd experienced the same trials, fought the same fights. She couldn't help wondering, again, how he would have reacted to the malpractice suit against her.

He looked at her perceptively, but chose not to ask about her sudden shift in mood. Instead he smiled and pointed out a family sitting at a distant table. "The way small towns work is simple. You're everyone's doctor, but you're everyone's friend first. If you don't win their trust, they won't treat with you." An older woman caught his attention when she entered the diner. "Good evening, Mrs. Marks."

"Good evening, Dr. Larson."

"Have you met Dr. Wexler yet? She's considering moving to Duck River and becoming my partner."

As Sheridan answered the usual questions about her specialty, where she was living, and how she liked Duck River so far, she thought about Chase's wording. She was on a six-month trial with the clinic. At the end of that time, they would sit down with Ted and Carolyn to decide if she would make a good addition to the clinic. He made it sound as if, after two months, it was a done deal. She guarded against false security as she continued her conversation with Mrs. Marks. The clinic meant too much to Chase for him to take the decision of getting a partner lightly.

"Will we see you in church, Dr. Wexler?" Mrs. Marks asked.

She looked to Chase for the right answer.

"She'll be there, Mrs. Marks. She's been settling in. You understand. But she'll be there this Sunday. I'll escort her myself."

"The Reverend and I will expect you both for dinner afterwards."

"Did I mention Mrs. Marks is the reverend's wife?" he asked Sheridan, unexplained mischief gleaming in his eyes.

"No, you didn't," Mrs. Marks scolded. "Dr. Wexler, Chase has known me and my husband since he was a youngster, and sometimes he takes liberties with that fact. He was a very," she paused to search for the right wording, "precocious child."

Chase's gaze never wavered from hers. "She's warning you to be careful around me." The right corner of his mouth lifted in a grin that said he enjoyed teasing Mrs. Marks. Underneath his professional manner was man who liked to play.

Mrs. Marks frowned at him. She silently asked many questions as she looked between the doctors. Probably wondering the same thing Sheridan was wondering: Was he flirting with her?

That would be bad.

Or very, very good.

Looking across the table at Chase's rugged good looks made her want to forget she was in Duck River to revive her career, not start a romance. But he was built with lean muscle, and had the sexiest strut. His black hair was always trimmed neatly. His wavy sideburns begged for her touch. His lips looked soft and able to please. She could listen to his sexy drawl late into the night. He was a gentle, intelligent cowboy who would throw her over his shoulder and carry her to his bedroom as quickly as he would read a philosophy book to her.

"Dinner on Sunday then, Dr. Wexler?" Mrs. Marks confirmed.

"I look forward to it."

Mrs. Marks said her goodbyes and left to meet her friends.

Chase shook his head as he watched her walk away. "Another key point about small towns: if you have any chance of surviving, you have to be accepted by the church. The reverend and Mrs. Marks hold a lot of clout in Duck River. You'll get to know all the players soon enough."

"You were a precocious child, huh?" She could see it in him.

He grinned, but didn't answer. "Another piece of chocolate cake, please." He signaled the waitress.

"I couldn't. I'm stuffed." She leaned back and patted her stomach.

"Of course you can. We shared the last one. You can share one more with me." The unruly right side of his mouth lifted upward. How could she say no to a smile like his? His perfectly aligned teeth shone at her behind full lips made for speaking words of seduction. In the hectic pace of the past year, she'd forgotten the importance of a good smile. His was genuine, meant to brighten the receiver's day.

"Help me eat another piece?" Chase asked.

"You're very persuasive."

"And precocious."

Sheridan grinned. "That, too."

"I like making you do the things that are good for you."

"Goofing off from work and eating too much cake are good for me?"

"Absolutely. It's my personal prescription for you."

The waitress delivered a thick slice of cake.

"And what would you prescribe for me, Dr. Wexler?"

Sheridan watched the fork disappear between his enticing lips. She stared at him, mesmerized by the rhythmic working of his jaw.

"Well?"

"A dose of humble pie might be in order."

He placed his hand on his chest, splaying his manicured fingers wide. "Are you calling me arrogant?"

"Not exactly. I haven't found the exact term I would use to

describe a man who uses his persuasive powers to get me to do what he wants."

As Chase's hand slid from his chest, the bright smiled disappeared, and his lips pressed together in a serious straight line. He leaned forward and whispered, "I'd call me very lucky."

He covered her hand with his and an unexpected warm thrill moved up her arm, catching her off guard. She stared at the connection, marveling at how his heat traveled, wrapping her in a warm glow. His touch was soft and gentle. He had the pampered hands of a surgeon, which were a contrast to the raw masculinity of his physique.

She let her eyes move up his arm, over his wide chest, past broad shoulders, ending at his smiling face. As if diving into a pool of warm water, she toppled into the depth of his gaze, completely submerged in his heat. He shamelessly held her captive. "Damn lucky," he added.

A young woman sitting at a table of teenaged girls detected their connection and giggled, breaking Chase's hold. Sheridan pulled her hand away and placed it in her lap. "Your admirers are shocked, Dr. Larson."

He turned to the table of giggling schoolgirls. He nodded hello and turned back to her. "We should get out of here. Don't want to encourage the high schoolers, what with their raging hormones and all."

"I agree we should be going—me to my house and you to yours." She reached for her purse. "Don't want to scandalize the new doctor and all."

He laughed, a warm, rich sound filled with promise.

She reached for the bill. Calculating her portion of dinner

would be a welcomed distraction from the effects of his laugh.

"Dinner's on me."

She stood and headed for the door. "Thank you."

"Sheridan, wait. Let me drive you home." Chase pulled bills from his wallet, tossed them on the table, and hurried after her.

"I can walk." The last thing she needed was to be alone with him. Halfway through dinner she'd begun imagining potential outcomes of spending more time with him. His undivided attention during their meal had validated her daydreams. He was a sexy man, easily able to tempt her physically, but what made Chase different was that he could seduce her mind. His subtle flirting could take her somewhere she wasn't prepared to go.

"Don't forget Sunday," he called after her.

She turned to wave goodbye. Chase stood next to their table, his large presence usurping the room. He made her think of rough and tumble play, long kisses, and lingering caresses. His eyes met hers with the distinct look a man gives a woman when he has intimate things on his mind. "Sunday?"

"Church, and dinner with the reverend and Mrs. Marks. I'm looking forward to it."

"Sunday." She watched the left corner of his mouth lift in satisfaction before making a hasty exit. Dr. Chase Larson could get her into more trouble than she could handle.

Chase led a charmed life. Coming from a family which had built its wealth the hard way, he marched out into the world and completed medical school, mastering the curriculum with ease.

His mother and father were in good health and very supportive of their only son. He had four beautiful older sisters with whom he got along wonderfully well. Most women considered him a quality specimen, and he worked hard in his gym to keep his body in shape so he didn't disappoint. He was liked in Duck River. He lived in a beautiful home and drove a nice vehicle. He didn't want for anything.

Yes, he had led a charmed life. So it appeared to outsiders.

Building wealth the hard way had taken its toll on the entire family. He loved his sisters dearly, but they had fought terribly as kids. He was the only boy, and the baby, and jealousy ran deep when his father showed him favor about certain "manly" things. Medical school came easy to him, but his social life suffered because of the long hours, making it difficult to compete against the star quarterback for popularity and female affection.

He enjoyed practicing in his hometown and gaining their respect as an adult, but he carried a heavy burden in being responsible for an entire town's health and well-being. The women loved him—on the surface. A thirty-two-year-old, single physician made good marriage material. Truthfully, they loved the son of one of the wealthiest families in town. He lived in a house built to his specifications, and it was gorgeous. But it was empty. He suffered silently, longing to fill his home with a dynamic woman who loved him for who he was inside; a woman he could cherish without fear of being the conductor of the train that would take her to housewife land.

Chase closed his eyes, conjuring up a glimpse of Sheridan. He was looking forward to Sunday. It would be his best opportunity to impress her. As intelligent as she was beautiful, he was instantly attracted to Dr. Sheridan Wexler. She appeared to be a little stressed, maybe even uptight, but he could remedy that. As far as he could see, it was her only fault. Very thorough in her patient's care, he often passed her office on his way home for the evening and saw her hard at work preparing for the next day. It could all be a show for his benefit—she hadn't been offered the partnership yet—but he sensed she was acting sincerely. She was a professional, hardly ever displaying her playful side. If Sheridan ever became involved with him, it would be because she was genuinely attracted to him, not because she was looking for her ticket out of Duck River.

Lester Wexler sat in his in-laws' living room, smug in his ability to mold them to his will. From the day he'd walked into their daughter's life three years ago, they'd formed a bond. He was the perfect catch for their strong-willed daughter: handsome, intelligent, wealthy, and on the fast track with his medical career. When he'd said his vows to Sheridan, he joined with her family, giving them the son they'd lost in a difficult childbirth. He enjoyed filling that empty space for them. They were good people. And Sheridan was just what he needed to balance his life.

Still, he'd been wary about coming. After all, he was the one who had asked for the divorce. He had told Sheridan unequivocally that she had to leave their practice before they lost all their patients. He worried her parents wouldn't understand what he'd been forced to do, but as he sat in the parlor, sipping his tea, he knew he'd always be their "son."

"Mother," Lester placed his tea cup carefully atop the china saucer, "I have truly enjoyed talking with you this afternoon."

Mrs. Anderson lit up, happy to have a link to their only child in her living room. Sheridan's leaving had been hard on her parents. She was exceptionally close to her mother, and held her father's heart in her hands. Lester watched the older woman with genuine affection. When he looked at her, he saw his future with Sheridan. An older version of his ex-wife, Mrs. Anderson had a pug nose, round brown eyes and dark lashes. Her skin remained flawless, often causing people to mistake her for Sheridan's sister instead of her mother. And she insisted on staying in shape. She worked out religiously, spent quality time with her lifelong friends, and exercised her mind by taking courses at the local college.

Mrs. Anderson placed her tea on the end table. "We're always glad to see you, Lester."

He nodded in thanks. "It's getting late and I haven't told you why I've come."

"You want to know if we know where Sheridan is," she interjected shrewdly.

Mr. Anderson joined them, taking his place next to his wife on the sofa. "She still hasn't contacted you?"

"No, she hasn't, and, well," he paused for effect. "Sir, I don't mind telling you I miss her terribly." He looked pointedly at Mrs. Anderson. She was the romantic. He would win his case by playing on her sympathy. "I've made a terrible mistake ending our marriage. I see it clearly now."

"It took you long enough," Mr. Anderson muttered.

His wife quickly put her hand on his knee. "The media attention and the possibility of losing the clinic was enough strain to end a marriage."

"Those things are not important when you love someone," Mr. Anderson added, determined not to be silenced. "You should have supported Sheridan more."

"You're right." Lester sat forward on the edge of his seat. He'd come prepared to humble himself if that was what it took to get the information he needed. "Nothing should have kept me from protecting my wife. I should have been stronger. I have to make this right. I need to speak to Sheridan." He looked between them, unable to determine their collective state of mind. In order to succeed, he had to win them both over. The Andersons made all major decisions as a marital unit. If one was against revealing Sheridan's whereabouts, he wouldn't get the information.

"Son—"

"Yes, Dad?"

"Give us some time to discuss it." Mr. Anderson stood up, effectively ending the conversation and the visit. "We'll call you with our decision."

Lester Wexler was a good man. He had his faults. He knew this. But he did love Sheridan. Sometimes his career and marriage goals were in conflict. He knew this, too. Many days he and Sheridan would return from a long day at the clinic just to continue workday arguments late into the night. He'd slept on the sofa more nights than he could count.

His medical career was important to him—sometimes more important than his wife. He came from a long line of physicians. His roots could be traced back to a man who served as medicine man to the slaves on the plantation in South Carolina. One of his ancestors had founded the first medical school in Mississippi to train black physicians. His mother and father were both neurologists. His sister practiced obstetrics. His little brother trained physicians in the military. Every generation of Wexlers spawned a pioneer in medicine, and his father was determined Lester, the oldest child, would be the benchmark of his generation.

His success as a physician had been programmed in his mind at an early age. Never was he allowed to consider exploring a career other than medicine. This didn't bother him. He embraced his parents' goals. He loved having the godly power to heal. It soon became apparent he'd leave his mark on medicine in the area of research. His lifelong goal was to find a cure for sickle cell anemia. Practicing in family medicine exposed him to families struggling with the disease. With family medicine being Sheridan's love, they should have been a perfect fit.

Sheridan loved the satisfaction of spending quality time with her patients. She often fell behind in her schedule because she was talking with a family in her office. She delved into the minutest complaints, ordering extensive tests until the problem was resolved. She'd uncovered several obscure disease pathologies that might have gone untreated if not for her diligence. Her patient's loved her, and she loved her patients.

On the surface, these seem like good qualities. Sheridan was the humanistic, altruistic physician, while Lester was driven and passionate to succeed in technological advances that would benefit a significant portion of the population. But Lester's work required funding. And Sheridan didn't care if the HMO's denied a claim—as long as her patients had the treatment they needed, the clinic could pick up the tab. This prompted them to take on more physician partners to meet the financial burden. More physicians brought more insurance companies and their regulations. The clinic had to be managed as a business, not as an extension of an intimate partnership between husband and wife. So when Sheridan's mistake threatened to end the clinic and all that he'd worked for, he had no choice but to pick his career over his marriage.

A week after sitting in his in-laws parlor, Lester answered Mr. Anderson's page.

"My wife and I made this decision because we're worried about our daughter. We won't take sides in your marriage, but we do believe a man should have a chance to right his wrongs."

"I will, Dad."

"We believe you love our daughter."

"I do. I want to make this right with Sheridan. I love her and I need her. I know she still loves me, too. We can work everything out and save our marriage."

"I've made bad decisions in my own marriage. My wife gave me another chance. Sheridan is a reasonable girl. She'll hear you out, but it's up to you to be sincere in what you want from your relationship with her."

Lester danced from foot to foot, anxious to make preparations to reclaim his wife. "Yes, sir."

"You'll tell Sheridan we're worried about her and to call her mother?"

"Absolutely. It'll be the first thing I say to her."

"When will you leave?"

"Today. As soon as I can arrange for a doctor to cover my patients."

CHAPTER 3

Chase hadn't dressed up for church in ages. Today, he'd pulled the most impressive suit he owned from the back of his closet. He matched the navy blue fabric to a powder blue shirt and striped tie. He'd spent thirty minutes trying to remember how to knot his tie. His hair was freshly cut and his mustache neatly trimmed. He'd oiled his body carefully and doused himself in his best cologne before leaving the house. He checked the polish on his brown wingtips as he got out of his truck. Satisfied he was at his best, he stepped up to the porch to ring Sheridan's doorbell.

He watched in frozen fascination as she approached. She seemed to come toward him in slow motion, giving him time to take in every curve of her sweet body. She wore a clingy, scoop neck blue dress closely matching the color of his suit—they were on the same wavelength. His eyes traveled down her body to the spike heeled shoes accentuating her calves. He fought to remain composed, finding his voice as she unlocked the screen door. "Good morning," he said, stepping inside.

"Good morning." She walked away, giving him the rear view of her spectacular body. "I just need to grab my purse."

Her generously rounded bottom swung rhythmically back and forth, hypnotizing him. Unable to speak, he nodded. If all doctors looked this sexy, insurance carriers would drop their coverage rates; the view alone would be enough profit. He silently scolded himself. If he didn't pull it together, he'd never make it through dinner. "Do you mind if I get some water?" he called.

"Help yourself."

Chase found the kitchen and poured himself a glass of water. There weren't many dishes in the cabinets. The refrigerator was stocked with healthy foods: vegetables and lots of fresh fruits. As he gulped his water, he noticed the entire flat seemed sparsely decorated. It didn't seem the norm for a woman. Most were good at decorating and coordinating. They kept their refrigerators stocked and brought extra sets of dishes in case unexpected company arrived.

Is she planning to stay? The answer had become more important to him than just finding someone to assist him at the clinic. There was a quiet quality to Sheridan that made him want to get inside her head—and explore the area around her heart. She seemed in need of a gentle stroking and a protective embrace.

"Ready?" Sheridan joined him in the kitchen.

"You look great."

"Thank you."

He placed his empty glass in the sink and followed her out. "You didn't bring much with you."

"What?"

"Your place has only the bare minimum."

She became uneasy, her step faltering.

He reacted quickly, realizing she might have found his comment tactless. "Believe me, I understand. You didn't want to move everything here when you weren't sure you'd be staying permanently."

"Everything I own is in Nashville in storage."

"Well, I want you to know everyone at the clinic thinks you'd be an asset. The six month trial is pretty much a formality on our part. We hope you feel the same way."

She watched him as he sputtered on, silently challenging him. Women usually fawned over him, captivated by his every word, eager to impress him. Sheridan simply watched him, waiting to be wowed.

"I'm putting you on the spot. I don't mean to. I'd hoped to make you feel more secure. Coming to a small town without any family can be stressful. I wanted to give you some sense of security."

Her expression softened appreciatively. "Thank you, but maybe we should see it through before we make any decisions."

"Fair enough." He didn't like her hesitation, but he didn't want her to feel pressured. Instead of appearing suave and irresistible, he'd come off as too anxious. They walked to his truck in silence, him berating himself for appearing desperate. "Looks like I keep doing the wrong thing today. I never considered you'd be wearing a dress and couldn't climb up into the cab of my truck."

"I love big trucks." She ran her fingertips across the shiny black paint job. "Maybe you could give me a hand."

He seized the opportunity to touch her and show off his strength. He grasped her waist, his hands swallowing her tiny waistline. "That I can do."

"Oh my goodness," she gasped.

He lifted her easily; bench-pressing two hundred pounds every day had finally paid off. He turned, slowly, in a complete circle before gently placing her in the passenger's seat.

"You're strong."

"I'm a big ol' country boy." He smiled, feeling he had made

amends for his lack of consideration.

Her eyes softened, roaming the length of his body. He puffed up his chest, accentuating the best part of his body for her inspection. The gesture made her realize she was staring, and her head snapped forward. He leaned into the truck and pulled the ends of the seatbelt together at her hip. His face came close to hers. He took in a deep, discrete breath, savoring her flowery fragrance.

"Buckle up." He snapped the belt together and closed her door, confidence in his ability to seduce her growing.

"Nice truck," Sheridan said as they started for the church. "I didn't know they were this luxurious inside." She ran her hand over the soft leather seat.

"You'll need a truck or a SUV if you expect to survive the rainy season in Duck River."

"I'll keep that in mind."

Another answer he didn't want to hear when he was trying to read her for signs of mutual attraction. She insisted on remaining noncommittal. He wanted her to be determined to become a partner at the clinic, moving past that issue and onto examining the possibilities of spending her personal time with him.

She pointed to the stereo. "Do you mind?"

"No, not at all."

Sheridan played around with the buttons until she punched the one that filled the cab with Luther Vandross's velvety voice. She relaxed, letting her head fall against the seat. Her hands rested on her thighs, calling his attention to their lean outline beneath the sheer fabric of her dress. "Do you like Luther?"

"*A House is not a Home* is my all-time favorite song." His voice remained strong despite the rasp in his throat caused by her innate sexuality.

"I like that one, too." She closed her eyes and hummed along with the music. She was a picture of erotic perfection: pretty face and amazing body, wrapped in the leather cab of his testosterone-driven F150. Songs had been written about these moments. She opened her eyes, catching him staring.

"Do you sing?" he asked, covering for his unrestrained observation of her figure.

"I sing all the time. I just can't carry a tune."

He laughed at her easy humor. He hadn't seen this side of her before. She insisted on being all business at the clinic. Maybe she was beginning to loosen up around him. Seizing the moment, he asked, "What would need to happen to make you want to stay in Duck River?"

She watched his profile as he drove. "I don't know if there's any one thing that will do it. I want to fit in with the philosophy and mission of the clinic. The town would have to accept me and trust my skills, or I wouldn't be any value to you."

Just having her near was priceless. "But what do you need to persuade you to stay? What's important in making your decision?"

A touch of sadness revealed itself in her answer. "I want my skills validated. I want to be accepted."

Why would anyone question her medical skills? The town would love her. She was smart and focused. She took her duties seriously and cared about her patients' outcomes. He hadn't penetrated her protective shell, but he was sure that when he did, he'd find a woman as beautiful inside as out. As he listened to her talk about the course of her career thus far, he wondered about her personal life.

Has she experienced her one great romance? Has she sacrificed a love affair for school? For her practice? Does she have plans for marriage and a family? Or has she given up hoping for those things because of the demands of caring for others?

They arrived at the church just as he had decided to delve into Sheridan's personal life, saving him from crossing the boundaries of their professional relationship. But once they were inside the church, he decided very quickly that he'd have to cross that line if he wanted a chance to explore a relationship with the new doctor. At first his chest swelled with pride when every man in the sanctuary watched him, envious of Sheridan on his arm. A throng of curious townspeople greeted them; his plan to make her part of the town had worked better than he'd anticipated. The men tripping over themselves to get an introduction was what made his possessive side flare. Mrs. Marks had told everyone about the charming new doctor, and they couldn't wait to meet her and assess her for themselves.

Scott Stoner parted the crowd of eager men. "Dr. Larson, please introduce me to this beautiful lady."

He should have expected the young, pompous, self-titled "Best Catch in Duck River," to make an appearance once he heard about Sheridan. Begrudgingly, Chase introduced them. Scott took Sheridan's hand between his with too much familiarity. "Dr. Larson should have brought you out to my ranch as soon as you came to town. He has told you about me, hasn't he?"

Sheridan glanced in Chase's direction, intuitively catching the negative vibe. "I'm sorry. I've met so many people..."

"Of course you have. I'd imagine every eligible man in town has scheduled a check-up with you." He laughed—guffawed, actually. "The Stoner family supplies the feed and grain to all the farmers in this vicinity. They come from miles and miles away to buy our product." He continued in a self-assured, arrogant manner that made the hair on Chase's neck stand up. "The Stoner family keeps the Larson family's champion horses alive and well. Hmm. I'm surprised Dr. Larson didn't mention that to you. Anyway, you must have dinner with me after service."

Chase wished he could read Sheridan's mind, but he couldn't, so he went with what jealousy dictated. He placed his arm around her waist and pulled her away from Scott. "We have plans for dinner." He looked down into Sheridan's questioning eyes. "We should find a seat."

It took a moment for him to stamp out his jealousy. It was inappropriate, he told himself. But he was a man, and he didn't like men hitting on the woman he planned to get to know better. Scott had always been the wealthy jock who got everything he wanted. Chase was not about to let him upset his chances with Sheridan.

She tried to hide her grin behind the program.

"You don't have to look so amused. I embarrassed myself back there."

"Yes, you did. Town jock?" She tilted her head in Scott's direction. He was sitting across the aisle—and he was watching her every move.

"Don't look at him."

She raised an eyebrow.

He cleared his throat, backing down. "Unless you're interested in him."

"He's a bit too arrogant for my taste."

"You said I was arrogant at the diner."

She placed her finger against her chin. "Did I?"

He felt like throwing a temper tantrum. Scott had succeeded in taking away all the points he had scored with Sheridan. He wondered if inviting him out back for a good old fashioned butt whooping would win a few back. "Well, if you'd prefer to have dinner with *Scott Stoner*—"

"I wouldn't." She let the moment settle before going on. "You do understand this is two colleagues spending the afternoon together, don't you? This isn't a date."

He debated the right way to handle her question. He could tell the truth and risk coming on too strong. Or he could smile and nod, letting Sheridan set the pace of their relationship. He thought of how distant she had been when she first joined the clinic and decided the latter approach would be the best. His lips curled into his broadest smile. He nodded. "Of course, colleagues spending the afternoon together. Me, helping you, become familiar with the town."

Sheridan watched Chase's mischievous smile brighten his face, and she knew she was in too deep to walk away. For two months she'd successfully kept her guard up against his charms. Thinking she had it all under control, she'd allowed herself to walk right into his seductive web. It all happened too quickly. It might have happened over dinner, or during the emergency in the clinic with Reggie. Maybe even the moment he wrapped his arm around her shoulders and possessively whipped her away from Scott. It could have even been when he took her hand at the reverend's house during prayer before they began eating. Whenever it occurred, the attraction was strong, and it was undeniable.

Chase felt it, too. He couldn't stop watching her. When he lifted her into the cab of his truck, his fingers lingered on her waist a little longer than necessary, and he brought her face a little closer than needed when he hoisted her up. Not to mention, she had to remind him twice that she had learned how to buckle a seatbelt many years ago.

She folded her hands in her lap to keep from wringing them. They were sitting in the darkened cab of his truck on the way to her temporary home. The silence had become thick a few minutes into the drive. She searched for something to shatter the quiet and keep her mind occupied, but pictures of Chase in compromising positions kept creeping into her head.

What woman could blame me for having salacious thoughts about him? No woman with eyes, that's for sure. She marveled at his silhouette. It was too dark to make out the fine features of his moustache and sideburns, but no problem—she'd memorized those during dinner. There *was* enough light in the cab of the truck to make out the chiseled strength of his jaw.

Chase lifted his hand and scratched the side of his nose, bringing new appreciation to how straight and perfect it was. "Mrs. Marks gave you the lowdown on everyone in town."

"What did Scott mean about your family and horses?"

"Duck River's main export is feed and grain. Everybody around here is connected to horses in some way; breeding them or racing them. My family runs the largest horse ranch in this part of Tennessee."

"Breeding or racing?"

"Racing. One of my father's studs finished fifth in the Kentucky Derby last year. He swears he had a winner this year, too."

"Really? It must have been great growing up in the middle of all that excitement."

He shrugged one broad...muscular...well-developed shoulder. "I suppose," he answered modestly.

"Why did you choose to pursue a career in medicine? It seems you would have followed in your father's footsteps."

"I love riding, but I don't like the commercialization of the horse trade."

"Ouch."

"Yep. My philosophy didn't go over well with my father. It's all gravy though. My four older sisters work in the family business. So do their husbands."

"You're the youngest and the only boy?"

"Before you say it," he chuckled, "I was never spoiled. My mother will tell you I was just well loved." He pulled into the dirt drive next to the house she was renting. He cut the motor and turned to face her. "Would you like to go riding?"

"I don't know how to ride."

"Now there's a tragedy. I can picture you atop a strong, black stallion."

The cab of the truck heated up fifteen degrees.

"I'll have to teach you to ride."

Why did that sound obscene? She shook her head, clearing her mind. She was projecting all her midnight fantasies onto him.

Every word he muttered seemed to have double meaning.

"Are you up for it?"

"I don't know. Horses are big, scary creatures."

"Horses are beautiful, graceful animals."

"I'd be afraid to touch one, let alone get on one."

"The secret to life is to have no fear. Weren't you paying attention to Reverend Marks' sermon?"

"He did say that, didn't he?"

"Yes, he did. And he speaks the truth. We'll start off slow. I'll take you out to the ranch and show you around. Then we'll let you touch a horse. Work our way up to riding."

"It could take quite a few visits before I'd actually ride one."

"I'm not going anywhere," Chase answered a bit too quickly. Noticing this, his eyes dropped.

"I'm not either. At least not for a while."

Chase looked at her through thick, dark lashes which were unable to hide the heat of his wishes. "Good. I'll have time to get to know you. We can start with me teaching you to ride."

"I'm willing to give it a try as long as you promise to be patient and not push me."

He held up his hands in surrender. "I won't push." He gave her the brilliant smile, full of self-confidence, but fringed with modesty. "We'll start next weekend."

Sheridan found herself hoping the workweek would fly by quickly. "I should go inside."

"I've kept you all day," he said.

"Work in the morning."

"Work in the morning," he echoed as he got out of the truck.

She watched him walk around to open her door. His rugged

body was graceful beneath the elegant cut of his suit. He was made of hard angles, but moved stealthily with a glide that could only be natural. She could see him sitting astride a stubborn horse, demanding its obedience.

He opened her door and looked up at her with dark, hopeful eyes. "I had a good time, Dr. Wexler."

"It was fun." She swung her legs around toward him.

Chase reached up and grasped her waist. He had helped her in and out of the truck several times, but she still reacted as if it were the first time he'd touched her. His tapered fingers engulfed her waist, spreading their heat throughout her body. His hold was authoritative and sure, leaving no doubt about his ability to thrill. She felt safe and protected…aroused, and in great danger of falling under his spell. He lifted her high, setting her gently on the ground. He did not step back, effectively blocking her between his body and the truck. Her stomach fluttered in anticipation of his next move.

"You were right," Chase said.

Slowly, cautiously, Sheridan looked up at him. "Right about what?" she dared to ask.

"Perceptive. Maybe I should say you're very perceptive."

She found it hard to maintain eye contact with his intense gaze. He stepped closer, his body applying a light pressure against hers. "Aren't you going to ask me what you were so perceptive about?"

She cleared her throat. "What was I so perceptive about?"

"I hoped you thought this was a date." He pressed closer. "And I was jealous as hell when Scott hit on you."

Before she could answer, Chase dipped his head and pressed

his lips to hers. The softest lips she'd ever tasted assaulted her with gentle determination. His hands wound around her waist and pulled her into his solid mass. The tip of his tongue pushed against her lips, tenderly asking permission to invade her mouth. His kisses were cherry flavored, and warm, like homemade pie. He hummed as he deepened the kiss, letting her know he was enjoying what she gave in return. Her feet left the ground as he lifted her, holding her captive to the charms of his kiss.

His right hand came up to cup her face as he brought her back to the ground. He wasn't finished exploring her, or displaying the depth of his attraction. He pulled her into his kiss with his grip on her waist, and his touch on her cheek. His left hand slipped lower, bringing her entire body into his by the hold on her bottom.

Her eyes were closed, her body melting into his. For a dangerous moment, she gave herself completely over to Chase and the way his kisses made her feel. She dropped her guard and released caution. She stopped her mind from computing the consequences and analyzing possible outcomes. As he raised her up on tiptoe, she felt as if she were flying, without a worry in the world. She inhaled the musk scent of his cologne, and her body reacted to the sensual aroma.

She wanted nothing more than to stop pretending she wasn't attracted to him.

She wanted to invite Chase inside and ask him to make love to her all night long.

"Stop!" She shoved him away.

"What?" He looked as confused as she felt.

"This can't happen." She pointed at his chest, and then her

own.

"Why not?"

"It can't." She pushed past him and sprinted to her door, but Chase followed. She held out her hand, stopping his pursuit. "Thank you for introducing me to the town, but this won't happen again."

"Can't. Won't. What are you talking about, Sheridan? It did happen. It will happen again."

She shoved her key into the lock and rushed to open the door. "Good night."

"No good night. We have to talk about this. We can't leave it like this. Let's talk about whatever is bothering you."

Sheridan closed the door, shutting him out.

She felt like such a fool! Not only had she made out with her boss, she had handled the situation childishly. He wanted to talk, which would lead to his wanting explanations. Explanations she couldn't give him. She couldn't explain her apprehension about having a relationship at work without telling him about the malpractice suit. Once she had divulged that much information, he would insist on knowing all the details. He wouldn't take a chance on losing his clinic because of a brief moment of attraction.

How did she let herself get into this mess? Hadn't she learned with Lester that mixing a relationship with work could only lead to disaster? She had come to Duck River to start over, not upset her life more.

Sheridan was still leaning against the door contemplating a way to correct her mistake when the phone rang. Chase had given up and driven away in his truck ten minutes ago. The phone continued to ring—stopping and starting again. He wasn't the type of man to give up easily. He'd want to dissect every one of her arguments about pursuing a relationship. It would be better to work this out with him outside of the clinic, before they returned to work. She should make it clear the only thing she was looking for was a place to practice—not a relationship complicated by work with the town's doctor.

She mustered up enough courage to tell Chase how she felt and ran to answer the phone. "Hello?"

The line went dead.

All for the best. She needed time to formulate an apology. She had to find just the right words to explain why she couldn't get involved with him. Most of all, she needed time to convince herself she would be able to carry on a professional relationship with a man who made her heart melt whenever he walked into her space.

CHAPTER 4

No woman had ever affected him this way. Closing the door in his face after the most sensuous kiss in his life should have been enough to shame him into never dating again. It had the opposite effect. The emotional impact of holding Sheridan in his arms, however brief, taunted him throughout the weekend. Now he'd barricaded himself in his office, careful to dash down the corridor to the exam rooms, avoiding her. He wanted to barge in on her and demand answers, but if there was any chance of salvaging their "relationship," he had to behave calmly, exerting maximum self-control.

"Can I come in?"

He looked up and saw his dream materialized. Her hair bounced as she stepped up to his desk. She hid her femininity beneath a sterile-looking, white lab coat. He had experienced her heat, and a modest gray pantsuit could not hide it. Her eyes glittered with sensuality while her mouth was set in an expression of serious contemplation.

In that moment, something as innocent as the glide of her stride helped him decide he would pursue Dr. Wexler until he conquered her heart.

He pushed back slightly from his desk and waited for Sheridan to continue.

"I wanted to clear up any misunderstanding from this weekend."

"Misunderstanding? That's an interesting choice of words."

She shifted her weight onto her right foot. She'd prepared her speech, and his interrupting threw her off balance.

Good.

"What exactly did I misunderstand, Sheridan?"

She tossed her head to the left and pushed her hair behind her ear. It shined like rich velvet. The next time he kissed her he would weave his fingers through it, testing its softness.

"I had a good time this weekend," she said, "but I'm not looking for anything other than friendship. Especially with my boss."

"I'm not your boss. I'm your colleague."

"I'm not looking for an office romance."

He nodded slowly, studying her.

She shoved her hands in the pockets of her lab coat. "Then we're all right?"

"We're fine. Can you tell me exactly what kind of romance you *are* looking for?"

"I'm not looking for—I'm not looking for any kind of romance right now. I want to concentrate on my career."

He rose from his chair, rounding the desk in three long strides. "I just need clarification about a few things."

Sheridan cleared her throat and fought to meet his eyes. "Yes?"

"I misunderstood everything that happened between us this weekend?"

"Well, I wouldn't—"

He stepped closer. "What I thought was a man and a woman having a good time together—connecting—was only business for you."

"It—I—"

"When we kissed, the connection wasn't so strong that it was almost scary? Scary enough to make you run in the house and shut me out?" He stepped closer and gave in to temptation. He threaded his fingers through her hair and cupped her face. "I had it all wrong."

Sheridan looked up at him with a warm expression that openly displayed the internal battle she was fighting.

"There's no connection between us. The way you're looking at me means nothing."

"Dr. Larson." Ted knocked on the door. "Your next patient is ready."

Sheridan stepped back and away from his touch.

"I'll be right there, Ted." He turned to Sheridan. "We should finish this conversation later."

"Chase." She stopped him as he placed his hand on the doorknob.

"Yes?" He turned to her, giving her his full attention. His eyes roamed her face, lingering over her lips. Lips he knew from brief experience could bring him great pleasure.

Sheridan arched her back: a cat raising her hackles, a kitten needing to be petted. "I'm firm on this."

"Really?"

She cleared her throat. "Really. To continue this conversation would only make working together awkward."

"And you really want the partnership position here."

"I do."

"You've made that clear." He stepped up to her, shattering her three feet of comfort zone. He wanted her off balance, unable to form logical arguments. He would not allow her to buffer her feelings for him. "I don't know why you turned me away Sunday. Maybe some guy broke your heart. Is that it? He didn't treat you right, so now you've taken a holy vow not to give your heart to another man."

"You're being arrogant again."

Laughter rumbled in his throat and tumbled past his lips, but didn't touch the seriousness of his eyes. "Maybe. Maybe not. Could be I know mixed signals when I see them."

The day she had walked into the clinic a piece of him latched onto her. She seemed to always be on his mind. He sneaked glances at her during the day, heard her voice when he lay down to sleep at night, and hadn't been able to eat a good meal in two months because of the butterflies swarming in his stomach.

The way she kissed him revealed she felt the same way. He didn't understand why she was fighting his efforts, and he didn't care.

Sheridan crossed her arms over her chest. "I'm not expressing myself very clearly."

Before she could continue, he stepped up and took her in his arms. She went soft, confirming his suspicions; she wanted him as badly as he wanted her. He caressed her cheek with the tip of his nose, bringing his lips next to ear. "Tell me this doesn't feel right."

"This is not why I came in here," she answered breathlessly.

"I know." He pulled away and smiled down at her. "I think you came in here because you missed me." He tightened his arms around her waist, bringing her into his body. "I've been avoiding you all day because all I've wanted to do is take you in my arms and kiss you again." He lowered his head and placed a light kiss on her lips.

She blinked, unable to speak.

"You turned my head the first day you walked into this office." He kissed her cheek. "Now, if I can only get *you* to admit you noticed *me*." He slowly released her waist and stepped backward out of his office, leaving her dazed.

The last thing Lester needed right now was a ditzy woman behind the counter of the rental car agency. With her running the place, he understood why his reservation was screwed up.

He had planned to be in Duck River yesterday. He couldn't find coverage for his patients until the end of the week, which meant he had to see everyone on his schedule. *Well, it might not be such a bad thing.* It gave him a few days to formulate a plan. Sheridan was no slouch. Winning her back would be more complicated than showing up and declaring his love. She would make him prove his sincerity, and then he'd still have to convince her they could start over and build a new life together. Sheridan was intelligent and independent. She didn't need a man to take care of her. There would have to be a benefit to falling in love. Love was a wonderful thing, but the man couldn't enhance her life in some way, she wouldn't give her heart over to him.

"Okey-dokey, Dr. Wexler. We have a car for you. It's coming from the other lot and should be here in less than fifteen."

And then he could be on his way. He checked his watch. It

was still possible to arrive in Duck River by the afternoon. Everything was in place. The town was so small he could stand at the northern county line, spit, and hip the southern county line. Finding Sheridan would be too easy. The problem would be settling in without her seeing him until he wanted her to. He wanted to learn her routine and find a way to insinuate himself into it.

He pulled out his wallet and flipped past photos of his relatives to find the one he kept of Sheridan. He swallowed a thick lump. He missed her. He still loved her.

Sheridan released the deep breath she was holding. She wasn't doing a good job of ignoring the extra attention Chase was giving her, or the blaze of his suggestive gaze. Every time she looked up, he was watching her. Ted and Carolyn attended the patient care meeting, seemingly not noticing the heat radiating between them.

She placed her fingers against her lips, remembering the gentle kiss he'd given her earlier in his office. That conversation did not go as planned. She had rehearsed over and over again just the right words, firm words that were not insulting. She had even practiced the right tone to use, one that would get her point across without sounding preachy or confrontational.

Once she walked into his office, everything changed. She immediately pictured him in the dark blue suit he had worn to church. She remembered his strength when he lifted her from his truck. She could still feel the steel bands of his arms as he pulled her into him for a kiss that made her see fireworks.

"Do you have anything, Dr. Wexler?"

Ted watched her curiously, awaiting her answer to Chase's question. If anyone would notice the romantic pull between her and Chase, it would be Ted. He and Chase had been friends since high school, Ted told her the first week she joined the clinic. They were in the "nerdy" classes together—physics, calculus, Shakespeare—but didn't become good friends until Chase decided to re-open the local clinic. Ted had been more than happy to give up the long drive into Nashville for work everyday and joined Chase's team the day the doors of Duck River Family Medicine opened.

Sheridan opened the medical record she'd been reviewing earlier. "This patient has me stumped."

"Who?" Ted asked.

"Mrs. Harvey."

"Ah, Mrs. Harvey," Chase said. "Her husband died last year. Since then she visits the clinic once a month or so with vague complaints. She comes mostly for the company. I usually recommend she spend time volunteering at the elementary school, or prescribe a visit to the church support group."

She proceeded carefully. "She expressed concern you may not be taking her symptoms seriously...because you're a man."

Carolyn's head snapped in Chase's direction. She looked ready to defend and protect all women everywhere. Easily excitable, and a little rigid when it came to policy and procedure, Carolyn was an excellent office manager. She juggled the schedule, ordering supplies, handling insurance billing, and any other tasks she noticed needed to be done. If she had a concern, Chase would take it seriously. She'd earned respect with her staunch professionalism and unquestionable reliability. She wore flowery dresses covered with a dark blazer everyday. She kept her hair wound tightly in a severe brunette bun. Having Carolyn as a ally would work to Sheridan's advantage when it came time to vote on her winning the partnership.

Chase ignored Carolyn's unhappy pucker and addressed Sheridan's concerns. "I'm sorry Mrs. Harvey is unhappy with the care she's received, but it has nothing to do with my being a man."

"Or her being a woman," Ted added with a coy smile directed at Carolyn. If he wanted to get a rise out her, he would if he continued down this path. "Oh, c'mon Carolyn, you know Dr. Larson doesn't discriminate."

Sheridan responded. "I didn't mean to imply—I was relaying the patient's concerns."

Chase left his chair and took the vacant seat next to Sheridan. "Can I?"

She pushed the file over to him.

Her attention was drawn to his manicured fingers as he flipped though the last several pages. As handsome as Chase was, the gentle touch of his long fingers most aroused her. During their kiss he had held her with authority, hardly exerting a fraction of the strength that lay beneath his large hands.

"I've done a full battery of blood work," he pointed out the results, "all normal. Her complaints are vague and they're so sporadic. Believe me, I spent a great deal of time trying to substantiate her symptoms. There's nothing physically wrong with her. After a while, I attributed her symptoms to grief—and loneliness."

"If you don't mind, I'd like to take a second look at her case."

"Sure." He lifted one broad shoulder. "See if I missed something."

"It's nice having another woman around here," Carolyn added, her lips still puckered.

Chase smiled, not at all offended by Sheridan's requesting a second opinion, or Carolyn's defensiveness. "Ted, I think we're getting ready to be ganged up on."

"On that note, it's time to end this patient care conference." Ted moved to the side table where Carolyn had set up lunch. Carolyn joined him, discussing the next supply order for the clinic while selecting a dessert.

"When will you see Mrs. Harvey again?" Chase asked.

"She's on the schedule for next week. I'll search the physician database and see what I can find."

"Let me know if I can help." He stood and pulled out Sheridan's chair.

"You're not upset about my wanting to take a second look at Mrs. Harvey's case?"

His shoulder lifted again. "Should I be? Maybe you'll find something I didn't."

She mentally compared Chase to her ex-husband. Both physicians, their philosophies of how a clinic should be run, were radically different. Whenever she had tried to make an independent decision with Lester, her effort resulted in a huge blow-up. And if she had dared question his treatment plan for a patient, she might as well have packed her bags and moved to a hotel.

"I have a one o'clock," Chase said, moving to the door. "I'll see you before the end of the day."

"He's prepping for his patients now?" Carolyn asked with some disdain. "Or should I say primping?"

"You saw the schedule," Ted added.

Sheridan's curiosity peaked. "What's the deal?"

"She hasn't met Ms. Reese yet."

"She never will. She's a woman." Ted wiggled his eyebrows over a bright smile.

"Who's Ms. Reese?"

"*Candy*," Carolyn corrected. "Words can't adequately describe Candy, but you'll see for yourself soon enough."

Carolyn and Ted left the lounge together, their conversation quickly switching back to supplies count. Sheridan watched them move down the corridor together. She swung around the other way to try to catch a glimpse of Chase. His office door was closed. She decided to shrug off Ted and Carolyn's comments as office gossip. She gathered the files she'd left on the conference table.

There was usually some grain of truth in gossip. *Candy* didn't sound like the name of the average patient. *Madonna, Pink*—they went by one name. People from Duck River, Tennessee had three or four names, they didn't call themselves *Candy*.

Sheridan marched down the hall to her office. She closed her door with too much vigor, had second thoughts, and opened the door wide. Since when was it her concern what went on between Chase and his patients? She had gone to him this morning and told him they were colleagues only—no personal involvement was in their future. Still, she was unhappy about Candy's one o'clock appointment. *Not my business*, she kept reminding herself.

After scanning three pages of medical text on an Internet physician database and not remembering one thing she'd read, she cut off the computer. She left her desk and paced to the window. She watched the citizens of Duck River go about their day. Anything to keep her mind off Chase and his personal life and how her life would be different if she'd met him before she married Lester. Reliving her relationship with her ex-husband aroused such intense emotions she thought she saw him walking down the street. She pressed her eyes together, and when she opened them, the man was gone. No way Lester Wexler would be caught dead in this small town. He was all about big city flash, notoriety and money. There was nothing in Duck River he wanted.

She pulled herself away from the window and tried to distract herself by making her grocery list. Somewhere between pineapples and oranges, her grocery list shifted to a listing of Chase's most attractive qualities. Tall, dark and handsome were a given. Sensitive, intelligent and compassionate were a pleasant surprise. Sexy strut, seductive smile, great kisser...she crumbled up the "grocery" list and tossed it in the trash. Then she left her office and wandered to the front desk to "check her schedule for the afternoon," she told Carolyn.

"I place a printout of your schedule on your desk every morning, Dr. Wexler."

"I misplaced it." Actually, she'd used the back of it to make her grocery/Chase's attributes list. She used the tip of her nail as a guide as she checked the schedule. A thirty minute block had been crossed out for Candy's visit. "I need to speak to Dr. Larson.

Is his one o'clock here yet?"

Carolyn nodded toward the front door of the clinic. "Here she is now."

Sheridan turned, and hot-red blinded her vision. Candy strutted into the lobby on tall heels, wearing a tight dress made of shimmering scarlet material. She clutched a sequined purse in her left hand and finger-waved her way past Carolyn's desk with her right.

"That's Dr. Larson's one o'clock." Carolyn rolled her eyes.

"Does she always just walk back without checking in?"

"I've tried to break her of the habit, but the doctor has a soft spot for her."

Or a hard spot.

"All the men in Duck River do," Carolyn added. "She'll see him in his office first then Ted will show her into the exam room."

"Who is she?"

If Carolyn noticed her jealousy, she didn't call attention to it. Her eyes narrowed for a moment, gathering information, but she answered honestly. "Candy runs a little house on a big ranch with a lot of single women that none of *us* women are supposed to know about."

She turned in the direction of Candy's perfume trail. "A brothel?"

"Shh." Carolyn held a finger up to her lips. "We're not supposed to know," she added sarcastically.

"Do you know why she's here?"

Carolyn's lips pursed. "Patient confidentiality, Dr. Wexler."

Damn propriety! Candy was alone with Chase in his office—

behind closed doors. They could be doing anything. She whizzed around and returned to her office, passing by Chase's door as slowly as possible, hoping to overhear what was going on inside.

Ted popped out of one of the exam rooms. "I placed tomorrow's patient files on your desk, Dr. Wexler."

"Thank you. Hey, Ted. I need to speak to Dr. Larson. Is he busy?"

"He's with *Candy*."

"So he's busy."

Ted gave her the same inquisitive look Carolyn had just given her. "Is there something I can help you with?"

"No." She was distracted by a noise from Chase's end of the corridor.

"I can interrupt him if you'd like."

Chase's door swung open and the doctor poked his head out. "Are we ready, Ted? I'll need exam room 3."

"Three's ready." Ted hiked his thumb toward Sheridan. "Dr. Wexler needs to speak with you."

"It can wait." She retreated to her office before Chase could reply. *Exam room 3!* Exam room 3 was strictly reserved for gynecological examinations. The implications of Candy's visit turned dramatically torrid. Sheridan closed her door with a slam that clearly demonstrated her red-hot anger.

She went back to the window and tried to cool her anger by watching the townspeople. It didn't work. Her mind kept picturing what was going on in exam room 3. Although Candy probably didn't wear underwear, Sheridan's panties were definitely in a bunch. She closed her eyes and rubbed her temples. Dr. Chase Larson's personal life was none of her business. He could see who he wanted, when he wanted. If he wanted to get involved with his patients, it didn't concern her.

She pressed her finger to her lips for the hundredth time that day. There was passion behind Chase's kiss. More than passion, there was possibility. She pushed her shoulders back. She had two choices. One, she could abide by what she'd decided earlier and not get involved with Chase. Or two, she could admit Chase stimulated her mind and body and that she wanted to see where a relationship with him could go if she lower all the barriers around her heart.

"Dr. Wexler?" Ted wrapped on the door.

"Come in."

"Dr. Larson needs a female in the exam room with him."

Oh, great. In her jealous flurry, she forgot policy dictated a female needed to be present during the gynecological exam of a female patient by a male physician.

"He's ready now," Ted added.

What did they do before I arrived? she wondered. Why hadn't they asked Carolyn to join the good doctor? She used the tip of her finger to smooth away the wrinkles marring her forehead. She could never play poker because her emotions were readily displayed by the bunching of skin on her forehead. She put on a professional face and joined Candy in exam room 3.

Chase glanced up when she entered the room. "Candy, this is Dr. Wexler."

Candy looked outright obscene lying on her back on the exam table in the paper gown. She lifted her head and gave Sheridan a quick looking over. "This is the new doctor I've heard so much about."

"Yes, and now that she's here Carolyn doesn't have to stand in the wings."

"You're causing quite a stir in the men around here." Candy went up on her elbows so she could see Chase clearly. She smiled, revealing perfect teeth and two deep dimples. "Business at the ranch has doubled since she came to town."

Sheridan's mouth dropped open. She looked to Chase. He was grinning. Her cheeks began to burn. The lines in her forehead deepened. "Are we ready here, Dr. Larson?"

His mouth moved up in a perfect smile, his eyes nearly closing in dazzling fascination. "Yep. Let's get this show on the road."

She stuffed her hands into disposable gloves and pushed the bedside tray within Chase's reach.

"Feet into the stirrups, Candy," he instructed.

Sheridan chewed her cheek to keep from screaming.

"Scoot your bottom to the end of the exam table."

Candy did as Chase asked, wiggling her hips down to the end of the table and making an elaborate show of putting her feet into the stirrups.

"Jeez," Sheridan mumbled.

"What was that, Dr. Wexler?" Chase asked as he rolled closer to the exam table.

"Nothing."

Chase's country-flavored drawl addressed Candy as he alerted her to his every move. "Can you hand me the speculum, please?"

Now she was his assistant? Or did the glint in his eye prove he knew what this whole scene was doing to her? She handed him the speculum and hurried along the process by being ready with the culture tubes. He changed his gloves, tossing the old in a nearby garbage can.

Her cheeks reddened and she stood mute as Chase told Candy to prepare for the penetration of his fingers. Well, maybe he didn't use the word *penetration*. She felt like going up on tip-toe to see exactly how many of those perfectly manicured fingers he was using when Candy moaned. He apologized for hurting her. *Hurting her?!* Finally, after what seemed like ten minutes, he withdrew his hand and returned to his seat on the stool.

She stepped up. "I can finish up here, Dr. Larson."

He gave her an inquisitive look, but would never question her in front of a patient. "Okay, Dr. Wexler." He stood, removed his gloves, and washed his hands at the sink. When he finished, Candy was out of the stirrups sitting on the edge of the exam table. "Ted will call you if there's a problem. Otherwise, I'll see you in six months."

"Or sooner, Doctor." Candy winked at him.

Sheridan's mouth did drop this time.

Chase looked embarrassed. "I'll have Ted come in to send those cultures, Dr. Wexler."

Her eyes must have reflected her anger because he backed out of the room without another word.

CHAPTER 5

Chase grinned behind the closed door of his office. Dr. Sheridan Wexler's mouth said she didn't want to get involved, but her actions showed the opposite. Candy's visit couldn't have been more perfectly timed. Sheridan turned two shades of jealous purple when Candy winked at him. Normally, he would have lectured Candy on the inappropriateness of her flirtatiousness, but he had enjoyed Sheridan's reaction. Candy was flirtatious by nature of her work; she didn't have any feelings for him, but her wild personality had sure worked in his favor today.

He'd gone about getting Sheridan all wrong. Bowling her over with his charm wasn't going to impress her. She had too much to offer a man to be placed in a humbling position. If he wanted Sheridan, he had to let her decide he was what she wanted and allow her to make the first move. She needed to retain her independence. She needed to be in control.

Playing this game could be dangerous—he could lose Sheridan before he even had her. He had to move carefully, cleverly guiding her in the direction he wanted her to go. Trying to win a woman was new to him, but he rather liked this new challenge. If the experience thrilled him as much as Sheridan did, he couldn't lose. He'd never been in a relationship with a woman who didn't fawn over him, hoping her passive nature would endear her to him. The goal always seemed to be getting to the altar with a doctor. Letting Sheridan take charge of their destiny would be interesting. She'd still need a little behind-the-scenes guidance, but he was willing to let her have her way with him.

Before his fantasies about Sheridan could distract him further, there was a knock at the door. "Can I speak to you?"

Here was his chance to try out his new approach. "Of course. Ted told me you needed to see me about something."

"This doesn't concern the clinic." She came into his office, closing the door, determination etched into the wrinkling of her forehead. She looked so sexily disheveled, he briefly considered tossing his bright idea, grabbing her, and kissing her until she fully understood his purpose. He wouldn't survive letting her dictate the pace of their relationship—especially when they hadn't even agreed on having anything more than friendship. Fate placing Sheridan at the clinic could turn out to be a cruel trick, or a blessing—it hadn't been decided yet. For now, he'd stick to his original plan, hoping she'd come around soon.

"Really? What *does* this concern, Dr. Wexler?" He came around and sat on the corner of his desk, folded his arms, and waited for her to proceed.

"It has to do with our conversation this morning."

He watched her intensely, purposefully flustering her.

"I've had time to think about what you said."

He angled his head in question, enjoying the cute way she squirmed.

"I'd like you to forget everything I said."

"And what was that?" He dipped his head until he could hide his excited grin.

Sheridan marched up to him. "You know what I'm talking about."

"We've had several conversations today."

She exhaled, frustrated. "I've changed my mind. Seeing each other might not be a bad idea."

"Gee, thanks."

She blinked twice. "I meant—"

"Sounds like you're settling."

"I didn't mean it that way."

His eyes lingered on the hollow of her neck. He wanted to kiss her there, taste her skin, and leave his scent behind. He agonized over his decision to let her run things, but pushed ahead. "How did you mean it?"

"I—"

"Are you suddenly attracted to me?"

"I—"

Just a little push…"What is it, Dr. Wexler?"

She eyed him suspiciously, but no less determined to finish what she'd come to do. "I'll admit I enjoyed our time together Sunday, and…I'm…yes…I'm attracted to you."

He shifted his jaw, fighting a smug smile. Game over! So soon? The challenge had just begun to appeal to him. "Would this have anything to do with Candy's visit? Because if you're only changing your mind about us because you're jealous—"

"Jealous!" She folded her arms over her chest. "Dr. Larson, you are too conceited for your own good. I don't even know what possessed me to come in here."

She turned to leave, but he caught up her arm, stopping her. "I'm as observant as you are perceptive. You were green in the face the entire time Candy was here."

She wiggled out of his grasp and he wondered if severing

their connection was playing fair. "You were flirting on purpose."

He pressed his fingers to his chest, emphasizing his innocence. "Me?"

"Yes. You."

He watched her with a glimmering smile. "No, I didn't do it on purpose, but I sure did enjoy knowing you're jealous over me."

She stepped up, grabbed his face and brought her lips to his. He'd been trying to make her squirm a bit, but he was no dummy. He wrapped his arms around Sheridan's waist and pulled her into him. Sitting on top of his desk brought them face to face, which was a perfect position for kissing. He maneuvered her between his thighs and took control of their kiss, sliding his tongue into her mouth.

Sheridan had another agenda. She wrestled his tongue, becoming the aggressor. He gladly acquiesced. Mental shrug, *Let the woman have her way.* He held her waist tightly, following her willingly as she released her sensuality.

When she pulled away, he was breathless, imagining intimate possibilities. He was also speechless when she gave him a teasing smile and sauntered out of his office.

CHAPTER 6

Within days, Lester had settled in to a daily routine. He moved around Duck River discretely, not yet ready for Sheridan to know he was in town. When he approached her, he would clearly know his mind. He would have a plan to win back his wife. *Ex-wife*, he corrected himself. He was going to present himself humbly. He had to remember she was no longer his wife, and he had no legal hold on her. He prayed the emotional bond would be enough to make her want to start over with him.

The first thing he'd done was find a place to stay for an extended amount of time where no one would ask too many questions. Or spread the word of his presence. Small towns were notorious for gossiping. He doubted this town was any different.

"I have a room for you, mister, but as you can see my rooms are in use." She spread her arms wide, drawing his attention to the half-dressed women and their patrons bustling in the parlor.

He pulled out his leather money clip and began to peel hundred dollars bills from the stack. "How much would my staying here for a month cost you in lost income?"

She sat up straight, shimmying her hips deeper into the tan leather recliner. "That stack of bills you have in your hand might cover it."

He sat forward and handed her the bills. The amount he offered was more than any one of her girls made in a month. It should be enough to buy discretion—and uninterrupted time to work on his research.

"The cost of the room rental is extra," she added before taking the wad of money.

"Of course," Lester mumbled and peeled off three hundred additional dollars.

She took the money with a wide smile.

"And this is for keeping my presence here quiet."

She tucked the five hundred additional dollars he handed over down the front of her dress. He'd given her a nice chunk of his monthly salary from the clinic, but being from a wealthy family afforded him some extravagance. He'd never splurged on anything in his life, but getting Sheridan back could not be valued monetarily.

"Use of the girls is extra. Although, you've been quite generous, so take one on the house. Tonight only."

"The woman in my life wouldn't like the idea of me sleeping with one of your girls." He stood and offered his hand. "I'll move in immediately."

"I'll introduce you to the girls. They should know who you are if you're going to be hanging around here."

"Fine." Everything had been handled in a very businesslike way. Whorehouses were always safe havens for men with nowhere to go. No one would snoop around in his affairs. They wouldn't bother him while he worked. As long as he kept the money coming, he'd be able to stay in seclusion as long as he needed.

"What's your name, mister?"

"Lester."

"Lester, I'm Candy. Enjoy your stay in my home."

CHAPTER 7

Okay, so she could have climbed up into Chase's F150 by herself, but it certainly was much more fun to have him lift her up into the truck. He didn't remark on the fact she was wearing jeans—as he had requested—and that there was no excuse for him having to wrap his sexy hands around her waist and hoist her up with gentle care. Sheridan placed her hands on his shoulders and squeezed for effect. If he thought she was too comfortable in his arms, she wanted to appear to have some concerns about him dropping her one hundred and thirty pound, five foot five frame. When he leaned inside the cab of the truck she didn't remind him she was a physician and knew the intricacies of fastening a safety belt; she batted her eyes and let him take care of her.

She liked Chase taking care of her. She liked being a "girl" with him; not always having to be in charge of the situation or search for topics of discussion. This was her time to enjoy herself. Her intention was to have as much fun as possible. They were equals, but he beat her out in the physical strength department, and she was going to reap the benefits.

She watched Chase come around the front of the truck. His dark jeans were slightly worn, faded around the knees, and outlining the generous haunches of his behind. A real cowboy in black boots, a white tee was molded to the muscles of his chest. Over the tee he wore a dark blue button down shirt. The edges flapped open when he walked, and she could see the outline of his erect nipples. The beaten cowboy hat had fallen to the ground when he kissed her hello. She griped the brim as she remembered the way her lips sizzled when he'd kissed her. He climbed into the truck, every muscle clearly defined as he hoisted himself up. He was a walking *Playgirl* poster—the southern hunk special edition, of course.

The motor flared up with a masculine growl. He looked over at her with his teasing grin. "Are you ready to go, Shameless?"

"Shameless?" She couldn't help laughing.

"Yes, Shameless. Do you think I believe a woman who kisses me the way you do can't get into my truck by herself?"

"You've got me." She hid her blush behind his hat.

"Umm, hmm." He leaned across the seat, plucking the hat away. "Shameless or Sassy—I don't know what to call you." He kissed her lips. "Ummm," he hummed appreciatively. He put on his hat and pulled out of the driveway, spewing gravel. His chest expanded, puffing out as he tried to impress her with his manly maneuvering of the truck.

"What's on the agenda?" she asked as Chase drove them deeper into the countryside.

"I thought we'd start by letting you get used to being around the horses. If they since you're afraid of them, they'll never let you ride."

"I needed all of these things just to visit the horses?" She hiked her thumb toward the duffle bag packed with a change of clothes and shoes, plus the other things he'd told her to bring.

"Here's your opportunity to call me Shameless."

"What are you up to?"

"I want you to have fun today. Drop your guard and trust me

to show you a good time."

"What does that mean? Drop my guard? What are you going to do?"

"No questions." He pushed the rim of his hat up. "No questions. Just enjoy yourself."

"You're not going to tell me what you have planned?"

"No. Partly because I don't have it all figured out. Partly because I don't want you to overanalyze or prepare. I want you to learn to relax." He glanced at her. "You're the tensest person I know. You have to learn to have fun."

"I'm not tense. What makes you think I'm tense?"

"Look at what I had to go through to get a date with you. Instead of accepting the fact we were attracted to each other, you started analyzing and supposing. Sometimes I watch you at work and—"

"You watch me at work?" She'd been watching him so much she was sure she would've noticed him watching her.

He tugged at the hat. "Sometimes I watch you at work, and you're so absorbed in studying a medical record you go into a zone shutting everyone out. You need to loosen up."

"Loosen up?"

"No one ever told you that?"

"Learn to have fun, huh?" She rested against the seat. "If you were wrong, I'd put up an argument."

Chase stopped, allowing a farmer driving a tractor at a creeping speed to clear the road. "You're going to cooperate?"

She studied the features of his face beneath the black hat. The hat couldn't hide milk chocolate skin, a straight nose, and dark eyes that seemed to see right through her insecurities.

"Your mind is racing like a computer," Chase said after a few minutes. "Stop using this," he tapped her forehead, "and start using this," he pressed his finger in the dip of her cleavage.

A slow smile spread over her face. She wrapped his hand in hers and slid it to the left and below her breast. "My heart is over here, Doctor."

He drew a small heart beneath her breast. "Shameless."

"You make me this way."

"Good." He threw his head back and laughed.

Chase turned onto a private road, and, within minutes, they were passing through an enormous wrought iron gate with the words "Larson Ranch" above it. The grass was green and lush. The leaves on the trees were beginning to turn early October red. Ranch hands worked diligently to keep the grounds perfectly manicured. A mile onto the property, Sheridan spotted the first house.

"My oldest sister, Sarah, lives there." Chase pointed to the large Tudor. "Sarah set the bar by going to Olds College in Alberta, Canada. She majored in Equine Science, which assured my father he'd exerted enough influence over his children when it came to their educational choices. Sarah aced college. She returned home with a top-notch education, her husband, Howell, and a bun in the oven."

"How did your parents feel about that?"

Chase shrugged. "My mother was glad to have her oldest daughter home. My dad was glad she'd be able to take over the ranch one day. Both were happy about their first grandchild. It took Howell a little while to adjust." He rolled his eyes, but a playful grin danced on his lips. "He's Canadian, *eh*."

"How old is the baby?"

"The baby is now a teenager who is a senior in high school. They have four teenagers."

A half mile down the twisting road, Chase pointed out a white house trimmed with black shutters hidden in a thicket of trees. "My second oldest sister, Jayme, lives there with her husband, Neil. They're both horse doctors. My mother says they both have old souls that brought them together."

"Why does she believe that?"

"They're hardworking, serious-minded people who don't smile much." He shrugged. "They're very happy together. It's their way." He pointed out a matching cottage situated close enough to Jayme and Neil's house to be their garage. "Brenda and Hugh live in the little place tucked behind them. Brenda and Jayme are closer than twins. They're both vets and they both have two kids only months apart."

"I'm sensing a theme here."

On the opposite side of the road was a sophisticated modern ranch made of dark brick. "That's the number four sister, Alison's house. She and Dwayne have only been married a year."

"What does she do?"

"She's a professional rider. She's placed first in too many shows to count. She started riding young—she has a natural talent for it. I don't think she's ever considered doing anything else with her life. Dwayne was her first coach. He's ten years older than Alison, which caused my father to blow his stack when he found out they were seeing each other." He glanced over at her. "I think he feels a little guilty about missing the signs."

"What signs?" Sheridan was finding his family fascinating.

"Signs that Dwayne might have been making moves on her when he was still her coach."

She nodded in understanding.

"Alison is older than me, but she's like my little sister. Very sweet. Not wise to how the world works, so I had to step in and intervene on her behalf quite a bit when we were young. She was always busy with training and shows, so she had a private tutor. Not going to school and being a regular teenager deprived her of the experiences she needed to mature. But she turned out all right."

"Your entire family works with horses."

"All except me."

"And they all live here?"

Chase nodded. "On the Larson ranch."

"Like *Dallas.*"

"Without a JR."

"How does that work out?"

He shrugged. "We're a close family, but we each relish our privacy. We lead separate lives, but are close by if needed. My parents worried about us growing up and growing apart because our personalities are all so different. Neither of them is close to their siblings, but value the family bond. When you meet them you'll get the *how American society is deteriorating because of the lack of family values* lecture."

"I bet you can guess my next question."

"Yes, I can. You want to know why I'm not married with a family of my own. I won't keep you in suspense. I haven't found the right woman. Every family in Duck River knows every other family, and that makes dating hard. Especially when women see my greatest asset as my career or my family's wealth."

She listened to him talk about the cause of his last failed relationship with interest. Actually, she was going to ask him where his house was since it wasn't situated in the same cluster as his sisters'. She heard a touch of loneliness in his voice as he told her about giving his heart to a woman who he discovered was telling everyone in town she was only attracted to him because he could take her away from the tiny town in lavish style. The public embarrassment wasn't enough to deter him from seeking his perfect mate. He'd just changed his strategy.

She swiveled in her seat to face him. "Tell me about your perfect mate."

He glanced over at her with wolfish curiosity. "She's intelligent, feisty, and has big plans for her life. She doesn't need me, or my career, to define her. She'll have a gentle, caring soul. She'll want marriage and kids and be able to handle the closeness I share with my family." He paused, his voice roughening to a more serious tone. "Most importantly, she'll love me for who I am. When I mess up, she'll forgive me. If I need to be pampered, she'll recognize that and do it with a smile because she loves me. Our time together will be full of laughs, trips to exotic locations, and hot, steamy sex."

"I was waiting for you to get around to the sex."

His grin challenged her. "What's wrong with wanting a healthy sex life?"

"It's always about hot, steamy sex with men."

"Really? Has that been your experience?"

"You know what I mean."

"You didn't answer my question. Is there something wrong

with wanting a healthy sex life with the person you love? Exactly how long do you think the perfect relationship would last without sex? Good sex?"

He'd roped her into a corner. Every time she watched him strut across a room, she thought of how making love with him would be. His kisses ushered her down the road of erotic touches. Naturally, when he wrapped his hands around her waist and lifted her into his truck, she thought of him lifting her in his arms and carrying her away to a canopy-covered bed.

"Well?" he prompted. "Do you think it's possible to have a good relationship without a healthy sex life?"

"Okay, I give."

He tugged at his hat, grinning in triumph. "You didn't ask me to describe my perfect sexual partner."

"Do I want to know this? Why would you think I need to know this?"

He gave her a long, assessing look. "You'll need to know for future reference."

She had never been a blusher, but since meeting Chase, her cheeks were always on fire. She turned toward the passenger window, eager for him to describe what a night with him would be like. She'd caught herself more than once picturing it. "Keep it clean," she warned him.

"When it comes to sex, this woman is comfortable with her body. She is sensual and not ashamed of it. And she's the aggressor when there's something she wants. Shy and inhibited doesn't do it for me." He turned, catching her gaze. "I'm willing to offer the same to my woman. All of it. I couldn't love someone without giving everything."

A huge white house rose from the horizon, catching Sheridan's attention. The grand home monopolized the Larson Ranch, clearly its centerpiece and serving as the hub for all operations. People buzzed outside the home, manicuring the lawns and pruning trees. The house screamed authority and southern charm. "Did you grew up in this house?" she asked in awe. "It's larger than Disneyland."

"It felt like Disneyland when we moved in. My family is from what locals call *new money*. My parents built their business from nothing. We were very poor. My father spent a lot of time on the road while my mother cared for five kids all alone." At the fork in the road, he veered right. "My mother found out my father wasn't taking care of business like he should be. Women started showing up at her door claiming my father as their children's father."

She thought of her own parents and how close she was to them. She would die if her father cheated on them. She was aware there were problems between her parents when she was younger, but they kept the details of their disagreements from her. Whatever had happened, they resolved the problems, and the whispered arguments behind closed doors stopped.

Chase continued. "Do you know my mother never cried? Not once. She sent for a distant relative to stay with us, and she went looking for my father. It was unheard of for a woman to leave her children to go chasing after a man when she didn't even know where he was." He paused, reflectively. "I don't know the details of what happened between them, but they came home together and my mother took over building my father's career. She gained a certain measure of respect from the town, and they supported her business. Next thing you know, my mother signs a huge contract and we're moving into Disneyland."

"Did you have a good childhood?"

"I had a great childhood. Even when we were poor, we had each other. My father insisted we hold our heads up. My mother insisted we get an education so we wouldn't have to live in poverty. My sisters and I got along well—just minor sibling stuff."

The truck bounced as Chase took a side road. "Tell me about your family."

"I'm the only child—"

He groaned.

She punched his shoulder before going on. "I'm very close to my parents. I always wanted a bunch of sisters and brothers. I used to pretend my dolls were a schoolhouse full of kids who were related to me. I'd like to meet your sisters."

"You will. I'd like to meet your parents." He maneuvered the truck down a winding road. "We're going to come up behind the stables."

He parked his truck in the shelter of a barn while he introduced her to the workers responsible for caring for the property and the animals. He explained the tools used to break the new horses. They watched the horses trot around the chorals, learning the feel of their riders. He brought her into his world, familiarizing her with the care of the horses in an attempt to ease her anxiety. They ended their tour at the stables. With him at her side, the horses weren't as intimidating. At the end of her first day of instruction, she accompanied Chase into the barn while he fed his favorite stallion apples from a metal bucket.

"He likes you," Chase remarked as he stroked the golden

brown stallion. "If you're comfortable, the horse is comfortable." He looked at her over the horse's mane. "One more visit and you'll be ready to ride."

"Not quite. It's a long way up there to the saddle."

"We'll take it slow." He walked around next to her. "How about brushing? He likes to be groomed."

"I don't know."

"I'll be at your side the entire time." He placed the bucket on the ground so the horse could continue to eat. He took Sheridan's hand and led her to stand beside the horse, showing her the safest place to stand in case the horse got spooked.

He grasped the stiff-bristled brush. "Place you hand over mine."

Tentatively, she placed her hand atop his, covering the network of veins that twisted up his arm along the path of his muscles. She watched the muscles of his back ripple as he made long strokes with the brush. He was gentle, but firm; attributes she'd recognized in his nature. "Okay," he said softly, "I'm going to let go now."

The horse took a step toward the bucket.

"Wait."

"You've got it. Remember, don't be afraid or the horse will pick up on it." He slipped his hand from beneath hers and took a step back. "Good. Long, firm strokes."

She continued to brush the horse, her heart jumping whenever he moved.

"Very good," he complimented her. He grabbed another brush and joined her while she brushed the horse.

"This is pretty neat," she said, feeling more comfortable. The horse paid her little attention as she applied light strokes to its coat. She, on the other hand, couldn't keep her eyes off Chase. He distracted her by shrugging of his button down shirt and tossing it to a nearby fence. His back muscles rippled with the simple action. He stooped down low and his thighs strained against the fabric of his faded jeans, clearly outlining their raw power. He worked his way around the horse, bringing the elegant coat to life with the magic of his commanding hands. His rhythmic strokes brought him to stand next to her.

"You've overcome your fear of horses." He took the brush from her hands, his fingers gently brushing hers.

"I don't know if I'm completely over it yet."

"You're well on your way." He grabbed the horse's bridle and led him into a stall. The cowboy doctor worked with quiet authority. He was gentle and fair, but anyone who would mistake him as a pushover would pay a hefty price. The intensity behind his eyes could be mistaken for unjustified anger until the mellow tone of his voice displayed the depth of his compassion. "Are you hungry?"

"I didn't realize it was so late." They had been together since dawn, and it was now late afternoon. "Lunch is on me."

"Next time." He whispered to the stallion, patting its mane. The horse settled into his stall as if his words had woven a magical spell. "Today, we'll have lunch at my place." He sauntered up to her, his strut more noticeable in the rustic setting. "It'll be your reward for being so brave." He removed the Stetson from his head and placed it on hers. She wanted to keep this little piece of him with her always. He dipped his head, wrapping his arms around her waist and pulling her into him. He nibbled patiently at the corner of her mouth. When she sighed, he captured her bottom lip between his teeth and gave a small tug. She wrapped her arms around his waist, wanting to experience the completeness of his kiss. He joined her beneath the brim of the hat, converging on her lips as if it were their first kiss after being separated too long.

They never heard the patter of hoofs approach.

"Son, who's this girl all the hands are gushing over?" The man pulled up on the reins of his horse when he came around the barn, startled by the intimate scene.

"What a first impression," Sheridan murmured as she disentangled herself from Chase's grasp.

Chase smiled, not fazed by his father's unexpected appearance. "Dad, this is Sheridan Wexler. Sheridan, this is my dad, Martin."

"The new doctor?" He dismounted from the horse, keeping a firm hold on the reins. This horse was the biggest she'd seen yet. It bucked and snorted, shaking it's mane in protest of being made to stand still. She stepped behind Chase.

Martin looked between them.

"She's not comfortable around horses yet," Chase offered.

He nodded, winding the reins around his hands to tighten his hold on the impatient horse. "You're causing quite a stir on the ranch today, young lady." He stood a few inches shorter than his son, but his booming voice made up for the lost height. "Now I see what the stir was all about. Larson men have a weak spot for pretty women."

"It's true. All of my four sisters are horribly spoiled. My dad has always been hardest on me."

"You're damn right." He stepped forward, dragging the snorting horse with him. He punched Chase in the shoulder. "It did you good, too. Look how good a man you turned out to be."

"Yeah, Dad." Chase laughed, humoring him.

"Listen, your mother sent me down here to see what all the talk was about. You two want to have lunch with us?"

Chase reached around behind him and hooked Sheridan around the waist. He pulled her from behind him. "Step back, Dad."

"Oh. Sorry." He stepped back a few paces, leading the horse a safe distance away.

"Thank you," Sheridan said, clinging to Chase's hand. His perfect fingers would be crinkled by the death grip she held on them.

"What about lunch?"

"Sheridan and I are going to have lunch at my house." Chase pried his hand out of her grip and placed it on her shoulder. "She's not comfortable with me either."

She elbowed him.

Martin's eyebrows shot up, but returned to normal as a satisfied smile spread across his face. "Maybe we'll see you later, then." He prepared to mount. "Your mother will want to meet this one."

CHAPTER 8

"You live here alone?" Sheridan stood in the domed foyer of Chase's home, her mouth agape. From the outside, the brick and stone home appeared compact and cozy, like a country cottage. Inside told a different story. The rustic exterior was met with a contemporary interior. The foyer was two stories high with a large window over the door drenching the entryway in sunlight. The foyer led into the great room with three doorways framed in exquisite molding. The furniture groupings highlighted the fireplace, patio, and tall bookshelves. The room was dark and warm, carpeted with Berber in multi-colored shades of brown. The sofa and chairs were several shades of tan, perfectly matching the carpet.

"Good afternoon, Dr. Larson." A woman appeared from nowhere. Her heavy Spanish accent and colorful garb revealed a Mexican heritage.

"Good afternoon, Ms. Fluentes. Meet Dr. Wexler."

They exchanged pleasantries, but Sheridan was distracted by the lavish house. She could easily picture herself curled up in one of the seating areas with a good book, relaxing after a long day at the clinic. She'd always dreamt of having a professionally decorated, large home, but Lester had been too busy to make a home. Their compact apartment was cluttered with the accumulation of two people's belongings—they never got around to combining their things, or their lives. They had two bedrooms—one of which was used as Lester's office. When she had complained about his spending too much time at his research, coming to bed after she'd already fallen asleep, he purchased a new bed and began sleeping in his office most nights. As she recalled those times, she realized Lester's buying the bed had been the beginning of the end of their marriage.

"I'm starving," Chase said. He turned to Ms. Fluentes. "Dr. Wexler and I would like lunch after we get cleaned up."

"Yes, Doctor." She reached for his hat and hurried off.

"Ms. Fluentes," Chase called after her, "Dr. Wexler is a vegetarian."

Sheridan should not have been surprised he noticed the smallest details about her, but it made her feel good to know she'd garnered so much of his attention. She'd seen him probe into his patient's complaints until he found the root of their problem, but she thought his concentrated intensity an occupational hazard. Now she knew Chase's scrutiny carried over to other aspects of his life. It seemed such a small thing, but for her it was an enormous declaration of his attraction to her. "You noticed I'm a vegetarian."

"How could I not? I've been worried about you working too hard at the clinic and not eating right. Whenever I do see you eat it's always rabbit food."

"Are you making fun of me, Dr. Larson?"

He lowered his face next to hers, shrinking her universe, positioning himself as the center of her world. It amazed her how he could enter a room and become its central focus, all seemingly without conscious effort. "You have the right amount in the right places." He accentuated his point by grabbing her bottom and pulling her into him. "But then a little meat on your bones wouldn't hurt."

"Wouldn't hurt, huh?"

"It's my prescription for you."

"I wonder what places you would be referring to."

"I thought I spoke clearly." He squeezed her bottom, sharing his preference.

"You really are bad for me."

"Or very, very good for you."

She giggled with the enthusiasm of a schoolgirl. He made her feel young and alive with pulsating energy. He opened a new world, pushing her to explore things that were previously foreign to her. He showed her she could be a good physician who was devoted to her patients' needs without sacrificing her own life. With him, she began to believe doing her best was enough, and the opinion of the insurance company in the malpractice suit had been wrong—it wasn't her fault and patients would be safe in her care. Maybe it would be all right to back off of the hours she spent researching and analyzing her patients' medical records. Being a physician meant knowing the intricacies of her specialty, but it also meant trusting your instincts enough to rely on them when textbooks couldn't provide an answer. That was the most harmful outcome of the malpractice case—she didn't trust her instincts anymore. And not just in relation to medicine. She didn't trust her instincts in personal relationships either.

"Hey," he pulled back to see her clearly, "are you still here with me?"

"I'm here."

"You left me for a minute. Why do you do that? Zone out?"

"I thought I was *in the zone*."

"Not in *my* zone." Before she could come back with a snappy rebuttal, he pressed his lips to hers. Every kiss was addictive, leaving her needing more. Her body had started to protest, cursing her for not giving it more satisfaction. Chase's kisses held unspoken promises of passion. Sneaking in a kiss or two at the clinic would never satisfy Sheridan. She had thought this date would cure her of her jealousy about Candy, but she was wrong. This date was the beginning of something she hadn't prepared for. The somersaulting of her belly promised sensuality beyond her dreams.

Chase pulled away, taking his hands off her bottom and cupping her face. "You're a great kisser. I can picture us sitting on a Caribbean beach kissing all day."

She smiled, happy to know she was weaving a little magic of her own. By the dreamy expression on his face, he wasn't prepared for where this date was taking them either.

"Let me show you where you can change." He took her hand and led her out of the great room, down a short corridor to the left. She had a thing for his hands: Long, slender, strong fingers with capable fingers that would leave no area of her body unexplored. Every time he touched her, a warm current rushed through her body, instantly relaxing her.

They moved down the corridor in silence until shimmering greens and blues reflecting off a distant wall caught her attention. "What's down there?"

Chase took her into a blue rainbow. "My favorite room," he told her, stepping aside so she could experience it all.

Her breath caught. "This is…" She stood into the middle

of the room, turning in a slow circle. "This is a tropical paradise." The walls were aqua, the carpet the color of the deepest sea. Crystal statues and artwork monopolized the room. Multiple skylights opened the ceiling up to the sun, which hit the crystals and filled the room with twisting rays of green and blue. The color scheme continued with the furniture, strategically placed to allow its occupants the full show.

"This is great, Chase," she whispered, not wanting to violate the purity of the room.

His body cast a tall shadow over her shoulder. "I redecorated this room after my first cruise to the Bahamas. There's something about being out on the ocean that is so relaxing. I wanted to bring a piece of it home with me. To last me until my next cruise."

He went to the statue, the centerpiece of the room. The large blue dolphin displayed a combination of strength and serenity—much like Chase. "Everything in here was brought in the Bahamas," he said. "Every year, I add a piece."

"How many times have you gone?"

He thought for a moment. "Fifteen. I'd like to buy a house there, but my mom flipped when I mentioned it."

"They don't want to lose you."

"She wants me to settle down, preferably in Duck River."

"There's nothing wrong with being close to your family. This room is spectacular. The whole house is great."

"Thank you. Let me show you my second favorite room." He led her out and down the corridor. Enclosed in glass, the heated kidney-shaped pool glistened. "Do you know how to swim?"

"I was on the swim team in college." She smiled.

"Then you'll make good use of my pool."

They rounded the pool and entered a glass enclosed extension of the pool area. "This is my workout room. Every morning, I come down here and lift weights. Then I swim two laps."

"Family medicine has been very lucrative for you."

Chase's eyes dropped in embarrassment.

After his aggressive pursuit, she hadn't thought him a man of modesty. "I shouldn't have said that."

"It's okay." He took her hand, leading her back to the main hall. "My father gave me this acreage. I built the house of my dreams here. I've worked hard. I'm not ashamed of what I've accomplished."

"But it embarrasses you when someone calls attention to it."

"It embarrasses me when you call attention to it. I want to make a good impression, but I don't want you to think I'm bragging."

"I don't." They climbed the staircase to the second level.

"And I don't want you to be impressed with me because of what I *have.* I want you to be impressed by the way I treat you."

He had no idea how impressive he was. His mere presence impressed her. If he did anything more to impress her, she'd never leave.

"You had this house built?" she asked, switching to a safe subject.

He led her down the hall. "I looked at several designs, but

couldn't find what I wanted so I hired a man who could listen to my descriptions and put them on paper. He built it; a decorator came in and did the rest."

"This is a big house to live in all alone."

His grip tightened.

Sheridan worried she had hit a nerve, but forged on. "You didn't build it for yourself, did you?"

He turned to her. The good humor filling his eyes disappeared. "No, I didn't."

"Sorry."

"It's not what you think. I built this house in anticipation of—not because of."

"You're looking for something."

His eyes raked her body. "Yes. I'm looking for the right woman to move in here and make this place warm and loving."

Sheridan wondered how many men would admit they were searching for the right woman to share a life with. She picked up on a hint of loneliness in Chase. She wanted to pull him into her arms and promise him a man as righteous as himself would find the perfect woman and have the perfect life. She couldn't. She was supposed to have had a good life with Lester and everything turned out badly. The only way she could guarantee Chase would have a storybook life was to make it her responsibility to give it to him. She couldn't do that.

"Are you feeling sorry for me?" There was a tight pinch to his tone.

"No."

"Good. Don't. I couldn't stand it."

She couldn't look at him without showing how sorry she felt for herself. She wanted this man. She wanted him, but she doubted she was good enough for him. Although he was only two years older than her, she had lived twice as long, twice as hard. She hid her emotion and lifted her eyes.

Chase blinked, ducking his head back in surprise.

She hadn't hid her emotions well enough.

He watched her for a long moment, clearly debating whether he should ask about her sudden sadness. She hung in the balance, waiting to see how much he wanted to know. If he asked, would she tell him about the malpractice case? Her failed marriage? Caught up in the closeness blossoming between them, she could have shared her most devastating mistakes with him. He would hold her and tell her she would get her life back on track. He would promise her everything would be okay and he would make it so.

Chase cleared his throat. He politely changed the subject. "Would you like to take a swim before lunch?"

"I don't have a suit."

A wolfish grin cut through the thick emotion, returning them to familiar ground. "It is a private pool." He wiggled his dark brow.

"No way."

"Loosen up. Listen, I won't wear a suit either, that way you'll feel more comfortable."

Just imagining him nude made her entire body tense.

"Don't look so scared. I'll let you off the hook this time. My sisters leave suits here. You can borrow one of those." He draped his arm around her shoulder. "The next time you forget your suit, you'll have to pay the penalty."

"Penalty?"

"Yes. My penalty. It begins with you swimming nude and ends who knows where."

Sheridan stood underneath the jet spray of the best shower she had ever taken in her life. Everything about Chase Larson was big and luxurious, in a subtly disguised way. She wiped the big grin from her face. Okay, so Chase was handsome, kind, sensitive, intelligent, and rich. He couldn't be *perfect.* He was a little arrogant and maybe a bit too sure of himself. He didn't walk, he strutted. She caught herself grinning again. Chase even wore those faults well, turning them into sexy features that attracted her to him like a bee to honey.

She stepped out of the shower, afraid she had lingered too long. She debated over which swimsuit to wear, deciding being as *un*sexy as possible was the way to go. She selected a wild, geometrically designed one-piece swimsuit from the three Ms. Fluentes had laid out across the bed. There was absolutely nothing sexy about this suit. It looked like something a teenager with gelled blue hair might wear. Good. The way her stomach rocked, she needed to put up as many safeguards against Chase's charms as she could. She wrapped her hips in a white beach towel with the Pink Panther's picture on it and headed to the pool.

Her first view of Chase made her sway. He was coming out of the pool when she walked in, his hands gripping the ladder as he pulled himself up. Every bulging muscle was boldly displayed for her viewing. He wore nothing. Well, if you could call the dark scrap of material covering his manly essentials a suit then he wasn't completely naked. Her eyes went to the dark material. She bit down on her bottom lip as she tried to ward off the power of his bulge. She was in serious trouble here.

"You look cute." He slipped his wet fingers through her hair and kissed her lips. "The Pink Panther has all the luck."

To keep her eyes from going to the blue scrap of material again, she discarded the towel and jumped into the pool. She swam around the side of the pool, avoiding contact with Chase's physique. When he approached, she swam faster in an attempt to work through her lust. Somewhere between going to church and learning about horses, her initial attraction had developed into real feelings for the doctor.

"Got you!" Chase grabbed her from behind, pressing every silky inch of his flesh against her. He turned her to face him. "You're a good swimmer." He pulled her closer. "You zoned out again. I've been trying to catch you since you dove into the pool."

"And now you have me." *Why did I say that? This is not the time to flirt.*

"Yes," he stroked her face from temple to chin, "now I have you." He maintained eye contact as he pressed his lips against hers. When he pulled away, his eyes were hooded, shielding her from the full blast of intense emotions. One simple kiss, nothing more than the meeting of their lips, was intimate enough to warm her to the core. She pushed away, swimming to the edge of the pool, and disrupting the heady arc of attraction between them. He followed silently, climbing the ladder and reaching back for her.

Two of Chase's sisters dropped by while they were having lunch.

"Sarah, I expected you, but Alison?" Chase said when Ms. Fluentes showed them into the dining room. He removed the linen napkin from his lap and rose to kiss his sisters hello. Sarah, the older, watched Sheridan inquisitively.

"You told me I could swim today. Remember?" Alison gave him an innocent look and he instantly softened, reminding Sheridan he was very protective of her.

"Where's your suit?" Chase asked, teasingly.

Alison started to sputter but Sarah took over. "Dad told us the new doctor was here and we wanted to meet her." She approached Sheridan with an outstretched hand. "Welcome to Duck River."

Sheridan took her hand with a smile, not finding any malice in their unexpected visit. "Would you two like to join us?"

"No!" Chase answered. The women turned to him. "My sisters are a little nosy."

"It's okay," Sheridan assured him. "You're the youngest, and the only son. It's okay for your sisters to be curious about me."

"Right," Sarah agreed. "Naturally, we want to know everything about who you're dating." She glanced at Alison, and they rushed to take a seat as if they feared Sheridan might change her mind.

Alison filled her plate with chicken salad while Sarah fired questions at the new doctor. "Where are you from?"

"Nashville."

"Nashville is good for shopping, but Duck River is where you want to raise your family. Have you found a place to stay yet?"

"I'm renting right now. My partnership with the clinic hasn't been decided."

Sarah turned to Chase, wiggling her eyebrows.

"What?" Chase snapped.

Sarah ignored him. "I'm sure it's just a formality. Do you like it here in Duck River?"

"It's great."

"Where has Chase taken you?"

"Sarah," Chase warned.

"How long have you two been dating?"

"Sarah," Chase's forehead wrinkled. "Enough with the questions."

His sister sighed. "All right. I have to meet Howell anyway." She spoke to Sheridan. "Howell's my husband. We'll have to have you over for dinner soon."

"I'd like that."

Sarah and Alison looked at each other, twin smiles spreading over their faces. "We would too," Alison answered.

Sarah stood. "It's a date then. I've got to get going. I have an appointment in town." She kissed Chase's forehead. "Bye, little brother." She whispered something in his ear before strolling out of the dining room.

Chase turned to Alison, who was absorbed in her food. "Aren't you supposed to go with her so you can discuss my date?"

She stopped eating long enough to catch his annoyance. "Bye." She hurried after Sarah.

Chase waited until the front door closed before he spoke. "As you can see, Sarah has to always run the show."

"It's cute how they check up on you."

"I'm thirty-two years old. It's not cute anymore."

Sheridan bit down on the tomato to hide her smile.

"And you didn't make it any better by encouraging her."

She sent her most sensuous gaze across the table. He watched her, waiting for any hint of teasing. When he didn't find any, his mouth rose in a lopsided grin.

"Excuse me, Dr. Larson." Ms. Fluentes entered the dining area carrying the cordless phone. "Your father wishes to speak with you."

Chase apologized for the interruption before speaking briefly on the phone. "Do you want to help me deliver a calf?"

"What?" Sheridan became excited by the opportunity to experience the birth of a horse. She'd delivered a few babies during her residency, but now she referred her clients to OB once they became pregnant.

"My sister, Jayme, the veterinarian is out of town at a convention. Her husband is at the delivery, but needs help. My father thought since we were doctors..."

"We could assist."

"What do you think?"

"I'm there."

Chase is the most amazing man I've ever met. As Sheridan stood in the background watching Chase assist his brother-in-law deliver the foal, slithers of her heart floated into his back pocket.

"My brother's pretty cool, huh?" Alison joined her outside the corral.

"Yeah, he's pretty cool."

She'd forgotten how big horses were until she entered the barn, full of enthusiasm but short on experience. She had stepped up to the horse from the wrong side, startling the mare. She quickly learned that starling a horse in active labor could be dangerous. The horse reared and nipped at her. Chase pulled her out of the way, seconds before the mare bit her. She stayed at a safe distance after that, but not far enough to keep her from heaving when the first signs of a baby horse emerged. Delivering babies in a hospital with other residents and a staff doctor wasn't the same as what she was witnessing now. Seeing the baby horse—not pony or foal, it was too large to be described that way—begin its way down the birth canal made her nauseous. Before she could run out of the barn, she threw up. Chase hadn't said a negative word. He covered her mess with hay and told her he'd done the same thing the first time. He asked one of the ranch hands to help her get cleaned up. When she returned, he relegated her to a safe distance away. But only after she had assured him she would be all right and didn't want to leave until the calf had been born.

Having gathered her wits and worked through her embarrassment, she stood next to Alison watching the miracle. Chase stepped into the situation with quiet authority as he doled out orders to the ranch hands. He was a natural leader and people didn't mind following him because they understood his intentions were good—honorable.

An increase in the level of excitement called Sheridan from her musing. Seconds later, the new foal emerged, wobbling and trying to walk. The ranch hands started to applaud. Sheridan joined them, her heart bursting with pride she wasn't sure she was entitled to have. Her eyes met Chase's over the group of people congratulating him and Neil. In that moment, they connected, and she realized her feelings for Chase were too strong to continue the pretense of denial.

A couple of hours later, they were standing on her front porch, Chase having changed into a pair of faded jeans that looked like they had been specially molded to his thighs. The night was cool, but he didn't wear a jacket and his shirt was unbuttoned deep enough for Sheridan to see his dark and curly chest hair.

"This was quite an adventurous date." She grasped the ends of his shirt. His eyes narrowed in surprise.

"Next time we'll do something more conventional—dinner, a movie, or play."

She flattened her hands on his chest, bracing herself against the power of his muscles.

"Good night, Dr. Wexler."

"Good night, Dr. Larson." Suddenly, she pulled him to her face. She kissed him hard, wanting him to smolder. She wanted to place heavy thoughts on his mind. She wanted his body to react as violently to her and hers had to him.

When he drove home, he would relive the kiss. He would feel her grip tighten on his shirt, pulling him—pulling him into her world, not giving him room to get away. He would want to make a U-turn and kick down her door to get more kisses. He would begin to imagine what else she could do to his body. Her hands slipped inside his shirt, caressing his back as she deepened the kiss. Tonight, he would picture her in his room made of blue and green rainbows. When he crawled into bed and turned off the lights, he would wish she were there with him.

CHAPTER 9

Chase felt the vibes growing between them, so he took a chance. He stood on Sheridan's doorstep, unexpected, hoping she would welcome him. They'd been the picture of propriety all week long, passing each other as they made their way to the exam rooms, calling each other "Doctor." By Wednesday, he couldn't stand it. He watched Sheridan work, and when she was in between patients, he'd slip into her office and steal one of those kisses that made his knees buckle. Sometimes, he'd take two, careful not to stay behind closed doors long enough to raise Carolyn and Ted's suspicions. But even two was not enough. He needed to be alone with her, uninterrupted, to explore all she had to offer.

"Chase."

"Trick or treat."

She laughed and her eyes sparkled.

"Trick or treat?" he demanded with a smile.

"I want the treat."

"You can't just demand the treat. You have to give *me* a treat or I give you a trick. Haven't you ever done this before?"

"Been giving out treats all evening, but none of the kids have looked as good as you."

If he could blush, he would have. "Shameless, are you going to give me a treat or what?"

She opened the screen door and sashayed her curvy body up

to him. She braced herself by placing both hands on his chest, rose on tiptoe, and kissed him.

"Very nice, Dr. Wexler. You're giving out the best treats in the neighborhood."

She cocked her eyebrow and stuck out her hip, crossing her arms over her chest to emphasize her displeasure. "And just how many houses have you visited before mine, Dr. Larson?"

Possessiveness—he liked her spunk. Belonging to Sheridan could be a lot of fun. "This is the only house on my list. With the way you greeted me, I don't mind going down the walk and coming back for seconds." He gave her a quick kiss. "I have a treat for you, Shameless."

She lost the attitude, her face lighting up in anticipation.

"I won't keep you in suspense." He pulled the garment bag from behind his back.

"What's that?"

"Your costume. I'm taking you trick or treating."

She scanned him from head to toe. "And what are you supposed to be?"

"An Arabian prince." He extended the garment bag toward her. "You're one of my harem girls."

She doubled over in laughter. "I am not dressing up like one of your prostitutes."

"Who said anything about being a prostitute? You're a harem girl. You're trained in the arts of seduction. Your only desire is to please me."

"In your dreams."

"Exactly."

The heat flared up between them.

"Okay. If you want, you can be the queen and I'll be your...I don't know what they call it."

"You can be my man-slave."

"Whatever." He rolled his eyes. "Whatever it takes to get you into this get-up because I'm feeling pretty silly about now."

"Come in."

He settled in front of the television while he waited for her to change. His mouth dropped when she pranced out doing her version of a Middle Eastern belly dance. The pink and burgundy scraps of material left her midriff bare and punctuated the flare of her hips. Her hips gyrated and she hummed an upbeat tune as she danced around the room. The gold waistband of her pants defined her tiny waist and made her skin glow. She twisted and strutted, ending the provocative dance by falling into a sprawling pose at his feet.

He shifted uncomfortably in an attempt to hide his arousal. "That was—" he sounded like a frog. He tried again after clearing his throat. "That was great. Did you study dance?"

"Four years in high school. Dance and swim. My parents wanted me to be well-rounded."

Looking down into her soft, sensuous features became too tempting. "Get up from there." He took her elbow, helping her onto the sofa beside him. His size made her seem delicate and in need of his protection. Hard to believe she was a powerhouse of knowledge, tough when she needed to be, and shameless to boot.

"Are we going to a Halloween party?" she asked.

"No. We're going trick or treating."

"As in door-to-door?"

He nodded. "We'll have a little fun introducing you to the

good people of Duck River."

"If I show up dressed like this, they'll think twice about having me take care of them."

"Seeing you having fun makes you seem more ordinary; more like them. They'll love it. Trust me." He expected her to try to wiggle out of it.

"Let me get my shoes."

He watched as she dashed off to her bedroom, her hips shifting and mercilessly provoking him. The stuffy doctor who insisted on remaining businesslike, hardly ever joining the clinic staff in chitchat, was bouncing off to get ready for trick or treating. He had been right: there was a hidden layer to Sheridan worth discovering. She was shameless and fun loving, ready to follow him into unknown adventures. He adored this side of her.

The first house they visited belonged to the reverend and Mrs. Marks. Both Sheridan and the reverend's wife gasped in surprise when the door swung open.

"Chase Larson, what are you up to now?" Mrs. Marks pursed her lips in disapproval, but he knew her well enough to recognize the intrigue in the furrow of her brow.

He held out his trick or treat bag. "Trick," he paused, "or treat, Mrs. Marks."

"How'd you let him talk you into this, Dr. Wexler?"

Sheridan stuttered. "It seemed like fun at the time."

Chase nudged her with his elbow. He jerked his head toward the bag with the huge orange pumpkin drawn on it. Sheridan giggled and mimicked his stance. "Trick or treat, Mrs. Marks?"

"And look at how you're dressed!" Her eyes zeroed in on Sheridan's bare midriff.

She shifted.

He inched closer for support. "She's a harem girl and I'm her master."

"I'm the queen and you're my man-slave."

"We never agreed on that scenario."

"I sure didn't agree to be your harem girl," Sheridan retorted.

"Well, I won't play into this foolishness," Mrs. Marks huffed. "Chase, you haven't changed one bit." She turned her scolding eyes on Sheridan. "I'm surprised at you, Dr. Wexler. I thought you'd be good for Chase—help to stamp out some of his mischief."

"Trick or treat?" Sheridan asked again, her voice tight with devilish intent. Chase grinned—now she was learning to have fun.

"Umphf!" Mrs. Marks slammed the door.

Sheridan turned to him. "I thought you said people would get a kick out of this."

"They will," he answered as they made their way back to his truck. "You've met Mrs. Marks. She's a little stuffy."

"To say the least."

He placed his hands on her waist, ready to lift her into his truck.

"Wait."

"What is it?"

She smiled, her eyes full of mischief. She gathered her purse from the floor of his truck.

"What are you doing?"

She whipped around, producing a roll of toilet paper.

"What are you doing with toilet paper in your purse?" he

laughed.

"I thought it might come in handy."

"You said you've never gone trick or treating before."

"I watch television. I know the rules."

He leaned into her, imprisoned by her playfulness. "We can't TP the reverend's house."

She watched him, persuading him with her smile.

"I haven't done anything like that since I was ten years old."

She challenged him with her eyes.

"We're doctors!"

She stood on tiptoe and kissed his lips.

"You're shameless," he said, taking the toilet paper from her hands.

CHAPTER 10

Sheridan completed her examination of Mrs. Harvey and peered down at the chart, pondering the findings and searching for a logical conclusion.

"You cain't figure out what's the matter wit' me, can ya?"

Sheridan wanted to answer honestly, but hesitated. She remembered the malpractice case that had destroyed her career and her marriage. Admitting Mrs. Harvey's complaints perplexed her could jeopardize her newfound happiness in Duck River. If she could just word it right—saying, but not saying at the same time, that she had no clue why the woman was sick. No, lying was unethical. No matter what she'd been through, she couldn't lie to her patients.

Mrs. Harvey peered at her, as if waiting for a royal proclamation.

"No, I haven't figured it out."

"I ain't makin' it up."

She dropped the clipboard next to the sink. "I believe your symptoms are real, Mrs. Harvey."

"Ya do?"

She nodded. "I do. It's just going to take me some time to figure this out and come up with a diagnosis." She sighed heavily, unhappy she couldn't give the woman a more definitive answer. "I want you to feel assured I'm doing all I can to discover why you're sick. Once I do that, I'll be able to prescribe a treatment."

Instead of just medications to ease the symptoms, she wanted to add, but knew it wouldn't be wise.

"I trust y'all are doin' all you can—now. That's all I need, Doctor. Just need somebody to believe me."

Mrs. Harvey's comment alluded to the discussion they'd had at her last visit. She thought Chase wasn't taking her seriously because she was a woman. Sheridan started to argue in Chase's defense, but thought better of it. She'd established a relationship with Mrs. Harvey based on her willingness to listen and not ignore her complaints. Chase didn't discount Mrs. Harvey's sickness either. When he couldn't find a plausible explanation for the vague symptoms, he'd attributed her illness to grief over her husband's death. It was a reasonable diagnosis, but something about Mrs. Harvey's sickness made Sheridan want to dig deeper. She was missing something. After reviewing the woman's medical history, she had started at the ground floor, rechecking labs and ordering new tests when those came back negative. The common illnesses had been ruled out. Now she would test Mrs. Harvey for rare diseases.

"I'm going to renew the prescriptions Dr. Larson gave you initially." She reached into her lab coat for her prescription pad. "Continue taking everything as you were. I also want to run more tests. Depending on what they show, I'll probably send you to Nashville to see a specialist."

"Keep takin' this here medicine and see the specialist," Mrs. Harvey repeated. Sheridan had suggested she use the technique to test her understanding when talking to physicians about her care. She had been clear with Mrs. Harvey that she was ultimately in charge of her medical care, and to make informed decisions she needed to understand all the facts.

"Right. I'll call you after the blood work comes back. I'll give you the details about the specialist then too." She looked up from her prescription pad. The woman was clinging to her every word. "You don't hesitate to call me if anything changes." She handed Mrs. Harvey the prescriptions with a smile. "Hang in there a little while longer. We're going to find out what's wrong with you."

Mrs. Harvey tucked the prescriptions into her purse. "I 'preciate what you're doin' for me, Dr. Wexler."

Sheridan took the woman's hand between hers and gave her a reassuring squeeze. "Wait here. Ted will come and draw your blood." Sheridan left the exam room, puzzled by Mrs. Harvey's illness. She had no doubt the woman's symptoms were real, but she hadn't encountered this particular pathology before.

Mrs. Harvey perceptively picked up on her good mood. Sheridan hadn't known trick or treating could be such sexy fun. She and Chase ran from house to house, racing onto porches and ringing the doorbells. They were met with questioning stares that soon turned into ripples of laughter. Chase had been right, the townspeople found the new doctor endearing and welcomed her into their close-knit group. They had collected pounds of candy, which Chase took into Nashville to donate to a children's shelter sponsored by the hospital.

She returned to her office, determined to find the pathology of Mrs. Harvey's symptoms. She settled behind her desk and logged into a physician database. As she tapped the keys and clicked the mouse, searching disease pathologies, she wondered how Chase was doing in surgery. She missed being able to catch glimpses of him in between examining patients. Although they remained professional at work, it was comforting to know he was only down the hall. Sometimes she would catch him staring and a slow smile would spread across her face. He would duck his head and try to hide his lopsided grin, and she would slip away, satisfied he was thinking of her.

"Carolyn?" Sheridan impulsively phoned the reception desk. "Is there some way to get hold of Dr. Larson?"

"I can page him. Is it an emergency?"

"No, it's not an emergency." She held onto a stoic, all-business face. "I'd like to speak to him, please. When he's out of surgery."

"I'll transfer the call to your office."

Sheridan returned to her study of Mrs. Harvey's case. She scanned page after page of data, finding most of the diseases had already been ruled out. She began to wonder if there was some credence to Chase's theory about Mrs. Harvey's grieving causing the mysterious symptoms. The phone rang, startling her out of considering the theory any further. "Dr. Wexler."

Carolyn's voice sang, "Transferring Dr. Larson."

"Thank you, Carolyn."

There was a faint click and then Chase's baritone voice came across the line, sending shivers over her palm. "Hello, Dr. Wexler."

"Very professional." She mimicked his tone. "Hello, Dr. Larson."

"Carolyn said you needed to speak to me. Is something wrong?"

She dropped her voice to a seductive whisper. "I was wondering what time you'd be returning to Duck River this evening.

I'd like to cook you dinner."

Quiet on the other end of the line.

"Are you there?"

There was some rustling and then quietness again. "I'm here, Shameless. Had to duck into the doctor's office for some privacy. You want to cook me dinner?"

"Yes."

"You miss me."

"Are you asking?"

"No. I can hear it in your voice."

She did miss him, but she didn't want to give him the satisfaction of admitting it. "I can't seem to stop thinking about your man-slave costume."

"Arabian prince, my little harem girl."

"We'll call it a draw." He filled her with laughter. "Can you make dinner?"

"I can. I'll be back in Duck River before you see your last patient. I'll meet you at your place."

"Okay."

"How's everything going at the clinic?"

"Good. I'm even staying on schedule today, much to Carolyn's delight." She continued to click the mouse as she spoke. "Mrs. Harvey came in today. I'm running some more tests and I'd like to send her to Nashville to see a specialist."

"Consider her financial situation. She's had a little trouble supporting herself since her husband isn't around. She has decent medical coverage, but she never learned to drive and her husband was her only family. If you want her to see a specialist here, talk to Carolyn about taking some money out of the indigent fund to get her transportation."

Sheridan's finger froze, hovering over the mouse. She should have known about her patient's financial difficulty, but as Lester had told her many times, she never considered the headache she caused the bean counters. Indigence was a dirty word in the practice she'd built with him. Every research dollar was strictly allocated. Charity had no place in the wondrous world of discovery. Many of their arguments stemmed from the free services she offered patients in need. Hearing Chase not only support her treatment plan, but recommend she provide care despite the patient's financial circumstances confirmed her high opinion of him.

"Are you still there?" Chase wanted to know. "I don't hear the mouse clicking."

"No," she answered. "You didn't lose me." She recovered from Chase's ability to make her speechless through his kind actions. She started clicking the mouse again, quickly scanning the computer screen as the pages rolled by. "I didn't ask you how your surgery went."

"Just like riding a bicycle. I worked with a great team." He paused, reflecting. "You know, I made the right decision to return to surgery."

"Did you have any doubt?"

"Briefly. I worried about leaving the clinic in the wrong hands. I wondered if my operating skills were still there."

"Do you feel better now?"

"Much. I see how much you care for your patients. Ted and Carolyn are the best at what they do, so I know the clinic will run smoothly when I'm not there."

"And now you've proven to yourself your surgery skills are still sharp."

"Exactly."

"I never doubted your ability to operate, or your ability to make the best decisions for your patients here."

Chase was giving her the details of his surgery when something on the computer caught her attention—a list of symptoms closely matching Mrs. Harvey's complaints.

"What is it?" Chase asked.

"I think I've found something on Mrs. Harvey's symptoms."

"Go. Finish your research. You can tell me about it tonight over dinner."

"Okay," she answered, distracted by her findings. "I bet the residents are getting restless."

"Waiting for words of wisdom from their fearless leader. Bye, Shameless."

She didn't want to hang up, didn't want to give up the warm and fuzzy feelings he brought.

His voice dipped to a whisper. "Shameless?"

"I'll see you tonight. For dinner. My place."

"I'm a meat and potatoes type of guy, so cook me some meat and potatoes."

"No can do. Vegetarians rule." She smiled, knowing she'd made the right decision to call him. He brightened her day, and she hoped she had the same effect on him.

"You force feed me veggies, and I'll force feed you steak."

"A perfect match."

"Perfect." With one word he steered the conversation back into deep emotional waters.

"Goodbye, Dr. Larson." She reluctantly disconnected.

The computer screen consumed her attention again. The list of symptoms read: muscle spasms, nausea, vomiting, diarrhea, and abdominal pain. She pulled Mrs. Harvey's medical chart in front of her. At one time or another, Mrs. Harvey had complained of all those things. The unusual, tell-tale sign that had caught Sheridan's eye as she scanned the screen was the garlic breath. She'd noticed the odor on Mrs. Harvey's breath today, but thought she'd probably just come from lunch at the diner.

Sheridan clicked the link, which displayed the cascading severity of symptoms. Hypotension—Mrs. Harvey's blood pressure had not been low. She checked the trend over the past few visits; all was normal there. The next set of symptoms set her heart racing. Cardiovascular collapse, aplastic anemia and eventually death. She cautioned herself not to panic. The symptoms were the same, but no definitive diagnosis had been made.

Arsenic poisoning. It sounded like the bad plot from a B movie. Mrs. Harvey lived alone, miles outside of town. By Chase's account, she wasn't a wealthy woman, so who would want to poison her? Sheridan had been scolded by Lester more than once for coming up with dramatic, rare diagnoses without enough medical evidence to back her up. This time she'd be vigilant, but not reckless.

Ted knocked on the door. "Dr. Wexler, the next round of patients is waiting."

Sheridan printed the information she'd found and placed it in her desk drawer. She'd read it more thoroughly at the end of the day.

"Dr. Wexler, you're on time and delivering service with a

smile," Ted said when she joined him. "What happened to loosen you up?"

"What do you mean?"

"Two months ago you were grim and scary. Now you're happy and fun-loving."

"I'm getting to know you better."

Ted took the clipboard from her. "You're getting to know *someone* around here better."

She and Chase had never talked about keeping their relationship a secret. It just seemed the right thing to do. She didn't want Ted and Carolyn to feel pressured when giving their vote about her partnership at the clinic. With Chase, the issue was sticky, but above all, he loved his patients and he wouldn't let anything jeopardize their care. If he felt she wasn't right for Duck River Family Medicine, he wouldn't offer her the partnership.

"Do you see it as a conflict of interest?"

Ted grinned. "If I wasn't married..." He ducked into the exam room, leaving his thought unfinished.

The rest of the day went smoothly, with Sheridan finding a good rhythm with Ted. He had learned the idiosyncrasies in her delivery of care that made her practice unique, and together they had perfected a routine that helped them give the best care in a timely way. They could read each other, click without words.

Sheridan bumped into Carolyn after lunch in the lounge filling her coffee cup.

"Good job today, Dr. Wexler."

"Thank you."

"I give you a hard time about staying on schedule, but the lobby can be a hard place to work. Sick people can be mean people."

"I understand." She grabbed a cranberry juice from the refrigerator.

"Do you mind if I leave after the last patient is placed in the exam room? Ted has agreed to check her out."

Nothing could dampen her mood today. She'd had a blast with Chase last night, and she had a lead in Mrs. Harvey's case. "No problem."

"Then I'll say good night now." Carolyn left, stirring her coffee frantically. Working the reception desk must press on one's nerves. Little by little, she was winning over the stoic receptionist. Carolyn would never embrace her in a hug and welcome her into the family. Her acceptance would be more subtle, quick conversations in the lounge, a vague compliment here and there, asking for a favor—those were signs the older woman liked her.

Sheridan downed her cranberry juice in between seeing the last three patients of the day. She would end on a high note. She was going to tell a newlywed couple they were expecting. They'd been trying to get pregnant for six months, and Sheridan would give them the good news today that they were successful.

"Dr. Wexler," Ted stopped her before she entered exam room three. "Dr. Larson's sister is here to see you."

"Me?" She didn't ask which of the four; it was surprising any of them would seek her out.

"She's in your office. I told her it might be a minute, and she said she'd wait."

Sheridan consulted with the newlyweds. She gave them a stack of brochures to read before the woman's first appointment with the gynecologist in Nashville. The doctor would send regular reports to Sheridan. With Nashville being a good drive away, she might be called on to deliver the baby in Duck River. She remembered the adventure with the calf's delivery on the Larson ranch and realized she had some brushing up to do.

During her consultation, her mind wandered, guessing what Chase's sister could possibly want with her. Maybe Sarah and Alison had told Jayme and Brenda about her and they wanted to warn her off. If that was the case, she'd keep her cool, discuss it with Chase and let him handle his family. Anticipation had her stomach tied in knots by the time she made it back to her office.

She took a deep breath and opened her door. "Alison." She'd put her money on it being Sarah.

"Hi, Sheridan. I hope you don't mind me coming like this." She was pleasant, but cautious—hiding something.

"It's fine." She sat behind her desk, pulling the chair forward. Alison had the element of surprise on her side. Sheridan needed the position of authority. "What did you want to see me about?"

Alison's eyes went to her lap. She clutched a purse against her belly, wringing the leather strap between her fingers. She was pretty with angelically soft features. Their meeting at the ranch gave Sheridan the impression she was a little immature and very vulnerable, as if she hadn't experienced enough of the harsh realities of life yet. She could understand why Chase worried about her.

"Alison?" she prompted.

She lifted her head and started in the middle of the conversation she was having in her head. "You haven't met my husband Dwayne yet. My family doesn't like him. They don't think I know, but I do. Dwayne's a little...he's a dominant personality.

The opposite of me. So they worry he'll take advantage of me."

"Are you sure you want to talk to me about something this personal?"

Alison went on, ignoring the question. "Dwayne is good for me. My family will learn that in time." She paused then got up and went to the window, staring but watching nothing in particular. "I'd like to speak to you as a patient." She turned, catching Sheridan's confused expression. "It gives me the right to confidentiality, right? Whatever I tell you stays between us?"

Sheridan wasn't certain she wanted to be placed in a compromising position, entering blindly into an agreement she might regret. If Alison wasn't Chase's sister, she would not hesitate to offer her patient anonymity. She put away her growing attraction to Chase and remembered she was a doctor, and as a physician, she owed confidentiality to her patient. "Whatever we discuss is private."

Alison's shoulders rose and when they lowered, the tears began to flow. "Last night," she choked out. "Last night I was making love with my husband, and he found a lump in my right breast."

CHAPTER 11

Returning to the operating room was exhilarating. Chase was surprised by how easily it all came back to him, how quickly he regained his confidence in his surgical skills. He acclimated himself to the surgical suite and hospital policies by assisting the General Surgeon with his OR cases. Once he was fully comfortable, he worked solo. Appendectomy—no problem. Remove a kidney—snip, snip and it's done. He even assisted with an emergency splenectomy. The rush of adrenaline accompanying saving a patient's life reassured him he had made the right decision in changing the direction of his career. He'd been growing stagnant in his practice at the clinic.

Working in Nashville three days a week would rejuvenate his medical soul. And Sheridan would rejuvenate what made him a man.

She had made his day, calling and inviting him to dinner. He couldn't wait to tell her about the way the eager residents scribbled notes during rounds. Or express his surprise about how skilled the nurses were, many directing the residents with patient care issues. With Sheridan he could speak freely, not stopping to explain medical jargon. She would understand his enthusiasm and understand what it was like for him to return to work at the medical center.

He went over his day as he showered and shaved, hoping not to forget one detail. He wanted to share it all with Sheridan.

Wearing a suit for dinner might be a little excessive, but he was proud of his accomplishments today and wanted Sheridan to be proud of him, too. He labored in the selection of a tie, and then spent too much time pondering which cologne fragrance would be most appealing to Sheridan. Maybe she didn't like men to wear cologne—she'd never voiced an opinion one way or the other—but he wanted to be his best for her. That meant shaving, and wearing a suit and cologne, even if they were staying in.

Dating another doctor definitely had its up sides. When Sheridan spoke about her day at the clinic, he would be genuinely interested. Not plastering on a smile and trying to be supportive of a profession he knew nothing about. Then they would move the conversation on to more intimate things.

Chase reflected on his feelings for Sheridan during the drive to her house. His initial physical attraction had grown into something much more substantial over a relatively short period of time. He tried to explain his hastily developing feelings by attributing them to the fact that they spent so much time together during work, and now dating, but somehow it didn't seem accurate. Simply, Sheridan was a dynamic, beautiful woman and he had connected with her spirit the moment he'd met her. He smiled at the concept of love at first sight. He'd never been a believer. *Love at first sight really means lust at first sight,* he'd told Ted when he announced his marriage after two months of dating. Many years and many babies later, Chase had to admit Ted was on to something.

"You look spectacular." Sheridan's eyes roamed appreciatively over the terrain of his body, and he knew the suit was weaving its magic. "Very handsome."

Still smiling about the unpredictability of love, he handed her a bouquet of flowers and a bottle of sparkling grape juice.

"Such a gentleman," she said, burying her nose in the mixed bouquet. "And you remembered I don't drink."

He knew all her favorite things, her quirks, likes and dislikes.

"Come in and have a seat in the living room."

He started for the living room, but the rocking of her hips in black slacks and the intermittent peeks of creamy flesh revealed by the burgundy cashmere sweater, called him to follow her. He walked in the trail of her perfume, wishing he could lick the bitterness from her pulse points. "You're pretty—glowing."

She glanced at him, the corner of her mouth moving upward into a slight smile as she searched her cabinets for a vase. "I'll bring you something to drink."

"You didn't kiss me hello."

Her sculptured brow shuffled. "I was distracted by the suit."

He stretched above her head and retrieved the vase. "Have the effects worn off because I would really like a kiss."

She laid the bouquet on the countertop between the vase and the sparkling grape juice. "The suit. The flowers. The sparkling grape juice. The least I can do is give you a kiss." She swished her hips, bringing her body next to his.

"Did you miss me today?" He caught her chin in his palm. "Don't try to deny it. You wouldn't have had Carolyn page me if you didn't."

She tossed her head back, jutting out her chin in defiance. "I did," she confessed.

He rested his hands on the curvy fullness of her hips. "I thought about you all day."

"Really?" Her voice lifted in pleasant disbelief.

He nodded, squeezing her hips. "I wished you were sitting in the observation deck, watching me so I could make you proud."

She laughed softly, a quick chuckle of approval.

"Did you hold down the fort today?" His heart leapt at the possibility of their being a permanent team—in and out of the clinic setting.

"I hope I made you proud."

He watched her in disbelief. Did she not have a clue how crazy he was over her?

"What is it? Did Carolyn say something?"

"What could Carolyn say other than you're a great doctor and a wonderful person?"

Relief made her head drop. He immediately caught her chin, not wanting to lose sight of her for one moment. She licked her bottom lip, and he traced her tongue's route with his finger. A soft shiver ran through her. She liked his hands. More importantly, she liked his hands on her.

"Can I have my kiss now?" Before she could answer, he bent to kiss her.

This kiss was different from their others. His tongue told her he'd missed her today. Her hands told him she wanted to know what she was missing. Everything around them faded away, leaving them alone in a small house in Duck River, Tennessee. As colors swirled above their heads, they were abandoned in the center of the universe.

Cherry, red, and cotton candy pink colored Chase's vision. He savored her. She tasted like a woman—soft, warm, sweet, rich and delicious. Their chemistry mixed—pheromones gone wild.

Their personalities merged through the perfect kiss, and he never wanted to let her go.

Sheridan pulled away first. Her eyes were hooded. She weaved. He placed his hands on her shoulders, steadying her.

"Did you feel it, Chase?"

"I made the earth move for you."

She angled her head, watching him. He wished he could take his flip comment back—she wasn't playing. He started to apologize, his nervous tongue twisting the words.

Sheridan stood on tiptoe, grabbed the lapel of his suit, shifted her body weight against his, and made him see stars. Her heat radiated through his clothing. The designer suit melted away. Her sweater vanished, leaving him naked against her power. He was her man-slave and she was the queen. No argument from him.

She ended the kiss, tilted her head up, and entered his psyche through his eyes. "I want you."

A million thoughts raced through his head. The sanest one made it past his lips. "It's too soon."

"I want you." She applied her body deeper against his chest, forcing him to take a step back to keep his balance.

"A few weeks ago we were acting like strangers."

She pushed again.

He took another step back.

"We're not strangers now." Her fingers pried open the knot of his tie.

"Two weeks ago you were singing the *somebody-done-me-wrong* song."

She started on the buttons of his tan shirt.

"The arteries feeding your heart were too clogged to even consider letting anybody in."

She pushed against his bare chest, sending him back another step.

"Sheridan," he caught her hands as she pulled his shirt from his slacks. "Talk to me."

She released him. Breathing hard, she gathered her thoughts, refueling her argument.

He stroked her cheek. "I can't let one kiss lead you down the path of no return."

She dropped her eyes, and her hair formed a curtain, concealing the beauty of her face. It annoyed him. He needed to see her expression and hear her thoughts. He tucked her hair behind her ear and lifted her chin. "What's going on?"

"I want you."

"I heard you say that. What's going on?"

"You told me to live without scrutinizing every move I make. You told me to have fun."

"Damn. If you think we're going to have quick sex and walk away, you're out of your mind. I won't go for it."

She moved into him, and he had to take another step back to see her need clearly. "Don't analyze the moment away. I want you. It's enough."

"Enough for what? What are you running from?"

"I want you," she rebutted, annoyed. "You don't want me?"

"I won't answer that question." It would take the conversation in the direction he was fighting against with every gentlemanly bone in his body. "Are you using me to get over another man? The *somebody-done-me-wrong* man?"

"No." No hesitation.

"Am I diversion?"

"Where are all the questions coming from?" She maneuvered him another step backward.

"I don't want you to wake up and start crying because you made a mistake."

"I want you," she answered with conviction.

Another backward step. With each step his resistance waned. He was trying to be honorable, to remain a gentleman. He wanted to take things slow—anticipating they'd have their entire lives together.

He looked down into her face, inhaled her flowery perfume, and reveled in the feel of her body pressed against his. She was beautiful. She had a lovely body. And his heart still did the flippy-floppy thing when she was near.

"You want me?" He couldn't believe it.

"Yes."

"Tell me why."

"Do I have to explain—"

"Tell me why."

She tossed back her head, brazenly meeting his gaze. "I care about you, Chase. I like the way I feel when we're together. Even if we're at the clinic, I feel like we're the only two in the building."

Words from his own heart. Words he needed to hear.

Sheridan's fingers wrapped around his belt buckle, and he didn't stop her. She applied a little pressure, and he took a step back.

She pressed her forehead against his chest. "There's a warmth surrounding you that has to be real. The way you look at me makes me feel special." She opened his belt buckle. "You kiss me with such tenderness, but underneath there's wild passion waiting—patiently waiting for the right time."

His body responded to her seductive words, but his heart craved more. "I'm looking for something real with you." He cradled her in his arms. "This can't just be about sex." He paused, fighting sexual urges. "If you can't give me more, I'll leave right now." His manhood grew, betraying his need.

"I can't promise you a future."

Desperation. "You can tell me it's on your agenda to try."

"I don't know if I have what it takes to be in a committed relationship." The crack of her voice told him she believed what she said.

"Let me be the judge. You care about me. I'm crazy about you. We'll build from there."

"We'll build from there," she repeated. She nudged him with her hip, and he crossed the threshold into her bedroom.

"And I care about you, too, Shameless."

"You make me laugh. Now I want you to make me moan."

CHAPTER 12

"I have never wanted a man this badly in my life."

Chase chuckled, his baritone conveying tiny sparks across her neck. He removed her sweater and pants. "This is more than sex." He spun her around, releasing the hooks of her bra. "This is a beginning, not an end."

"An end?"

"Putting an end to our lust."

"Our?" She'd never seen signs of his lust. She glanced downward, his bodily need was evident, but his desire came attached to emotions.

From behind, he grasped her waist and tugged at her panties, pulling them down—over her thighs, past her knees, across her calves. He sent her a heated look, and she used his shoulders as an anchor as she stepped out of her final piece of clothing.

After he undressed her, he started kissing her. Kissed the top of her feet, her calves, her knees, her thighs—stopped to seek silent permission, and then kissed her there, too. His lips roamed over her backside, the center of her back, her spine, her shoulders. He held her around the waist with both hands in order to keep her from swooning as she kissed her neck, her ears, the nape of her neck.

He kissed her *to* the bed. Kissed her *onto* the bed. Kissed her *underneath* the sheets.

Chase stood next to the bed and shrugged out of his jacket.

"I lust for you." He unbuttoned his shirt, revealing a muscular chest covered with a splattering of wiry hair. "I keep my lust in check because it's not the most important emotion I feel for you."

Sheridan watched in fascination as he undid the cuffs of his sleeves. He slid one sleeve off and then moved to his belt buckle. Suddenly, she felt naked as she anticipated him joining her nude, in her bed. He bent down and consumed her lips as he removed his shirt and slacks. He'd found she liked it when he sucked her neck, just to the right of the hollow. He sucked the tender skin until she squirmed, stopping only after he stepped out of his briefs.

"I like your kisses," Sheridan said as the mattress tilted under his weight.

"I need more of your kisses," he answered as he hovered over her.

She wiggled her hips until the length of his hardness pressed into her inner thigh. His hips gyrated, giving her a preview of what he would do once he was inside of her. She liked having the hard planes of his muscles cover her body. He placed his hands on the bed next to her head, lowering for a kiss. She inhaled the spicy fragrance of his cologne as it mixed with the scent of their arousal. She felt warm and protected in the cocoon of his body.

Sheridan bent her knee, bringing their interconnecting parts into alignment. He hissed above her, bringing to her attention the sound of her own ragged breathing. She reached between them and cradled the length of him in the palm of her hand. His breath caught. He was soft and hard and masculine and daunting, yet tempting. He cradled her cheek in his hand, still suspended above her. She lifted her head and stroked his chest, tasting the salty fresh flavor of him. He shivered, his hand dropping next to her face as he caught his weight. She showed him she was ready by placing the tip of him at her opening.

"Condom?" he asked.

She cursed.

"Sheridan!"

"Sorry," she apologized for her brash language.

"I might…" he stretched his long arm out, grabbing his slacks. While he searched his wallet, she let her fingers dance over his perfect body. Sculpted by the gods, his muscles were as hard as granite, his skin soft as fine silk. The hair on his chest left feather kisses on her breasts. The wiry hairs of his groin left abrasions on her thigh. As she touched him, her arousal grew.

"I have one," Chase announced, holding the package up for her to see.

"Just in time," she breathed relief.

"It's been in my wallet for awhile." He examined the beat up package. "It's a little bruised, but intact."

"Just one?" she squeaked. Her arousal was at its highest ever; one would not put out the fire.

"Just one."

Her eyes scanned his virile erection. "We can only do it once?"

He laughed. "This time." He lowered his body, curve to curve, against hers.

"We'll have to put it to good use."

Sheridan placed her hand on his forearm and concentrated on the texture of his skin as she ran her finger to his hand. "Your hands turn me on." She took his hand and pressed it to her breast. She splayed his fingers and lifted her head to watch him holding her.

"I picked up on that, but why?" He pressed lightly, causing the indentation of her breast.

"The veins running across the back of your hand show your strength. The way you touch me shows your gentle nature. Your nails are always manicured. Long, slender fingers. Yes, your hands turn me on."

The fingers of his free hand cascaded over her lips. He slipped one slim finger inside her mouth. His expression showed he was surprised by the heat he found there. She latched onto him, suckling vigorously. His body reacted violently, stretching and pushing for entrance.

"The condom," she said around his finger.

He handed her the condom and slithered down her body, letting her feel every muscle of his abdomen as it flexed. He threw her thigh over his shoulder and stroked her with those long, slender fingers. He pressed his finger against her lips until she opened her mouth and allowed him back inside. The moisture from her mouth made his exploration easier. He slipped his finger deep inside, rotating it to give her more pleasure. "Am I putting my hands to good use?" His hot breath scorched her thigh.

She moaned.

"Does having my fingers deep inside you turn you on more than looking at them?"

In answer, her feet dug into the mattress, lifting her up for his full consumption.

"You can say my name now." His other hand joined the mission, and soon her body was quivering.

"Chase. Chase. Chase," she chanted as her body returned to normal. When the earthquake ended, Chase dipped his head, used those perfect hands to part her sea, and drank and drank until she begged him to let her experience ecstasy again.

He let her recover before he rose up and pried the condom from her hand. She heard paper ripping and wondered if her body could stand being over nourished with pleasure. He balanced himself above her, his pecs bulging. He slipped a hand between them and started to slowly descend. In no hurry, he filled her with a sure and steady downward stroke. He breached her barrier and she sighed, her head falling back and exposing her neck. He converged on the flesh, finding an area he hadn't licked.

Chase made love to her. There was no lust in his strokes or his touches or his kisses. The combination of unbridled sensuality and tender emotions made Sheridan's head spin. She entered into this joining with Chase to fulfill her body's craving. Somewhere along the way to seduction, Chase had taken control and refused to let her reduce the experience to bodily fulfillment. She lay helpless beneath him as he made love to her, subject to the assault of his tender words. He maneuvered her in a direction she hadn't anticipated, making his body's movements more potent with every stroke.

He found her mouth and kissed her lovingly while he penetrated her with heavy strokes. Slow, even, in and out. "I know what you want from me." He brought her to the brink of chaos. "I want it, too." She wrapped her legs around his waist, dug her fingers into his back and rode him from below. "Shameless," he scolded. He pulled away to control the rhythm. No matter how aggressively she pursued, he remained sure and steady, slowly giving her what she needed. He never stopped kissing her. "You are so special to me."

She whimpered.

"This is the difference between real emotions and lust," he told her through gritted teeth. Still he maintained his self-control.

"Chase," she panted as his stroke massaged her.

He nipped at her ear, igniting a frenzy of delightful sensations throughout her body.

"Chase, please."

He showed her mercy, shifting his body so his shaft rubbed back and forth over her swollen nub. "Come for me again," he demanded.

She exploded at his brazen words. She panted, her chest heaving, trying to regain her senses.

Chase stopped whispering his feelings in her ear, and took her breast between his lips. He tasted her as his orgasm built in intensity. He struggled to control his rhythm. He fought the battle between emotion and lust until his hips jerked.

"Chase, it's all right," she whispered into the falling darkness. "Let go, baby. It's okay."

He found her lips again, pumping his hips with uncontrolled fervor. He froze, pushed hard, muscles tensed; he moaned and his body shook. Sheridan pulled him down on top of her and wrapped him in her warmth. "It's okay." She kissed his temples as he struggled to slow his breathing. "Lust has its place, too." She used her foot to work up the sheet and covered them.

"Do you want me to go now?" Chase's voice shattered the silence.

"No."

He spooned with her. "Damn. Only one condom."

She snuggled back into his hard chest. "Had to make it count."

His arms tightened around her waist. "Are you okay?"

She nodded in the darkness.

He kissed the area behind her ear. "I didn't think it would happen between us so soon, but I'm glad it did. This was about more than sex. I really care about you."

She twisted around to face him. "What time do you have to be at the clinic in the morning?"

He let her change the charged subject. "My schedule starts after lunch. You?"

"My first patient is at nine."

He kissed her forehead. "Go to sleep, Shameless."

"I've never been shameless with anyone but you."

"I know." He kissed each cheek. After a long pause he asked, "Why is your place so bare?"

"It's not permanent."

She felt him tense against her. He fought to relax before he spoke again. "It may not be permanent, but it's your home right now. You should make it more like a home, not an empty rental unit."

A funny quiver ran through her stomach and a pain shot through her heart. She didn't belong anywhere. Her life was unstable and she'd just complicated the situation at the clinic by sleeping with the medical director. She was keeping secrets from her lover: the lawsuit, her divorce, his sister's possible diagnosis. These were not the actions of a person who had promised to give her all to having a relationship with him. She could tell him everything about her past, but he had never asked. He didn't care about what baggage was in her closet. He cared about her happiness now; in this place and time.

"Chase."

"Yeah?" He yawned. "Tomorrow after work we'll go shopping." He yawned again. "Make this flat into a home." He tightened his arms around her waist. "What were you going to ask me?"

"I was going to say goodnight."

"Goodnight, Sheridan."

CHAPTER 13

"Thank you for calling Duck River Family Medicine, how may I help you today?"

"Good morning, Carolyn." Chase's bare feet slapped the kitchen towel. Sheridan had no decorative rugs to cushion his step, but he'd take care of that today on their shopping trip.

"Good morning, Dr. Larson."

"Can I speak with Dr. Wexler?" *Shameless*, he thought as he remembered their intimate time together.

"Yes. Don't keep her too long because my lobby is overflowing out the front door." Carolyn was prone to exaggeration; her way of tattling without tattling. Sheridan did have a problem with keeping on schedule, but it was because she spent so much quality time with each patient.

Chase searched for breakfast in the refrigerator as he waited for Sheridan to come on the line. The wet towel hanging around his neck swiped at his naked chest, reminding him of Sheridan's skillful work the night before.

"This is Dr. Wexler."

"You don't have anything to eat in this refrigerator."

Her smile crossed the phone line. "Plenty of fruits and vegetables."

"No caffeine?"

"Orange juice. Fresh squeezed."

"Where is the bacon? A man needs protein after last night."

He settled for an apple, closed the refrigerator and stepped into the living room. "You didn't wake me before you left."

"Thought a man needed his rest after last night."

He laughed as he chomped down on the apple. "When I come to work are we going to pretend like last night didn't happen?"

"Yes."

"Just wanted to know the game plan."

"You understand, right?"

"Um, hmm." He took another bite of the forbidden fruit. "You should see the way I'm eating this apple."

"Why is that important, Dr. Larson?" she asked, playfully.

"It would give you a preview of what I plan on doing to you the next time we're alone…in bed…unclothed…with the lights out."

She giggled, whispering, "Unclothed?"

"Unclothed, Shameless." There was a short pause. He could hear her shuffling papers. "Carolyn says you're a little behind today."

"I am. I'm working on it."

"Catch up. We're going shopping after work."

"I will. I don't like it when Ted and Carolyn are mad at me for working too slow."

"Ted doesn't get mad and Carolyn just likes to gripe. We all appreciate how much you care about your patients."

"I'll speed along."

Carnal pictures flooded his mind. "Not too fast, Shameless."

"I'd better go. Ted is signaling me. All the exam rooms are full."

He tsked. "Better get your act together before the boss arrives."

She laughed. The dial tone ended their conversation. He'd talk to her about that; never hang up the phone without saying goodbye. She was a little rough around the edges when it came to relationship rules, but he'd have fun tutoring her.

He finished the apple while he absentmindedly flipped through the television channels. Lord, the girl didn't even have cable. No furniture. No cable. No decent food in the cabinets. She needed him badly. He smiled at the thought. There were no personal belongings except a photo of who he assumed were her parents on the otherwise empty mantel.

He completed a visual inspection of Sheridan's place from the sofa, trying to feel her in it. It was as if she had no past. It didn't fit. The rental flat was not where she should be. Waiting for him in his home—that's where she fit.

He returned to the bedroom, made the bed and tossed the towels on top of the washer. She didn't have a hamper. He added it to the shopping list. He put on the chocolate suit he'd worn the night before to impress her. It had worked. His belt was thrown across a chair made of dark wood with oriental cushioning. He liked the chair. She could decorate the room around the theme of the chair. He imagined soft lighting and the fragrance of mystic flowers filling the air. Today they would shop and make the room their private love nest.

Chase dug his socks from beneath the bed. He was slipping on his jacket, ready to leave for work when the doorbell rang. If he answered the door and one of the town's gossips found him at the new doctor's home alone, their relationship business would be spread all over town by nightfall.

He looked out the curtain and saw a Lincoln with rental plates parked next to his truck. Could be someone lost and looking for directions. Could be a relative from out of town coming to surprise Sheridan.

He opened the door, cautious of seeming too familiar, in case it was one of her relatives.

A man near his age wearing an expensive Italian suit and Italian loafers stood on Sheridan's stoop. Chase's instincts made his stomach curdle. He gave the man a curt nod.

"I'm looking for Sheridan Wexler."

"She's not here. Would you like to leave her a message?"

"Dr. Wexler lives here, right?" The man's eyes moved over his shoulder, searching for proof.

"Yes." He didn't want to give up too much information.

The man leaned to the right, looking past him. "Are you living here with her?"

"I'm a friend. Who did you say you were?"

"I'm her husband."

Chase's game face reflexively slid into place to hide the riotous emotions thumping in his skull. He couldn't give over the advantage of surprise. "I guess you should come in." He pushed the screen open and watched the man as he walked by, visually sizing him up. Some women would go for his type. Rolex, expensive suit, three hundred dollar hair cut. One of those light skinned brothers that had too many groupies telling him he was the—

The man spun around and extended his hand. "Lester Wexler. Dr. Lester Wexler."

"Dr. Chase Larson."

Lester's eyes narrowed in surprise. They were on even ground once again.

Chase took his hand, offering a firm handshake. Lester cut it short. He moved around the flat, examining Sheridan's space, searching for something. After he took it all in, he opened the buttons of his jacket, sat on the loveseat and spread his arms along the back. "You're Sheridan's *friend*?"

Chase sat across from him on the sofa. "Yes."

"Are you gay?"

Chase laughed, loud and hearty, leaving no question about his answer.

"Then we have a problem."

"I didn't know Sheridan was married."

"She hasn't told you everything about her life." Lester's smug smile showed he thought this important.

"She's told me everything about her life that is significant."

This surprised Lester. His game face wasn't as potent as Chase's. He took his arms off the back of the sofa, lost his relaxed stance.

"Why wouldn't Sheridan tell me she was married? Where have you been all the time she's been in Duck River?"

"We divorced not long ago." Lester paused. "She didn't mention me? How good of friends arc you?"

Their lovemaking the night before flashed through his mind. "More than friends."

Lester nodded. He sized Chase up from head to toe with a disdainful grimace. "How long?"

"I have to get to work."

"Not long," he smugly deduced.

"How is it important to you?"

"She's letting you stay here when she's not home."

"Sheridan and I have plenty of time for her to tell me everything I need to know."

They declared a silent challenge in the meeting of their eyes.

Chase wanted to ask a hundred questions. He asked only one. "What are you doing here?"

Lester leaned forward and placed his hands on his knees. "I came to take my wife back home."

Paralyzed, Chase stared blankly at Lester.

"I want her back."

"That's impossible," Chase said, stunned by the idea it might just be a possibility.

"Impossible?"

"Sheridan is with me." He felt protective, jealous and hurt.

"I can see there may be…complications."

"I'm more than a complication."

Lester sat back, nodded. This would be a gentlemanly fight. "You see, Chet—"

"Chase."

"Chase." Lester's jaw moved back and forth as if it hurt to say his name. "Sheridan and I were married. We have history. You can't fight history. I'm her past and her future. You're the transition guy. You're in the picture because she needs a diversion from the hurt she feels over our break up."

I can't promise you a future, she'd said.

We'll build from there, he'd replied.

"You know I'm telling the truth," Lester gloated. "You may

be involved with Sheridan, but not on an intimate level. If there was a bond between you, you wouldn't be looking so worried right now."

"What Sheridan and I have is new, not weak."

He nodded, patronizingly. "Sure about that, Chase? She didn't even tell you she had been married before."

"You can go now," Chase demanded.

"We're not done here."

"I asked you to leave." He moved to the edge of the sofa. How quickly this could escalate from gentlemanly to rowdy behavior.

Lester stood, buttoning his Italian jacket. "Oh, I'll leave, but we're not done here."

Fighting words.

He stood, not wanting to be in a vulnerable position. "I'm not giving up Sheridan."

"Neither am I."

CHAPTER 14

"One of you is floating on air and the other is spitting nails," Ted said, annoyingly as observant as ever. "What's going on between you and Dr. Wexler?"

"Stay out of it," Chase snapped, and marched into his office. He reached behind him and pushed the door shut, intending for it to close with a slam.

"Hey!" Sheridan caught the door and closed it quietly behind her. "I thought we were going to act like strangers. Not like we hate each other."

All the anger he'd built up from the moment Lester announced he was Sheridan's husband threatened to explode. He balled his fists, crumpling his anger inside. He counted to ten, and then to twenty, before he regained control of his emotions.

"What's wrong? Are you mad at me?" Sheridan asked, reading him correctly.

He swallowed hard, fighting to maintain the tone he should with the woman he wanted to make his steady lover. Between gritted teeth he said, "Your husband stopped by your house today."

All the color drained from her face. She stood frozen in the middle of his office, pale and stunned. He peered at her mercilessly, applying mental pressure. He would demand answers and Sheridan would be open and honest with the information he needed.

"What did he say?" Her voice shivered, and he felt his sympathy growing.

Despite how angry he was, he wanted to comfort her in his arms. Afraid he would cradle her and tell her everything would be okay before getting any answers, he placed his desk between them. "What else is there?" he snapped.

"What did he tell you?"

"Nothing much. Just that he wants you back."

Her mouth dropped.

"Damn, Sheridan." He shoved some files across the desk, wishing he'd handled the situation with Lester differently. "You didn't tell me you were married?"

"Divorced."

"What?" Arguing semantics? "What did you say?"

"Lester and I are divorced."

"So he mentioned, which is more than you mentioned."

"You never asked. You never asked any questions about my past."

He sat down and started making notes in a patient chart. "I see. I didn't quiz you or have you fill out a questionnaire, so somehow this is all my fault."

"I didn't say that. You're accusing me—"

"Did you know he was in town?"

"No." She tried to shield her curiosity behind a frown.

"Did you know he still wants you?"

"No."

He slapped the chart closed and reached for the next.

"What happened?" she asked.

He looked up. His gaze was stern. She stepped back.

"What happened between you two? Did Lester start a fight with you?"

"Don't worry. We were gentlemen. He told me he was your husband and that my services were no longer needed. Seems I'm the transitional man in your life. Now that he's back, I'm dismissed."

"I'm sorry. Lester can be—"

"Don't worry. I can handle my own business."

"Your business?"

He stood up slowly, gripping the edge of the desk. "I told him I wasn't going anywhere."

"Doctors," Ted's voice called out on the other side of the door. "Patients in one, two and four. I'd like to have dinner with the wife and kids tonight."

Sheridan wrung her hands. "Can we talk about this later?"

"Later," he answered, tightly. "We'll definitely talk about this."

She followed him out into the hall.

"Dr. Wexler," Ted said. "You have a visitor. I was going to take him into your office. The exam rooms are filled." Both doctors got the hint.

Lester Wexler stepped around Ted. Chase turned back to see Sheridan, anxious to watch her reaction. He had to see the surprise to know if what she'd told him was true: she didn't know her ex-husband was in Duck River—she didn't know Lester was still in love with her. Her expression was unreadable. Her face didn't light up at first sight like Lester's did. Chase couldn't tell if they had parted enemies, friends, or lovers with unfinished business.

Lester froze when he saw Chase, blatantly staring before tear-ing his eyes away to look at Sheridan. The awkwardness made Ted stop and watch the scene unfold.

"I've been so worried about you." Lester greeted Sheridan with outstretched arms, his smile growing with each step. Chase watched him wrap her in a hug as he kissed her cheek.

Sheridan squirmed out of his embrace, but Chase couldn't help wondering if the move was only for his benefit.

Lester turned to Chase, not letting Sheridan's snub rattle him. "Dr. Larson. We meet again so soon."

"Doctor," Chase acknowledged curtly. Afraid of wringing Lester's neck, he moved away from the reunion, sure everyone could see the steam rising from his lab coat. "Who's next, Ted?"

Sheridan watched as Chase disappeared into exam room two.

"Do you have a minute?" Lester stood too close. She couldn't breathe.

"I have patients waiting."

"I know how that goes." He laughed debonairly for Ted's benefit. Sheridan knew him too well not to see it was a dig to upset Chase. "One minute? I came all this way. You can give me one minute, Sheridan."

She pulled her eyes away from exam room two, fully aware Ted was still standing with them.

"I won't keep you long."

She led Lester to her office. He wouldn't go away without making a scene, and she couldn't have him making a scene in front of Chase, or when she was still under consideration for a partnership position. She closed her office door and swung around ready to pounce on him for disrupting her new world. Chase was not a part of the mess she'd made with her life. How dare Lester involve him in it?

Lester played dirty. "Your mother and father are worried about you. They want you to call." Mentioning her parents melted her anger. She missed them. How were they were doing? Had they planted the tulip bulbs for next year? Did they remember to get their yearly check-ups? She warmed with memories of shopping with her mother and watching March Madness with her father.

"I've been worried about you, too." Lester's voice was a fluffy blanket of warmth for a rough cold soul.

"What are you doing here, Lester?"

"I was worried." His caramel eyes searched hers, bracing her for his next blow. "And I missed you."

"You were glad to see me go." She moved to the window, away from Lester, away from raw emotions. "Save the clinic, or save your marriage. The choice was yours, and you made it without hesitation."

He followed her, standing too close. Lester always refused to be ignored. His issues, his needs, his concerns always took precedence. "Mistakes, Sheridan. I've made a lot of mistakes."

"One of them was coming here today."

He gripped her shoulders, turning her to face him. "I'm here to repair my mistakes. I still love you, and I want you back in my life."

"What?" Chase had warned her, but she still couldn't believe what Lester was saying. He had discarded her in the name of research. She had been sacrificed for the good of all men. His sickle cell research was more important than their marriage, and he couldn't save both.

"My work—my research—means nothing without you in my life. I understand that now. I want you to come back to Nashville. Come back to your life."

"I'm trying to make a life here."

"In Duck River, Tennessee?"

"I hadn't planned for my life to turn out this way, but yes. Things are going well here."

"By things you mean the good doctor."

"Leave him out of it."

"How?" He paced away from her. "He was at your place. Alone."

"You had words with him? What made you think you had the right to question anyone in my house?"

"I'm your husband—"

"Ex-husband."

"Ex-husband. I'm your ex-husband, but I still care about you. Some strange man answers your door when I—and your parents—haven't talked to you in weeks. Of course I wanted to know who he was."

"Don't come here trying to ruin what I'm trying to build, Lester."

"I came here to win your heart back."

She was shocked by his admission. Lester was a practical man; expressing emotions wasn't his strength.

"I want you back, but I won't play dirty, Sheridan. I won't interfere with you work in any way."

She expected no less.

"But when it comes to Chase Larson," Lester squinted irately, "I won't play fair."

She wanted to defend Chase's manhood, but if she knew anything about men, she knew he wouldn't appreciate the gesture. She wanted to dismiss Lester, but she had loved this man enough once to marry him. Her personal life had collided with her work, and she wasn't emotionally prepared to handle with the fallout. "I can't deal with this right now, Lester. I have patients waiting."

"I don't want to interfere with your work. Have dinner with me tonight after you're done."

She moved to the door. "I can't. I need time to digest this."

"I'll call you tomorrow."

She looked at the gorgeous man who used to own her heart and something stirred deep inside. Then she thought of the way Chase had kissed her for an hour before he'd made love to her, and suddenly her past with Lester seemed insignificant.

"Sheridan, can I call you tomorrow? I'm asking for one conversation. One conversation and I'll leave you to your life."

She had to preserve what she was building with Chase by heading off any trouble Lester would cause. If one conversation would satisfy him and get him out of Duck River, she could grant him what he asked. "Yes." She hurried out the door before she regretted her decision.

CHAPTER 15

Sheridan stood underneath the hot shower spray, thinking about the two phone calls she had to make. She owed her parents an apology. She owed Chase an explanation. Neither call was a call she wanted to make. Talking to her parents would take hours. They would want to catch up on the latest goings on in her life since she had moved to Duck River. Then they would have to tell her about any news in the family. And then they'd have to discuss Lester's sudden appearance.

He wouldn't casually visit a town like Duck River. His finding her had to have been a well calculated plan—assisted by her parents. They still cared for Lester. It must have been easy for him to get them to fork over all the information they had about her whereabouts, which is why she remained so vague in her letters home.

She turned and let the hot spray rinse the suds from her back. Rightfully, Chase was angry. She had some ground to stand on though, didn't she? He'd never asked her about her life before coming to Duck River.

Thank God, Lester hadn't mentioned anything about the lawsuit. He'd told her he wouldn't in her office. He would keep his promise if he wanted any hope of winning her back.

Winning her back.

She'd just made a promise to Chase. She would try to have a committed relationship with him. Was she having doubts because Lester showed up talking reconciliation? Or were her doubts about having something real with Chase?

Sheridan stepped out of the shower, turning off the water as she wrapped herself in a towel. As she dried herself, she remembered the sensations that pricked underneath her skin when Chase touched her. She had been hungry for his body—dressed in the brown suit, he looked like a walking chocolate bar, and she'd been eager to get a taste. Admittedly, she had hungered for his body, but he had quickly dismissed the concept of meaningless sex and elevated the encounter to something more. Exactly what she truly wanted, but could not admit to herself.

As she dried, she formulated the words she'd use when she called Chase. As she dressed in a hip hugging pair of jeans and a cotton top, she decided she needed to have this conversation in person. She owed him more than a phone call explanation.

"Chase, it's Sheridan."

"Hi." Not his usual jovial spirit.

"We need to talk."

"Yes, we do."

"Can I come by?"

His answer was tight, as if speaking between clenched teeth. "Dinner in an hour?"

"I'll be there."

She grabbed her purse and started out for Chase's place. It would take her that long to remember how to get to the Larson Ranch. She stepped out onto the front porch and closed the door behind her just as Lester pulled into the drive behind her car. As usual, it was about what he wanted. Not what she needed.

"We agreed you would call me tomorrow," Sheridan said,

crossing her arms over her chest.

"I know." He stepped up on the porch. "Your parents called. Your dad made me promise to come see you immediately and to have you call home." He smiled sheepishly. "They're really worried about you."

She studied him closely for signs of insincerity.

"Would you like me to leave?"

She remembered she'd stood in front of God and taken vows with this man. Vows that had been broken, but all the same, there was a connection between them that would never be severed. Not to allow him inside was childish. "No, come in."

He followed her inside, going directly to the sofa and making himself comfortable. He'd been in her house before. He'd made himself familiar with her life when she wasn't around. She could only imagine what he and Chase had talked about. She dropped her purse and grabbed the phone, stabbing at the number keys.

"What's wrong?" Lester asked.

"You shouldn't use your relationship with my parents to get at me. They really love you."

"Your parents are as important to me as my own are. You know that. And I really love you, which is why I'd do anything to win you back."

Her mother answered the phone, deterring her answer. "Hello? Hello?"

The conversation with her mother and father was played out just as she imagined. It lasted so long Lester went into the kitchen and made himself something to eat. He sat down at the dining room table and leisurely ate dinner. She watched him, his features softening and reminding her why she'd fallen in love with him.

His business savvy was the stuff of legends for future generations of the Wexler family. He had been the one who taught her the benefits of vegetarianism. He'd taught her a lot of things over the years, and she was grateful.

Lester looked up, catching her staring. He smiled innocently while chewing his food.

"Mom, I have to go." She promised to call in a few days, sent her love to her father, and disconnected. She crossed the room and took a seat opposite Lester. "Why'd you come here?"

He put his fork down, swallowed, wiped his mouth on a napkin, and met her challenging glare directly. "I love you."

Her heart plummeted as she saw the reflection of truth in his eyes. She couldn't make sense of it. He was there when her life crumbled, and now he'd returned just as she began to rebuild the wreckage. "We're divorced," she whispered.

"I made a mistake. A big mistake. I want you back."

She shook her head. "It's not possible."

"Why not?"

"Too much water under that bridge."

"Really?" He pushed his plate away and folded his arms on the tabletop. He leaned toward her, shattering her piece of mind and confusing the issue further. "I had to do the right thing. The right thing isn't always the easiest thing. Sometimes innocent people get hurt."

"You chose the clinic over our marriage."

He nodded. "I chose to opportunity to save many lives over our relationship. At the time I thought I was doing what was best. If I had to do it all over again, I'd try to find another solution. You can't tell me you would *not* have done the same thing...if the choice had been yours."

"We've been through this a million times. I wouldn't have thrown you to the reporters and lawyers, or made you face the medical review board alone. I would have stuck by you."

He watched her for a moment, absorbing the truth. "You would have. You would have thought with your heart. You would have let sentimentality persuade you to choose love. And in the meanwhile, hundreds—thousands—hundreds of thousands—of people would be suffering from the effects of sickle cell while we huddled together in our love nest."

This was the point he'd argued for months until it was clear they'd never see the situation in the same way.

"What's different now, Lester? I'm still poison, according to the people who fund your research."

"What's different now is that I miss you more than I could have possibly imagined." His cool slipped away. "So we can't work together. Maybe it was too much, mixing a new marriage with a new clinic. This time we'll keep our marriage and our careers separate."

"I like it here. Are you going to give up the clinic to move here to Duck River with me?"

The truth moved behind his pleading expression. "I thought—if we worked things out—you'd move back to Nashville. Your parents are there—"

"And the clinic is there."

"And plenty of opportunities for you."

"No." She shook her head vehemently. "No, there aren't any opportunities there for me. The publicity surrounding the lawsuit has made practicing there impossible."

"We'll find something. There's a solution."

She moved across the room, not willing to face the pain. "There is nothing. If there was a solution, we would have found it before we met with the divorce attorneys."

Lester joined her, gently placing his hand on her shoulder. "Then we'll make something from nothing. I'm on a lot firmer ground now. The clinic is generating income. The investors are convinced about my research and more are signing on. I have resources and connections now I didn't have then."

She moved away from him. "You can't just show up and ask me to leave. I'm building something here."

"With Dr. Larson?" His jaw twitched.

"Leave Chase out of this."

"How?" he snapped. "I came to talk to you and this guy is in your house. Alone." He took a deep breath, forcing calm into his lungs. "He doesn't matter. This is about *you* and *me*. What we had and what we can have together."

Sheridan felt her armor slipping.

"How serious are you about Chase?"

She heard pain in his voice. She looked over at him, and it was confirmed. "He's a nice guy." She didn't want to inflict pain on Lester. His coming to Duck River, declaring undying love, confused her feelings for Chase.

"I'm not leaving without you."

"Lester—"

"Spend time with me. Let me prove to you I've changed. I know what I want now, and I'll fight to get it."

The continuous headboard banging, moaning, and groaning made it impossible for Lester to work. He tried to push pictures of what was going on in the surrounding rooms away, his fingers poised above the keyboard of his laptop. He couldn't get behind in his research. If he wanted Sheridan back, he had to prove he could balance their relationship with his career. He couldn't forget the burden of making family history, or the thousands of people with sickle cell praying for a cure to the disease.

He clicked the mouse, producing a quick succession of blood cell images. He'd developed an eye for spotting the abnormal with just a glance. He mindlessly scanned the pictures, frame by frame, blocking out the noises from the next room.

His conversation with Sheridan hadn't gone as he had hoped, but it had gone well. The best scenario would have been for him to apologize, then she would admit she still loved him too, and they would return to Nashville before dark. It hadn't gone that way, but at least she hadn't thrown him out. She'd given him a glimmer of hope by not shutting him out of her life. She'd agreed to see him and discuss their relationship. It was a short thread, but he was hopeful.

The only thing bothering him was his promise not to mention the lawsuit to Chase. He understood why Sheridan didn't want anyone to know about the malpractice case—she'd lose her patients. What bothered him was how she protected Chase. She didn't want to hurt him.

A sharp, rapid knock disrupted his thought pattern. He ignored it. Many johns had stumbled upon his door by mistake during his stay at the whorehouse. Someone would come along and direct the drunkard to the right room. He enjoyed the privacy staying at Candy's place afforded him, but with the privacy came the knowledge of what was going on in the other rooms. He was a man, and listening to the sounds of carnal lust long into the night definitely had an aching effect on him. The sharp, rapid knocking persisted, catching him before his mind could lead him down a dissolute path.

"Lester, it's Candy. I brought you dinner. Can I come in?"

Curiosity made him snap the lid of his laptop closed. He'd been adamant about having privacy, and she had respected his wishes up until this point, but he had to admit the woman intrigued him. How did someone as beautiful as Candy get involved in this line of work? She couldn't be much older than him, yet she was running a brothel—a position he'd thought was reserved for an older woman. Late at night, when the creaking and moaning kept him awake, he wondered where she was in the house and what she was doing. He'd never seen her take a man, but he'd been so absorbed in his work he hardly ever left his room.

Candy walked in the room, her hips swaying to a rhythm that only played in her head.

"You didn't have to go to the trouble of bringing me dinner." He cleared away his laptop and his research papers from the desk she'd had brought up from the basement for him to use.

"It's no trouble." She placed a silver tray in the vacant spot and backed away, waiting for him to inspect the contents.

He removed the covering to find a gourmet meal. "I expected a cold sandwich."

Candy smiled, slow and easy. He'd seen her smile for the guests, but this was different—this was a sincere gesture. "My cook has studied in France."

He raised an eyebrow in surprise.

"Let's just say he had certain legal *problems* that forced him to move to our tiny town. He's paid very well for his services here, so he's happy enough. I want the best for my guests. I run a classy place."

He had been dropped in the middle of an old western movie. He inhaled the savory aroma. "I'm trying to remember the last time I had a good meal." He wanted to come home every night to a well prepared meal and the glowing face of his gorgeous wife. Even when he and Sheridan were happy newlyweds, their life had not been about cozy meals together. They were both driven, intent on making a career out of their medical training. Time at home was about crunching the finances of the clinic, paying a maid to come out three times a week, and flipping a coin to decide who would bring home take-out. "Thank you."

"You're so busy up here working, I thought you might be hungry."

He rubbed his stomach. "All of a sudden I'm starved."

"I'll leave you to eat then."

His hand shot out and touched her arm. She jumped, as if the contact was electrified. His touch was soft, but he pulled away, afraid to offend her. "I didn't mean to startle you," he apologized. "I'm starved for company, too." She searched his face suspiciously. He could only imagine what she was thinking. He didn't want her to think he was a pervert—holed up in his room all day tapping away on the computer, oblivious to what was going on around him, until the madam visited and he tried to take advantage of her. He softened his approach and poured out the charm through his smile. "If you have the time to join me, I'd love the company."

Candy watched him for a moment longer before she floated over to the bed and sat gracefully on the edge of the mattress.

"Do you mind if I eat while we talk?"

She nodded, still watching him cautiously.

"I'm a vegetarian," he offered as an explanation for his removal of the steak on his plate.

"I'll let the cook know."

He chomped down on the crisp green beans and showed his appreciation with a low hum. Candy was amused by his boyish response. Her laughter broke the tension between them, instantly propelling them from awkward strangers to comfortable companions. As if she'd been waiting for someone to share her life with, Candy conversed easily about the importance of the services her girls provided to the town.

"How did you—how did you decide—" Lester stammered.

"My story isn't much different from anyone else's in this business. I had a rotten childhood, grew up too hard too fast and had to learn how to take care of myself with the assets I had available to me."

"You didn't have anyone to look out for you?"

"Nope." Her lashes dipped. "It's the past, but it still hurts."

"I'm sorry. I didn't mean to—"

"It's okay. I don't mind talking about my life. Just not my childhood."

"I won't mention it again."

Candy shifted, lifting one dazzling leg over the other. "I'm luckier than most who get into this business."

"How so?" Lester didn't want to pry, but he was curious, and she seemed to need to talk to someone as much as he did.

She chortled sarcastically. "Don't get it wrong. I took my bumps when I was out on the street. What I mean by lucky is that I got it—I *have* it—" She smiled. "I'm working on my English." She continued. "I have it better than most who have been in the business as long as I have been."

"How long?" he asked when she did not readily supply the information.

"Since I turned twelve. I'm twenty-seven now."

Candy swished her hips over to the window and started out. "Don't look at me like you pity me." She whirled around. "It's my life. I'm not proud of parts of it, but I survived." Sorrow softened her voice. "You never know what all you'll do until you're forced into a position where the only thing you're worrying about is surviving."

Lester nodded, forcing himself to swallow his food and his judgmental words.

Candy crossed the room with the grace of a soulful jazz song and reclaimed her seat on his bed. "I have enough money saved up now, so I can walk away. But I ask myself, where I'll go." She extended her arms out behind her and leaned back, staring at the ceiling. "Duck River is my home now. I've found some stability here."

"Yes, but," he ventured carefully. "Life should be about more than stability. What about happiness and family and being proud about the contribution you're making to the world?"

Candy dropped her head, meeting his questioning eyes straight on. "Those things don't apply to my life."

The muted light in her eyes told Lester she wished they did.

Candy abruptly changed the subject. "You're not the type we usually get around here. You're an educated man. I can see that. And you're always up here in your room working. That tells me a coupla things about you."

He stopped eating, intrigued to learn she'd been studying him. "Really? What?"

"Well, even though you don't go to work, you dress in slacks and a tie everyday. You're a workaholic. Probably something very important. Politics, or something like that. A lot of politicians come through here."

"Pretty good."

"You live in a whorehouse, but you haven't looked twice at my girls. Either you're gay, or you're happily married." Her lashes dipped again. "I may not have finished high school, but I know men."

He laughed, confirming her astute assessment.

"How close am I?"

"I'm working on something very important in the medical field. And I don't look at the women here because I'm in love with a very special woman."

Growing more comfortable, Candy leaned back on her hands and relaxed. "What kind of medical work are you doing up here in your room?"

"I'm conducting research in the area of sickle cell. Are you familiar with it?"

She hesitated to answer, fighting to mask her reaction. "I know a little about sickle cell."

"It's a terrible disease. The red blood cells don't get enough oxygen, so they morph into the shape of a sickle. The shape doesn't allow them to flow through the blood vessels, depriving the body of blood and oxygen. When there is no blood or oxygen to a body part, it dies. It's a very painful disease and those afflicted with it are forced to alter their lifestyles. When they go into *crisis* they require large amounts of pain medicine, and even hospitalization. The life expectancy of someone with sickle cell is—"

"I know about sickle cell disease," Candy cut off his diatribe. She sat up, tense again.

"I'm sorry. I enjoy my work and will bore anyone who will listen to the details about it."

"Sickle cell killed my mother."

Lester had met many whose lives had been destroyed by the disease, but none touched him so personally. "I didn't mean to be insensitive."

Candy waved away his apology with manicured fingertips. "How would you have known?"

He tried to offer some solace. "My research is for people like you. People who had suffered firsthand."

A sad smile lifted Candy's red lips. "Why are you working in Duck River? This place is known for horses, not life saving medical research."

"I came to try to win my ex-wife back." He finished the last of his dinner.

"Your ex?" She sat forward, curious.

"Dr. Wexler."

She watched him with wide eyes, blinking rapidly.

"Have you met her?"

"Yes." She cleared her throat. "I met her at the clinic."

"Now you know all my secrets. I came here to win her back and take her home. As soon as I do, I'll be leaving Duck River. As a matter of fact, now that she knows I'm in town I should be moving out of here. I don't want to take advantage of your hospitality."

"Afraid your wife won't like you living in a whorehouse?"

"No. My wife is a good person with a good heart. But staying here has to be disruptive for you."

Candy watched him for a long moment in which he wondered if he'd said something wrong. "You're welcome to stay as long as you'd like. It's nice to have a man around to talk to—one who doesn't expect anything more than good conversation."

He picked up a pang of sadness in her voice—loneliness maybe.

"Hey," Candy perked up, "I could help you."

"Help me how?"

"No one knows more about seduction than I do. I could help you get your wife back."

"Sheridan won't be won over easily. Flowers and sweet talk aren't important to her."

Candy stood and approached him, her hips singing. "If you think a woman doesn't like flowers and sweet talk, you do need my help. Every woman wants to feel wanted by her man. She wants to know he thinks she's attractive and can't wait to make love to her, but he will because he respects her." She lifted the tray. "You need my help—badly."

"Why would you volunteer to help me?"

"I'm a sucker for happy endings."

He looked up at her. Candy was a gorgeous woman, cursed

with a perfect body. Cursed because no man would ever take the time to talk with her and learn what was beneath the beauty. During the past hour, they'd talked like old friends. She had a wonderful sense of humor. She may not have graduated from high school, but she spoke intelligently on a variety of subjects. He suspected underneath the cool exterior was a lonely woman looking for her own happy ending.

She moved to the door. "What do you think?"

"I think I need all the help I can get."

She smiled, her sadness earlier completely gone. "Get back to work. We'll talk tomorrow."

CHAPTER 16

Chase was sitting at the dinner table with his hands folded in front of him when Mrs. Fluentes showed Sheridan into the dining room. His plate was empty and a linen napkin had been dumped there. The muscle in his jaw jumped, but he didn't look at her when he spoke. "You're late."

"I know. I had to—"

"Sit down and eat."

"I'm not hungry." Her stomach roiled.

"Sit down," he grounded out with unmistakable authority, "and eat."

She took the seat across from him.

"You skip too many meals and when you do bother to eat, you hardly eat a thing."

Mrs. Fluentes stepped up. She'd been standing there all the while, watching her employer's anger directed at the new doctor. "I'll heat this for you." She removed two colorful vegetable dishes from the table and disappeared.

"You're late," Chase repeated.

"I'm sorry."

"Were you with your husband?"

"Ex-husband."

"Sorry. He didn't introduce himself that way. He was very clear about letting me know he's your husband." He mumbled, "He was clear about a lot of things."

"What did Lester say to you?"

"The most important thing he said was that he came here to take you home with him."

Mrs. Fluentes returned, placing a steaming hot vegetarian plate in front of Sheridan.

"Thank you."

"Thank you," Chase echoed. "You can leave for the night, Mrs. Fluentes. I'll take care of the clean up."

Sheridan waited until she called good night from the kitchen before she continued their discussion. "I owe you an explanation."

"You never bothered to mention you were married."

"Divorced. I'm divorced. And you didn't ask."

"Come on, Sheridan. Don't ask, don't tell?" He pushed back from the table. "Do I have to ask you for every detail of your life? I can't depend on you to tell me about the things that are important to our relationship?" His eyes narrowed. "Do you really want me to start *questioning* you?" His tone told her it would be a drilling she would not survive.

"No. I should have told you about Lester. I didn't want you to find out this way."

He took a deep breath and passed his hand over his face, reclaiming his clam confidence. "How long have you been divorced?"

"Eight months."

He looked as if Mike Tyson had punched him in the gut. She quickly added, "Our marriage was over long before we were divorced."

"It wasn't what Lester wanted."

"He filed for the divorce. It was his idea."

"It wasn't what you wanted."

"It was the right thing to do."

He motioned for her to continue eating while he contemplated his next question. "What went wrong?"

She took another bite of her casserole before answering. She considered telling him about the malpractice case and relying on his good character to accept her and her faults. She looked across the table and saw him fighting to contain his anger about Lester's sudden appearance. This was not the time to pile more issues on his shoulders. "We worked together and had radically different concepts of how our clinic should be run. It spilled over into our home life."

"You owned a clinic?" Incredulity seeped between his words.

"Lester and I were partners."

"Partners." He mulled over the concept. "And you couldn't work together so your marriage fell apart. Work was more important than your relationship."

"For Lester, yes."

His jaw flexed. "It explains why you were hesitant about seeing me."

She sipped from her water glass as she carried on an internal debate. She could tell him everything now, put it all be out in the open. "Chase—"

"How do you feel about me?"

She went to him. "I care about you." She sat in his lap and wrapped her arms around his neck. "You have to believe me. Lester's showing up doesn't change the way I feel about you."

Chase scrutinized her with weary eyes. "How do you feel

about Lester?"

She'd known he would get around to asking that difficult question, but she still hadn't prepared a diplomatic answer. "Lester is—"

"Be honest, Sheridan." His demand was earnest.

"Lester was my husband."

"I know. What I don't know is how you feel about him. Are you still in love with him?"

"I knew you would ask me this, and I worked hard to come up with an answer that wouldn't upset you, or ruin what we've started."

"Just tell me, Sheridan, dammit."

"I don't know if I still love him."

Chase set her on her feet and crossed the room, moving as far away from her as possible.

"I can't lie to you, Chase. I care about Lester. He was my husband. There will always be a bond there."

"You care about me. You care about Lester. How is one different from the other?" He didn't like her silence. He shouted, "What are you going to do?"

"I don't know."

"The look on your face tells me you know exactly what you're going to do. Did you come here to tell me you're going back to him?"

"No." She came to apologize, to make things right between them. "You have it all wrong—"

He lifted a hand, quieting her then covered his eyes while he took several deep breaths before he looked at her again. "It's been so long since I met someone I could talk to. I can't remember ever being attracted to a woman's body *and* mind. I've never cared about anyone the way I care about you, Sheridan."

Sheridan felt small and evil.

"These are the words I want to hear from you. Not that you care about me *and* your ex-husband equally."

She never wanted to hurt Chase. If she had any idea that Lester would show up declaring his love, she would have fought her feelings for Chase, not wanting to drag him into the middle of a love triangle.

"Sheridan, I know I should be the bigger man and tell you I'm going to leave you to get your head together. I'm not that man. I want you. I want you, and I'm afraid that if I back off you'll decide you want to be with Lester again."

"I don't want this to be a competition. My focus has been on building my career. I never thought Lester would show up and complicate things between us."

"Tell him to leave."

"I feel like I should hear him out."

"Why? Didn't you 'hear him out' before you divorced?"

"I have to clear up any lingering feelings between Lester and me so he can go on with his life…and so you don't have any doubts about us."

He leaned against the wall and folded his arms over his chest. His easygoing nature was gone, replaced with turmoil. "You make it sound so logical. Like being rational is the civilized way to handle the situation."

"I don't know a better way to handle it."

"Forget being civilized. Forget being rational. Tell that arrogant pri—"

"Chase!"

"Tell Lester to go back wherever he came from."

"You would always wonder."

"*You* would always wonder."

She looked away.

"Sheridan, I know relationships take work. I'm not naïve, but I didn't think we'd have to deal with *these* types of issues in our relationship."

"If I could change my past, I would. I don't like you being angry."

"But you can't change your past, which is why you should have told me about Lester up front." He studied her. "What do we do now?"

She slowly approached him, suddenly needing to know it was all right for her to touch him. "Nothing changes between us. I want to keep seeing you."

"You just want to see Lester, too."

She shook her head. "I'll listen to what he has to say, because he deserves as much. I'm not dating him."

"Why do I feel like he won't understand your intentions?"

"Lester can seem difficult to those who don't know him."

His jaw locked in boldness. "I don't want to talk about Lester when we're together."

"Okay."

They watched each other for a long time. She didn't like the implications of his silence. "I never meant to hurt you, Chase."

"I know," he whispered.

She reached up and cupped his face.

"Don't."

"You're such a handsome man."

"We're not through arguing."

"It's done," she whispered with conviction.

"I don't like this."

"I know."

"The thought of you spending more time with him—"

"It's done," she whispered.

"He's so arrogant. What were you thinking when you married him?"

"Chase, it's done." When he didn't challenge her, she stroked his jaw line. "When I say you're handsome, I don't mean just on the outside. You're a good man—in your heart."

He placed his hands on her waist, touching her for the first time during her visit. "I'm not giving you up without a fight."

"It's not a contest."

"Not a contest," he grunted. "Don't be mistaken, Sheridan. This is a fight to the finish. And I plan to win."

"It doesn't have to be a contest, or a fight."

"Then go tell Lester to leave—right now."

She covered his lips with her fingertips. "Chase, it's done. We're not going to argue about this anymore."

"Enough for today," he conceded.

"Take me upstairs."

He lifted her into his arms. "I'm not giving you up, Sheridan. Starting now, I'm on a mission to conquer your heart."

CHAPTER 17

Tiny firecrackers exploded beneath Chase's skin. He loomed over Sheridan on his bed, tracing the soft lines of her face with his finger. He tugged at her chestnut colored hair, fanning it across the pillow, framing the perfection of her face. Eyes he once thought were naively innocent stared back at him with sizzling desire. He placed a kiss on each of her high cheekbones, again wondering if she were part Indian. A bead of perspiration sat atop the flare of his nostrils. She was burning for him. His fingertips passed over the mark near the notch of her right jaw. "How'd you get this?"

"I fell off the swings when I was little." She removed his hand from her imperfection and cupped it between hers, tracing each vein, fascinated.

"You like my hands."

"You have strong, masculine hands, but they're soft and gentle at the same time." She brought his palm up to her mouth, pressing her lips to the center, teasing him with the circular motions of her tongue.

Her simplest actions turned him on. The way she studied the computer screen at work. Her intensity in reviewing medical records. Always running behind schedule, oblivious to how nuts she made Carolyn on those days. Her enthrallment with his hands. The small smile that escaped her when he passed her in the hall at the clinic. The sincerity behind each of her kisses.

He felt the tiny sparks beneath his skin, outdone by the massive explosion around his heart. He opened the first button of her blouse and kissed the newly exposed area. He released the next and the next and Sheridan's eyes fluttered closed. He pushed the ends of her blouse apart to expose her small breasts nestled white lace. He wasted no time removing the barrier. His hand hovered over her breasts, barely touching her. She arched her back as if he had squeezed her with all his strength. He rewarded her unrestrained reaction by massaging her breasts until she moaned. He took the puckered nipple between two fingers, rolling it with his thumb. She gasped. He pinched harder. She squirmed below him.

He kissed the other breast, supporting its weight with the tip of his tongue. He circled the dark areola, moving toward the center. He broke his rhythm, sucking the second puckered peak into his hot mouth. He laved and suckled in response to her reaction. Her hands were in his hair, pulling him in closer, demanding more.

He broke away. Her eyes flew open in protest.

"You're hot."

"Always with you," she panted. "Kiss me."

He brushed her lips with his. She wrapped her arms around his shoulders, wanting more. This woman belonged to him. He possessed her body with his touch. He'd conquer her heart with his love. He kissed her several more times, tiny pecks meant to build her anticipation. She moaned in protest. He pressed their lips together, opening his mouth to taste her fully. She accepted his tongue heartily, meeting it with her own.

As they kissed, his hands explored the length of her body. Her back snapped into a bow, and he encircled her waist, pulling her into him. His fingers danced upward, slipping inside her mouth. She latched on, her lashes drifting downward as she swirled her tongue around the tip. Chase pulled his finger away, sharing her flavor before crossing the intersection of her V with a wet thrust. With polished expertise, he peeled away the moist folds, finding the spot that made Sheridan bend her knees and push off the bed.

"Your fingers are magic," she moaned. "You're working my *e-f-and g* spot."

"Look at me," he demanded.

She opened her eyes, but struggled to hold his gaze when his finger swirled around her weeping bud.

"You shouldn't talk like that."

"I should tell you if what you're doing makes me feel good."

"You should tell me how you feel about me." He increased the pressure.

She backed away toward the headboard.

"Don't move."

"Im-im-impossible," she panted.

"Don't move," he ordered through clenched teeth. He added another finger, lower, deeper. Sheridan scrambled away from the intensity. He grabbed her leg and pulled her back. "Don't move."

She hummed in sweet agony, struggling to obey him.

He threw her leg over his thigh, giving him better access to her wet treasures. He found the right rhythm to make her twitch. He strummed relentlessly, patience his greatest asset when making love. He watched her fighting the urge to wiggle away from the sensations possessing her body. He inhaled deeply, swimming in her heated scent. She writhed below him, begging for an end to his torturous stroke. He unfolded the petals, searching deeper. She jerked, but did not move away. She ground her hips as he used his thumb to vibrate the tiny, weeping nub. Her body tensed, every muscle as tight as a bow, and he told her, "Okay, Shameless." He whispered, "Let it go." She did, her body jerking and shaking. His fingers remained inside her heated cove, along for the rocky ride. He pushed her to the limit and beyond.

"Chase," she panted. Her lashes were dark curtains, shading the deep brown of her eyes. He continued to massage her, caressing her until she was too sensitive to tolerate his touch. "It's enough now, Chase." She reached for him, but he had exhausted her. Her arms were limp, her grasp on his shirt weak.

He reached up and pushed her disheveled hair from her face. He could wait until she could give him her all. This woman belonged to him. "Get some rest, Shameless."

Sheridan's eyes fluttered closed. Chase cleaned her with a warm cloth, moving slowly with a tender touch, trying not to disturb her as she drifted off to sleep. She didn't eat right and she didn't get enough sleep. Habits picked up from med school and never remedied. He covered her with the sheet, knowing he'd fall asleep with the fragrance of her perfume on his mind for days to come. She needed someone to take care of her. He lay down next to her, his arm resting lightly across her belly. She needed to know she wasn't in the world alone. She didn't have to fight every battle solo.

Lester had been her nemesis, not her other half, and certainly not her support system. They had fought about work, letting it come between them until divorce was the only answer. And

Lester had asked for it and served her with the papers.

But Chase couldn't imagine the clinic coming between him and Sheridan. Their styles were different, but they meshed well. Reggie and Mrs. Harvey's cases were prime examples. They recognized each others strengths and weaknesses and complimented each other accordingly. What had been so hard to work through that Lester wanted to end their marriage?

And now he reappears, just as they were coming together, to rectify his mistake. Too damn bad. Sheridan was his now.

Chase spooned her naked body, relishing in her touch. How had he fallen so deeply so quickly? Physical attraction had grown into a mental connection with Sheridan he wasn't ready to let go of. They had so much more to explore. He was still teaching her how to have fun. She needed someone to remind her to take care of herself. How could she heal others if she was worn down and suffering from malnutrition?

Sheridan pushed against him. "I'm cold."

He left the bed to retrieve his pajama top. He helped her into it, and she quickly fell back asleep. He covered her with a blanket, tucking it securely around her. When he climbed back into bed, she scooted over to him like a magnet. He held her tightly to his chest, kissing her chestnut hair. How could Lester compete with this?

CHAPTER 18

"Candy, come tie my tie," Scott barked.

The sheet fell to her waist, leaving her naked and vulnerable as she climbed down from the four poster bed he'd insisted upon buying her.

This was their routine. Scott Stoner was a regimented man who liked things done with military precision. He tolerated no variance from routine. He visited Candy once a week, demanding special and immediate service. She had tried to explain once that she no longer slept with the patrons, but he would not recognize her *retirement*. His lovemaking consisted of choreographed movements that never varied in order to offer her pleasure. He displayed no passion with his touches or his kisses. After sex—always two rounds, the positions predetermined—Scott showered, donned his business suit and waited for her to knot his tie.

"Who's the guy you have staying here?"

Candy's head snapped up at his angry tone.

"I know about everything that goes on in this house," he reminded her. He had his spies.

"Just a man passing through."

"Make sure he keeps moving."

She nodded, taking the ends of his tie between her fingers.

"You're not sleeping with this guy are you?"

"Never." She gave him a seductive smile she hoped would

end the discussion.

"Remember who pays the Sheriff and the State Police to overlook your little business venture."

She went into super-seductive mode. "Baby, Candy never forgets how good you are to her."

She had begun to hate *Candy*, and all she stood for. She wanted to be Doreen Miller again. The innocent teenager who trusted the wrong man to save her from a life of poverty and serial foster homes. She wouldn't be so innocent, so stupid this time around. She'd make smart choices. She'd get an education, a small house all her own, and plan for a future with a husband and kids.

No decent man wanted her now. She was damaged goods. Sure, the men who visited the house were always propositioning her. But they wanted sex. They wanted to taste the forbidden fruit in the garden only Scott Stoner had permission to sow.

She mindlessly looped the tie as Scott droned on. She drowned out his possessive ranting—this had become a part of their routine, too. She pictured Lester huddled over his computer, typing furiously, his concentration at a superfine point. Her vision was so vivid she could hear the tapping of his computer keyboard. He oozed sex appeal when he was absorbed in his work. Often she would peek in on him, but he would never notice her watching.

Lester dressed too old for his age. His clothes were made of fine, imported materials. Even in sensible Italian loafers, he was five inches taller than her. He should be wearing snappy designer jackets that hugged his lean arms and snazzy slacks to show off his muscular thighs. He suffered from man-without-a-woman-in-his-life syndrome.

Why had she offered to help the man whose voice made her quiver find love with another woman? At the time, it seemed the perfect excuse to spend more time with him. As she offered suggestions on how to win Dr. Wexler back, she imagined Lester doing those things for her. The small acts of kindness every woman wants from her man, but would never ask for. She wanted every minute of his existence focused on her. Even when they weren't together, she'd know he was thinking about her, worrying about her, wanting her to be happy. She wanted him to embrace her with the warm feeling he gave her every time he looked up from his computer and smiled.

"Some guy is always sniffing around trying to get his turn at you," Scott was saying. "Where were these idiots when you were sitting in jail waiting for your low-life pimp to bail you out? I'll tell you where. They were nowhere around. Scott Stoner had to step up and rescue you."

"I know, baby."

Over the years, Candy began to know Scott in a way few people did. The upstanding, egotistical businessman who tried to run Duck River liked decadent things. He liked to sneak away from his latest girlfriend and find comfort in Candy's arms. Scott was hotheaded, eager to start a fight after downing two glasses of hard liquor for courage. Sometimes his buddies would drag him into her bed to sleep off his latest drunk—couldn't let the town see him at his weakest, he would tell her the next morning. He liked to dictate the way things should be in bed, allowing for no variation, and stifling any chance she had of making the act pleasurable.

Candy had long realized Scott had an unbreakable hold on

her life. When she first arrived in Duck River, she couldn't afford to pay the local law enforcement's *look the other way* fees. Once she established her business, they wouldn't take her money. Scott had informed them everything concerning her should flow through him. Duck River was a good town, but like anywhere, there was an element of corruption that always seemed to find its way to Candy's doorstep. Her work wasn't exactly legal, so she had learned to play by the rules in order to survive—like she had done all her life. Like she was content to go on doing until she met Lester.

Scoot pulled his wallet from his back pocket and began to peel off crisp one hundred dollar bills. He walked over to her dresser, opened the top drawer, and placed two thousand dollars inside. She didn't need to count it—it was always two thousand dollars in hundred dollar bills.

"You don't have to give me money."

"You're my Candy." He slid the drawer closed, slowly, with calculated meaning. "Wouldn't want you to forget it."

"I know, baby," she said sadly.

"Alison, it's Sheridan."

"Just a minute."

Sheridan heard rustling on the other end of the telephone line. Alison's voice became muffled and then disappeared. Shortly, she came back on the line.

"You have my test results."

"Yes, I do. I'd like you to come to the clinic so we can go over them."

"Oh, God."

"Don't panic."

"If the tests were normal you would have said so. Instead you're telling me to come in to the clinic. You know how risky it is for me to come there. You wouldn't ask me to come unless it was bad."

Sheridan didn't deny the obvious. "Have you talked to your husband yet?"

"No. I don't want my family to know until I know for sure what's happening to me. What did the tests show?"

"You need further testing."

Alison whimpered and Sheridan's heart sank. "Further testing? What does that mean? Don't go all doctor on me. What kind of tests, Sheridan?"

"You need to have a biopsy."

"A bi…" her voice faded.

"Alison?" If she passed out and hit her head—

"I'm here. You need to do a biopsy of the lump…the lump in my breast."

"I need to refer you to a specialist in Nashville. He'll have the proper equipment to perform the biopsy in his office, and his lab resources will be more sophisticated."

"And doing a biopsy at the clinic will be too hard to hide from my brother."

"Alison, I have to insist. You *have* to tell your family. Talk with Chase, he'll help you tell Dwayne and the rest of your family."

"No. I appreciate the position I've put you in, but I don't

want my family to know yet. I'm not going to upset my parents if there's nothing for them to worry about."

Sheridan twisted the phone cord around her fingers, trying to find a convincing argument. "You need someone with you as you go through this. Your family would want to support you."

"No. They can't know."

"What about Dwayne?" Sheridan persisted. "He found the lump. He'll ask questions."

"Dwayne, like most men, doesn't want to discuss women's medical problems. I told him I had the lump checked. He's satisfied with that."

"How could he be satisfied with that unless you told him everything was fine?"

"Sheridan, you're my doctor. You have to respect my right to privacy."

"I do respect your right to privacy, but—"

"You're my brother's girlfriend, so it places you in a hard spot." She paused. "I need to know, can you do this? Can you be my doctor and support me through this? Or should I find someone else?"

Sheridan contemplated her options.

"I don't want to do this alone. Another doctor won't care the way you do."

"I'm still your doctor," Sheridan conceded. "But I want it on record that I think you should tell your family."

Sheridan burst through her front door, rushing to catch the

phone before the answering machine picked up. She hoped it was Alison, calling to tell her she'd talked with her husband about the biopsy and next she would tell her family, taking Sheridan out of the middle of a very sticky place.

"Sheridan, this is your father."

She pulled up, stopping quickly when she heard the authoritative tone come from her answering machine. After a long day at the clinic, she did not need to hear a lecture from her father.

"Your mother and I are disappointed we haven't seen you even after our last phone call. I spoke with Lester a few minutes ago, and I made him promise to bring you home for dinner this Saturday." He brooked no argument. "We'll see you two this weekend."

Sheridan muttered a curse word as she dropped her purse and headed for the shower. Her father had a way of making her feel like a little girl, afraid of disappointing him. She adored her parents and missed them terribly. Dinner would be nice, but she was still confused about how to handle Lester. Until she had heard out his best argument and sent him back to Nashville, she didn't want to be placed in an intimate position with him. Too much chance for misunderstanding. Sitting down to dinner with her parents like they used to do sent the wrong message to Lester, and her parents.

She and Lester would be confined together in the car during the long drive to Nashville. They would have nothing to talk about but their past, and the possibility of building a future. Without asking, she knew they were pulling for them to reconcile. They didn't believe in divorce. They felt once you married, you had to work out your problems, and divorce was a coward's way out. They never outwardly suggested she stay trapped in a marriage where both people were miserable, but they hadn't been happy to see it end.

"You left the front door open."

Sheridan jumped, grabbing her chest.

"Whoa." Chase enveloped her in his arms. "I didn't mean to scare you. You were deep in thought. Gone to that place you disappear to again. What's up?"

She shook her head. "Nothing. My parents want me to come to dinner Saturday."

"Why is that a problem?"

"We were going to continue my riding lesson this weekend."

"We can always reschedule." He kissed her forehead.

"What are you doing here?"

He released her, taking a short step back. "I couldn't take my eyes off you today. Did you notice?"

"I felt your red hot gaze burning into me every time I passed you in the hallway."

"And you didn't sneak in my office and give me a kiss? Shameless, you're slipping."

"I'll give you slipping," she laughed, swatting at him. He ducked her hands, letting her chase him around the living room. She connected, her tiny hand barely making an impact on the sinewy muscles of his chest. He grabbed her in a bear hug and tossed her to the sofa, landing solidly on top of her. She giggled, struggling beneath him until they landed in a heap on the floor. A tactical move on her part, she scrambled until she was riding him piggyback style.

"I heard the screams."

Sheridan and Chase were both startled by the intrusion.

Lester was standing over them, watching the intimate play with disdain.

Sheridan slid down from Chase's back.

Chase stood, extending her hand to help her up. "Does he just walk in here?" he asked, gritting his teeth.

"Does she answer to you?" Lester retorted.

They stood on either side of her: Lester, with years of intimate history—Chase, with hope of building a future. Together they said, "Sheridan, what is he doing here?" Their eyes met above her head, and they engaged in a stare down that scorched her hair. Together they asked, "Sheridan, can I speak to you in private?"

She looked at Chase. His jaw seesawed back and forth, his eyes locked on Lester.

She looked at Lester. He wore the smug expression of a man sure of himself.

Together, they both looked at her, waiting for her to make a choice. She made the only choice she could. "I just came home from work, and I'm very tired. You both should leave."

Lester tore his eyes away from Chase. To prove he hadn't lost the silent challenge, he rubbed her back possessively. "Okay. I'll call you later. We need to talk." He threw Chase another heated glance.

Chase leaned down and pressed his lips to her cheek, lingering until Lester shifted.

"Goodbye, gentlemen," Sheridan said with conviction.

Lester left first.

Chase followed closely behind. When he reached the door, he

closed it firmly behind Lester. "Before you say a word, I'm not leaving." The furrow of his brow told her he meant it. "When are you going to tell that clown to leave town?"

She spoke in the quiet tone she used to sooth an irate patient. "We discussed this, Chase."

He stomped across the room. "He walked in on us."

"We were just playing around."

"I was about to seduce you."

"Seduce me?" She tilted her head to the side, amused by his choice of wording.

"Don't you dare laugh."

"I'm sorry. I know this isn't funny." She walked over to him. "What I should do is tell you I can't see you until this thing with Lester is resolved."

"Don't even suggest it, because it's not going to happen. Nothing is going to change between us just because your ex-husband came to town."

"If you want it that way, you have to be tolerant—"

"Tolerant? Dr. Wexler, you've been dipping in the narcotic cabinet." He stepped closer, looming over her. "I will *not* be tolerant. I want you to hurry up and tell him you're with me and he doesn't have a chance in hell at getting you back. Tell him to jump in his rented Lincoln and go back to Nashville pronto."

"I can see you're upset." She pressed her hands to his chest, placing a comfortable distance between them.

"You haven't seen me get upset yet. If Lester walks into this house one more time like he lives here, you'll see me upset."

"All right, Chase. I'll tell him not to come over unannounced."

Winning the small battle calmed him enough for him to pause and get his thoughts together. "We need ground rules."

"*We*," she pointed between them, "don't make ground rules about *my* life. You're not my boss once we leave the clinic, Chase."

He quirked an eyebrow. "Then we're not playing fair?"

She studied the expression behind the words and found something venomous there. "We're playing fair," she agreed.

"Rule number one: he doesn't come here to see you."

She opened her mouth to protest, but his brow furrowed, signaling the rule was a deal-breaker. "I can live with that."

Another small battle won. His shoulders relaxed.

"Rule number two," Sheridan said.

He crossed his arms over his chest and nodded for her to continue.

"You can't grill me about what Lester and I discuss."

"Out of the question."

"What Lester and I discuss is private, just as what we discuss is private."

He shook his head. "It's not the same thing, and you know it. I have the right to know what he's saying to you."

"I won't agree to that, Chase. Telling you what Lester and I talk about will only make everything harder."

"Harder for who?"

"For you! Look how upset you are right now."

He noticed his stiff stance and locked jaw, and backed down. "Okay, but you're not going on any dates with him. Meet him for coffee, talk, and then cut him loose. No need to prolong things. And I don't even need to mention sex."

"Wait a minute. If I can't date, you're not dating."

"I haven't thought about seeing anyone else since I met you, sweetheart."

"Really?" She smiled, savoring a triumph of her own.

He softened. "Did you think I was seeing other people?"

"We never discussed it."

"Do you think I'd be going nuts about Lester if I were seeing other women?"

She shrugged. "Men are strange creatures." She sauntered up to him, pressing her body against his. "I'm the only woman in your life?"

He nodded. "Does that please you?"

"Very much."

He wrapped his arms around her waist. "Our relationship is a bit lopsided."

"I'm going to hear him out, and then I'm going to explain to him we won't be getting back together."

He pulled her close, burying his face in the crook of her neck. "When I think of you and him—"

She remembered going a little nuts herself as she had watched him with Candy. "Shhh. Don't think about it."

"Last rule." He pulled back and lifted her chin. "I want you to work through whatever you have to work through with Lester so we can get serious about us."

"I will."

"I can definitely live with that rule."

He lowered his head and sealed their agreement with a heated kiss.

CHAPTER 19

An accident on the expressway made Sheridan and Lester an hour late for dinner with her parents. They made polite, awkward conversation for most of the ride, but the accident brought back painful memories for Sheridan.

If she had looked away and left the screaming woman standing in the street, she would still be married to Lester. She should have considered the possibility of being sued for acting as a Good Samaritan—Lester and many of their colleagues would not have faulted her. She hadn't been able to save the baby, and the accident had destroyed her life. She pushed those rationalizations away. She was a physician. It was her duty to provide aid if she could. She'd done the right thing. She couldn't second guess herself anymore than she already had.

"Why couldn't you take my side?" she reflected aloud. "All I wanted you to do was to stand up for me one time." She turned in her seat to face him. "It's all a woman ever wants, really. She wants to know her man will defend her against men who shout lewd remarks when she walks by. When the cashier gives her a hard time, a woman wants to know her man will take it up with the manager."

Lester gripped the steering wheel. "You wanted to be protected."

"Exactly."

He concentrated on the highway. "Did you really want me to

walk away from my work? All the good it will do?"

"I never asked you to walk away from your research. I know how much your work means to you."

"What did you want, Sheridan?" His voice was low and calm like he had been preparing for this confrontation.

"I wanted..." She didn't know what she wanted him to do. They'd argued for hours and hours before their marriage had finally ended. She was no wiser now that they were divorced.

"How much should I have sacrificed to save our marriage? How much were you willing to sacrifice? The bottom line is, neither of us was willing to give an inch." He glanced at her. "We both behaved selfishly, and I resent you putting it all on my shoulders."

The truth stung deeply. Sheridan turned and watched the minivan in front of them inch forward. Lester was absorbed in thought, too—he never drove behind minivans, SUVs, or trucks. He had a phobia about the oversized vehicles. Something about them rolling over in an accident.

"We destroyed our marriage—together," Sheridan admitted.

"I apologize for my part in it. It's all I can do. Apologize and try to make things right between us."

She watched his profile. This was the opportune time to tell Lester they could be good friends, comfortable with their past mistakes, but nothing more. They would not rekindle their romance. They'd had their shot and it hadn't worked out.

"Does he know we're together?" Lester asked, taking the conversation in another direction.

Guilt drew her attention out the window. "He doesn't."

"Why didn't you tell him?" She detected a trace of hope in his whispered question.

"I didn't want to upset him."

"He doesn't look fragile." He made a sound between his teeth. "I don't know what you see in those kind of men."

She turned, ready to defend her relationship with Chase. "What?"

"You know. The big, strong, overbearing type who drinks beer and scratches himself in front of the TV."

She rolled her eyes. "What about Chase gives you the impression he's a scratcher? He's a surgeon who owns a clinic."

Lester made the annoying sound with his teeth again. "I don't like him. He's opportunistic."

"Stop. Just stop. You don't like anyone who doesn't worship you. Chase doesn't give you an inch, so you don't like him. It's so Lester Wexler."

"And you still have your head stuck in a fairy tale book. Be a do-gooder and all doors will open for you. Right makes might. It's bull, Sheridan. Life is not fair—a fair is an amusement park. Life is hard. You have to fight for what you want."

"If you truly believe what you're saying, why do you want me back?"

"You need someone to look out for you."

"I can take care of myself."

They continued the drive in uneasy silence. Sheridan watched the scenery go by, saddened by the fact that a love between two people could deteriorate into the inability to hold a civil conversation. She tried to pinpoint the exact moment it had all started to fall apart for them. It wasn't the malpractice lawsuit. The lawsuit unleashed hidden unrest, giving them an outlet to express their unhappiness.

She watched Lester. He had loved her. He never gave her reason to doubt it. He never looked at another woman, although they openly flirted with him. He was a handsome man— smart with a good heart. He wanted to help people. It was his life's mission to ease the suffering of sickle cell patients. His family was tight-knit, as blue-blooded as African American slave descendants could be.

Lester turned into her parents' driveway, and they rushed out onto the porch. Her heart burst with love. She hadn't realized how much she missed them until she saw them again. She grabbed the door handle.

Lester stopped her by placing a firm hand on her forearm. "You asked me why I want you back. I still love you, and I want you in my life. It's very simple."

The men went out to the garage to look at Sheridan's father's new car while the women cleaned the kitchen.

"This is so stereotypical, Mom." Sheridan handed her mother another plate to rinse and dry.

"I know, but I wanted some time alone with you."

"You had this all planned?"

"I asked your father to keep Lester busy for a little while."

She playfully elbowed her mother. "Clever. Why did you invite Lester if you wanted to speak to me alone?"

"We adore Lester. You know that. I just wanted a minute alone with my favorite daughter."

Sheridan filled her mother in on the last few months of her life. She told her about the funny characters of Duck River and how serious they were about the horse trade. She described the small town and all its quaint attributes.

"So you're seriously considering settling down there?" her mother asked as they sipped green tea at the kitchen table. The men had returned to the house, but didn't dare intrude on the mother-daughter moment.

"I really am."

Her mother tapped her teacup with the edge of her silver spoon. "What about your marriage to Lester?"

She stared into her drink. "I'm trying to rebuild my life. I had finally worked past a lot of those demons and then Lester shows up wanting to get back together."

Her mother watched her intently.

"There's someone else."

"Someone else?"

"He owns the clinic where I'm working. Dr. Chase Larson. He's great, Mom."

"But you're here at dinner with Lester."

"And that's the problem." She added extra lemon to her tea. "I'm confused. I talked with Chase. The plan was to hear Lester out and tell him we don't have a future."

"But?"

She looked toward the archway. Lester and her father were just beyond it, wondering what the women were discussing, yet knowing all the time.

"Lester was my husband," Sheridan whispered, conspiratorially. "Marriage is supposed to last forever. If I couldn't make it work with Lester, can I ever make it work with another man? Is it fair to Chase to pursue a relationship with him when I don't know if I can make it work? Is it fair to Lester not to try again?"

"Marriage should last forever, but would you torture yourself by staying in a relationship that's not working? Maybe this Chase is the right man for you. Maybe it's meant for you to get back together with Lester." She shrugged. "I don't know."

She wearily restated her mother's logic. "So maybe I should be with Lester or Chase."

"Maybe. Maybe neither is right for you. What I do know is that you'll know the right man for you without question. Your instincts will help you decide. He'll give you all you need. You'll want to sacrifice everything to be with him. Your heart will jump whenever he comes near."

"Sounds like a movie."

"Don't discount the magic of true love," her mother answered. She leaned forward and lowered her voice. "Most importantly, there will be fireworks when you make love to him."

"Mom!"

They deteriorated into giggles so violent the men came to check on them.

Sheridan's father pulled up a chair beside his wife. "Are you two okay?"

"We're fine. Sheridan and I were having a little girl talk."

Lester clasped Sheridan's shoulder, amused by her happiness. "Can I steal you for a little while?"

When they were dating, if they wanted to escape the watchful eyes of her parents, Lester would take her to the neighborhood park. A nine block walk through the upper class neighborhood ended at a small park where kids played on seesaws, sandboxes and swings. The sun had gone down by the time they reached the park, but it was no less charming. Maybe more so since it was deserted, making it their private playground.

"It's not a bad thing—us arguing," Lester said after a long period of silence. "It shows there's still a great deal of passion between us."

She ignored the remark, climbing up two rungs on the jungle gym instead. She took a seat on the cold metal bar, swinging her legs back and forth until she found her balance.

Lester looked up at her from the ground. "I love your parents. I miss our weekend dinners at their place."

"What happened to make you so sentimental?"

"Nothing in particular." He kicked the dirt. "I didn't have an epiphany—me wanting you back—I never really wanted you to go."

"We should talk about—"

"Do you remember our wedding day?"

"How could I forget it?"

"Come down. You're making me nervous."

She grasped the metal bar overhead and hung in midair, using her legs to swing her body. Lester circled her thighs with his arms and lifted her down. He held her close, pressing his nose into her hair. He inhaled deeply, bringing his arms up around her waist. Not wanting to fall into a cloud of emotion fueled by sentimentality, she stepped back.

"Let's walk," Lester suggested. They had walked several feet before he returned to the original conversation. "Our parents wanted the biggest wedding Nashville had ever seen. Remember, all the planning made us so anxious we decided to run off to Las Vegas."

She laughed. "My father and your mother were racing through the airport, screaming at us. 'You better not get on that plane, young lady,'" she mocked her dad.

"'After everything I've done for you,'" Lester mimicked his mother.

"They were so outraged, security escorted them out of the terminal."

Lester joined her in laughter. "My mother beat me with her purse all the way to the long term parking lot."

She doubled over, remembering the hilarious scene.

Lester took her hand and led her to sit on a bench. "The start of a marriage that was never boring."

"Never." She remembered the luxurious honeymoon cruise. The yearly ski trips to Aspen, courtesy of Lester's parents. Fancy parties with dignitaries and politicians. They appeared to be the perfect couple: handsome, young, in love. Everyone wanted to know them. They were well-respected physicians with promising futures.

"I know what you're thinking," Lester said, obliterating her thoughts. "But it was good between us at first."

She nodded. "It was very good at first." It was only when work got in the way that things started to fall apart. Were they as good as they thought if work could cause their demise?

He turned to her, taking her hands in his. "We could get back to where we were."

"How are we going to do that, Lester? I'm not giving up my career. You know your partners would never let me back into the practice. Their liability insurance would shoot through the roof. Your sponsors would pull their funding…and you'd withdraw your love from me…again."

"Never. It would never happen. I've talked to people who are willing to help you rebuild your career."

She pulled her hands away. "I thought you were going to say you would never choose your career over me again."

His eyes widened in surprise. "Of course. It doesn't need to be said."

She moved away from him. "Don't you see? It does need to be said. More than that, you need to prove it."

He went to her open armed, leaving his heart vulnerable. "I *will* prove it. I'll do whatever it takes to prove it."

"I'm not sure I want you to prove it." She looked away from the hurt consuming his face. "I'm not sure I want this life anymore. The hustle of the city, working under the rules of insurance companies who have no connection with the patient…"

"Me."

She watched as he turned his back on her. It was never her intention to hurt him, but still she had. Even through the arguing and the divorce, they had maintained some level of respect for each other. Months after the divorce was final, she'd been forced to crush his hopes and break his heart.

He composed himself before facing her again. "Is it impossible for you to love me again?" He stood anxiously poised to receive words of encouragement. No matter how badly things had turned out between them, they shared a bond built on past love. She couldn't shatter him.

"I didn't say it was impossible."

Relieved, he rushed up to her. "Then there's hope."

"What about your work?"

"I'm learning how to balance my work with my personal life. You have to give me time. Just as I'm willing to give you time to decide if this is what you want. My family has instilled certain values in me since I was a baby. Those values are now my values. I can't walk away from what's expected of me. From what I want to accomplish."

"I understand."

"I'm asking you to be open to the possibility."

Chase's words hit her in a heated rush. *"I'm looking for something more with you. This can't just be about sex. If you can't give me more, I'll leave right now."*

"I can't promise you a future."

"You can tell me it's on your agenda to try."

She shook away Chase's haunting presence to find Lester standing inches away from her. "Do you know what you're asking of me?"

"I wouldn't ask if I wasn't serious. I've thought about it for a long time."

She looked away, suddenly feeling as if she were betraying Chase by even considering it.

"What's holding you back? Have you formed such an attachment to Duck River in three months? Or is it Dr. Larson you're attached to?"

"Off limits."

"How do you feel about him?" Lester pushed.

She turned away, but he moved quickly, maneuvering himself in front of her. "I have the right to know."

"I care about him," she admitted.

"He'll hurt you."

"You have no basis—"

"I see the way he looks at you. Proprietary. Not with love."

"You want to drag him into the middle of what's wrong with us. He wasn't there when our marriage ended."

"But he's here now to pick up the pieces."

"I won't listen to this." She walked quickly toward her parents' house.

Lester caught up to her, stopping her by grabbing her arm. "I was out of line. Sorry." His voice was tight, obviously saying the words she wanted to hear, but not necessarily believing.

She accepted his apology with a curt nod. "We should be getting back. It's starting to rain, and it's getting chilly."

CHAPTER 20

Something happened at Sheridan's dinner with her parents. She denied anything out of the ordinary when Chase asked, but he had come to know her. She was *different*. Her personality hadn't changed. The way she behaved toward him had changed. He couldn't label it good or bad, just different. A safety net had been erected between them, keeping her emotions firmly separated from his. She'd taken an emotional step back and away, and he didn't know why. He did know he wouldn't let her put an insurmountable wall between them.

"You look terrible," he said, concern throwing him into doctor mode.

"I've never handled the common cold well." Sheridan's voice was thick and heavy, gravelly. She let him inside and trudged off to her bedroom wearing thick white socks and a flowery flannel gown. Her hair was disheveled. She was unpolished, without her usual professional makeover.

He set the two grocery bags he was carrying on the dining room table and followed her into the bedroom. He pulled up a chair, placing his medical bag on his lap. "What's your temp?"

She snuggled underneath a pile of blankets and closed her eyes. "It's high."

"How high?" He was already searching his black bag. He found his thermometer and placed it in her ear. He frowned at the reading. "101."

She turned on her side, facing him. "It's gone down."

"It was higher than 101? Why didn't you call me?"

"Relax. It's just a cold."

"Have you gotten a flu shot this year?"

"Chase," she moaned, clearly not wanting to be nagged when not feeling well. "I'll be fine."

"You look awful."

"Thanks." She turned her back to him.

"Have you eaten anything?"

She shook her head no without opening her eyes.

"Fluids?"

"Some."

He counted two water bottles next to the bed. The bedside table was filled with over-the-counter cold medicines and decongestants. The wastebasket overflowed with Kleenex.

"What are your symptoms?"

She huffed.

"What are your symptoms?" he asked more sternly.

"Muscle aches, headache." She sneezed.

"Do you have a cough?"

She nodded. "A dry cough."

"I want to check your vitals."

He ignored her protesting moans as he applied the blood pressure cuff to her arm. Her BP was within normal limits. He checked her pulse: slightly elevated. He palpated her skin and her eyes flipped open. She didn't protest when she saw the serious set of his brow. "Your skin is hot, clammy." He pulled down her lower eyelid, right then left. "Sclera's red. You look a little dehydrated. Open your mouth."

She moaned again.

He removed a tongue depressor and penlight from his medical bag. "Open your mouth and say 'ahhh.'"

She crossed her eyes but did as he demanded.

"Your tonsils are red and edematous. Might be a mild infection."

"I have a scratchy throat. You'd expect a scratchy throat with a cold."

"Ears?" he asked.

"No problem."

He flashed his penlight in her right and then left ear. "No drainage, but I'll have Ted bring my scope so I can take a look inside."

"You're making a big deal out of nothing. I have a cold."

"And antibiotics. I'll have him bring some antibiotics to help you shake this."

"Antibiotics don't help with a cold."

"I don't like the way your throat looks."

While she was still protesting, he left the bedroom and dialed Ted at the clinic. He asked for the appropriate antibiotics and supplies, and told Ted to have them delivered.

Sheridan appeared in the doorway. "It's just a cold, Chase. Don't bother Ted."

"Back to bed," he pointed the way, continuing his telephone conversation with Ted.

She crossed her arms over her chest in defiance, but a sneezing fit encouraged her to heed his words.

He finished talking with Ted before moving into the kitchen. He boiled noodles and filled the teakettle, sitting it on the electric eye to heat. His mother had given him simple instructions for making a soup of vegetable broth and noodles. While he waited for the noodles to cook, he found a tray table he could sit next to Sheridan's bed. He puttered around the kitchen, finding places to put the groceries he had brought. Vegetables of all shapes and colors for her. Two steaks for him.

He left the soup bubbling while he checked on Sheridan. She was snuggled beneath the covers, the sniffles plaguing her in her sleep. He tested her temperature with the back of his hand then returned to the kitchen. For a paralyzing moment, he let his mind imagine the worse case scenario. A fever gone wild, antibiotics that did not work—he called himself ridiculous, blaming his crazy imagination on his intense feelings for Sheridan.

A little while later, he placed the vegetable soup and a steaming cup of tea on the coffee table. He garnished a plate with tiny crackers and fresh fruit.

"Sheridan," he whispered, shaking her softly. "Wake up. I want you to eat and drink something."

"I really don't feel like it," she mumbled. "When I get like this I need to sleep."

"I'll let you sleep." He threw back the mountain of blankets and lifted her in his arms.

"Hey!"

"You can go back to sleep later. First, you need to eat and drink. You're losing a lot of water through your perspiration. I don't want you getting dehydrated."

"Do you treat all your patients with a cold this way?"

"You're more than my patient."

He carried her into the living room and propped her up on

the sofa.

"I reserve the right to refuse treatment." She tipped over, ready to take a nap.

He pulled her upright. "Do you want me to have Ted bring an IV set-up?"

She came fully awake, the threat enough to refuel her appetite.

"Eat your soup and then you can go back to bed." He left the room and returned with a blanket to cover her. "You're not eating." He lifted the soup bowl and reached for the spoon.

"I can do it," she snapped, grumpily.

He handed her the bowl and watched as she took the first bite. "How is it?"

"I think it's good, but everything tastes bland now. No sense of smell, no sense of taste."

"Might be for the best. I'm not the greatest cook. Eat up." He left her to complete his mission. He started a hot bath running while he cleaned her bedroom. He tossed the trash, and removed the various medications. He piled the blankets in a chair, and pulled the sheets from the bed. They were warm and damp from her fever. He searched several closets until he found clean linen in the bathroom. He found matching sheets—women were sticklers about that sort of thing—and remade the bed.

When all was done, he went to check on the patient. "You finished it all. Good."

She looked up at him over the rim of her teacup. "Can I have a little sugar? Please." He happily met her request.

"Thank you," she mumbled. "I'm not good company when I'm sick."

"I've noticed."

"You should go before you catch my cold." She let her head fall lazily against the back of the sofa.

"I'm resilient. I never get sick. Very seldom catch a cold or get a headache." He chuckled. "Well, you give me a headache sometimes. Like when you won't let me take care of you."

"You forget I'm a doctor, too."

"You're vulnerable when you're sick. You might need something." He sat beside her. "You don't look very good at all. I want to keep an eye on you." He placed a comforting hand on her thigh. "Besides, I don't want to leave you."

"I don't like having people around when I'm grouchy."

"I'm not people."

She watched him, searchingly. His resolve was clear. She asked, "Can I go back to bed now?"

"After your bath." He lifted her and carried her into the bathroom.

"I can walk."

"I like carrying you around."

"You like to be in charge, don't you?"

"Yes! And when it involves you, I so rarely get the chance. I have to take advantage when you're sick."

"That doesn't seem gentlemanly."

He nodded toward the bathtub. "Normally, I wouldn't ask, but seeing that you're sick…do you want me to stay?"

She rolled her eyes at the hidden innuendo. "I can do *this* myself."

He left her to undress, standing outside the door and waiting to hear the splash from her sinking into the tub. While Sheridan soaked in the warm water, he moved the television from the living room into the bedroom. Next, he pulled the recliner into the bedroom, arranging a sitting area where he could keep a close eye on his favorite patient. He didn't want to be a room's length away from her.

"Sheridan?" He knocked lightly on the bathroom door.

"Come in."

"Are you doing okay in here?"

"I'm fine." She sagged forward, wrapping her arms around her drawn up knees.

He sat on the rim of the tub and took the washcloth from her hand. "Let me bathe you." He invaded the water, soaping the cloth, rinsing and repeating the cycle. He alternated between boyfriend and physician mode. He scrubbed her tenderly like an adoring lover, while analyzing the nature of her cough and sniffles.

Gradually, Sheridan gave over all control to him. She relaxed into his touch, her eyes closing while he cascaded warm water over her back.

"Time to go back to bed," Chase said, removing the stopper from the tub.

Sheridan stepped from the tub, stepping into the fluffy white towel he held open for her. She didn't protest when he dropped to his knees and dried her. He helped her slip into clean pajamas before lifting her and carrying her back to bed.

"I hate you seeing me like this," she said as he laid her across cool, dry sheets.

"You're beautiful." He pulled the sheets up to her chin and covered her with one blanket, ignoring her request for two. "Let me check your temperature again." Satisfied with a temperature several degrees lower than before, he kissed her forehead. "Get some rest."

"Are you leaving?"

His heart did that crazy flippy-floppy thing when he heard the twang of desperation in her voice. "Not on your life." He pointed to the sitting area he had arranged for himself. "I'll be right here until you feel better."

She closed her eyes, visibly relieved.

He kissed her forehead again. "I'm not leaving you."

Chase remained quiet and determined while keeping his two day vigil. His bedside manner was flawless, never showing any signs of annoyance or fatigue. He gathered Sheridan up in his arms and placed her on the sofa while he changed her bed linens, then he carried her back to bed and covered her with a sheet. He made sure she took her medication every six hours, no matter how much she grumped about it being unnecessary. He made her meals, and insisted she eat them. He sat in the recliner he had pulled into her bedroom for two days, leaving only to go to work. He used his lunch hour to check on her and called whenever he had a five minute break. Every night, he held her in his arms and hummed to her until she fell asleep.

"Thank you for staying with me," Sheridan said, feeling well enough to join him at the dining room table for dinner. "I know this has been an inconvenience. I didn't make it too easy for you, either."

He smiled, extended his arm across the table, and stroked her face with his long finger."What is that song you've been humming?"

"It's a special song. I only hum it for you."

"You're sweet." She smiled into her bowl of soup.

"You need me to care for you."

Very simple for him. He wanted her and she wanted him, therefore they should be together. He didn't dwell on past mistakes. He didn't have an ex demanding equal time. He had no secrets.

Sheridan let her emotions grow, but fearing she would cry, she suppressed them. "Thank you," she squeezed out.

He ate several bites of his steak before he spoke. "You want to tell me what happened when you went to visit your parents?"

She continued eating while pretending to be unfazed by the question. "What makes you think something happened? I get along very well with my parents."

He wasn't fooled by her mental shuffling. "If you don't want to tell me, you don't have to."

She looked up, earnestly. "The last thing I want to do is tell you," she answered honestly.

He watched her, trying to shield his hurt and keep his composure. He was sticking to the rules. She had broken them by going on a date with Lester.

"Are you upset?" she asked, hoping the question would force him not to be.

"Very." He sliced off another piece of his steak. He chewed slowly, diverting his eyes from her. Looking at the painting on the far wall, the curtains, the vacant space where the television used to be. Anywhere but into her eyes. She felt guilty. She felt alone.

"I'll go home tomorrow. If you don't mind me staying tonight." He still avoided looking at her. She could tell by the aggressive working of his jaw he hadn't lied when he'd said he was angry.

"I hate making you feel this way," she confessed.

He dropped the fork and knife. "Then don't."

She placed her palms flat on the tabletop and leaned forward, wanting to crawl over the table to him and place her nose against his. She wanted to press their lips together and swallow up his warm, easygoing, old fashioned ways. "Do you have any idea how much I care about you?"

His eyes latched onto her soul and searched for truth. "No," he whispered, "I don't."

She shrank back in her chair, stung by his brutal honesty. The only thing that made her feel worse was the damage she was inflicting to their relationship. She hung her head, whirling the spoon through her soup. "Why haven't you just walked away?"

He waited for her to look at him before he answered. "Because I know how much I care about you."

They went to their neutral corners, politely avoiding any discussion that might delve into the issues facing them. Sheridan needed to make a decision. She needed to clean up her past and go to Chase with a heart free to love him. Cleaning up her past meant not only finding peace with Lester, she had to tell Chase about the malpractice suit. Having Lester share her secret and expecting him not to use it as leverage against Chase was like expecting a house of cards to withstand a tornado. Her shaky medical practice history could destroy Chase's clinic.

She worked up her resolve, numbering the reasons she had to tell Chase—tonight. He cared about her, and he wasn't Lester. He would understand why she hesitated telling him. He would pull her into his arms and thank her for telling him now. He'd speak about trust and support. He'd tell her it didn't matter. And she would agree that nothing mattered as long as they were together.

"You okay?" Chase brushed a lock of hair away from her forehead and tested her temperature.

"I'm fine." She removed his hand and held it tightly.

"I want to give you a full exam tomorrow morning before you see any patients."

She didn't bother to argue. She wouldn't win. "All right."

"I'm going to bed." He peered down at her. "Are you sure you're feeling okay?"

"Yes," she whispered.

He kissed her forehead. "Good night. Don't stay up too long. You need your rest."

She watched him pad away from her, his bare feet sinking into the carpet. She idly wondered where he found pajama bottoms long enough to fall to the arches of his feet. He toyed with the drawstring, humming a soft tune. His white tee bunched atop the haunches of his firm behind.

He felt comfortable going to bed without her. The last two nights he'd slept in the recliner in front of the television, his long legs hanging over the bottom and his lanky arms dangling off the side. He didn't want to disturb her sleep, he'd told her. At dinner, before things went quiet between them, she'd insisted he sleep in her bed tonight.

All rational thoughts of being honest with Chase disappeared when an image of him snuggled in her bed appeared. She needed a little longer. She had to be sure he wouldn't walk away from her. She dug her fist into her thigh out of frustration. He should have left her long ago—the moment she showed any signs of indecision about sending Lester back to Nashville. She was a hypocrite, and as long as her feelings for Chase continued to grow, she would be. She didn't want any woman vying with her for his affection. She selfishly wanted all of him for herself.

Sudden sadness befell her. Once in an argument, Lester had told her she had been spoiled so badly she believed the world should work by her crazy, convoluted rules. She pressed her palms to her temples, fighting confusion. What she felt for Lester mimicked obligation. To Chase she freely gave her heart. Maybe she did want them both on some level. Her past and her future together made her whole. She needed to right things with Lester to prove she could—she wasn't a failure at marriage. She couldn't let Chase go because he had come to mean so much to her.

How could she be trained to make life or death decisions in a split second and not be able to decide what was the best path for her life? How much longer would Chase wait for her to figure it out? She immediately sobered. The consequences were too painful to think about.

She stood in the archway of the bedroom, watching Chase. He snored lightly, his head turned into the pillow. He lay on his stomach, legs together, but arms stretched the length of the bed. Her heart strummed. She would never get used to how handsome he was.

She slipped out of her gown and tipped over to the bed. She carefully pulled back the sheet—he never slept beneath a blanket—and climbed onto his high haunches, covering his body with hers. The hardness of his muscle-clad back offered security and comfort. She snuggled into his grooves, fitting her softness to the ripples and mounds of his posterior. His skin warmed her, his breathing lulled her into a safe place. She planted quick kisses at the nape of his neck.

"Umm," he moaned, turning his head to the left. "You're feeling better."

She pressed her hardening nipples into his back.

"Are you naked, Shameless?"

Her body thrilled at his private nickname for her.

"You'll catch cold again." He flipped over unexpectedly, covering her body with his. "You need to keep warm."

"I'm rather hot right now, Doctor."

"I see." He pressed his erection into the warm depths found between her thighs.

She slipped her hands underneath his tee and pushed it up above his head. "If you're going to share your body heat you have on too many clothes."

He kissed the tip of her nose before tossing his shirt and pushing down his pajama bottoms. He kicked them off, but froze when he saw the look in her eyes. "What's wrong? We don't have to do this if you're not feeling up to it."

She couldn't face him.

"What is it?" He placed his finger beneath her chin and turned her head.

She pulled away from his tender touch.

"Sheridan, you're scaring me."

After all the turmoil she was bringing to the relationship, he was scared for her. He was too good for her. One day, he would tire of her baggage and indecision and leave her. She couldn't bear the thought.

"Sheridan, look at me right now." He clicked on the bedside lamp to find her face bathed in tears. "You're scaring me. Tell me, what's going on?" He sat up and started examining her body. "Are you feeling bad?"

She stilled his hands beneath hers. "I'm not sick."

He cupped her face between his hands. "Then what's wrong?"

"I don't want to lose you," she managed.

"Lose me?"

"Everything is so confused right now. I'm not handling this situation the right way. I do care for you and you don't understand—"

"Shh." Chase kissed her lips lightly. He caught her tears on his tongue, humming as he swallowed the salty emotions. "Shh." He moved his body against her in small circles. He pressed his erection into her, waiting for her erotic response. He slipped his tongue in her ear and applied two fingers of pressure to the spot that made her back arch. He wound his arm under the small of her back, melding their bodies together so tightly her breath caught. He dragged her with him as he stretched to reach the bedside table. With a minimal shift of his body, he unrolled the latex.

Her tears were gone when he eased inside of her, rocking his pelvis and holding her tightly. She wrapped her arms and legs around him, wanting to pull his strength inside her.

"Breathe, baby," he whispered into the darkness.

She took a deep breath, inhaling the unique aroma of his soap and cologne mixture.

"Breathe," he said again, pushing deep inside. He rocked his hips, kissing her neck with each stroke. When she writhed beneath him, her climax coming down, he inserted his tongue into her mouth. He kissed her until he felt the last jerk of her body, until he heard the final moan.

He grasped her calves, pulling them upward and bending her knees. His fingers locked into place, his tongue licked her breasts in sync with his long strokes. With sudden urgency, he hammered into her, hard and fast. Completely out of control of his emotions, he pushed her to the top of the bed with the force of his thrusts. His body stiffened. He groaned long and loud. He grinded their pelvises together, savoring the good feeling. He collapsed on top of her, their rapid breathing combining as one.

Sheridan lifted her head and kissed his lips.

He pressed his mouth to her ear. "I know how much you care for me."

CHAPTER 21

"Welcome back, Dr. Wexler," Ted said with a knowing smile. He stuffed his stethoscope into the pocket of his crisp white uniform. "We missed you around here."

"Thank you. And thank you for bringing the antibiotics."

"Anytime." He exchanged glances with Carolyn, but it did not deter Sheridan's energetic bounce.

Missing three days of work put her behind on reviewing test results, but skipping lunch would help her catch up. Her office visits went smoothly, making Carolyn happy because she stayed on schedule. She had to hide her face when she passed Chase in between patients. She'd catch a whiff of his cologne and be bombarded with memories of the intimacies they'd shared late into the night. He'd flirt with her a bit, whispering in her ear when they were in the lounge alone, or patting her behind as she entered an exam room. He kept her on edge and aroused at the same time.

"Dr. Wexler?"

Sheridan looked up and saw Carolyn standing in the doorway of her office carrying a white bag. The flowery polyester dresses she insisted on wearing made her look several years older than her true age. The tight bun atop her head added a few years, too. Sheridan often wondered about the woman's personal life, but other than mentioning her husband a few times, Carolyn kept her home life private.

"Dr. Larson said you're to stop and eat lunch." Carolyn handed her a bag containing the diner's version of a vegetarian plate. She knew from experience the special was colorful and well presented, but not very tasteful.

"Has everyone had lunch?" she asked, hoping Carolyn might volunteer information about Chase's lunch plans. She imagined a private lunch in his office. They could spread a blanket across the floor and feed each other fresh fruit. In between tasting cold strawberries and grapes, she could taste his juicy lips.

"Everyone but you," Carolyn answered before the fantasy got out of control. "Dr. Larson had me bring this back when I went out. He worries about you."

"Yes, he does," she answered cautiously, concerned about Carolyn's reaction to their relationship. The older woman prided herself on being the watchdog of ethics and propriety for the clinic.

"We all worry about you," Carolyn added staunchly.

Sheridan knew it would be the best compliment she'd ever get from her. "Thank you."

Carolyn nodded and swiftly left the office. Ted caught the door with his palm. "Dr. Wexler?"

"Yes, Ted?" She smiled up at him, knowing he was the keeper of her secrets when it came to her romance with Chase. He might not know all the details, but finding Chase making soup at her house told quite a bit.

"I wanted to check the orders you wrote for Mrs. Harvey." He held the chart up for her inspection. "Are these the correct tests?"

She scanned her orders. "Yes. The tests we performed at her

last visit still haven't pinpointed the problem. I did some research, and decided to look in a different direction."

"The lab we use can't run these tests. They can take the specimens and ship them out. Or Mrs. Harvey can go the medical center in Nashville."

"Which is more economical?" she heard herself asking, remnants of Lester's medical philosophy escaping from her mouth. Somehow, it didn't seem unethical this time. Probably because she knew finances would not preclude Mrs. Harvey from receiving the tests, even if the clinic had to bear the costs. Chase would insist she obtained the best care available. Finances would be a second thought.

"It's more cost effective for our lab to take the samples and ship them out. But…"

"Yes?"

Ted spoke frankly. "This requires a sophisticated testing procedure. I would want the best possible lab—a lab familiar with running this sort of test—to handle it."

"You would send Mrs. Harvey to Nashville."

"I would."

"Make the appointment. I'll clear it with Dr. Larson before I call Mrs. Harvey and explain."

He turned to leave the room.

"She'll need transportation. Can you arrange it for her?"

Ted gave her an approving smile while jotting down a note on his clipboard.

"Ted, can I talk to you for a minute?"

"Sure." Sensing she wanted to have a private conversation, he closed the office door.

She wheeled in tight to her desk, her fingers strumming the desk calendar. "You probably have questions about why Dr. Larson was so comfortable at my house the other day."

The corner of his mouth lifted in amusement, obviously enjoying watching her squirm. "It had crossed my mind a few times."

"It's not what you think."

"It's not?" He crossed his arms over his chest.

"It depends, I guess, on exactly what you think." Her fingers tapped the corner of the calendar.

"I think you and Dr. Larson have been hot for each other since the day you started here."

"Ted!"

He laughed, putting her at ease. "Look, Dr. Wexler, what you two do after hours is nobody's business."

"I don't want my relationship with Chase to influence your vote about my becoming partner."

"I can remain completely impartial." He chuckled. "I wonder if Dr. Larson can."

"You're certain you're not bothered by my seeing him?"

"Not at all. Dr. Larson and I are fairly good friends. My wife and I have him over for dinner a lot. He's my kids' godfather. He's a good man. He deserves to be happy. If you do that for him, who am I to have an opinion?"

"Thanks, Ted."

"Anytime." He went back to work, oblivious to the anxiety she'd had before talking with him.

Chase wrapped on the doorframe. "Are you eating?"

"My office has become Grand Central Station," she teased,

warmed with the delight of knowing she was a part of the team.

He planted himself in front of her desk. "Eat. I don't want you getting sick again. Besides, you need to keep your strength up for me."

"You take such good care of me." She lowered her voice to reflect seductive intimacy. "In and out of bed."

His lashes dipped. She'd succeeded in embarrassing him, but he recovered quickly. "Would you like some company tonight? I'll bring dinner."

She squirmed in her seat, thinking fast. "I can't. I'm having dinner with Alison today in Nashville."

His lifted a thick, dark brow. "My sister? Since when did you two become an item?"

"I like her. She's sweet."

Concern gripped his handsome features. "Are you up to it?"

"I'm back to normal. One hundred percent. Stop worrying."

"Um-hmm," he hummed. "When did you make these plans? You never mentioned them."

"She called just last night. It's been so busy we haven't had a chance to talk today."

"It's good you're getting along with my family, but don't let Alison grill you. My sisters have a habit of sticking their noses in my personal business. Just tell her you have strict orders from me not to discuss our relationship."

"I think I can handle Alison's questions." She shook her head. "You worry too much. I'm sure we can find something else to talk about besides you."

"I thought I was your favorite subject. I'm wounded." He placed his hand over his heart, and Sheridan's body responded as she remembered the things he had done with those fingers a few nights ago.

"The things I want to say about you are too hot for Alison's ears."

He smiled. "You're forgiven."

"I didn't know I was in the doghouse."

"You were for a minute there, but its all gravy now." He stood, his height casting a protective shadow. "Call me the minute you get back into town. And tell my sister not to keep you out too late. You're still recovering. Doctor's orders."

"Yes, sir," she teased.

"I want a rain check on dinner." He leaned over the desk and stole a kiss.

Sheridan's insides warmed to a wicked glow. "I'll be back in time to have a late dessert."

"I love the *Planet of the Apes* movies."

Sheridan lowered her magazine, giving Alison her full attention. A young couple huddled together in the far corner of the waiting room. Soft muzak played in the background, unsuccessful at soothing the patients waiting to learn their fate. Tall plants decorated every corner of the room, blending in well with the sand and brown motif.

"They fascinated me as a child." Alison turned her reflective gaze to Sheridan. "When Dwayne and I got married, he gave me the complete box set as a wedding gift." She laughed at a private memory. "I've watched them so much I know all the lines." Her eyes welled with tears.

Sheridan squeezed her hand. "Why does that make you sad?"

"I wanted to share them with my children some day."

Sheridan dug a Kleenex from her purse and held Alison through her quiet tears. "You *will* have the chance to share special moments with your kids. You have to think positive. Even if the biopsy is positive, your life isn't over. You can't claim the negative."

Alison rambled through her nervousness. "I know it sounds silly—to want to pass on the *Planet of the Apes* movies to your children—but they gave me a lot of joy as a child. Did Chase tell you how poor we were as kids?"

"He did."

"My mother didn't allow us to watch too much television. We didn't even have one until the horse business took off, so we used to race home and sit glued to the tube for hours. My mother said we were ingesting too much junk, so she allowed each of us one hour of TV a day. The rest of our time had to be spent doing chores, playing outside, or reading."

"That explains why you're all so successful."

Alison nodded. "My mother knew how much *Planet of the Apes* movies meant to me, so she used to let me watch the entire movie—regardless of her rule. Most times, she'd watch with me. We bonded over those cheesy movies."

"There's nothing cheesy about bonding with your mother."

"True. I want to share moments like that with my children. Now I may never have the chance."

"We're jumping ahead of ourselves here, Alison. Let's just wait until we have the biopsy results. Stay positive."

"You're right." She sat up, dabbing at her tears. "I'm being paranoid," she sniffled.

"You're not being paranoid. Finding a lump in your breast is scary business."

They watched the nurses moving behind the glass at the reception desk.

"Where does Chase think you are?" Alison asked.

"I told him you were taking me to dinner."

"But you didn't tell him about coming here?" Alison's eyes widened.

"No. I wouldn't do that without your permission, but I don't like keeping this from him. It puts me in a bad place—in the middle of family business."

"Maybe you'll be family soon," Alison fished for information.

"Don't change the subject." Sheridan tried to remain stoic, but thinking of Chase made a goofy smile cross her lips. "You shouldn't be keeping this from your family. I know your husband would want to be here with you. He loves you. He'd want to support you."

"I'm not ready yet. I'll tell everyone if we find out there's something to worry about. Otherwise, there's no reason for everyone to get upset."

"You shouldn't go through this alone."

"I'm not." She grasped Sheridan's hand with icy cold fingers. "I have you here with me."

Ninety minutes later, the only sign of Alison's ordeal was a small bandage on her right breast. While waiting for her in the lobby, Sheridan had a chance to consider the advice she'd given her. There were some things she needed to come clean about with

Chase. Keeping Alison's confidence was adding one more secret she'd have to account for sooner or later.

She had no reason to believe Chase would be anything less than supportive—his unconditional support had been one of the first things to attract her to him. But still she hesitated. The clinic was important to him. Remembering how excited he had been after his first day back at surgery confirmed it. The clinic was the result of his lifelong work. She wasn't sure his feelings for her could compete. With Lester around to ruffle him, she didn't need another problem coming between them.

Alison was unusually quiet in the car, but by the time they reached the restaurant where they'd agree to have dinner, she was returning to her bubbly self. "What did my brother have to say?" she asked when Sheridan returned to their table.

"He asked how much longer we were going to be in Nashville." She slipped into her chair and placed her linen napkin on her lap. "He's going to grab dinner at the diner before he heads home. We're meeting for dessert later."

Alison fished an ice cube from her glass of water. "My brother is ga-ga over you. And it looks like you feel the same way." She crunched down on the ice. "I've never seen him like this with a woman. Don't get me wrong. There have been women." She rolled her eyes dramatically. "Let me tell you, my family was glad to see them go."

"I don't think Chase would want you telling me this. He gave me specific orders not to discuss our relationship with you."

She waved away the thought. "Chase has four older sisters. He knows the drill. If he really didn't want me to talk to you about something, my phone would have been ringing before we left Duck River."

The waiter interrupted long enough to take their orders.

"I would be hungry all the time if I only ate fruits and vegetables," Alison observed.

"It took some getting used to at first, but now I don't miss meat at all. And I feel a lot healthier."

"Really?" Alison leaned forward. "Maybe I'll give it a try." She smiled. "Starting next month. Today, I'm going to enjoy the filet mignon I just ordered. But I admire you for sticking with it. How'd you get started anyway? Did you just wake up one morning and shout 'Save the cows!'?"

Sheridan laughed at Alison's free-spirited nature.

"Seriously, what made you give up meat? Because I have a fur coat at home, and I'm hoping it won't end our friendship."

"You're funny." She remembered Lester encouraging her to join him as a vegetarian, making a friendly bet she would feel much better within thirty days. Then he became more serious, telling her he wanted to have her in his life permanently and he would do anything to prolong their time together. She cleared her throat, pushing the memory of his adoring face away, feeling she betrayed Chase by recalling it while at dinner with Alison. "My ex-husband encouraged me to give up meat."

"I didn't know you'd been married. Chase didn't mention it."

"You've talked about me with Chase?"

"Of course." Alison gave her a look of incredulity. "He tried not to say much, but I have my ways."

Sheridan shook her head, not wanting to know how the conversation went. Chase was guarded about his personal life when it came to his sisters, but Alison had a way with sweet relentlessness. "My family is skeptical of Dwayne. We've made it our mission to prove to them we were made for each other."

As Sheridan listened to Alison prattle on about how she met Dwayne and the development of their relationship into marriage, she contemplated a future with Chase. Deciding whether to give Lester another chance wasn't about his needs or his newly found regret over the demolition of their marriage. The decision had to be about her happiness. She'd spent hours listening to Chase and Lester each tell her what they wanted. The real question was what she wanted, and what she needed to be happy.

"You're very quiet. What's on your mind?" Alison asked.

She lifted her spoon and polished it with a napkin. "It's about your brother."

"It stays between us."

She hesitated, considering Chase's need for privacy. She felt she could trust Alison. There was a way to discuss her problem with her new friend without embarrassing Chase. "I like him a lot," she began.

"Everyone who has seen you in the same room together knows that."

"Is it that obvious?"

"To anyone who's watching. His eyes stay trained on you. You smile whenever he walks by. It looks like a case of puppy love."

Sheridan thought back, searching for the truth in what Alison said. She hadn't realized she was so obvious.

"So what is it about my brother that's bothering you?"

Sheridan hesitated, folding the corner of her napkin. "There things about me he doesn't know, and…I'm afraid his opinion of me will change if I tell him."

Alison's easy nature turned serious. "Do you not care about him like he cares about you?"

"No," she answered emphatically. "He knows exactly how I feel about him. It's just—I've made some mistakes in my professional career he should know about. Mistakes that could have an impact on his career."

"Why haven't you told him up to now?"

"At first I felt it was in the past and nothing would come of telling him. I didn't tell him after we became involved because I felt ashamed I hadn't told him up front."

"You said it might affect his career."

"It could."

"Would he break up with you if he knew?"

Sheridan pondered the possibility. She was most attracted to Chase because he was compassionate, understanding and forgiving. From the moment she met him she'd made comparisons between his character and Lester's, wondering how he would have handled the lawsuit if he'd been her husband at the time. She pulled herself up taller, sure of her answer. "No. I don't think he would. I think he'd tell me it didn't matter."

Alison observed her for a long moment before offering any advice. "You know, women always feel the need to confess. We always want to be open and honest. We loathe ourselves for keeping secrets from the man we love." She cocked an eyebrow. "Let me tell you something. Sometimes there's nothing wrong with keeping a little information to ourselves. Whatever it is hadn't affected his career so far. If it's not going to hurt him, and it wouldn't change anything, what's the point of digging up the past?"

Sheridan latched onto the advice, justifying her actions with Alison's words. She ignored the nagging voice in her head telling her a good relationship had to be built on honesty. She let fear of losing Chase dictate her decision.

Alison lifted her glass in salute. "I say, ignorance is bliss."

She lifted hers in agreement.

CHAPTER 22

They ate red velvet cake sprinkled with nuts in the middle of Chase's blue-green ocean. Soft music helped them float over the waters as Sheridan finger-fed him each mouthwatering piece. She inhaled the ocean breeze—woodsy cologne and testosterone. Her fingers dipped into the cool waters, and she painted Chase's lips with orange jubilee.

She liked being the aggressor when they played. It pleased him, heightening his arousal. She gave him cake and fed off his reaction to her touch. She pushed his broad shoulders until he lay on his back in the man-made sea of greens. The waves shimmered around her, guiding the rhythmic movements of her hips. She rode each wave, bracing his thighs to keep him from catapulting from the ship.

Chase palmed the back of her neck. He gripped her waist and shifted their positions, placing her beneath him. He held her hands, and used them to fan her arms out from her body. "Slow this boat ride down," he told her. "Make love with me."

The intensity of their connections, bodies and minds, was too overwhelming to add raw emotions. But Chase took control and steered them into calmer waters. He stayed at the helm, moving slow and deep, taking Sheridan where he needed her to go.

"This is good," he whispered. He toppled forward, trailing

his tongue up her neck, nestling it in her ear. "This is good."

She nipped at his neck as she lost control of her lips.

Chase took her hand and placed it next to his heart. "Look at me." He stroked her face.

She did.

"Don't let go of my heart." He pressed her hand against the muscles of his chest. "Don't let go, Sheridan."

"I won't."

Chase began to rock his hips wickedly. He moved slow and deep with a confident command of her body. He grasped her bottom, lifting her from the floor into each sure thrust. His body dripped sex appeal. The way the muscles of his abdomen flexed as he drove into her. The drops of perspiration raining down on her. His roughened voice. The bulge of his thighs as he knelt between her legs, feeding her his essence. It was all a testament to what made him a virile man, able to steer her into the waters of ecstasy.

"Make love with me," he demanded, his voice steady and controlled.

Sheridan let her mind join him in a place too warm for sex, but not hot enough for the love they were making. She watched his face as it contorted into a session of emotions. Her heart beat in time with the soft music coloring their background. The blues and greens absorbed her, wrapping her in a cocoon of sensuality. She inhaled the scent of their conjoined bodies, and shivered at the magic of it.

"Come to me," Chase said. The power and speed of his thrusts carried him closer to the orgasmic border.

"Come with me." She pressed her fingers to his chest. "I'm

not letting you go."

"Together," he told her.

She moaned, overwhelmed by the sentiment.

"Together."

She maintained her hold on his heart as he brought her to the edge of the shore, joining her before giving her permission to disembark. Their bodies jerked for a long time, until every ounce of emotion was drained. He collapsed, rolling over on his back and dragging her on top.

She giggled.

"What's funny?" he panted.

"You're covered with cake." She ran her fingers through the icing clinging to his shoulders and placed it in her mouth, licking the sweetness of him.

He cradled her in his arms. "Look in your heart and tell me what you need from this relationship to make you happy."

"I am happy."

"Tell me where you'd like this to go. How far would be far enough?"

She lifted her head to look at him. "Sounds like you've been thinking about his for a while."

"I have."

"I'm very happy with the way things are between us. I have never been this happy in my life."

"Where are we going?"

"It can't be predicted."

"Don't be cautious with me, Sheridan. Tell me where you'd like to see our relationship go. You've been married, you know the possibilities."

"We keep moving forward. We go as far as we both want it to go. Why are you pushing this?"

"I wanted you to tell me how you're settling into Duck River, and even if you didn't become partner at the clinic, you'd want to stay here—to be with me."

"Is it an either or situation?"

"Not as far as I'm concerned. I want you to have everything you need to be happy. I just don't know what it is you need."

She traced her finger around his puckered nipple. "Don't try too hard to please me. You're a good man, with a good heart. Everything you do makes me happy: the time we spend together, the way you make me laugh—it's all good."

"Is it enough?"

"Can't you feel it? Can't you tell by the way it feels when we're together?"

"I do." His fingers gathered her hair. "I know how I feel. I'm not sure what's going through your mind."

She lay her head on his chest. "Where is all this coming from?"

"Your ex-husband is still in town. It makes me wonder if you're having trouble telling him to go home."

She gripped his waist. "I know this isn't fair to you."

"I don't want you to apologize. I want you to clear up the situation with Lester so we can go about building our relationship."

"I will. I promise."

They lay on the floor, entangled in each other's arms in silence. Sheridan's finger moved through the grooves of his rippled abdomen. He was troubled. She could feel it in the tension of his muscles. Nothing she could say would put him at ease.

Until Lester went back to Nashville, he would always have doubts about her commitment to their relationship.

"This is such a great room," she told him.

He stroked her hair. "My favorite."

"Mine too," she said. "Mine too!"

CHAPTER 23

"I need to turn up the heat." Dinner with Sheridan's parents hadn't been a total disaster, but it hadn't helped Lester's cause. Every time he thought of her kissing *that* doctor, his blood boiled. Minute by minute, they were growing closer which meant she was growing out of him.

Lester sought Candy out. Her advice would be helpful. His way hadn't gotten the results he wanted. He found her in the sitting room off her bedroom. She spent most of her time here, hiding from the sins of the house. He often wondered why she stayed in the business when it made her so unhappy. He never pried though—it wouldn't be polite. They'd grown to be good friends. She'd talk to him about it if, and when, she wanted to.

"Am I disturbing you?" he asked, entering her room.

"No. Come in." She perked up, sitting upright on the settee and straightening her dress. The sexy chiffon number fit her curves perfectly. She always dressed as if she were waiting to shoot a layout for *Playboy*. He believed, beneath the makeup and fancy dresses, Candy was a natural beauty who used her looks to cover up the pain of her life. He wished he could reach out and touch the pain, flicking it away as easily as she gave unhappy men pleasure.

"What are you doing?" he asked with an amused smile. He lifted the book she was reading. "Toni Morrison."

"I'm just looking at the pictures."

"I've read everything Toni Morrison has written, and I've never seen any pictures."

"You like her stuff?"

He nodded, taking a seat next to her.

"You probably think it's stupid for a—for me to be reading her."

"I think Morrison is a great writer, but her literary style is a challenge for anyone to read. You should be commended for daring to try."

She lowered her head, self deprecatingly. "If I get stuck—"

"If you get stuck, call on me." He gave her a broad smile. "It's the least I can do since you're helping me get my wife back."

Candy shut the book and moved into her bedroom to tuck it away in her dresser. When she turned back around, her eyes had lost the brilliance of their shine. "Where are we now?"

"I haven't spoken to Sheridan since we had dinner with her parents."

"And that was a disaster."

"I wouldn't say *disaster*."

"I would." She tapped her temple with an extra long manicured nail. "The trip down memory lane didn't work out. What you should do is build new memories with her. Happy memories. Make her forget the past and want to start again."

"Our past? Our history is what makes us special." It was his trump card against Chase.

"Your history destroyed your marriage."

He mulled over her words. "You're right."

"Candy knows all about romance." She said it with a smile, but she sounded sad.

"Why do you do that? Refer to yourself in the third person?"

"I don't know. I didn't notice." Her sagging expression told him otherwise.

"You're a beautiful, intelligent woman. You shouldn't have a low self esteem."

A bitter laugh threatened her cool persona. "I'm very sure of myself."

He let the argument die—his point had been made, and no matter if Candy wanted to acknowledge what he'd said, she'd reflect on it when she was alone. She was a proud person who didn't like to be looked down on, or embarrassed, but she strived to better herself, and she valued his opinion. "Have you eaten?" he asked.

She shook her head.

"Let me take you to dinner."

"You want to take me to dinner?"

"We can finish talking." He checked his watch. "I have a lot of work to do, so we can't go far. The diner okay?"

"The diner is excellent."

"Bring Toni along."

The glow returned to her eyes. "Okay."

"I want to change my shirt and tie. Meet you downstairs in fifteen minutes."

"I'll change, too."

"See you downstairs."

"This is almost like a date."

"Yeah," he laughed. "I guess it would be if we weren't going to talk about you helping me get my wife back." He left with the renewed hope of mending his relationship with Sheridan making him hum—unaware of the shattered expression on Candy's face.

Candy leaned forward with her chin resting on the temple of her fingers, mesmerized by Lester's every word. He had answered all her questions about Toni Morrison's book without hesitation, never making her feel stupid or uneducated. He'd even read his favorite passage to her. The diner was quiet. The few patrons who were there when they had arrived had already finished their dinners and gone. Being virtually alone with Lester, she couldn't help closing her eyes and picturing them in a different time—with her as the center of his universe.

She envied Dr. Wexler for having such a tight hold on his heart. If he were in love with her, she would be the best wife he could ask for. She would encourage his work, happy to make a real home for him. She'd be delighted to serve dinner for his doctor friends. She'd support him in every way for the opportunity to have him smile at her with love in his eyes.

"Tell me about your research," she said.

"I don't want to bore you with complicated medical talk."

"It's okay. I want to hear about it." She touched his hand across the table. "Brag a little on yourself." She persuaded him with a seductive flutter of her brow.

"Stop me if I start to go on. I'll start with the pathophysiology of the disease."

"Patho—?"

"The origin of the disease."

She nodded, encouraging him to go on. He liked to talk

about his career and his research. He pulled out a pen and illustrated the development of the disease. He placed an arrow at the point his research was meant to intervene.

"Am I getting too technical?"

"No. Go on. You're like—like a genius."

"Hardly."

She crossed her arms on the table, pushing her empty vegetable plate out of the way. If being a vegetarian would keep her young and healthy, she was willing to give it a stab. "One day I'll be watching TV and they'll be interviewing you on some news show."

"Bringing honor to the family name is important, but it's really about easing the suffering of those with sickle cell anemia." He explained the familial responsibility to accomplish great things in the medical field. His enthusiasm was contagious, making her want to learn more about the disease that had claimed her mother's life. Until now, she had suppressed all memories of her mother, shielding herself from the pain the best way she knew how.

He sensed her melancholy. "Your mother died from sickle cell. It must be hard for you to hear me go on about it."

"Strangely," she admitted, "it's comforting to know someone is trying to do something about it."

"Do you want to talk about it?" He lowered his voice respectfully.

"There's not much to talk about. I was eleven when she died. Once she went into the hospital, I never saw her again. My mother, the dearest person to me, went into the hospital one day and never came out. After that, I moved from relative to relative until

I ran out of family. By the time I was twelve, I was placed in my first foster home. It was a nightmare."

"I can imagine."

"No one should have to imagine."

He covered her hand with his, sending warm feelings to her heart. "I didn't mean to upset you."

"If you had been born twenty years earlier, I might still have my mother."

"You inspire me."

She couldn't begin to tell him how much he'd inspired her to become a better person. More and more, the parade of lusty men in and out of her house was becoming a nuisance. She had begun to dream about a normal life with a husband and children.

"Do you have the trait?" Lester asked.

She nodded. "Another reason I will never have a child."

"Don't be discouraged. You just have to be careful about who you marry."

"Marry?" she asked sarcastically. "Who would marry me?"

He sat back not hiding his surprise. "Any man would be lucky to marry you. You're beautiful, sensual, funny." He laughed. "You're a good listener. Believe me, the right man will come along."

She'd found the right man, only he didn't know it. "I can't believe I'm having dinner with such an amazing person."

"You're pretty amazing yourself." He stroked the back of her hand. Her eyes dropped, pondering his touch. He pulled back slowly, not overstepping his bounds, but showing her the value of her friendship.

"Why in the world would any woman leave you?"

He cleared his throat, embarrassed. "I take full responsibility for destroying my marriage."

"It takes two to make it work and two to destroy it."

"Maybe." He sipped his water, the intimate moment between them lost.

"What happened," she prodded gently.

"My research was more important than my marriage. When Sheridan needed me, I chose my work over our marriage."

Candy dipped her head. "I don't understand it." She lifted her head and held his gaze. "If I were married to a man like you, I would want to support him and his work. I would keep the perfect house, cook for him, love him at night when he came home. I wouldn't bother him when he was working, but I'd be there when he needed me on his arm. Having the love of a man like you would be enough to fill my days."

Lester watched her unblinkingly. Unwittingly, his mind had begun to picture a scene: him working late, and returning home tired and beaten. He'd step into their cozy home and find her there ready to soothe him.

Male laughter pulled his attention away. He turned and saw Chase and his nurse enter the diner. The nurse went to the counter to pay for his take out order, leaving with a bag large enough to feed an army. The doctor talked with the owner for a few minutes, making sweeping gestures with his arms. They shook in agreement and the doctor took a seat near the window. He immediately picked up his menu and started perusing it. The waitress came over, making small talk that caused him to laugh. She left him with a light brushing of his shoulders.

Lester shredded his napkin into tiny pieces. "I don't like to think about Sheridan being with him, but if he hurts her, I'll—"

Suddenly he jumped out of his seat, and marched across the diner in Chase's direction.

Chase looked up, his face souring. Lester represented the only thing he disliked about Sheridan: her marrying him of her own free will. The man was pompous and rude. He insisted on exercising some bizarre right he believed was his to reclaim Sheridan. If not for his reputation, and his fear of Sheridan's reaction, Chase would pummel the guy.

"Stay away from my wife."

He folded the menu and laid it neatly on the table beside his glass of water. "Sheridan is not your wife. Get over her. Go live your life."

"We're working it out."

He sagged back in his seat, mimicking Lester's pompous attitude. "She's trying to let you down easy."

Lester snickered. "You're delusional. Sheridan and I are working through our problems. We're spending time together, trying to get back on track."

He sat upright out of his swagger. "What do you mean, 'spending time together?'" His ears burned to hear the words repeated. Sheridan was not supposed to be *spending time* with Lester. They had agreed she would hear her ex-husband out, and then send him home heartbroken.

"What medical school admitted you if you can't understand simple English?"

Chase pushed back his chair. He'd had enough of Lester and his mind games.

"Hello, Dr. Larson." Candy appeared, wrapping herself around Lester's arm. "Lester, I paid the check, and I'm ready to go."

Chase zeroed in on the way Candy held Lester. He questioned their relationship with the narrowing of his eyes. He and Candy had never been involved, but he knew about her past and how vulnerable she was because of it. Her relationship with Lester caused him a degree of concern—especially if Sheridan would be dragged into the middle of it. "What's going on, Candy?" he asked.

"Lester and I were having dinner."

"You're friends?"

"Do you have a problem with it?" Lester asked, on the verge of breaking the limit of Chase's patience.

"I do if you're using her."

Chase stood with the calculated grace of a cougar waiting to pounce. Candy cringed, but he had a feeling it didn't have anything to do with his sudden movement. "When have you spent time with Sheridan?"

Lester fought the smile of triumph. "Sheridan is my wife. I don't answer any of your questions about our relationship."

"Relationship? Sheridan and *I* are in a relationship. *You're* begging her to take you back."

Candy tugged on Lester's arm. "People are watching. You don't want to make a scene here."

"No," Chase agreed, "you don't want to make a scene here. Listen to Candy."

Lester disentangled his arm. "Are you dismissing me?"

"You're dismissed. Leave Duck River and go back wherever you belong, because it's not here. Sheridan wanted to let you down easy, but you're too stuck up to understand you're not wanted here."

Lester lurched forward, intending to grab him around the neck. He welcomed the challenge and the ability to tell Sheridan he'd only been defending himself. He stepped into Lester's path, his hands balling into fists. Candy stepped between them, pushing against their chests to keep them separated. "Guys, stop it."

"Listen to Candy," Chase taunted.

"Let's go, Lester." She pressed her palms to his chest. "Lester. Let's go."

His eyes slid down to her.

"Let's go."

Chase watched as Lester let her lead him out of the diner. He glanced around, measuring how much attention they'd drawn. He hadn't been in a fight since wrestling with his oldest sister, Sarah. He cursed underneath his breath, upset he'd let Lester goad him into an argument. He should be sure of his relationship with Sheridan. No one should be able to come between them with a few meaningless words.

Lester couldn't resist turning around and getting in one last dig. "You're the transition guy. Don't forget your place."

"I can't believe you started a fight with Dr. Larson," Candy scolded Lester from behind the wheel of his rental car. He had been so upset after his conversation with Chase, she didn't believe he was focused enough to drive them home. "Chase is a good guy." She'd always had a fond place in her heart for him. He cared for her and her girls, never being judgmental about their chosen careers. Lester, she had grown to know, was a good man, too. They were very different men who loved the same woman. "I'd hate to be Dr. Wexler." Choosing between two handsome, educated, passionate men would be impossible for her. "You messed up back there."

Lester watched the scenery of winter-beaten trees and grazing horses out his window. "I know. He'll tell Sheridan, and she'll be upset with me for making a scene."

"Exactly."

"He gets to me. Who does he think he is coming between me and Sheridan? I don't blame him for falling for her, but once I told him I was back, he should have gotten out of the way. Instead, he wants to make this personal."

She tucked a lock of hair behind her ear. "I don't think Chase is playing games. He's a decent man. He's never been the type to fool around, or deliberately hurt someone. He must really care about her."

"I thought you were on my side."

"I am." She would help him because he was her friend. She prayed he wasn't successful because she loved him.

"It doesn't sound like you're on my side. Sounds like you're taking up for Chase Larson."

"I'm telling you Chase is a good man. You won't win Sheridan back by trying to prove he's not. Or by trying to prove you're the better man. It won't work."

Lester crossed his arms over his chest, trapping his tie beneath them. "You're supposed to be helping me here."

"I'm trying to help."

"How is telling me how wonderful Larson is helping me?"

"If you want to win Sheridan, you're going to have to find another way. You're going to have to prove to her you deserve another chance. She's going to have to realize that Chase is a good man, but so are you and all things being equal, it's better to save what she had with you, instead of taking a chance with a man with too many unknowns."

"How am I supposed to do all this? Sheridan and I can't have a civil conversation without arguing about my past mistakes. Chase won't get out of the way. I'm lost here. I know about medicine—not women."

"I'm trying to help you." She wished she could help Lester see her feelings for him.

"What do I do?"

"Go back to where it fell apart." She inhaled deeply, giving honest advice that diminished her chance at happiness. "Fix the thing that broke."

"I appreciate you agreeing to see me," Lester took a seat on Sheridan's sofa. He'd worn black slacks and a charcoal gray sweater for his last attempt at winning back his wife. After trimming the tuff of hair on his chin, he slapped aftershave cologne on his face and marched off to claim Sheridan.

"We need to talk this out, Lester." She wore a look of determination, confirming she'd already made her decision.

He hadn't talked to her for several days—he could only imagine what Chase had told her about their confrontation at the diner. Maybe he hadn't mentioned it at all. The doctor could be sitting back, waiting for him to mention it so he would look like the instigator. If Sheridan knew, she would have scolded him for causing a scene in the diner, embarrassing them all. No matter. He hadn't come to see Sheridan to talk about anything negative. Let a discussion between men remain between men. Yes, that's how the country doctor would play it—all full of pride and chivalry, he'd protect the little lady from the fallout of combat.

"I haven't been fair," Sheridan said. "I should've talked to you about this a long time ago."

"You needed time to think. Please, sit with me." He waited for her to join him before continuing. "I completely disrupted your life by coming here."

She looked surprised. There weren't many times in their relationship that he'd admitted to doing something wrong.

"I barged into your life, declared my love for you, and demanded you take me back. Then when you didn't fall into my arms, I went about finding ways to trick you into loving me as much as I love you. This wasn't the right way to handle this situation. I apologize."

Sheridan swallowed hard, taken aback by his self depreciating honesty. The determination setting her lips in a frown disappeared. He locked onto her eyes, reaching for her hands. He released a tension filled sigh when she curled her fingers around his. "The bottom line is I love you and I want you back. The best way for me to win your heart is to show you I've changed."

"Lester, I –"

"No, wait. Let me finish. This is hard for me."

She searched his face for a long moment before allowing him to continue.

"I want to go back to where the problems between us started and fix what went wrong." The next part was painful. He hesitated, completing an internal review of his reasons for making the greatest sacrifice of his life. He rested his palms on her shoulders, and her silky hair brushed the back of his hands. He remembered the warmth of her embrace, the way she loved completely and unselfishly, and the nights they stared into each other's eyes as they made love. He reached out and trailed a finger across her high cheekbone. "I'm giving up my research."

"What?" She bolted from the sofa. "You can't give up your research."

Lester matched her height. "I had hoped for a different reaction."

"You can't give up your work."

"I can—for you. My research is far enough along that the backers will be able to find someone to continue it relatively easily. I've made a list of suggested candidates. I'll help them find a suitable physician they'll be happy with."

"Your backers won't be satisfied with you making a list. They've invested too much time in your work. You've invested too much time in your work. No one can duplicate the hours you've devoted to this project. What are you doing?"

"I'm prioritizing—like you told me to do when our marriage was falling apart. I was too pigheaded then to do it. Now that I've had to live without you, I understand what's really important to me."

She wrapped her arms around her middle, placing her back to him.

"Sheridan?" His gut twisted and burned. Giving up his research had far-reaching consequences he couldn't even consider without feeling nauseous. So many were affected by his decision: the afflicted, his family legacy—it was too overwhelming to entertain. He had to focus on one thing at a time to remain sane, and right now he was anxious to know what Sheridan thought about his ultimate sacrifice.

She turned, wearing her professional physician's face. "You can't give up your research."

"I want you back in my life. My work is the thing keeping you from me."

"The research, the lawsuit—those things were the catalysts to ending our relationship. If two people love each other—truly love each other—they can work through anything. We should've been able to work through anything."

"Are you saying you never really loved me?" The thought crushed him.

"I'm saying we need to consider the possibility we aren't right for each other. Why should either of us have to give up what's important in order to be together? How are we supposed to rebuild on regret?"

"There'll be no regret. I've taken a long time to think this through. I'm willing to sacrifice my research in order to have you."

Her eyes softened. "I understand what you're doing, but it isn't right. Finding a cure for sickle cell is your life. I could never live with myself."

"This is what you wanted. Why is it what you wanted then and not now?"

She came to him. "I never wanted you to give up your dream. I wanted you to support mine. Instead of saying it's us, or your work, I wanted you to say it's us first and I'll find a way to continue your research. I would have supported you in that decision. I could have helped you lobby the drug companies and universities—it's how we won the financing in the first place. You wouldn't hear it. It had to be your way or nothing." She pressed her palm against his face. "I needed the safety and security of knowing you'd stand by me while I fought to save my career. I needed you to believe I didn't do anything wrong—I needed you to believe I'm a good doctor."

He held her gaze. He couldn't let go of her. He couldn't be without her in his life. He'd realized his mistake the day the divorce became final. He needed a wife to support him. He needed help to make a home. He took a desperate chance, wrapping her in his arms. He pulled her in for a kiss. Pressing his lips to hers, he tried to delve deeper, but she pushed away.

"Please don't do that again."

"Even my kisses are revolting now?" He couldn't hide the anger stinging his chest. "Sheridan, there's nothing more I can offer you. I'm giving you my heart. I'll leave my research. I've been away from my practice for weeks, here trying to work it out with you. I'm cowering in the shadows while my wife plays around with the good country doctor."

"Stop right there, Lester. Calm down before you say something that puts a permanent wedge between us."

His fingers curled into tight fists. He breathed heavily—in and out, in and out—finding his composure.

She took his hand. "You're a good man, Lester."

"But?"

"But we don't work well together. Our professional goals are so far apart they interfere with our personal relationship."

"We can make it work. I'm trying to make it work."

"Would you be happy here? Living in Duck River while I work at a small family clinic? What would you do? You'd go crazy here."

"I'll go crazy without *you.* You don't even know if you'll get the partnership at the clinic. No final decision has been made. You can't plan your life around what might happen."

"It's what I want."

"Along with Dr. Larson," he added accusingly.

"Our professional goals are more suited, yes."

He had a thousand things he wanted to say about Chase, but he held back. According to Candy, putting down *Dr. Perfect* wouldn't make anything better for him. "What am I supposed to do without you, Sheridan?"

"Lester," she said softly, "go back to Nashville."

"What? That's it? You're not going to give us another chance?"

"The truth is, this wasn't a decision I had to make. It took me a long time to realize it, but it's true. You would never be happy if you gave up your research. You'd regret it, and resent me. And I don't want to start over again with you. I want to stick it out here and continue to rebuild my career. I want a chance to make a real home."

Lester scrubbed his chin. "I've lost you."

"Our divorce has been final for over eight months. What has happened that made you want me back after all this time?"

He dropped all pretenses, knowing he and Sheridan had been friends before they married. He could be honest with her. "I'm lonely, Sheridan. I need a woman in my life. I loved having a wife. Having a partner helped me make sense of everything."

"Lester." She hugged him. "You'll have someone special again. You just need to go and find her. Trying to put us back together when we both know it's not right would never give you what you need."

"No other woman could replace you."

She pulled away and gave him a sassy smile. "Well, of course not." She prodded him in the shoulder, encouraging him to laugh.

He gave in.

"You should go back to Nashville," Sheridan said when they stopped laughing.

"I will. Soon."

She raised an eyebrow.

"I'm getting a lot of work done here—away from the obligations of the clinic. Besides, I want to say a proper goodbye to you. We'll have dinner." He winked. "I'll give it one last shot at convincing you to come back with me."

CHAPTER 24

Chase jumped down from the horse and handed the reigns to the nearest farmhand. He patted the horse's mane, whispering close to its ear. He turned and caught Sheridan watching him from her place perched on the corral fence. The brown trench coat knocked against the back of his cowboy boots as he strutted toward her. He placed a gloved finger in his mouth and tugged, completing the removal with the help of the other manicured hand. She shivered, remembering the velvet softness of his touch as it caressed her naked skin. His dark eyes watched her as he removed the other glove and tucked them in his pocket. He continued his stroll toward her, a bright smile growing on his full lips.

Her heart pounded, knowing his smile was meant for her. He'd been cautious with her over the last few days. Their conversation was polite, not heated. Their kisses were too quick, not lingering. She'd wanted to get him away from work when he left an invitation for dinner on a prescription pad on her desk.

Duck River Family Medicine

Prescription for Sheridan Wexler

Horseback riding this Friday.

Followed immediately by dinner with Dr. Larson.

Refills: unlimited.

Signed: Dr. Chase Larson

She watched Chase as he rounded the fence, his eyes never

leaving hers. He marched up to her with sparkling determination lighting his brow. He grasped her around the waist, lifting her down. He held her against him, pressing their bodies together. The bulge of his muscular arms flexed beneath her as he placed his arms underneath her bottom to hold her steady. She wrapped her arms around his neck, and he stole her breath away. His tongue entered her mouth before their lips met. His facial stubble burned her chin as he probed her mouth. His belt buckle pressed into her belly as something harder rose to awareness between her thighs. A chorus of whistles and howls ended their affectionate display.

"Spectacular," she breathed.

The corner of his mouth quirked upward, and he let her slip from his embrace, sliding down the length of his body. She grabbed his muscular forearms, refusing to release him. "Don't let me go."

"Never," was his heated response. "Never." He wrapped his arm around her neck, pulling her to him and holding her face against his chest.

She'd been rescued from anything that could ever harm her. She latched onto his waist then she buried her face in his chest, inhaling the outdoorsy aroma of his clothing. He lifted her head with his finger, meeting her mouth for another fiery kiss. She barely heard the ranchers applauding their efforts. Her heart and mind were wrapped up in Chase. When he pulled away, she had no doubt she'd made the right decision about Lester.

"Are you ready for your first ride, Shameless?"

She tugged at her turtleneck. After his kiss, she felt she would burn up inside the heavy cable knit. "Ready."

"A little nervous?"

"Just a little." She breathed heavily, the cold air mixing with her sigh to paint the sky with white ribbon.

"I'll take care of you." Chase leaned forward and caught her smoke signal with his mouth. He kissed her again, and instantly, all her fears melted away.

"When's the next show?" one of the workers called.

"They wish they had what I have." Chase took her hand and led her to a considerably smaller horse than the one he had been riding. The horse tried to nuzzle Sheridan, but the movement startled her, and she jumped behind Chase. "It's okay." He patted the horse. "She remembers you."

Sheridan eased out from behind his protective girth. "I remember this horse. Rose. I fed her once."

"She's mild tempered and takes to strangers quickly. Pat her. Get to know her before you mount up."

Sheridan glanced at him before she reached out to touch the horse. She'd been spending weekends on the ranch with Chase as he continued her lessons about horses and riding. Today, she would "mount up" and go for her first real ride. Walking around the corral with Chase holding the reigns didn't count. She stroked Rose's shiny coat until they were comfortable with each other.

"You wanna try this on your own?"

"You mean ride without you in the saddle?"

He nodded. "You're doing well."

"Only because you were right there with me." She looked up at the brown, doe-eyed giant. "No. I want you with me the first time out of the corral."

"Okay. I'll put you in the saddle, and then I'll join you."

She clutched his arm. "No. You go up first."

"Hey." He lifted her chin with his finger. "If you're not ready—"

"I'm ready." Chase enjoyed horses and riding. If she wanted to share this with him, she had to learn to ride.

"We can take more laps around the corral."

"No, I'm ready. Can you go up first?"

He gave her a quick kiss. "Sure." He planted his boot in the stirrup and threw his long leg over the back of the horse. He waved for one of the workers who was standing by watching them. "Help the lady up, please."

The man answered in Spanish, lightly placing his hands on her waist.

Chase took her hand. "Put your foot in the stirrup." She did, and the man behind her lifted while Chase pulled until she was straddling Rose's back. "Are you on?"

"I'm on." She wrapped her arms around his waist and tried to settle comfortably in the saddle.

"We'll take it slow," Chase said, using his boot to encourage the horse into a lazy walk.

"How far are we going?"

"Not far. This isn't so bad, is it?"

She opened her eyes. "No, it's not."

Chase made a clucking sound with his tongue, and the horse sped up into a smooth gallop. "Too fast?"

"I'm fine." She pressed her face against the curvature of his back. Her fears mellowed as they went along. She hugged Chase tighter around his waist, drawn by his strength. This man had it all. He was a caring physician who could love her body with unprecedented skill. She would always be grateful for his patience with her indecision about their relationship. He remained humble, even though his family was one of the wealthiest in town. His interests were wide and varied, and Sheridan knew his riding ability was only one thing she could learn from him.

"Isn't it nice out here?"

"It's wonderful." She took in the wholesomeness of the Larson ranch. The greenery of the land was interrupted by clusters of trees. Horses were secured in separate groups according to their age and stage of training. Farmhands, trainers, riders, and businessmen swarmed the grounds, but the further they rode the more isolated the land became. Chase brought Rose to a slow trot as they reached a thicket of trees in an isolated area.

"We need to rest the horse," he told her as they came to a stop. After dismantling, he held her hand while leading Rose to a tree near a small creek. "I come here to fish a lot when the weather's warm. I'll teach you next summer."

"You plan on having me around next summer?"

"Oh, yeah." He secured the horse to the tree. "Look over there." He grasped her shoulders and turned her in the right direction.

"What's that?"

"Go see."

She left the comfort of his embrace to venture over to a white park bench. The grass was thick and lush beneath her feet. She entered the small picnic area enclosed by a circle of tall trees and wild flowers. The bench was covered with a vibrant red cloth. A huge wicker basket sat in the middle of the picnic table. Heat from a large bar-b-que grill warmed her face. Someone had come before them and prepared a secluded picnic for two.

Chase joined her. "I thought you might need to rest before we go back."

"Did you do this?"

His arms surrounded her waist from behind. "It was my idea, but Ms. Fluentes prepared the food. Check it out."

She opened the wicker basket and began removing its contents. She unpacked ice-cold juice and bottled water. A vegetable mixture had been carefully prepared and wrapped in foil, ready for the grill. Chase's favorite T-bone steaks were fragrantly seasoned, accompanied by a bottle of steak sauce. She pulled out a Tupperware dish filled with fresh fruits for their dessert last.

"I could do this everyday with you," Sheridan said as they tended the grill.

"Good. My mission will be accomplished."

She flipped his steaks. "If I can't make you a vegetarian, maybe you could give up beef."

He shook his head. "It's not going to happen. I weaned from the bottle to a steak."

"I bet your mother loves to hear you tell that story."

He laughed, dragging her over to the picnic table. He settled her in his lap and placed his finger inside the collar of her turtleneck.

She traced his top lip with her finger. "I talked to Lester. He understands that it's over between us."

His eyes widened. "He does? The last time I saw him he was going on about spending time with you. He made it sound like you were trying to patch up everything."

"You spoke to Lester?" All questions about where their relationship was going, and if she was happy with him now made sense. She couldn't figure it out at the time—why he would ask those things after they'd just shared the intimate moment together in his blue and green room—but now it all fell together. "When did you see Lester?"

"At the diner a few days ago. It was nothing. Especially now that I know you squashed all his hopes of reconciling."

"Don't sound so happy about it. Lester isn't so awful, and I don't like being the bad guy."

"When is he leaving?"

"Soon. He wants to do a little more work on his research project before he goes back to the clinic."

The muscle in his jaw jumped.

"What is it?"

"I won't feel better until he goes back to Nashville and leaves us alone."

"You've been very tolerant about everything, and I appreciate it."

He kissed her. "Maybe you can show me a little of that appreciation right here, right now."

"The steaks are burning," she said between kisses.

"You can *appreciate* me when we get back to my place."

One romantic afternoon was all Sheridan needed to confirm her decision to leave her failed marriage in the past and concentrate on building a solid relationship with Chase. They spent a lazy afternoon lying in the grass and kissing like they were teenagers. When dusk approached, they mounted Rose and headed back.

Sheridan pressed her cheek against Chase's back. "Your ranch is so beautiful."

"You're more comfortable riding now." He reached back and squeezed her knee.

"I know you won't let me fall."

"I would never let anyone hurt you."

"Chase?"

"Yes?"

"I don't know exactly where I want our relationship to go. I only know I want to take it as far as possible."

He turned, surprised by her candidness.

"I surprised you."

"Yes. A few hours ago you were still lost."

She kissed his cheek. "You found me."

"Hold on tight, because I plan on taking this further than you could ever imagine." He took Rose to a full gallop. Sheridan held him tightly as their laughter rippled the air.

After returning Rose to the stable, they went to Chase's for a swim. The swim quickly became skinny-dipping in his heated pool. Their suits were discarded, along with any inhibitions they might have had.

"Who is the shameless one now, Dr. Larson?" Sheridan asked as they kissed in the middle of the pool.

He peered through the water at her naked body. "Gotta say it's you."

"You have the cutest country drawl."

"I do not."

"You don't hear it?"

"I can't hear it because I don't have one." He swung his arm, splashing her with warm water. She shrieked and swam away. He pursued, easily catching up and pinning her against the wall of the pool. His dark eyes locked in on her, assessing every inch of her face. He lifted his hand, pushing the wet tendrils away from her face. "You are beautiful." He sounded amazed, in awe. It made her stomach flutter. "I have never felt like this about anyone before." He placed his face in the crook of her neck. "Never."

"I know. Alison told me."

He threw his head back in laughter. "I knew I would be the topic of discussion during your little outing."

"She told me *everything*."

"I'm not going to fall for it because there's nothing to tell."

"How come?"

"Same old story. Never found the right woman—until now."

"You're handsome, smart and successful. There must have been a big romance in your past."

He shook his head. "No. I've dated. Even had a high school sweetheart, but no serious relationships until I met you."

"I find that amazing."

"I was saving myself for you."

She kicked her feet, staying afloat as she cupped his face in her hands. "I'll choose to be blissfully ignorant, but only because the thought is so appealing."

"It's true."

"You were saving yourself for me?" she teased.

"All for you." He kissed the tip of her nose.

"Then would you make love to me now?"

"Yes."

"Let's get out of the pool."

"Why?"

Her face lit up. "You *are* the shameless one now!"

He propelled himself out of the pool and reached out for her. The water sluiced over his shoulders, abdomen, and legs, dripping off his burgeoning erection. Her stomach tumbled. He looked like a Greek god. A statue chiseled from dark marble. When she didn't take his hand, he knelt and lifted her underneath her shoulders out of the water.

She stood cheek-to-chest with him, looking up in wonder. "It amazes me when you lift me so easily."

He bent down and scooped her up into his arms. "Let me amaze you in another way." He carried her up the winding staircase, his breathing showing no signs of exertion.

"We need towels," she said as he approached the bed.

"Damn the towels." He placed her in the center of the bed and was kneeling beside her before the mattress recovered. He used his slender fingers to excite goose bumps on her flesh. His fingertips pulsated over the silky wetness of her skin, making her nerve endings come alive. He used his medical knowledge of the female body to find her hidden erogenous zones. He caressed them with the practiced skills of a surgeon, meticulously and methodically, bringing her to a quick orgasm.

Sheridan lay in an exhausted heap, her nerve endings raw and pulsing. She struggled to catch her breath, aware she was near hyperventilation. Just when the climactic waves were close to subsiding, Chase pushed her thighs apart and settled there. The first stroke of his tongue caused her to scurry to the head of the bed. His fingers formed a clamp on her thighs, trapping her in a position that allowed him the best advantage. He ignored her pleas and continued to lap at her, tasting her, consuming what made her a woman. Her back arched high as the next climax came down on her. Chase secured her to the bed, coaxing her to respond as brazenly as her body desired.

She heard the paper rip and had the presence of mind to lift her head. Chase knelt between her thighs, preparing to enter her for his own pleasure. "Come here," she panted. She reached for him, adding her fingers to the work of unrolling the condom. His erection twitched beneath her touch. He sighed, letting her know it wasn't a mindless nerve reaction. She finished unrolling the condom and guided his penis into her.

He braced her hips and went forward by careful degrees until he was completely absorbed by her heat. "Sheridan," he said between sharp intakes of air. "Sheridan." She moved her hips to meet his thrusts. She added a circular rotation when he began to moan. His head fell back, and she suddenly wanted to kiss his Adam's apple. She wanted to place her kiss there, suckling the skin until her burgundy mark was cast.

"Sheridan," Chase moaned.

She added extra bump to her grind.

"Sher—" His head snapped forward.

She gripped his thigh.

"She—"

Almost there. She wanted to watch the emotions wash over his face as he found his release.

"She—"

She surged forward, lifting her hips from the bed, pressing into him, pushing him deeper.

Chase's hips began an uncontrollable hammering.

"Chase," she called.

He exploded. Deep. Inside her.

He exploded deep inside her.

He exploded deep. Inside her.

Sheridan pulled him down to her. Holding him tight, she whispered in his ear, "That was incredible."

"Wonderful."

"Astonishing."

"This is getting serious." He pressed his elbows into the mattress, suspending his weight above her.

"My body is addicted to yours."

"I mean serious here." He drew a heart on her chest.

"And here." Sheridan returned the gesture.

"Definitely."

"Kiss me, Chase."

"The most intimate part of being with you is holding you afterwards." Chase's seductive words woke Sheridan. He wrapped his arm around her middle and pulled her back against the hardness of his naked body.

"The sun is coming up." She sounded sleepy.

"It's still early."

"I was asleep. Were you talking to me?"

"Yes."

She waited for him to explain. He didn't. "What did you say?"

"I always talk to you when you're asleep."

Surprised by his admission, she turned within the circle of his arms to look at him. "What about?"

"That's between me and your subconscious." He wrapped his arms around her again.

"Are you trying to hypnotize me?" She snuggled into his chest. There was early morning warmth there.

"Yes."

"To do what?"

"I'm not telling you." He smiled. "It's working already."

"Don't tease me."

He captured her mouth in a sizzling kiss before she could protest further. When he released her, she couldn't remember what they'd been talking about. He had the uncanny ability to erase her mind of everything but how she felt about him.

"You enjoy sex." It was his observation, not a question.

"Is it a problem for you?"

"Hell, no. It surprises me. Your first impression is of a woman who is too serious about her work and too disciplined to have fun."

"You've changed me."

He growled. "I didn't know I had such power."

"You ignited my sensuality."

His long fingers stroked her spine, and she curled her back in a feline arch. "There are some other things I'd like to spark in you, Shameless."

"Should I ask?"

"Hmm." He rolled his eyes upward and then back to her. "Maybe not yet."

"You worry about me."

"All the time."

"Why?"

His hands lazily cupped her bottom. "Because I care about you." He moved one hand to her chin and tilted it upward. "Actually, it's a lot more than that. I—"

Her pager jumped to life, startling them both. "It's me." She untangled herself from his arms and padded across the room through the early morning chill to retrieve her pager. She climbed back into bed before reading the display.

"Doesn't look like Carolyn's code," Chase observed. He reached for her. "Let it ring. I want to tell you something."

"I don't recognize the number. I should answer it. It might be an emergency." She smiled over her shoulder as she reached for the telephone. "I worry about my parents."

He fell back against the pillow, his arm draped over his eyes. He wanted to talk, but he'd let her deal with her parents first.

"Sheridan?" Lester answered on the first ring.

She pulled the sheet up to cover her naked body. Lester's intrusion into their intimate time altered everything, including her comfort level. "What is it?" She dropped her voice. "It's early."

Chase sat up, curious.

"I know. I know." Lester was excited, his voice higher than usual. "I think I've found something."

"What do you mean 'you found something?'"

"In my research. I think I have a breakthrough. I'm coming over to show you." His excitement cleared enough for him to realize he'd paged her. "Where are you? I've been calling your house for the past half hour."

She stiffened, and Chase read her body language. "This is a bad time—"

Chase's angry breath warmed her back.

"Did you hear me? I think I have a breakthrough. I need to run it by you before I get too excited. Meet me in thirty minutes?"

"Well." She had sacrificed her marriage for this research. She looked back at Chase. He wasn't happy about the interruption.

"Sheridan, please. You know how much this means to me. I want to share it with you first."

It was an impossible choice. Lying in bed with Chase for another hour or meeting Lester for possibly the most important discovery in medical science in over a hundred years.

"Sheridan?" Lester pleaded.

"Thirty minutes, but I have to go to work."

Chase threw back the sheets and leapt out of bed. He paced the length of the room like a caged bull.

"Thank you," Lester breathed. "I'll be there in thirty minutes."

She disconnected and turned to Chase. "I'm sorry."

"You're leaving my bed to go see your ex-husband."

"It's not like that." She rushed to gather her clothes. "He's had a breakthrough."

"I was about to have a breakthrough myself."

She zipped her pants. "What do you mean?"

"I'm not going to tell you *now*, when you're running out the door to be with Lester."

She pulled her sweater on as she slipped into her shoe. "We'll have dinner tonight. You can tell me then. We won't be interrupted. I promise." She hopped around the room while she jerked on her other shoe. "Where's my coat?"

"You're excited," he accused.

She stopped and took in his strained face and chiseled body. Her eyes lingered too long. He crossed the room and stepped into his pajama bottoms.

"Chase, don't give me a hard time about this, please. This *is* exciting. I've suffered through every minute of Lester's research."

"And now you want to celebrate his success with him."

"I want to share in it, yes. I want to know what he's found. Is it wrong?"

"Is it wrong to jump out of my bed in the middle of the night when he calls? Yes, it's wrong."

"It's morning. I was going to have to leave in a little bit anyway to get ready for work." She went to him to give him a kiss. "We had a good time. Don't send me home mad."

He begrudgingly kissed her.

"We'll eat lunch together today."

"We have the monthly clinic meeting today."

She snatched her keys from the bedside table. "I forgot. But we're on for dinner, right?"

"Dinner." He watched her go. "Right."

CHAPTER 25

Chase grumbled about two thousand curse words during his drive to Sheridan's place. She had jumped out of bed and fled the romantic scene he was trying to set the minute Lester called with his "breakthrough." He had been about to tell her he was in love with her. She may be unsure about what she wanted in the future, but he wasn't. He wanted her to love him as much as he loved her.

He was just getting over his boiling anger when Lester called her at work. During the entire monthly meeting, Carolyn had to keep calling her attention back to the matters being discussed.

And their dinner plans? What dinner plans? By the time he had wrapped up with his last patient, she was gone. She never finished up at the clinic before he did. She was notoriously slow in examining her patients and methodically thorough with her follow-up research. Today—"breakthrough day"—she had burnt rubber out of the parking lot an hour before him.

Well, enough is enough. He had been patient while she cleared up this whole ex-husband thing, but when Lester interrupted their intimate time together, he'd gone too far. Chase hadn't beaten the jerk into the ground when he had confronted him at the diner, but he didn't like the way Lester was quietly insinuating himself into Sheridan's life, and he aimed to let her know it.

His anger skyrocketed when he saw Lester's car parked behind Sheridan's in her driveway. He hastily parked his truck, jumping down from the cab before the key was out of the ignition. He stomped up onto the porch and used his fist to bang on the door.

Sheridan came to the door barefooted, wearing a pink jogging suit and snacking on a celery stick—completely relaxed and too damn comfortable for his liking. "Hi. I wasn't expecting you."

"We had a dinner date."

She slapped her forehead. "I completely forgot. Come in."

He stepped inside and saw Lester sitting at her dining room table plucking away at the keys of his laptop. Papers, graphs and folders were scattered over the table. A vegetable tray, dip and iced tea were at his elbow. A chair had been pulled intimately close to his. Intense in his work, it took a minute for him to feel Chase's heated glare. He glanced up for a second, but quickly returned his eyes to the screen. Chase didn't miss his taunting grin.

"What is he doing here?"

"He came by this morning to show me what he'd found. We hashed out some ideas and he went to work. When Lester works, he loses touch with everything around him. I went to the clinic, and he was still here typing away when I returned." She talked like Lester's focus was mystical.

Chase grabbed up her elbow and hauled her into the bedroom, slamming the door behind him. "Why is he here?"

"I told you."

"If he can't tell when it's time to go home, I can help him figure it out."

"He's working."

"So? Are you oblivious to how angry I am right now?"

She stepped away from him. "I'm getting a clear picture."

"Tell him to go."

"You don't know how Lester gets when he works. I can't interrupt him. It'll throw off his rhythm, and it'll take him days to get it back—if he gets it back." She gestured with passion. "He's right at the threshold of something big."

He watched her, dumbfounded by her oblivion to his level of anger. If she had any idea how his stomach was burning and his chest was tightening, she would run to the dining room to drag Lester from the house. She squirmed under his scrutiny.

"So what's the plan? Are you going to feed and house him until he makes this medical breakthrough?"

She took a seat on the corner of the bed. "He's not a horse."

"And I'm not a fool."

Her mouth dropped open in shock. "I never said you were a—"

"Lester is using every trick he can to get you back. Boy Wonder can work anywhere, anytime. He doesn't need to be *here*—occupying your space. He wants to be here so you can take care of him." His eyes narrowed to an accusing stare. "And I think you want him here."

"I've told him it's over between us. He's only here to get some work done. When he comes to a point where he can stop, he'll leave."

"You are not that naïve," he ground out. "What is it with you? Why are you so caught up in this whole thing?"

"Lester's research ended my marriage. I do have some interest in seeing how it turns out."

He shook his head adamantly. "No, you don't. Your relationship with him is over. Nothing he does concerns you. His research has no effect on your life."

She turned her back to him. The gesture annoyed him. It was as if she'd dismissed him and his feelings.

"Sheridan, what you're doing does have an effect on *us*."

She turned abruptly, caught off guard by the tone of his words. "What exactly are you accusing me of?"

He didn't bother to answer. His accusation was pretty clear. "I want him out of here."

"Enough of the 'I'm-the-boss routine.'"

"He goes." He planted his feet firmly, taking a defensive stance. "Now."

He'd succeeded in making her as angry as he was. As if it mattered. He understood Lester's game, even if Sheridan refused to see it. And the game was still on. Her telling him she no longer wanted him had not been effective—Lester still felt he had a chance to win her back. Chase wanted to crush all his hope. And he could start by having Sheridan throw Lester out. He widened his stance, but narrowed his mind. "Gone, Sheridan. Now."

"No. You can't barge in here and tell me to kick Lester out."

He took her declaration as a personal challenge to see what he could and could not do when it came to their relationship. The argument escalated into a fight, both vying for title of "being right." When she told him to lower his voice so Lester wouldn't hear, he doubled his volume. When he told her to do as he demanded because he was her boyfriend, she reminded him how quickly his status could be reduced to employer. She went round for round with him, never letting him fully justify his jealous arguments. The intelligence and spirit he admired in her had betrayed him. Docile and meek seemed perfect qualities about now.

"Listen, woman—"

"Woman! You don't address me like that."

Okay. He'd overstepped. Her entire face reddened. Her fists were balled at her sides. If he didn't back off, he *would* lose her from his life.

"I should go," he said in a considerably lower voice.

"You should."

"You'd put me out, but your ex gets to stay."

"I'm not putting you out, but we're not getting anywhere with all this arguing. I want you to understand why Lester is here. You won't hear me out."

"You'd never be able to explain it to my satisfaction."

He turned and left her bedroom, daring Lester to look up from his laptop when he passed. He continued to tap away at his computer, seemingly oblivious to the explosive argument. At one point, the neighbors next door could have heard their shouting. Lester was crafty. "Slick," his father would say. In this instance, Lester knew Sheridan better than he did. He'd handled her with the practiced finesse a husband learns after years of living with his wife. Lester knew what Sheridan's sympathy buttons were, and he'd pushed them until she invited him into her home—and denied her boyfriend.

Chase pounded the dash of his truck. What bothered him most was Lester's interruption of their dinner plans. Another chance to tell her he loved her blown—courtesy of Lester Wexler, ex-husband, genius, and pain in the butt. Twice, Lester had succeeded in demolishing the romantic mood Chase was trying to set for Sheridan. He could have blurted this out in the middle of their argument. Maybe she would have been more sympathetic about why he was upset. But he didn't want it to happen that way. He wanted the occasion to be special and romantic. He wanted Sheridan to remember the day he confessed his love for her forever. He wanted her to tell their children the story over and over again. He wanted to celebrate the anniversary as one more milestone crossed on the road to conquering her heart.

Chase looked at Lester's car parked in the driveway as if it were where it should be. "I wonder if it'll be there all night."

"Should I leave?"

Sheridan returned to her seat at Lester's elbow. "Don't you do it."

"What?" Lester asked too innocently.

"Try to be the good guy here. You're not. You could have left when Chase showed up, but you didn't. You wanted us to fight."

He pressed the button to put his laptop on STANDBY mode. "You could have asked me to leave like he wanted you to," he said quietly, careful not to tic her off.

"I should have," she snapped. "Don't think I didn't want to."

"Then why didn't you?"

"Because Chase has to learn he doesn't have the right to tell me what to do. We're equals in this relationship."

Lester nodded reflectively. "Does he lose his temper a lot?"

She narrowed her eyes, daring him to push his luck.

"I have to ask. We are still friends, and he was pretty angry."

She rested her chin on her fist with a thud. "I know." Understandably so. She had blown off their plans to be with her ex-husband—a man who had made it clear he wanted her back in his life. She'd have to make up with him—take responsibility for her part of the argument. But first he needed time to cool off. He wouldn't hear her when he was this angry.

"He shouldn't yell at you. As much as we fought, we never shouted at each other. It's disrespectful."

Sheridan remembered many heated arguments during their marriage. Lester had forgotten, retaining only the memories that made him happy. "Chase and I both did some shouting."

"I know, but you in response to him. I'm going to have a talk with him—"

"No, you're not. You'll only make things worse. Chase does everything with passion, which includes fighting. He reminds me of you in that way. Everything is full of wonder, no matter how simple or how complicated."

"How are we different?" His question was a search for more information. He was asking what had swayed her decision. If they had like qualities, and he was her ex-husband, why not choose him over Chase?

It was a valid question, but not one she would ever explain to Lester's satisfaction. They'd had their chance. It hadn't worked out. Nothing in their personalities showed her it would work out now.

She and Chase were good together. They complimented each other. He tempered her seriousness with his playfulness. Both being physicians worked in their favor. She could discuss her work with him and he would offer her reasonable solutions to her dilemmas. They were both passionate, taking their intimacy to a level she'd never experienced before. Most importantly, they cared about each other.

"Lester—"

"I know. Our marriage is over." He covered her hand with his. "I want us to remain friends. I can't imagine sharing this—" he made a sweeping gesture over the scattered papers—"with anyone but you. I had to tell you *first.*"

"I appreciate it. I'm honored to be here with you as you reach your goal."

He rose from his chair and hugged her tight. She felt him pressing into her, his body becoming pleasantly tight. She knew what his next gesture would be. They had done this hundreds of times before. He pulled back, searching her face for permission to proceed.

She let him down easy. "You're being a good friend right now." She placed a hand on his shoulder. "Let's finish up."

"I can't sleep knowing you're mad at me."

"Shameless," Chase's husky voice permeated the phone line. "It's 3:15 in the morning. We have to be at the clinic in five hours."

"I shouldn't have called." She was embarrassed, and saddened, by his response.

"No. I'm glad you called. I'm upset you haven't been able to sleep."

"I keep messing up with you."

"You're not messing up, Sheridan. It was a fight. One fight. Couples argue sometimes."

"Go back to sleep now. I just wanted to apologize."

"Wait," he stopped her. "I've had a rough night, too. Sheridan, I don't know why you affect me like you do, but you make me crazy. Sometimes it's good crazy, sometimes bad crazy. Today it was bad crazy and I acted like a wild man. I apologize for shouting at you, and throwing around ultimatums."

"I should have tried to see things your way." She thought of her jealousy as he examined Candy. "If the situation were reversed, I would have demanded you ask your ex-wife to leave. I want you to know nothing happened between Lester and me. He worked on his research—nothing more."

"I trust you."

"But not Lester."

"But not Lester," he repeated. "And I never will, so don't ask me to. I know how strongly I feel about you, and we aren't married. He's kicking himself because he had you, and he let you go. He's not going to stop trying to put your marriage back together until you make it *clear* it's not going to happen."

"I made it clear tonight."

"Good."

As long as she had his trust, she would not do anything to hurt him. Before she let this relationship go any further, she was going to have to tell him everything. He had the right to know all the details about the lawsuit that ended her career in Nashville. Despite what Alison advised, it was deceptive to keep the information from him, and she'd have to take responsibility for doing so. It was unethical not to disclose the information to her patients. The doctor-patient relationship had to be built on trust. She would find the right time, and she would tell him everything, placing her faith in him not to walk away from her.

"Get some rest, Sheridan."

"Okay, but I'll expect my make-up kiss first thing in the morning, Dr. Larson."

CHAPTER 26

"Dr. Wexler?"

Sheridan looked up and saw Ted standing in front of her desk. She'd been so absorbed in her work she hadn't noticed him come.

"The lab in Nashville called to inform you Mrs. Harvey missed her appointment."

"She did?" Sheridan really wanted to solve the riddle of Mrs. Harvey's illness. She needed all the pieces of the puzzle to do it. "Mrs. Harvey is really good about keeping her appointments."

"I know. I rescheduled with the lab, but when I called to give her the information, there was no answer. I'll send her a letter notifying her, but it'll take time, and I know you really wanted her to get this done."

She looked at her watch. "Can you give me directions to her place? I'm about done for the day. I'll drive out and check on her. I can give her the appointment information."

"I'll give you directions, but do you want me or Dr. Larson to go instead?"

"No. You go home to your family. Dr. Larson still has patients to see. There's no reason I can't go alone." She shut down the computer. "Just tell me the way."

"Dr. Larson doesn't really like anyone to make home visits alone. Some of these mountain folks can be *spirited.*"

She was already removing her lab coat. "Ted, you know Mrs.

Harvey. She's a frail, sickly lady. I'm sure I'll be fine."

Ted debated a moment more, but she wouldn't listen. It was her job to check on her patients if she was worried about their safety. Mrs. Harvey's health may have deteriorated. She might be in need of emergency medical care. She certainly wasn't going to wait until an impersonal letter was sent to see how her patient was doing.

Sheridan passed grand homes with huge ranches on the way to Mrs. Harvey's home. The further she drove into the mountains, the worse the neighborhoods became. Mrs. Harvey's small farm was separated by miles from her nearest neighbor. The land was rundown—it was obvious no one had been working it since her husband's death. The grounds were sopping wet, muddy from the last rain. Malnourished goats loitered in the front yard. Chickens roamed freely on the porch.

She knocked on the door of the wooden frame house, afraid her fist would cause the home to fall down. She heard a faint reply and determined she had permission to enter.

Mrs. Harvey was lying on a ratty sofa, covered in a tattered blanket. The sparse surroundings made Sheridan's heart lurch.

She placed her medical bag next to the sofa and knelt to talk with Mrs. Harvey. "Are you okay?"

"Just tired is all."

"You were supposed to go to Nashville for testing. You missed the appointment."

"I forgot. I ain't been feelin' too good."

"I want to check you out."

"I don't think my 'surance covers house calls, Doctor, and I ain't got no money to pay."

"Don't worry about it."

Mrs. Harvey let Sheridan examine her without further protests. Her symptoms remained the same. The woman just seemed more rundown than usual.

"Have you been eating?" Sheridan asked.

"Some. Not much appetite. And my bowels are botherin' me all the time."

She searched her bag for a remedy. "I'll leave something for you." She looked around the room. "Do you live here alone?"

"My people stop by from time to time."

"I want you to go have those tests in Nashville as soon as possible. Ted made you another appointment, and I'll find you a ride."

"Okay."

"Do you have a phone?"

Mrs. Harvey pointed it out.

"Water? Electricity?"

Mrs. Harvey nodded.

"I want you to call me every morning at the clinic and tell me how you're doing. I want you to call me before you leave for your tests, and when you get back. I'm going to ask for a rush on the results. If you're not feeling better in the morning, we're going to have to talk about admitting you to the hospital."

Mrs. Harvey unquestionably trusted her judgment. She nodded to every one of Sheridan's directives.

"I'm going to let you get some rest, but I want to hear from you first thing in the morning. Sooner, if you start feeling worse. Do you understand?"

"I do, Doctor."

"You're going to call me in the morning, right?"

"First thing."

"All right. I want to keep a close eye on you until you start feeling better."

Mrs. Harvey grasped her hand, squeezing it firmly. Tears appeared in her eyes. "Thank you, Doctor."

Sheridan warmed, fighting tears of her own. This was why she went into medicine—to help those in the most need, but often forgotten by people who wanted to make medicine about big business.

Sheridan tossed the last of the salad ingredients into the bowl and reached for the tongs. She listened to Alison chatter while checking the food in the oven. The white business envelope marked "Confidential" caught her attention. It still lay on the countertop where Alison had placed it when Sheridan gave it to her. She was anxious to open it and learn the biopsy results, but she had to give Alison time to ready herself for whatever news she would get. She knew Alison's propensity to avoid bad situations—she'd been prodding her for weeks to tell her husband about the test. Alison had to face the truth and take the necessary steps to move on with her life.

"Chase and Dwayne will be back any minute," Sheridan reminded her.

"I know." Alison moved around the kitchen, pulling dishes from the cabinet. "Help me set the table."

"I wasn't talking about dinner. I'm talking about your biopsy results." Sheridan followed her into the dining room. "If you don't want to do this today, we can meet at the clinic during the week, but you have to do it soon. Time is important."

"I don't want to do it at the clinic. The clinic is too impersonal." Her voice tightened. "If I'm going to die, I don't want to be told while sitting on an exam table."

"Nobody said anything about you dying. We need to see the test results before we come to any drastic conclusions. Even if the biopsy results are not what we want, there are options."

"Options," Alison said sarcastically. The stress was getting to her.

"You could come by my place. Or I could leave the results and you could open them with Dwayne."

Alison slammed the plate down on the table. "Don't push me," she snapped. "I'll do it when I'm ready. Or not at all. Maybe I won't ever look at those damn test results!"

Sheridan absorbed the sting of Alison's words. She continued setting the table, afraid she might have pushed too hard. Alison wasn't ready. It wouldn't hurt to give her a few days.

"I'm sorry," Alison said with her voice's normal sweetness.

"It's okay. You'll look at the results when you're ready. Whenever—you call me if you need me, and I'll be there for you."

Alison took a deep breath and exhaled it slowly. "Let's do it."

"Now? You're ready?"

Alison nodded. "Can you get the envelope and bring it to the sunroom?"

Sheridan watched her trudge off before retrieving the envelope from the kitchen counter. Her heart drummed with every step. She prayed the biopsy results would be negative. Alison was fragile, probably from her family's overprotection. A breast cancer diagnosis was traumatic for anyone, but Alison seemed less prepared to deal with it than others. She lived a dream life, her siblings removing all obstacles from her way. She married, and the baton was passed to her husband. He took on the responsibility of making sure her life was good, without any snags. Sheridan worried she just was not strong enough to deal with the physical and emotional trials a cancer diagnosis would bring.

Alison sat at the window seat, staring at the acreage behind her home. Lost in though, she didn't notice when Sheridan joined her. They sat in silence for a long time. Sheridan turned the envelope over in her hands, wishing she could use her medical skills to make everything all right. She'd found a friend in Alison, no matter how opposite their personalities seemed, and she didn't want to lose her.

Sheridan asked, "Do you want me to open it?"

"No, I'll do it." She placed the envelope in her lap. "Thank you for doing this. You're going out of the way to accommodate me." She reached for Sheridan's hand. "You're a good doctor."

"I'm your friend."

Alison smiled. "You're my friend. Now we need to work on making you my sister-in-law."

"Don't you have enough sisters?" Sheridan helped lighten the moment.

"I can always use a sister like you."

They shared a pointed look.

"Open it," Sheridan said.

Alison inserted her finger underneath the flap and tore the

envelope open. "My brother is a fool if he doesn't marry you."

Her declaration threw Sheridan off, but she quickly recovered when Alison pulled a single sheet of paper from the envelope. She glanced up at Sheridan, and then pressed the paper against her chest while she whispered a prayer. Meticulously, she unfolded the paper. She glanced at Sheridan again before scanning the lab results. Her eyes moved rapidly back and forth across the page. She couldn't interpret Alison's facial expressions. What did it mean when her brow shot upward? What about the small line at the corner of her mouth? Were these signs of good news, or bad?

"I don't know what this means."

"Let me take a look." Sheridan reached for the paper, but Alison maintained her death grip.

"All these medical abbreviations." She read, "Results have been verified by doctor—I can't read this scribble."

"Let me see." Sheridan tugged on the lab report, and Alison released it. She scanned the paper quickly, going directly to the bottom line. She then started at the top, reading each line twice.

"What does it mean?" Alison asked with a shaky voice.

"Negative. The biopsy was negative. You don't have cancer."

They stared at each other for a long time before both their faces blossomed into smiles. Alison shouted, jumping up and pulling Sheridan up with her. They danced around the room, celebrating the tests results.

Sheridan hugged her tight. "The lump is probably a cyst, and you need to follow up."

"I will. First thing in the morning, I'll make an appointment."

"And I want to see you again, too. It'll be very important for you to do monthly self breast examinations."

"I know. I know. If I had been doing the exams, I would have found the lump earlier."

"It could have saved your life if it had been cancerous."

"I've learned my lesson. Don't lecture me anymore today. I want to be happy without consequences right now. Let's get dinner on the table and celebrate."

Two deep voices invaded their bonding moment.

"Honey," Dwayne called. "Where are you?" He entered the sunroom with Chase close behind. "What are you girls up to?"

"What do you mean?" Mild panic filled Alison's voice.

He peered into the grocery bag. "The grocer hadn't heard of half the stuff on this list, and we checked the kitchen—dinner is done. It seems like you were trying to get rid of us." He turned and headed to the kitchen, mumbling all the way.

Chase remained behind, observing the shared glances between Sheridan and his sister. Dwayne had stumbled onto something, but was too distracted to notice. Chase didn't miss it.

"Wash your hands, Chase," Alison told him as she passed. "Dinner is ready."

He caught Sheridan's hand as she walked by. "You want to tell me what's going on?"

"You sound like Dwayne."

"Sheridan," he scolded.

"Girl talk. Alison can share it with you if she wants." She stood on tiptoe to kiss him. "Go wash up for dinner."

Chase studied her face, but she was smiling, too happy for anything to be wrong. He shook his head and left the room. Sheridan snatched up the forgotten envelope and stuffed it in the back pocket of her jeans. She'd add it to Alison's medical record, which was locked in her office file cabinet, in the morning.

She helped Alison bring dinner to the table. They were giddy, giggling whenever their eyes met.

"I want to know what's going on," Dwayne demanded.

Alison draped herself over him from behind. "What do you mean, sweetie?"

"You women are bouncing around here all silly—like you have a private joke. Something's going on."

Alison rolled her eyes. "Calm down and enjoy dinner."

Chase silently inquired about what was going on with a lift of his brow. Sheridan kissed his cheek. "Enjoy dinner."

"Alison," Dwayne called as she danced into the kitchen. "I'm going to get it out of you sooner or later." His harsh stare turned to Sheridan. "You know what's going on."

Sheridan placed her hands firmly on her hips. "The only thing going on is that Alison and I are having a good time. Now, for the last time, relax."

She effectively shut down further argument. When she and Alison returned from the kitchen, the men jumped up and pulled out their chairs. Dwayne, the self professed Testosterone King, softened as dinner went on. Alison's good mood made him more loving. Sheridan could see why she was attracted to him. He was handsome in the grunge-hair-too-long sort of way. He was a bad boy, mean on the outside, but a softie on the inside. He was dangerous, tamed only by his love for Alison. He rode his motorcycle when he should have been working, and worked when he should have beeen playing.

Chase learned from Dwanye's scolding not to push the issue,

but Sheridan caught him scrutinizing every interaction she had with his sister. He loved Alison, and wanted to know if she was in trouble. After dinner they watched a rental movie, but Chase's attention seemed divided, afraid he would miss a crucial sign.

At the end of the evening, Chase lifted her up into his truck and jumped into the driver's seat. "So, what do you think about my brother-in-law?"

"He's different, but nice."

He rolled his eyes. "You like everybody."

"You don't like him?"

"I haven't made up my mind yet."

Alison and Dwayne stood on their porch, waving goodbye until Chase was out of sight.

"I had a really good time tonight," Sheridan said, taking Chase's hand.

"I know my sister has come to see you at the clinic."

"How would you know that?"

"If you're thinking I'm spying on you, I'm not. It's natural that Carolyn or Ted would mention her coming by."

"She's stopped in a few times."

"What for?"

"You know I can't tell you."

"The only reason you couldn't tell me is if Alison is a patient of yours."

"She is."

He drove a short distance before he continued. "So Alison has come to the clinic, and you haven't bothered to mention it to me. I ask you about it, and you tell me you can't talk to me about it, but you admit she's your patient. I'm closer to her than any of my other sisters. It seems whatever is bothering her would've come up in conversation."

"Where is this going, Chase?"

"If something were going on with Alison, I'd want to know. Are you going to make me ask you outright?"

"No. I don't want you to ask me because I'm not going to answer. As her doctor, I can't tell you."

"I love my sister."

She placed a comforting hand on his knee. "I know how you feel about Alison."

"I'm worried about my sister, Sheridan."

She opened her seatbelt and moved closer, wrapping her arms around his neck. "The only thing I can tell you is I'm Alison's doctor, and she's just fine. There's nothing to worry about. If there were, I'd make her tell you."

He watched the road unfold in the darkness, heavy in thought. "You wouldn't let anything happen to Alison?"

"Never. Do you feel any better?"

"I know you'll look out for Alison, but I can't help worrying about her."

She buried her face in the crook of his neck. "One of the things I like about you is how close you are with your family. If there were anything, I'd make Alison tell you. Trust me on this."

"I'd trust you with my life. I'm trusting you to take good care of my sister."

"Shameless." Chase's sleep-roughened voice tickled Sheridan's ear.

She glanced at the clock next to her bed. "You're up late."

"Thinking about you."

She hummed, cradling the phone next to her ear. She wished he were lying next to her, whispering words of endearment. She imagined his powerful arms around her and shuddered. "What are you thinking, Dr. Larson?"

"I woke up and you weren't here…I became mildly distressed."

She laughed. "Mildly distressed, huh?"

"Maybe not so mild."

"Hmm." The thought had its appeal.

"This is a cool night."

"I'm under an extra blanket."

"Maybe you'd like to be underneath me."

She realized his voice wasn't roughened by sleep. Chase was a man with things on his mind.

"Well, Shameless?"

"It's late."

"I want to see you before I leave for the seminar tomorrow morning. I can be there in fifteen minutes…say yes."

"I'll be waiting."

Sheridan hurried to shed the flowery flannel she'd worn to bed. She rummaged through her drawers, delight sending tingles down to her toes. "This is it," she said, pulling a lacy pink nightie from the bottom drawer where the new purchase had been long forgotten. She freshened up, brushed her hair, and slipped into the clingy gown. Wanting to set the perfect mood, she scrounged up every candle in her home, placing them in her bedroom. She had just lit the last when Chase rang her doorbell. Butterflies invaded her stomach as she went to let him in. She stood frozen at the first sight of him.

His broad shoulders were covered with a black leather jacket. The smell of leather and suede were rich enough to fill her living room. Touching him would be a pleasure for all five of her senses. Beneath the jacket, he wore a white button down shirt. It was open to his navel, and every inch of exposed skin glowed, while his muscles rippled. Designer jeans, faded in *certain* places to accentuate *certain* male body parts, completed the outfit. Sheridan licked her lips. He was a chocolate dessert, begging to be eaten.

She looked up into his handsome face and found his eyes glued on *certain* parts of her anatomy. They made eye contact and fireworks went off. Chase pushed the door closed behind him, never taking his eyes off her. He approached with long-legged strides, scooping her up without warning. He carried her through the darkness, into her bedroom, the candles lighting his way.

He set her down gently atop the bed. His masculinity excited her. She watched as he lazily shrugged off the leather jacket. She reached for it, hugging the butter-soft material to her chest. It smelled of his cologne: woodsy and robust. She inhaled deeply, becoming more excited as he started to remove his belt.

The sound of his zipper being lowered pushed her over the edge. She scrambled to the edge of the bed, kneeling in front of him. She pushed his hands away. Tortured pleasure passed over his face as she slid his jeans down his thighs. She thought of large columns and virile animals when she worked his black jockeys off. He sprang free with a gasp, his anticipation having built to a peak during his drive to her place.

Her hands stroked his thighs, coming up to grasp his behind. His buttocks were taut and smooth, high and unyielding. He shivered. She let her fingertips dance over the length of his erection. He squirmed, placing his hands on her shoulders. He stroked her hair. She ran her thumb over the tip of his erection, catching one crystal drop of his essence. His lashes hooded his sexy brown eyes. Ecstasy was on his horizon.

Sheridan squeezed his behind, bringing him to her waiting mouth. He slipped inside, slowly, every ridge gliding across her tongue. His grip on her shoulders tightened, his body swayed. His response encouraged her to perform with more vigor. Her tongue swirled while her jaw applied suction. She pulled him in deeper, coaxing wild moans from his lips. She teased and tormented until the anguish of unbridled rapture covered his face.

He pulled away abruptly. He feverishly worked the pink lacy nightie over her head. She ravaged his pants, searching for a condom. Her gown flew across the room, landing on her dresser. She grabbed a condom, sighing as she ripped the paper open.

He grasped her shoulders and pushed her down on the bed. Sexual tension threatened to break him. He covered her quickly, snatching the condom from her hand. Sheridan giggled, delighted by his uncontrolled desire for her. He stopped the laughter with a heated kiss that made her head spin. He entered her quickly, sighing with relief as he sank to his hilt. She got caught up in the frenzy, lifting her hips to meet his thrusts.

They performed as if they hadn't been together in months, when actually it had only been days. The more Sheridan had

Chase, the more she craved him. They loved zealously. She lost account of her hands, his hands—after a while she couldn't tell the difference. They touched, licked, bit, squeezed until a climax washed over them so strongly that Sheridan thought she might blackout from the sheer pleasure of it all.

He collapsed on top of her, breathing heavily and sweating profusely. "Great…that was great."

She wiped the perspiration from her forehead, shifting beneath him into a comfortable groove. "Chase!" she shouted.

"What?" He lifted himself on his elbows, stunned by her alarm.

"My nightie is on fire!"

He cursed, jumping up to fight the flames. Her new pink lacy nightie had landed on a candle when he'd tossed it away. They hadn't smelled the smoke or seen the flames during their vigorous session. She ran to the bathroom and grabbed some towels.

"Do you have an extinguisher?" Chase hit the flames with the towels while she ran to the kitchen. When she returned, the fire had been beaten down to a controllable flame. He put the rest out using the extinguisher.

She stood back surveying the damage. There was nothing left of her expensive new nightie. The dresser was scorched. The wall above the dresser was burned, the paint already peeling from the heat. Chase stood with his feet planted in the carpet, breathing hard, the fire extinguisher gripped in his hand, and the spent condom dangling from his penis.

Sheridan doubled over in laughter.

Chase tilted his head in her direction.

She pointed at the funny picture he made.

He glanced in the mirror and joined her. "Shameless, we almost burnt down the house!"

She couldn't stop laughing long enough to answer him.

He opened the window. "Pull yourself together."

She fought her laughter, taking deep breaths until she could control herself.

He took her in his arms, giving her a kiss sure to re-ignite the fire. "You are truly shameless."

"Your heat almost incinerated the place."

He swatted her behind. "Get dressed. You'll stay at my place tonight."

CHAPTER 27

Chase tried hard to keep his mind on what the speaker was saying at the Biofeedback Seminar, but being away from Sheridan for two days was too distracting. He still hadn't told her he was in love with her, but he wanted to do it the right way. He wanted a romantic dinner with candlelight, and then he would make love to her until the sun came up. When she thought she had experienced all the happiness she could stand, he would tell her he loved her.

He thought of the small fire they'd set together. His face heated. He glanced around, wondering if anyone could see the blush on his dark cheeks. Sheridan was truly shameless—and he loved every minute of it. He'd had a hard time trying to explain the fire to the workers he sent out to repair the damage. Sheridan would deteriorate into laughter when he told her about that phone call.

The crowd erupted in applause, awakening him to his surroundings. Coming to the seminar had been useless since he'd spent both days daydreaming. People started to leave their seats. He gathered his belongings and headed up to his hotel room. While he was waiting for an empty elevator his pager buzzed.

"Carolyn, it's Dr. Larson."

"Are you bored to death yet, Doctor?" she asked with delight.

"Almost."

"Well, hang in there. Dr. Wexler asked me to page you. Hold on."

He held in anticipation of hearing Sheridan's voice. He was so far gone just a phone call lifted his spirits and brightened his day.

Ted came on the line. "How's the conference going?"

"It's over. I'll make rounds this evening and then head home. How's everything there?"

"Dr. Wexler is handling everything like a champ. She's even staying on schedule. You know, her six month trial is about up."

"I know. We'll meet next week—you, Carolyn and I—and make a final determination."

"Sounds good."

Chase was anxious to speak with Sheridan. "Dr. Wexler called," he told Ted, hoping to prompt him to find Sheridan.

"She's standing right here."

"Hi, Dr. Larson," Sheridan's chipper voice came across the phone line.

"Hi, Dr. Wexler."

"I miss you," she whispered.

"I miss you, too," he whispered back. "Why are we whispering?"

"I'm standing outside of room one, and Ted is in and out."

"Oh, I see. What's up?"

There was a brief pause and Chase heard papers ruffling. "Dr. Harper called me from the lab in Nashville. Mrs. Harvey's lab results came back positive for arsenic poisoning."

"Arsenic! What? How?"

"I took a look around while I was out at her place. She has a lot of pesticides stored near her water source. According to what I found out, arsenic is a common ingredient in some pesticides.

It could have gotten into her water."

"She could have been slowly poisoning herself to death."

"I have a call in to the authorities so they can investigate. Then we'll know what and how she was poisoned. Meanwhile, I arranged for an ambulance transport Mrs. Harvey to the hospital there." She paused. "I promised her you would meet her."

"I'm on my way." He whistled. "Arsenic poisoning? I missed it. What made you test her for arsenic poisoning?"

"The symptoms were so vague, and all the other tests were negative…when I saw the pesticides…I took a wild shot."

"And saved her life. Good going, Dr. Wexler. I'm proud of you."

She pulled in an audible breath. "You're *proud* of me."

"Yes. You're a great doctor. Don't sound so surprised. The clinic is lucky to have you. *I'm* lucky to have you."

"I can't believe you're proud of me."

"Believe it." He laughed. "Do you really not have any idea how much you've changed my life since you came to Duck River? Why do you think I was willing to fight Lester for you? You are a great doctor, and a wonderful woman. I don't know what I would do without you, Shameless."

"Chase." Her jovial tone was gone. "There's something I need to tell you."

"What is it?"

"I wanted to tell you when we were face-to-face," she hedged.

She was going to tell him she was in love with him. He braced himself for the impact, harnessing his own desire to blurt out he loved her first. "What is it, Shameless?"

"I should have told you a long time ago, but I…This is hard

for me."

"It's okay. What do you want to tell me?" He knew Sheridan struggled with how vulnerable her emotions made her feel. He wouldn't push, but encouraged her to go on.

"You mean so much to me, Chase."

"You mean a lot to me, too, Sheridan." The pager on his hip buzzed. "Just a minute." He checked the display. "It's the hospital. Mrs. Harvey must have arrived."

"Call me after you've admitted her."

"I will, but tell me what you were going to say."

"We'll talk later. I have a patient waiting, and Mrs. Harvey is probably scared to death. We'll talk when you get home."

"I can take a minute to hear you out." Hearing her declare her love for him was worth placing everything on hold.

"No. It'll keep. When will you be back?"

"Tomorrow, early."

"Call me later. Gotta go." She hung up before he could convince her to tell him what she wanted to say.

Chase used his short drive to the hospital to plan the perfect date for Sheridan. He couldn't wait any longer to tell her how he felt. Once he met with Ted and Carolyn—he was certain they'd approve her partnership—he'd be that much closer to having her in his life forever. Maybe he'd encourage her to move in with him. She'd need to give up the rental and find somewhere to live once she became his partner. Why not with him? He would encourage her to stay at his place while the fire damage to bedroom was repaired, and once she felt comfortable sharing his space, he'd ask her to make it permanent. She wouldn't settle for just living with a man. She'd want a commitment. He was more than happy to offer her one.

The hospital emergency room buzzed with activity. Firemen and paramedics delivered patients on stretchers. Patients sat in the lobby waiting to be examined. Chase navigated the halls, searching for the cubicle where Mrs. Harvey had been assigned. He'd never been cut out for the emergency department. He liked to work methodically, concentrating all his attention on one patient at a time. The ER was about saving multiple lives at a breakneck speed. Healthcare workers raced up and down the halls, the overhead pager announcing another medical code's arrival. As Chase watched the crew prepare for the patient's arrival, anxious to save another life, he appreciated their skills, but would never leave his specialty. He was happiest when closing after a particularly complicated surgery. He delighted in delivering care in a controlled atmosphere where he had advanced knowledge of the patient's condition and medical history.

"Dr. Larson." Mrs. Harvey reached out to him as he entered her cubicle. "Dr. Wexler said you'd be here." She looked pale and tired.

He noticed her take a breath between words. He'd missed her illness. If not for Sheridan's diligence, Mrs. Harvey may have died.

"They say I have arsenic poisoning. Someone tried to kill me!"

He embraced her hand while pulling a chair up to her stretcher. "Wait. Let's not jump to conclusions. Arsenic is a naturally occurring element in the environment. You may have been using it and not known it. It's in the pesticides you use on the farm."

"But someone would have had to put it into my food."

"Not necessarily." He shook his head, speaking slowly to calm her. "Dr. Wexler believes you were poisoned by accident. She saw some suspicious chemicals stored out on your place. It could have gotten in you water, or you may have inhaled it. It was probably just an accident. The authorities are taking a look around your farm now. We'll have more information soon." He stood, still holding her hand. "Right now we want to get you better. I'm going to take a look at you." He pulled his stethoscope from his lab coat. "We're going to admit you for a day or so."

"I have to stay here?" She looked panicked.

Chase knew she was leery of new doctors. "I'll be here to watch over you." He gave her hand one last squeeze. "Don't worry. We're going to take care of you."

After completing his examination, Chase went to the doctor's lounge to write admission orders for Mrs. Harvey. He called Sheridan to make sure he had covered all the tests and procedures she wanted. He was finishing up when Dr. Baylor, a surgery colleague, joined him in the lounge.

"Chase. Arsenic poisoning? When's the last time you've seen a case? I've never seen a case." He sat across the table from Chase. "I don't even know if I could have picked it up."

"I didn't." He smiled proudly. "Dr. Wexler, the other doctor in the clinic, discovered it." He closed the physician's desk referenced book. "She solidified her partnership with this one."

"Hmm. Dr. Sheridan Wexler as in Lester Wexler's wife?"

Chase wanted to correct Dr. Baylor; tell him Sheridan was his woman, no longer Lester's. He ignored his jealousy and remained professional. "Yes. Sheridan Wexler. She's under review for partnership at the clinic. We'll be lucky to get her."

"I only know her in passing. I've attended a few fundraising events for her husband's research. She's pretty. Very intelligent. She didn't deserve to be persecuted." He started reviewing a medical record. "I'm glad things worked out for her."

Dr. Baylor won his full attention. "What do you mean persecuted?"

"Well, I personally think she was shafted. I'm sick and tired of these bogus lawsuits that do nothing but drive up the costs of our malpractice insurance premiums. If she had done nothing and the baby had died, she would have been sued. She intervened, the baby dies, and she loses her practice." He shook his head, his attention on the medical record. "It's a shame. The other doctors should have stood beside her, but you know how it goes. Threaten their ability to make payments on the Porsche, and they run."

Chase's silence made Dr. Baylor stop writing. "I didn't know about this," he admitted.

"I shouldn't have said anything. It was a media circus. Dr. Wexler is probably trying to forget it all." He gathered up his work. "I have to get going. Let's have lunch next week."

Chase watched him go. After dropping half the story—enough to pique his interests—Dr. Baylor leaves. He wanted to run after him and get every detail—lawsuit, lost practice, media coverage—he could only imagine the worst. He thought to run out of the hospital and drive full speed back to the clinic. He had no idea who he had entrusted his practice to. He fought to remain calm. He had an obligation to his hospitalized patients.

After rounds, he could drive back to Duck River and ask Sheridan about what Dr. Baylor had told him. Right now, he had to consider it all rumor. He loved Sheridan. He trusted her with his life. She wouldn't keep anything from him that would threaten his clinic—his life. The least he could do was give her a chance to explain.

CHAPTER 28

Sheridan stood in her office window looking out at Duck River. When she'd made the decision to come to the small town, the best she had hoped for was to continue her practice—even if it was only patching up bumps and bruises.

The experience had turned out to be life changing. She'd regained her confidence in her medical abilities. She'd made new friends. She had met the man of her dreams.

Coming to Duck River was the best thing she could have ever done.

She waved at a group of school children as they passed by her window. They ducked inside the clinic. She shook her head, knowing they were standing at the front desk hounding Carolyn for free suckers.

Sheridan inhaled deeply. Her heart was heavy. She had to make things right with Chase. She had no doubt he'd understand why she kept her past a secret, but it didn't make her deception any easier to swallow.

She wouldn't allow herself to make any excuses. Tonight, when Chase got back home, she'd tell him everything. She'd apologize for not trusting him enough to tell him right away. She also planned on telling him how much he meant to her. Afterward, they would make the sweetest love she'd ever known and everything would be all right.

The residents of Duck River began hurrying past her window. She craned her neck in the direction of the diner. A small crowd had gathered. The situation didn't look urgent—no one had come to the clinic requesting medical help—but Sheridan's natural curiosity took her to the front desk.

"What's going on at the diner, Carolyn?"

"Ted's gone to check it out."

He entered the clinic on cue.

"What's going on?" Carolyn asked.

"The newspapers are here to talk to that doctor who is staying at Candy's place. You know, the one who came to see Dr. Wexler."

They looked at Sheridan.

"Lester." She didn't want them to connect him to her through last names.

"Yeah, him," Ted said.

"What are they coming to see him about? Is he in trouble or something?" Carolyn wanted to know. "I knew there was something wrong with a man who calls himself a Dr. Lester and stays in a whorehouse."

"He's not in any trouble. Seems he's some big shot from Nashville. He made a medical discovery. There's going to be a news conference at City Hall."

Carolyn looked reflective. "It must be something big to bring all this media attention to Duck River."

"The diner is full of news crews and reporters. The hotel is booked solid, and people are renting out their spare rooms. Reporters are interviewing anyone who has ever met the man. I even saw a truck from CNN."

Sheridan backed away in a daze. She left Carolyn and Ted to

try to figure out the riddle. Once she was out of their sight, she ran to her office, snatching up her purse. She had to get to Lester before the press conference. She had to stop him.

CHAPTER 29

"Let me straighten your tie," Candy said, stopping Lester before he went to greet the group of reporters who had swarmed around Duck River.

He stood nervously shifting his weight from foot to foot. "Do you understand why I have to leave?"

"Of course. One of the world's most famous medical researchers can't be found living in a whorehouse." She smiled self deprecatingly. "It would ruin your reputation. You have to be aware of things like that now that you're famous."

He worried she wouldn't understand why he had packed his belongings the moment he reported his breakthrough to his financers. He felt the burden of those suffering from sickle cell as an even greater weight on his shoulders since uncovering a possible predisposing genetic code. He had worked so hard to save lives. He couldn't let the public's opinion of his personal life interfere with continuing his work. He was so close to helping thousands of sickle cell patients.

"I want you to understand," he said again.

She placed her delicate hands against his torso. "I understand. Don't worry about Candy. Candy will survive." Her smile revealed the sadness hidden behind her words.

His stomach lurched. He would miss her. She visited him daily, genuinely interested in the work he was doing. She took care of him, seeing to it he ate right everyday. She reminded him to take breaks so he wouldn't suffer from exhaustion. And their conversations were delightful.

She would make someone a good wife.

"I recognize that reporter from TV. He's going to interview you?"

Impressing her made his chest swell. "He's going to ask questions of everyone on the panel."

"But the mayor said they want you to take the podium afterwards to answer questions."

"Less than ten minutes, Dr. Wexler," a stagehand said. "We need you to take your seat."

"Are you ready?" Candy asked, taking a step back to look him over one last time.

"Ready as ever."

Candy gave him a good luck hug. He took his seat on the panel, looking backstage to find her. She stood at the curtain, giving him the thumbs up. He absorbed her encouragement, again thinking she'd be a supportive, loyal wife. He shook the hands of his backers and lead assistant. He posed for photos, glancing at Candy's smiling face once more. The press conference was called to order, and he read a statement to the media.

The press furiously jotted notes, trying to understand the medical jargon. They clearly understood the significance of his findings. Once he had completed his statement, the panel took questions from the reporters.

After the panel discussion, he was called upon to answer questions. He received the usual inquiries. Why did he devote his life to sickle cell research? How long had it taken him to make this discovery? What was its significance for future research?

Where would his discovery lead him next?

"Dr. Wexler," the female reporter shouted above the crowd. "Dr. Wexler, over here."

Lester nodded in her direction, signaling her turn to ask a question.

"I understand your ex-wife Sheridan Wexler is practicing here in Duck River. Is that why you're completing your research here? What part has she played in this discovery?"

Before Lester could formulate diplomatic answers to her questions, she bombarded him with more. "Are you considering reconciling, and if so, will this effect the funding for your research? Are you afraid her malpractice will hinder funding for this project?"

The slander on Sheridan's character built to a frenzy. Every reporter in the room shouted questions about her past legal troubles. Many ran from the room, fact-checking and gathering the history of the incident. Then the assault on his character began. Reporters slaughtered his credibility by attacking his reputation.

"Dr. Wexler, is it true you divorced your wife when she was found negligent in the death of Baby Boy Doe?"

"If Dr. Wexler was truly innocent of malpractice, why was she forced to leave your clinic in Nashville?"

"Are you living in a whorehouse, Dr. Wexler?"

"Is it true you have a deviant sexual addiction?"

"Who's the woman you've been seen around town with? Does your ex-wife know about her?"

Lester stood stunned. The investors had wanted to jumpstart media interest right away in the hopes of getting more backers. Knowing his discovery was only the beginning, he'd agreed to any efforts to obtain additional funding for his continued work. Speechless, he scanned the crowd, looking into the faces of people who didn't want to celebrate his successes, but instead ruin him. At the fringe of the crowd he saw Sheridan standing horrified as the verbal assault continued. Candy frantically waved him toward her from backstage. She called to him. When he still didn't move, she came onstage and pulled him away from the podium.

"Those reporters are vultures," Candy comforted him behind stage. "We'll go out the back way."

"Lester!"

He turned to see Sheridan running toward them. Candy stepped away, and he felt embarrassed she didn't think she belonged at his side.

Sheridan had come directly from the clinic. She still wore her lab coat and her stethoscope dangled around her neck. Her face did not display the wonder of the day they'd worked on his research together. She was not happy about his success. His ex-wife was scared.

Sheridan stood between him and Candy. "Lester, the town is overrun with reporters."

"Sheridan, I'm sorry. I never thought they'd bring up the malpractice suit."

"You don't understand what you've done."

"I never meant to hurt you. You have to believe me."

Sheridan watched him, tears at the rim of her eyes.

Candy stepped up. "We should get out of here."

Running off stage made the reporters more determined to rehash the past and uncover new controversies. His research wasn't the news story of the day anymore. He remembered the old footage of Sheridan ducking reporters as she left the arbitration hearings. The local news had run the story over and over, building such interest the national news had picked up the story. The reporters would take over Duck River, digging for dirt. They would interview Sheridan's patients, bringing his mistakes to their doorstep again. There was a good chance another bogus lawsuit would be filed by one of her current patients—people liked to jump on the easy-money bandwagon. His success had brought about Sheridan's ruin.

He looked down at her trembling form. "I'm so sorry."

CHAPTER 30

By morning, every television and radio news show in the country was talking about Lester's findings. Sheridan quickly learned that as the scientific world struggled to build his reputation, the media world fought to tear down the man behind the scene. Every report about Lester's work on curing sickle cell disease was followed by file footage of his "wife's" legal troubles. They painted her as an albatross, strangling him and hindering his "great work."

Sheridan called Chase the moment she left the auditorium where the press conference had been held. He didn't answer her calls or return her messages. After talking to her parents and assuring them she was all right, she'd had to unplug the phone to avoid the barrage of reporters' phone calls. She considered going to Chase's house, and if he wasn't there, the hotel in Nashville, but if wouldn't take her phone calls, she was sure he wouldn't see her.

She tucked away her regrets about how she had handled the situation with Chase and left to face the consequences at the clinic. No matter how Chase felt about her, she had an obligation to her patients.

Sheridan detected something was wrong the moment she stepped through the clinic doors. Ten minutes before her first appointment, the lobby was empty. Usually, at least six patients would be waiting, leafing through magazines while drinking coffee. Even stranger, Carolyn wasn't manning the desk. She sat down behind the desk to check the appointment book. It wasn't there. She searched the desktop, and not finding it, she went to her office.

The clinic was too quiet, deserted. When she passed the lounge where they held their monthly conference, she heard voices. She entered the room, her eyes locking on Chase standing at the head of the table. He was flanked by Ted and Carolyn. His lab coat covered a crisp white shirt. A red tie punctuated his dark skin. He removed the stethoscope draped around his neck and placed it on the table. He cleared his throat. "Join us, Dr. Wexler." The bite to his formal tone told her they'd been talking about her, and he was very unhappy about the topic of discussion.

"Good morning," she said, taking a seat next to Ted.

Chase looked at her as if she were a stranger. "It seems all of our patients have cancelled their appointments." He took the appointment book from Carolyn and held it up for her inspection. "There are no patients for the entire week." He flipped through the pages to illustrate his point.

"This has never happened before," Carolyn added. Sheridan couldn't tell if she blamed her for the cancellations, or if she was appalled by their patients' behavior.

Chase was very clear about his stance. "There's no doubt that the cancellations are the result of the news reports."

"I'm sorry." Sheridan looked from Ted to Carolyn to Chase, trying to convey her sincerity.

"You had an obligation to this clinic, and your patients, to disclose the information about the malpractice case," Chase said. He raised his voice, and Carolyn cringed. "Not to mention your obligation to Ted and Carolyn—to me."

"Let me explain. The lawsuit—"

"The time to explain was when I interviewed you. What you have done is unethical and—"

Ted interrupted, tempering Chase's escalating anger. "What are we going to do now? The clinic can't survive without patients."

Carolyn answered. "I'm the one who took all the cancellation calls. Our patients are afraid. They've heard the news reports and don't know if it's safe to be treated here. We have to win back their trust."

Chase crossed his arms over his chest. "I can think of only one way to do it."

Everyone understood the unspoken words. The only way to regain the trust of the people in Duck River was to remove the problem. Chase had to show his patients he was a victim too, and as soon as he learned about Sheridan's history, he had rid the clinic of her. She was no longer wanted at Duck River Family Medicine. No six month review was needed. The only lingering question was if Sheridan would leave with dignity, or wait to be fired by her lover.

"Maybe we should take our time in finding a solution," Ted advised.

Chase watched her, unwavering.

Carolyn dropped her head.

Sheridan took a deep breath to fight off the tears. She gathered her pride, refusing to be reduced to sobbing in front of her coworkers. "I'm very sorry for what I've done. You're right,

Chase. I should have told you about my past legal troubles when I interviewed for the job. I made a mistake. I didn't know any of you then. I never meant to hurt anyone." She pushed herself out of her chair. "I'll get my things from my office."

She did not shed one tear. She'd done the wrong thing, and now she had to suffer the consequences. She packed up her office and left the clinic after saying goodbye to Ted and Carolyn. They were cautiously supportive, probably wary of their boss's wrath. Chase remained in his office, refusing to answer when she knocked.

She sat in her car with the motor running, trying to absorb the impact of it all. At thirty, she was unemployed without any prospects. Her medical career was probably over. She had no home. No direction.

And she had probably lost Chase. His behavior certainly indicated their relationship was dangling by a thin thread of hope. She peered at the window of his office. Did she have any chance of fixing things between them? Could they be a couple and not work together? She could only imagine what he thought of her. He was too angry to talk to her. Of everything she was losing, he was the most important. A tear dropped into her lap. Giving up Chase would hurt the most.

Sheridan swiped the tears away. She was not a quitter. She was a strong black woman who knew how to fight for what she wanted. She hadn't made it through medical school by giving up when things became difficult. She didn't survive the malpractice case by walking away. She hadn't lived through her divorce by cowering. Chase was important to her. She needed him. He had to hear her out. Impulsively, she cut the engine and marched back into the clinic.

"Dr. Wexler?" Ted asked. "Is something wrong?" She passed Ted and Carolyn, ignoring their curious stares, and barged into Chase's office.

"Are you going to let me leave without even talking to me about this?" she demanded.

"I'm too angry to talk to you right now." He sat behind his desk, his cold stare mocking her and everything they'd shared.

"You can't throw me out and not give me a chance to explain."

"You explained."

"I want to discuss this with you."

"I told you, I don't want to talk to you right now," he ground out through clenched teeth.

"Too bad! If you don't talk to me now, when?"

"All of a sudden you learn the value of communication." He rose slowly, using his desk as leverage. "You want to force me to discuss this? Fine." He lowered his voice to a menacing whisper. "Do you have any idea how long I've worked to build a reputation with this clinic? Do you know how hard it is to get the people around here to trust your skills and not keep using home remedies that are only making their illnesses worse?"

She opened her mouth to answer, but he charged around the desk and continued his tirade. "You lied to get what you wanted. I never pictured you as an opportunist. I thought your patients meant something to you."

"My patients *are* important to me," she countered. "What I did was wrong. I admit that, but I never placed my patients in danger."

"You placed this entire clinic in danger!" he shouted. "Our patients don't trust the care they receive here. My insurance premiums will skyrocket. We don't do big business here—the increase in premiums alone might be enough to shut the clinic down. You've jeopardized Ted and Carolyn's jobs. If we have no patients, I can't pay their salaries. They depend on this job to feed their families. Did you think of anyone else but yourself when you came here?"

Sheridan swallowed hard. The truth of his words were difficult to digest. "You're right. I didn't think about anything but having another chance to practice." She approached him, wanting to touch him, to absorb a little of his strength.

He stepped away from her.

She continued. "I didn't harm that baby. I did the best I could to save his life. The parents were angry and blamed everyone for their son's death. I got caught in the crossfire. Lester's investors refused to back me as I fought the malpractice case. Too much funding was at stake. The media got hold of the story and everything escalated."

"Sheridan, you should have told me this story during your interview. It doesn't matter if you're guilty or innocent now. The patients turned against you because you lied. You didn't allow them to make an informed decision. You hid the information, and now they'll never trust you again."

"What about you, Chase? Why are you turning against me?"

Her comment stunned him. For a fleeting moment, it seemed he might hold her—comfort her—in his arms. He stepped away.

Sheridan forged on, hoping she'd touched something in him. "You said yourself the biggest obstacle I had to overcome was gaining the trust of the people in Duck River. How could I tell anyone I was sued for harming a baby?"

"How were you ever going to gain their trust if you weren't honest with them?"

"You're right. How many times can I say it? You're right about it all. I did everything wrong." She approached him again, and this time he didn't move away. "Can you understand why I did it? At least try to understand that. Practicing medicine is everything to me. I just wanted a chance to start over."

Kindness was reflected in his eyes, but not his words. "I can't jeopardize this clinic to save your career."

She backed away, his words delivering the finality of his decision. She composed herself before continuing. "What about us?"

"You've made it clear your career is the most important thing in your life."

"I didn't say—"

"Am I supposed to believe anything you tell me? How do I know getting involved with me didn't have something to do with your securing the partnership here?"

She backed away, wounded. "I can't believe you just said that."

"I can't believe everything I've worked for could be lost in one day. Due to one bad judgment on my part."

"Now whose career is the most important thing in their life? What about us? Where do I fit in your life?"

"I don't trust you, Sheridan. Hell, I don't even know if I should trust my own judgment anymore. And without trust, there can't be any 'us.'"

CHAPTER 31

"You're packing." Lester stood in Sheridan's bedroom, watching her throw her things into the open suitcases atop her bed.

"There's nothing for me here now." Her insides were wound tightly, her head throbbed, and she felt she would melt into tears at any moment. Her goal was to stay focused. She wanted to get out of Duck River as soon as possible. Once she was away from Chase and the clinic, she cold let herself fall apart.

"I wanted you back, but not this way. I didn't know this would happen."

She spared him a glance. "I know."

He wasn't malicious. He was driven, but he would not purposefully hurt her. Their marriage had been a disaster because they were both too stubborn to work through their problems. She now understood she had to take responsibility for her part in its failure. As her life fell apart again, she wouldn't blame others for letting her down. She had to save herself.

"I want to help," Lester said. "I have a better foundation to stand on with the investors since the breakthrough in my research. I've asked for funding to start my own practice. It'll be completely devoted to finding a cure for sickle cell. We'll make the most advanced treatment around available to sicklers. We'll have only state-of-the-art medical equipment. The financial problems we had before won't be an issue."

"You're going to accomplish great things."

"I've made it clear to my backers you are to have a place in my practice. If you want to set up a family practice clinic in the same building, you can. Whatever you want to do—name it."

"They'll never go for it, but I appreciate you trying. We tried this before, remember?"

"Things were different then. They need me—instead of it being the other way around. They understand I can take my research to another investor. They're smart. They want to be a part of what I'm doing."

"They need *you*, not me."

"Sheridan, it's a done deal."

Ironic, their marriage had ended because they couldn't find a solution to this problem. Lester was now using the solution to bring them back together. For a brief moment, she wondered who was the more understanding—Chase or Lester.

"If you want to start your own practice, you just need to say the word," Lester continued. "I received a considerable bonus for the discovery I made."

"I don't know, Lester. It would be taking advantage." Chase had turned her away, but she was still hopeful things would work out between them. He needed time to cool off. She had to find a way to make him see things through her eyes. He would forgive her, and she didn't want to give Lester any ideas about their relationship. "I need time to think about it."

"What is there to think about? This is what you've always wanted. I can afford to give it to you. We made a good team once. This could be our second chance."

"When we were together, this is what I wanted. You backing me, and helping me to succeed. But we're not a couple anymore."

She locked her suitcase. "What do you want for helping me reestablish my career?"

He looked sheepish. "I've been clear about the terms since I stepped foot in Duck River."

"You want to put our marriage back together. Getting back together should be about us still loving each other, and wanting to make it work. I care about you, Lester, but not in the same way. Our marriage will never be repaired."

"Even with Larson out of the picture?"

She nodded. "I'm sorry."

He took her hands in his. "You still care about me. It's enough to build on. All the problems in our marriage were because of our career goals. If we've taken care of those, what could interfere with us making it work?"

"There's no magic." She thought of the way her heart pounded when she looked at Chase's naked body, and the way her stomach quivered when he touched her.

"The magic will come. Give us a chance, Sheridan. There was magic before. The magic will come again."

She wanted to explain magic was elusive. You couldn't just wish for it, and have it appear. All the elements had to be right. There had to be chemistry. Obligation wasn't enough.

"I don't know." She moved away from him. "I can't depend on you—or anyone else—to save me. I need time to figure out what's important to me."

"You take all the time you need to think about it. I'll be waiting for you when you decide."

She hugged him for his support. He was pushing a little too hard, but at least he hadn't turned his back on her.

"I'm going back to Nashville today. Do you want to leave together?" he asked.

"No. I still have a lot to do before I go."

"I could wait."

"I'll call you once I'm settled."

He smiled. "Don't disappear on me again."

"I won't."

An awkward silence moved into the room.

"I'd better go so you can finish packing."

Sheridan walked him to the front door.

"Think about my offer."

Candy felt as if someone had ripped her heart from her chest. She stood in the foyer, bleeding a slow death as she watched Lester load his bags into the trunk of his rental car. He'd made his grand play for Sheridan, and she'd still turned him down. What a fool! Didn't she see what a good man Lester was?

Candy wanted a chance to peel away his serious layers and reveal his playful side. They would make a good pair—him too serious, and her too sensuous. They could learn from each other, growing together every day. Even today, during his move, he wore a dark suit and matching tie. The man was in desperate need of someone who could show him what fun life could be.

"I guess I'm ready to go." Lester stood in front of her, larger than life. "Hey, don't look so sad. We'll keep in touch."

She smiled, knowing she'd never hear from him again. Everything was falling apart. "My world will never be the same."

He looked at her strangely, trying to read her signals. He seemed confused, flattered, and embarrassed. When he placed his hand against her cheek, she saw something unidentifiable in his eyes. "I'll never forget you."

She placed her hand over his.

"You're going to make someone a wonderful wife."

Candy burst into tears.

"What did I say?"

She waved him off, turning her back on him. "Go."

"Candy—"

"Go before I ruin your suit."

CHAPTER 32

Sheridan stood in nervous anticipation as Chase left the pool. Even as she fought to save their relationship, her body responded violently to his physique. He tempered his surprise at seeing her. She handed him a towel.

"Thank you." He secured the towel at his waist, and reached for another to dry his chest.

"Ms. Fluentes let me in."

"It's okay." He draped the towel over his shoulders.

"I'm leaving today."

"Going back to Nashville?"

"Yes."

"Alone?"

"Yes."

His gaze moved away from her. "Have a good trip."

She absorbed the sting and continued on her mission. "I don't want to leave you. If you ask me to stay, I will."

"We're not together anymore."

"Chase, you're angry. I understand. But you're not this cold. You're a caring, forgiving person. Why won't you give me another chance?"

"The clinic—"

"I'm not talking about the clinic. I'm talking about you and me."

"Sheridan, I don't know why I can't give you another chance.

I've struggled with myself about it. I still care for you, but I feel like I don't know you. Everything I thought you stood for, I'm not so sure about anymore. I've opened up my life and let you inside, but I'm not a part of your life."

"I want to change that."

"Believe me, I've thought about this for days. It's too late."

"I love you."

He froze. He searched her face, unable to respond. The declaration took him by surprise, but the muscle jumping in his jaw said it was more than just surprise.

"I love you, Chase."

"I have to rebuild my practice. It's going to take every bit of my energy—"

"I love you."

"I won't have time to work on us."

"*I love you*. Don't take it lightly."

"I'm not," he whispered. "I don't. You're the one who hasn't been taking me seriously—the clinic, our relationship—you didn't recognize how much it meant to you until you lost it. It makes me wonder if you're only finding value in what I offer because I don't offer it anymore."

"That's not true. Your reasoning is off."

"How do I know what's real with you?"

"I'm telling you."

"You come here telling me you're leaving town. Minutes later, you tell me you love me. I'm not certain what you want."

"I love you. I'm leaving town because I'm not wanted here. If you want me here, I'll stay. Now you know exactly what I want."

"You should have shown me—through your actions. Every

time Lester calls, you go running. Everything has always been about you—*your* medical career, *your* fears about entering into another relationship. You've never considered me, or my career, or how I felt about you."

"I'm trying to correct that now."

"You show up here on the way to Nashville and expect me to accept your apology? Everything's supposed to go back to normal because you're ready. You're not willing to put in the work to save us. You stop by and give me ultimatums—"

"This is no ultimatum."

"What would you call it? I have a few minutes to forgive you, or you're in your car going back to Nashville. I'm not ready to forgive you. You haven't done anything to fix what you've done."

"I love you, Chase."

"The words are not enough."

CHAPTER 33

Lester listened to smooth jazz while lying across the sofa, relaxing with a glass of cognac. He closed his eyes and relished in his newfound success. His parents were so proud of him. They'd thrown a party to celebrate his research findings, giving them a chance to brag to their friends. The legacy was safe for another generation. He'd enjoyed himself, but felt a little awkward when everyone kept telling him all he was missing in his perfect life was a perfect wife.

When thinking about having a wife, Candy came to mind. No woman had supported him so unconditionally before. She would be happy at home, making a warm home and raising their children. She would charm his backers with her sexuality and sultry personality.

He thought back to their discussions and the way she took care of him, seeing to his smallest needs without his asking. He replayed every one of their discussions, wondering if he might have missed a subtle cue. Her reaction to his leaving had taken him aback. He had never been the most perceptive when it came to reading women, but he felt sure he'd seen something more than friendship in her eyes.

He'd called her a few times in the month he'd been home, but she never came to the phone. One of the girls would make her excuses—obvious lies to avoid him. He hadn't done anything to offend her, he was sure of it. The more she avoided him, the more he thought about her. He'd written her a letter, sticking it inside Toni Morrison's newest novel. He asked Candy to visit him in Nashville. He offered her dinner and a show. He promised her they would discuss Morrison's new book late into the night, like they'd done before. He'd been sure the letter would entice her to call—nothing.

If he hadn't offended her, then what? Why had their friendship ended when he left Duck River? He considered the possibility of never seeing her again. It made him down the last of his cognac.

The doorbell rang just as his mind began imagining the ultimate intimacy with Candy. He placed his cognac glass on the side table, and turned on the living room lights before opening the door. He couldn't hide his surprise when he saw who was standing there with her suitcases.

"Can I come in?"

"Do you know what you're asking?"

She hesitated, her eyes going to the floor. She stiffened her resolve, lifted her head and answered. "I understand."

"I'll get your bags."

He stood aside as Sheridan walked back into his life.

CHAPTER 34

Sheridan was in the kitchen cooking dinner when Lester entered with flowers. "Hi." He kissed her cheek, handing her the bouquet.

"How was work?" she asked.

He gave her the details of his day, falling into their usual routine. Lester would come home from the clinic and tell her where his research was leading him. He'd share some funny stories about the people he worked with and tell her about any upcoming fundraising events. She would find a way to wiggle out of attending with him. They'd have dinner while making further small talk and then she'd sneak off to bed before their interaction could become more intimate.

When Sheridan came back to him, he knew things would be awkward at first, but he'd expected her to be more comfortable by now. He could see how unhappy she was. He'd catch her daydreaming, lost in thought for hours. She never told him what was on her mind, but he knew.

"Sheridan, sit with me for a minute."

She took a seat across from him at the kitchen table. The apartment wasn't very warm, but Lester had given her free range to redecorate. She never seemed to have any interest in making the surroundings more homey. They'd toss around ideas over dinner, but each day Lester returned home, the apartment looked the same—sparse and cold.

"You've been sleeping in the spare bedroom for two weeks."

"Lester, I—"

He held up a hand, stopping her. "Let me finish, please. You've been here two weeks and it's apparent you're uncomfortable when we're alone. We've been living together like sister and brother." He loosened his tie. "This is not what I wanted, and I bet you're not happy either."

She felt guilty—using him for the safe haven he provided, but being unable to love him. She would always care about him, but she was in love with Chase.

"You being here has made me think about what I want for my future," Lester continued. He took her hand in his. "You're not in love with me anymore."

"Lester—"

"I know. You've been telling me that or months. I'm just starting to hear it." He squeezed her hand, quieting her. "I'm not in love with you anymore, either. I'll always care about you, but I'm not in love with you." He took a deep breath. "I'm in love with someone else."

She raised an eyebrow. "You're in love with someone else? And you let me live here? How can you have a relationship with someone while living with another woman?"

"Now you understand why I wanted to have this talk with you." He waited for her to absorb the weight of his words.

"I'm interfering with your life."

"I like having you here, you know that. The problem is we're together, but not together. We share an apartment, but no emotions. I'm in love with someone else, and I think you are, too."

"I don't know what to do."

"You have to make some serious decisions about your life. I've provided you a place to hide when I shouldn't have."

"My career is over. I've lost Chase. I don't know what to do."

"What do you want?" Lester was always good at helping her sort through her problems. He was rational to a fault. He could dissect a situation, seeing all possible solutions. It wasn't until now she appreciated his logic.

She pulled her knees up to her chest, balancing on the chair. "I don't know."

"You do know. Tell me what you want. Be honest with yourself."

"I enjoyed my work at Duck River Family Medicine. I adored my patients." She smiled as she recalled her days at the clinic. "Ted and I were putting together a community health program for the schools. I left a lot unfinished."

"Then go get your job back."

"I can't."

"Since when do you give up so easily?"

"I ruined any chance of going back to the clinic. Duck River is a small town and they don't seek care with doctors they're afraid of. Besides, I need a majority vote to win the partnership. Chase has three votes, so even if Ted and Carolyn want me there, he can veto it."

"Convince him you deserve the partnership."

"How?"

"You'll have to figure that out." He removed his jacket and hung it on the back of his chair. "What about your relationship with Chase?"

"There is no relationship." She still couldn't discuss Chase without a lump forming in her throat.

"Is that okay with you?"

"No."

"Then why are you living here? Sheridan, you have to stand up and fight for what you want. The woman I'm in love with, we've never even been out on a date. I don't know if she has any feelings for me, but you know what? I'm driving to Duck River this weekend to tell her how I feel."

"Duck River? Who is it?" she prodded.

His lashes dropped and he answered bashfully, "Candy."

Sheridan lay in bed staring at the ceiling while going over all the mistakes she had made. There was no excuse for not telling Chase about the malpractice lawsuit. He was right: she jeopardized the clinic, his career, and Ted and Carolyn's livelihood. It had been selfish of her to keep the information hidden thinking only of her needs, trying to keep her career alive. She owed her patients the truth, giving them all the information they needed to make an informed decision about selecting her as their physician.

She had given the baby the best care she could have under the circumstances, but she had been penalized by the medical board and her insurance carrier. Her patients should have been allowed to form their own opinions—after they had been given all the facts. She had to believe in her proficiency as a physician. The people in Duck River wanted a good doctor to care for their families—just like everywhere else. She had to let her skills speak for themselves.

Her most regrettable mistake was not opening her heart completely to Chase. If she truly loved him, she would have disclosed all her faults, all her baggage, and allowed him to decide if she were worth taking a chance on. Instead, she had sucked up all his strength and hid behind his protective nature, taking and not giving back.

She called his name, wishing the simple gesture would make him appear.

A sharp pain pierced her belly when she received no reply.

Lester was right. She was a fighter. She needed to fight for what was important to her. She wanted a permanent partnership with Chase, and she wanted her job back at Duck River Family Medicine. She turned on her belly, racking her brain for solutions. Her breathing sped up, anxiety touching her heart when she considered the possibility Chase might never forgive her. She remembered Lester's words of encouragement. When it came to her relationship with Chase, failure was not an option.

She leapt out of bed and raced across the apartment to Lester's bedroom. She banged on his door, alarming him out of bed.

"What is it?"

"I want to go back to Duck River with you."

"Okay." He yawned. "You could have told me this in the morning."

"No. We need to go now."

"In the middle of the night?"

"Do you think Candy will let me stay in your old room?"

"I guess, but it's two in the morning. Let's wait until daybreak before we leave."

She put her hand on her hip and assumed a determined stance. "I can't wait another minute to reclaim my life. How long can you wait to start yours with Candy?"

He considered her plea. "I'll be ready in twenty minutes."

Candy's place was lit up with music and laugher—even at three in the morning. Lester had no idea what he would say to Candy, or how he would explain his falling in love with her without ever having gone out on a date with her. He remembered his advice to Sheridan. He had to seize the moment and go after what he wanted. He wouldn't make the same mistake with Candy he'd made with Sheridan. He never truly fought for her. When Sheridan had needed him most, he chose his career over his marriage.

Sheridan stood behind him with a black duffle bag stuffed with clothing over her arm. "Do we ring the bell?" she asked. They'd been standing on the stoop for a lengthy period of time while he gathered his courage and worked out his words.

"The door's open," he told her.

She watched him, allowing him to handle the situation in his own way.

"Maybe we should ring the bell," he said, but didn't move.

Sheridan stepped up and pressed the button that set off a chorus of chimes. "I see why no one rings the bell." She glanced at him, and his appearance made her do a double take. "Are you going to faint?"

He felt lightheaded and woozy. He wiped away the perspiration from his forehead. What had made him think Candy would want him? He was about to make a royal fool of himself. Hadn't he learned anything from trying to win Sheridan back? Candy was beautiful and smart and funny. What would she want with a nerdy doctor who spent all his time in front of a computer screen doing complicated research? He was about to tell Sheridan he'd changed his mind when Candy opened the door.

"Lester?"

Seeing her again made everything clear. His heart burst, happy to be near her. He had a million things to talk to her about, more to share. All the emptiness of the past weeks left in a rush. Without a moments thought, he wrapped his arms around her waist and pulled her across the threshold flush against his body. "Will you marry me?"

"What?" Candy and Sheridan said together.

Lester pressed his lips to Candy's and kissed her, dipping her backwards. She resisted at first, clearly surprised by his brazen actions. Then she softened. Her arms wound around his neck and she opened to his kiss. When he released her, most of the girls stood at the door, watching.

"I'm in love with you, Candy." The kiss made him more confident. He would not leave town without her. He grew surer of his feelings for her. He now understood why he'd lain in bed, unable to sleep because he was thinking about her. This was the magic Sheridan had told him about. "I want you to be my wife."

Tears were in her eyes. "I love you, too. Yes, I'll marry you."

Scott Stoner stormed through the crowd, rudely pushing the girls aside. "What's going on here?"

"Candy and Lester are getting married," one of the girls answered.

His face dropped, and then reddened with anger. "Candy's not marrying anybody. Candy belongs to me." He stepped out on the porch, pulling Candy out of Lester's arms.

"Don't touch her," Lester warned.

"You don't understand how things work around here, Doctor. Do you know who I am? I own this town, and everything in it. Including Candy."

Lester pulled his glare from Scott. "Candy, do you want to go with me?"

She didn't hesitate to answer. "Yes."

"Let's go." He held out his hand for her. As she reached for him, Scott knocked her hand away, calling her every vile name he could think of.

Lester didn't know what came over him. The woman he loved was being threatened. Without thinking, he hit Scott in the jaw, decking him. The girls erupted in applause. Candy wrapped her arms around him, pulling him away. Sheridan stood over Scott, unable to believe what she'd witnessed. As Lester watched Scott falter when he tried to get up, his testosterone soared. He wrapped a possessive arm around Candy's waist. "Get everything you need because you're never coming back here."

CHAPTER 35

Sheridan didn't let her nervousness get in the way as she pleaded her case to Ted and Carolyn. She gave them every detail of the malpractice case, showing them a copy of the arbitration agreement. She even told them how her marriage to Lester had ended because of the lawsuit. She took responsibility for not disclosing the information when she first applied for the partnership. "I'll say it again: I know what I did was wrong, and I'm sorry."

"What do you want from us?" Carolyn asked. After six months of working together, she still couldn't read the woman's nonverbal cues. She could be angry, impressed, or simply bored, Sheridan didn't know.

"I'm here to try to win your vote."

"You still want the partnership?" Ted asked.

She sat up proudly. "I still want the partnership. I've made a mistake, and I'm willing to do whatever is necessary to correct it. You have become my extended family. Duck River is my home. I want to continue working here."

Ted and Carolyn shared a look.

Carolyn spoke first. "I've been very impressed with what you've done here. Except for falling behind schedule, I think you're what this clinic needs—fresh ideas and a good work ethic."

Sheridan bolted out of her seat and hugged the older woman. She quickly returned the embrace, clearly uncomfortable with the emotional display. Sheridan ignored her staunch attitude and kissed her on the cheek. She composed herself and returned to her seat, waiting for Ted's verdict.

"Carolyn's right, and I think we should have stood behind you publicly when the media came down on you. If in the same situation, I probably would have done the same thing. I support you returning to the clinic. You have my vote."

"Having our votes isn't enough," Carolyn pointed out.

"Have you talked to Dr. Larson yet?" Ted asked.

Sheridan shook her head. "I didn't want to talk to him if you two didn't want me here."

"He's going to be harder to convince," Carolyn said.

"I know."

"This clinic means a lot to him," Ted added. "But not everything."

Carolyn blushed. "We heard you two arguing the day you left."

Sheridan couldn't back down now. "I came back for my job." She watched for their reaction. "And for Chase. I love him."

Ted grinned. "I knew it."

"And you didn't tell me?"

"Is my being in love with Chase a problem?"

Sheridan thought she saw a tear in Carolyn's eye. "He needs someone to take care of him."

She smiled. "I want that job, too."

Today Chase would fight for his clinic. Its survival depended on his ability to earn the trust of the residents of Duck River at the monthly City Council meeting. His schedule was so light he'd made an executive decision a week ago to only open the clinic half a day. The clinic would not survive financially if he could not persuade his patients to come back. It had taken a great deal of lobbying to be placed on the agenda so he could address the citizens—his patients—but he hadn't given up until the answer was favorable. He took no chances, stacking the audience with his entire family, his close acquaintances, Ted and Carolyn. He would need all the support he could get.

He dressed conservatively in a black suit with a white shirt and red tie. Sheridan's favorite tie. He wrote out his speech and practiced it in front of his bedroom mirror, making sure his expressions matched the sincerity in his heart.

As he sat in the back of the room, scoping out the location of his supporters, he wondered how Sheridan was fairing. It tore him apart to let her go—from the clinic, and his heart—but she'd given him no choice. If he had known all the facts up front, he would have been better prepared to deal with the town's reaction. He'd handled the situation with her badly because he'd been so surprised by it all.

Over the last few weeks, he'd asked himself hard questions. Would knowing about the lawsuit have kept him from considering her for the partnership? Probably so. Did he have preconceived notions about her when he offered her the temporary position at Duck River Family Medicine? Yes. His physical attraction to her had made him skip over the prudent steps of evaluating a new employee. He should have run a background check on her and found out all he needed to know. Did his love for her blind him to glaring signs he should have seen? Yes, on so many levels.

He ran through his speech as the City Council discussed the schools, drainage problems, and their economic forecast for the next year.

The one question he had asked himself repeatedly was if Sheridan really loved him. He couldn't be certain she hadn't said the words in an attempt to save her job. He'd asked her before what she wanted in life, and she hadn't been able to answer. He'd tried several times to set a mood to tell her he loved her; each attempt failing, and he now wondered if she hadn't sabotaged them purposefully.

He thought back, reliving every minute of their fast-paced courtship. He'd fallen for her the first time he saw her, and he wanted her to feel the same. He'd bulldozed right over her reservations and pushed her into the relationship he wanted. When Lester came into the picture, he pressed hard, not wanting her to have a minute to consider her ex-husband's reconciliation attempts. He set out to conquer her heart, solidifying his place in her life. He'd handled it wrong. He should have taken things slower. Given her time to adjust to a new job and a new home. Maybe then he would have built her trust in him and she wouldn't have kept any secrets from him.

The City Council finished a round of question and answer, signaling it would be his turn to speak next. He straightened his tie and waited his introduction. What happened next threw him off kilter.

Sheridan stepped up to the council table. Gawd, she was beautiful. Chestnut hair floated above her shoulders, begging for his hands' stroking action. Her five foot five frame supported thick curves, classically adorned in a navy suit. The top three buttons of her jacket were open, triggering memories how well her diminutive breasts fit into his palms. Her innocent, experienced eyes surveyed the audience. She cleared her throat and ran her hand over her cute little nose, drawing attention to the tiny mark on her right jaw. She wore the imperfection as a beauty mark.

He felt unrightfully possessive as the men in the audience watched her prepare to make a speech. He hadn't completed his exploration of her mind or body, and yet she was free to find another to delve into the complicated layers that made her who she is. He hadn't met her parents, who were so important to her. He hadn't taken her to the Kentucky Derby; an attempt to impress her by showing off his family's successes. There were areas on her body he hadn't tasted. Parts of her heart he hadn't penetrated.

The only way he'd been able to live through missing her was by concentrating on saving the clinic. Seeing her made him want to run to the front of the auditorium and whisk her away, his captive on a deserted island.

Sheridan reintroduced herself to the audience then launched right into why she had returned to Duck River. "I want to serve this community as your physician," she said assertively. "I have betrayed your trust, and today I'd like to try to get some of it back."

She crushed her note cards in her palm and dropped them on the council table. Chase leaned forward, sending his strength in her direction.

"I was involved in a malpractice lawsuit about a year ago that forced me to give up my practice in Nashville. I assure you I did nothing wrong, but sometimes lawsuits aren't won by proving the accused negligent. Lawsuits in medicine are big business for some attorneys, and meaning well and doing your best aren't enough."

She paused to scan the reaction of the audience. No one had left the auditorium. They were listening intently to what she had to say. They were at least willing to give her a chance to explain herself. In a small town, ruled by a group mentality, this meant a lot.

Sheridan continued. "Dr. Larson took a chance on me, knowing only about my education and work history. I did not disclose to him any information about the lawsuit. For that, I apologize. Please don't judge him by my mistakes. I apologize for not giving *you* all the information you needed to make an informed decision about selecting me for your physician."

She looked around the audience, searching for a reaction, a way to gauge how the citizens felt about her disclosure. Finding nothing, she braved the chilly reception and continued on. "I want to ask you to let my work serve as proof for my skills."

The room remained quiet.

"What I have done has hurt the clinic. It's in jeopardy of closing if you don't bring your business back. Dr. Larson told me when I came here that the citizens of Duck River are proud, and hardworking, and if I wanted to make it here I needed to earn your trust. Today, I'm asking for two things. One, support Dr. Larson the way he has been there for each of you. Don't hold what I did against him. He had no part in it. Secondly, I'm asking for you to give me another chance. If I don't have your support I'll leave Duck River, but with your support I can ask Dr. Larson for my job back."

Silence.

"Thank you."

More silence.

Sheridan turned and thanked the council for allowing her to speak and began to walk out, defeated and shamed.

"Dr. Wexler is one of the best doctor's I've ever worked with." All heads turned. Carolyn stood staunchly in the middle row, openly supporting Sheridan. She wasn't one to display her feelings about anything, so this got the crowd's attention. "Dr. Wexler, it would be a privilege to work with you again."

Sheridan mouthed a silent thank you.

Ted stood up, his youngest son on his hip asleep. "It would be Duck River's loss if you leave." He sat down.

Someone shouted out, "I heard on TV you killed a baby."

Reggie's mother bolted out of her seat. "She helped save my baby!"

Mrs. Harvey, still a little weak, stood with the help of her son-in-law. "I've been sick since my husband passed—rest his soul. After a while, I felt like everyone thought I was makin' up my sickness to get some attention. Dr. Wexler always listened to what I had to say, and she found out what was wrong with me. She saved *my* life. Wherever you go, Dr. Wexler, count me as one of your patients."

Chase tried to read the crowd as people started whispering. People continued to jump up, sharing stories of how Sheridan had helped them. Others rudely challenged her medical skills, relying on television reports for the information they would use to judge her. Sheridan had placed her fate in the citizens of Duck River, when truly she didn't have to suffer the humiliation. She could have approached Chase, persuading him to give her a second chance. Or, she could have moved on to another place where her skills would be appreciated, never looking back at the small town clinic. He had to admire her chutzpah in facing the crowd.

The reverend and Mrs. Marks stood together. "I support the doctor," Mrs. Marks said. Her brief statement carried a lot of weight. If Sheridan was to win the town's respect, she had to have the backing of the church. Several church members applauded Mrs. Marks's show of support.

The crowd swelled with whispers. As the debate escalated, the gavel was banged, bringing the audience to order. Chase almost fell out of his chair with the next turn of events.

Alison stood, and holding Dwayne's hand for moral support, testified on Sheridan's behalf. "Everyone here is persecuting Dr. Wexler because she kept her own confidence. Ask yourself if you've ever had a reason to visit the doctor and wanted him to keep your secret." She glanced down at Dwayne who stood up beside her, still holding her hand. "A little while ago my husband found a lump in my breast."

The crowd mumbled, but settled down quickly, awaiting the rest of the story. Chase sat forward, stunned by her disclosure. He remembered the secretive looks Sheridan and his sister shared, and it all made sense.

Alison continued. "I went to Dr. Wexler, and she held my hand through the entire process. She even went to Nashville with me when I had to have a biopsy."

A biopsy! Chase wanted to run to his sister. He needed to protect her. He watched the emotional bond between Alison and Dwayne, as Dwayne lovingly supported her. Everything had turned out all right with Alison—thanks to Sheridan.

"I asked her to keep my confidence," Alison continued, "and she did. Most of you are probably saying she had to as a physician, but she works with my brother. She could have easily given him information about my condition. She didn't do that." She turned, finding Chase seated at the back of the room. "We would be fools to let her go."

CHAPTER 36

Sheridan had been planning her play to win Chase back for a week. Once the town accepted her as their physician, she'd gone into seclusion at Candy's house, waiting for the right time to clean up her mistakes with Chase. The clinic's appointment book was filling up again with many patients requesting Sheridan as their physician. She'd heard through Alison that he had been asking about her, trying to find out where she was staying. Alison never told.

Sheridan had purchased a designer dress made of slinky fuchsia silk and matching three inch heels for Chase's seduction. She remembered the source of their break up—not showing him her true self—and returned the dress. She discarded the entire notion of seducing him and settled for a more straightforward approach. Beneath Chase's professional persona was a simple country boy who appreciated a good steak more than French cuisine. The way to prove herself to him was by being honest about her feelings.

The day she aimed to win Chase back, she went to Nashville and took care of her business. When everything was as she wanted, she drove to Chase's house. She grabbed what she needed and marched up to his door. She held her head high, looking more confident about her mission than she felt.

Chase was sitting in his darkened living room mindlessly watching television when his doorbell rang. Not expecting anyone, he checked the display on his pager, thinking maybe he'd missed a page about a patient. The screen was blank.

It must be Alison again, he thought, coming to encourage him to reconcile with Sheridan. She'd become Sheridan's champion, using every opportunity to point out how miserable he was without her. He'd decided as he watched her speak at the City Council meeting that he'd made a mistake in ending their relationship. He'd searched for her, but had no idea where she was staying. He thought she'd contact him once the town blessed her return to the clinic, but she hadn't.

Maybe it was Ted. They were having their official vote in the morning about whether or not to make Sheridan a partner. Not being able to contact her, he didn't know if she was still interested in working at the clinic. He flipped on the lights as he made his way to the door.

"Sheridan." He smiled. She stood on his doorstep dressed in faded jeans and a sweatshirt that had seen better days. A blue bandanna covered her hair. He'd pictured their reunion being a little more…sensual. She'd wear a provocative dress and lacy underwear. Her hair would be perfect and her lips painted a seductive red.

"Can I come in?"

"Sure."

He reached for the portable radio she was carrying, but she held firmly. She placed the radio on the floor at her feet and planted her hands on her hips. Her face displayed nervous determination, much like what he had witnessed at the City Council meeting.

She wasted no time. "Dr. Larson, I would like another chance at the Duck River Family Medicine partnership. I'm willing to start another six month trial—the same terms apply."

He crossed his arms over his chest and tried to match her stubborn determination. "I'll consider your offer."

"You've had more than enough time to consider my reemployment. I'll be needing your answer immediately."

He ducked his head back, surprised by her brazenness. He studied her, giving her his most intimidating glare, but she didn't back down. He dropped his hands to his sides. "I accept your terms."

She blinked rapidly. She hadn't expected him to give in so easily. She looked rattled. "Thank you."

"You're welcome."

She watched him, clearly trying to formulate her next move.

"Is there anything else, Dr. Wexler?" If she was finished, he had a lot to say.

"Yes, actually, there is."

He gestured for her to continue. "Please, go on."

"I want to dance with you."

"Dance?" She'd surprised him this time.

"Yes."

He studied her, confused as to where she was going. "Okay. I'll dance with you."

She pressed the PLAY button on her portable radio and Luther Vandross's *A House is not a Home* began to play. She stepped up to him, tentatively holding her arms open. He met her half way, taking her into his embrace. As Luther began to croon, he pulled her closer. She wore no perfume, but smelled sweeter than ever. Her natural scent touched a place inside of him, latching onto his heart. He leaned into her, pressing his body against hers, nuzzling his nose in the crook of her neck. She held him tight around the waist, her hands stroking his back.

"You asked me when we went riding what I wanted from you. I couldn't answer then, but I can now. I've thought about this every day since we broke apart." She pulled back to look into his eyes. "I want to make your house a home."

Chase stopped swaying to the music. He had wanted to hear these words from Sheridan for months.

"If I can't have you, nothing else matters," she went on, emotion making her voice quiver. "I'd rather be a stay-at-home wife than lose you. Practicing medicine is important to me, but not as important as having you love me."

"I have been so unhappy since you left." He cupped her face in his hands. "I love you."

She choked back a sob. "Do you believe me when I say I love you? That being with you is the most important thing to me?"

"I want to, but I think you still have some things to work out. When you come to me, I want you to be sure I'm truly what you want. I couldn't stand it if you realized this life isn't for you and you walked away."

"It won't happen. I've taken time to think. I've cleared up things with Lester." She pressed her face against his chest, clinging to him. "I want to be your partner at the clinic, and in your life. Forever."

"I want those things, too, but I pushed too hard before. Everything happened so fast. You just came into my life and took control of my heart. I want to take things slower this time around. I want you to be *sure* what I offer is good enough for you."

She stepped back, watching him incredulously. "You asked me. Now I'm asking you. What do you want from me, Chase?"

"I want to marry you."

Shock and relief washed over. A slow smile spread across her face. "But you have to be sure I know what I want?"

"Yes." He nodded. "Before I ask you to marry me, I want to know it's what you really want for the rest of your life."

"I love you. I want to be with you for the rest of my life...I can prove it to you."

He tilted his head in question. Maybe their reunion would start to be the norm now. He waited for her to start peeling off her clothes so she could seduce him. Instead, she stepped over to the window and pulled back the curtain.

"Come take a look."

He took slow steps to the window, suspicious about her blazing smile. He bent down, ducking his head so he could see outside. "What am I looking for?"

She peered out, and not seeing what she was looking for, she led him outside on the porch. "There."

Chase followed the direction of her finger to find a U-Haul truck parked in his driveway.

"Does this make it clear enough?" She dangled the keys in front of his face.

Laughing, he pulled her into his arms for a reconciliation kiss that would rock her world.

CHAPTER 37

Two Years Later

Nashville

Sheridan doubled over, pushing as hard as she could. Her mother sat on the bed, wiping away the perspiration from her eyes, and offering words of encouragement. The contraction passed, and Sheridan dropped back on the bed.

"Ice chips, please," she panted.

"Just a few," the nurse called out.

Sheridan's mother complied.

"Another contraction is coming," Sheridan gritted out. Her mother jumped into action, supporting her shoulders. She braced for another painful wave.

"I see the head!" Chase exclaimed.

Her mother laughed. "He's so excited! Nurse, you better have another doctor on standby for this delivery."

"I can handle it," Chase said from his place at the foot of the bed. He placed his hands on Sheridan's knees, lovingly, winking at her. "This push should do it, Sheridan."

She felt the tightening of her stomach muscles and gritted her teeth.

"Push!" Chase boomed. "Push!"

Everyone in the room gathered around, ready to take action. A chorus of "Push! Push!" encouraged her to bear down. She screamed. She pushed. She felt an unbearable pressure relieved.

Her mother's mouth fell open. The room became quiet. The nurse midwife moved in shoulder-to-shoulder with Chase.

Her baby cried.

"My baby," Sheridan sobbed.

"My grandbaby." Her mother hugged her, crying.

Chase stood and brought their baby to her. He settled next to her in the bed, wrapping his arms around them both. He was crying.

Sheridan wiped away his tears, then her own.

Chase kissed her forehead, bringing her closer. "Thank you for my son."

ABOUT THE AUTHOR

Kimberley White is a multi-published romance author. A Detroit native, she uses her nursing experience to address controversial topics in an entertaining, and informative manner. Please send your letters to: kwhite_writer @ hotmail.com

P.O. Box 672
Novi, MI 48376

Excerpt from

INTENTIONAL MISTAKES

BY

MICHELE SUDLER

Release Date: April 2005

CHAPTER 1

"Darn! Every time I walk past that table this happens," Tia said to herself as she rubbed the outside of her wounded foot, her already bad mood darkened.

She suspiciously eyed the old end table. It was in the wrong spot in the living room. It had been since she moved in and tried to decorate her new townhouse herself, but she didn't know where else to put it. Still, instead of half blocking the walkway by the steps, she needed to find a nice, cozy corner for it. It was her only prize project from shop class. Sure, one leg was slightly longer than the other, it had started to fade, and was a safety hazard, but she couldn't part with it. Besides, she seemed to be the only one that the table hurt.

Slowly, she began to fall into her morning routine: took a shower, dressed, curled and styled her hair then carefully applied her makeup. Tia made a bowl of cereal for her son, Kevin, who moved slower than she did in yet another attempt to delay the start of his school day. Since being placed in a five-minute time-out along with two classmates by his new teacher for throwing stones at the preschool center, his enthusiasm for school had drastically changed.

"Mom, I sink I sick," Kevin said, holding his forehead.

"You're not sick," she quickly replied trying to hide her smile. She knew it was coming.

"But, I got a feber."

"No, you don't. Besides, if you're sick, you can't stay with Mommom and Poppop tonight."

Kevin sat silently with a look on his face that told her he was carefully weighing his options. "Mom, do I got stool tomorrow?"

"No."

"I can tay with Mommom and Poppop afther stool?"

"Yes, you're going there right after school. Please eat your cereal, baby." She sighed and moved the bowl closer to him. "Okay. Mom, will you pick me up from stool?"

"Don't I always pick you up from school?"

"Yes."

"Okay, then."

"Mom, in a fuew minutes?"

"Kevin, I'll pick you up at five o'clock like I always do. Now, eat!"

This was pretty much their normal morning routine. After ten more minutes and a hundred more questions, Tia finally had him dressed and ready to start his day. But, she wasn't prepared to start hers. Thanks to the seven phone calls she had received during the night before finally turning off the ringer and the constant pounding on the front door, she'd hardly slept a wink all night. Now, with a monster headache and a hurt big toe, she was expected to make her way out the front door and have a cheerful workday. It wasn't likely to happen, not with the mood she was in.

It had only been six months since she had started her new job at the Teen Intervention & Community Center, but she loved it already. Every night when she left work, she felt as if she had made a difference in someone's life. It wasn't the perfect job, and it hardly paid a decent salary, but it gave her a lot of pleasure.

Fresh out of college with a BA in Psychology, Tia jumped at the chance to get her feet wet with some real life work experiences. She planned to go back and get her doctorate eventually and dreamed of having her own office. However, being a single mother, she decided it was time to make some money. Her parents supported her unconditionally, but she couldn't live with Mom and Dad forever.

With that in mind, after graduation, she used the money her parents gave her as a graduation gift to put a down payment on the small three-bedroom townhouse she'd had her eye on for a couple of months. Her brothers and sisters gave her enough used furniture to make her home comfortable, and she used the last of her meager savings to obtain the rest of her belongings.

Her parents had always been her backbone. Even when she popped up pregnant at nineteen, they insisted that she continue with her plans to go to college. And that's what they truly wanted for her, so that was what she did. Instead of going away, she enrolled at the local university. For her parents as well as her and her son, Tia had to succeed, and she would. It was important for them to be proud of her. Her home was her second step to independence. The job was her first, and she was thankful for it.

Although she hadn't been assigned any hard cases, a lot of the young women that came into the center saw her as a sort of confidante. Maybe it was because she was a lot closer to their age than some of the other counselors, or maybe it was her face.

She was always being told what a happy person she seemed to be.

Her supervisors loved her positive attitude, and they felt that she was a good example for some of the younger women. They saw her as a single young mother who took a negative situation and turned it into a positive lifestyle. The other counselors had no problems using her as a real-life example for their clients. If only they knew about the negative situation she hadn't turned around. She had so many regrets. Tia often wished that she could turn back the hands of time.

"Hey, girl, why the sad look?"

Tia automatically put a smile on her face as her best friend, Denise, who also worked at the center, walked into her office. This girl's life was always in some kind of chaos, Tia thought, according to Denise anyway. But all Tia could see when she looked at her friend was a beautiful, caramel-colored woman, who men constantly fawned over. She was tall, taller than most women at 6'1". Playing basketball and working out four days a week kept her in shape and looking like a goddess. But the best thing about Denise was that she didn't know she looked that good. She never talked about her looks, wasn't conceited, or even vain. She was just Denise, and that made her an even better person in Tia's eyes.

"Girl, I had another rough night," Tia said, unable to stop

the yawn that forced its way out of her mouth.

"What was it?" Denise held up one hand to stop Tia from speaking. "No, don't tell me. Adam again, right?" Denise stood in the doorway leaning to one side with her hands crossed in front of her. She appeared to be a no-nonsense kind of girl. But Tia knew that was her coverup. Deep inside, she was sensitive just like every other woman.

"Yeah, well, I guess. I didn't answer the phone or the door so I can't be totally sure." Tia leaned back in her chair, closed her eyes and let her breath out in one long stress-filled release.

"Well, I'm sure," Denise replied as she stepped away from the door and walked into the office. "Why don't you just call the cops on that creep? This has been going on for weeks now. If it's not him; then it's her. How much more of this can you take?" Denise's voice began to rise.

"Why are you getting loud with me?" Tia asked.

"I'm not getting loud, but I am getting mad."

"Why?" Tia questioned with a slight hunch of her shoulders.

She was just tired, too tired to be mad or to waste unnecessary energy.

"Exactly. Why aren't you doing something about this fool? Call the cops or something. Call your brothers and cousins. God knows there are enough of them."

"Because I don't want anybody to get into trouble because of me, and I can handle it myself."

"Can you?" she said, voice laced with sarcasm.

"Yes, I can." Tia snapped. "And I don't want to talk about it anymore."

"I'm not trying to argue with you, Tia, but…"

The receptionist from the front desk buzzed in startling both women.

"Tia, your nine o'clock appointment is here, and a bouquet of roses just arrived for you. Do you want them?" she asked. "They're from him again," she drawled.

"No, please put them in the trash for me, Carmen." Tia sighed, put her elbows on the desk and lowered her head.

"That's the third delivery this week. It's a good thing today is Friday." Denise laughed. "Anyway, we both need to lighten up our moods. I'm tired of being depressed. How about we go out after work? We could meet up around seven o'clock and get something to eat first, my treat. Hey, we could go to your cousin's new club. I haven't been there yet." A small smile formed at the corners of her mouth. The wheels in Denise's head were already turning.

"Would this by any chance be an excuse for you to get up close and personal with Chauncey, again? I know you aren't over him." Tia looked at her friend and waited for confirmation.

"Well, I figure I might as well kill two birds with one stone. I can get you out of this bad mood and get to see him, too." She looked at Tia. "And I am over him," she added, seeing the non-belief on Tia's face.

After giving it a moment's thought, Tia decided she deserved to relax a little, and she hadn't seen Chauncey in weeks. He was one of the few people who could put a smile on her face. She needed that. And, Denise was still in love with him no matter what she said.

"All right," Tia said hastily, "meet me at my place at seven o'clock. I'll see you then."

"See ya."

After a long day at work, the last thing Tia felt like doing was clubbing. She had to call the police on the abusive spouse of one of her clients after the woman came to her meeting with two black eyes and a busted lip. The new girlfriend of one of another client's husband followed the woman to the building. The two women began to fight all because the wife was taking her own husband—her own babies' daddy—to court for child support. It took three people to break the fight up. Then she had to straighten up her office. *You never know what might happen up in this place,* she thought to herself as she crawled around on her knees trying to account for all of her already limited office supplies.

All Tia really wanted to do was get into a tub of extra hot water and some Olay bubble bath. But she had given Denise her word, and unlike some people, that meant something to her. So, she dutifully picked up her son, took him to her parent's house, went home, bathed, took a very quick nap and then slowly dressed to go out.

Although Tia lacked enthusiasm about being out, it felt good to hang out with her friend again. She and Denise had decided to get something to eat at the club instead of wasting time waiting on someone to take their order. Friday nights at the local restaurants were always a busy time. And neither of them wanted to wait outside for an hour only to finally get inside and have to wait another forty-five minutes before actually getting their food.

Standing in front of the club, Tia started to get an excited and proud feeling at what her cousin had been able to accomplish.

As kids, who would have ever thought that Chauncey Avery would grow up and achieve so much. Most people probably still didn't believe that he was behind the idea and management of this highly successful night club. They would be shocked to find out that his dream of owning the nightclub began years before.

Tia and Chauncey came from a very large family. Their fathers were brothers. There were only five kids in all, but each of the siblings had married and had at least eight children.

Tia's parents had the least at eight, and she was next to the youngest. Chauncey's parents had eleven kids, and he was sixth.

Being one of the middle kids to older parents often left him lost in the crowd. A lot of the time he was either alone or left to the influence of his older brothers.

She remembered James and Timothy and how she and most of her other cousins were afraid of them. They were crazy and mean. With those two as his mentors, Chauncey couldn't have turned out any way but bad. Things had been hard for her growing up in such a large family, and she imagined that things were much harder for him because her family had at least managed to get out of the project housing unit they were born into on the lower eastside of Chicago. It was true that eventually the whole family had managed to move from the poorest section of the city into nice middle-class communities, but it took Chauncey's family much longer than the others.

By the time they were "better-off," he had already been involved in the gangs and had even been to prison twice. He and Tia had always been close, but to a lot of the family, he would always be the no-good, black sheep even though his brothers were worse than he was. They at least made enough money illegally to send this one or that one to college or to pay bills for their sisters, nieces, and nephews. Chauncey just kept getting caught, and then stayed away all together when he realized he wasn't cut out to be a criminal. She was glad the family could see what he had become and that he hadn't ended up dead like Timothy or in jail for life like James.

"Penny for your thoughts, beautiful."

Tia looked up into the eyes of one of the most handsome men she had ever seen, but before she could get "Hi" out of her mouth, a woman grabbed the man's arm and pulled him to her side.

Tia stood at the curb watching the scene unfold before her. Tia heard the woman cursing him loudly. She was so loud and embarrassing that he just walked to his car and nearly pulled off without her.

"Is it going to be one of those nights?" she asked Denise as they broke into laughter. They watched the girl in amazement trying to shut the car door as it sped off.

"Come on, let's get in here before all of the good tables are taken," Denise said. "If you weren't standing there in deep thought, all cute in that little hottie shirt and tight jeans, none of this would have happened."

"What's wrong with my shirt?" Tia asked looking down at herself. She pulled at the bottom of the shirt so that it covered her bellybutton, but it just raised back up when she put her arms to her side. "See, now, you've made me all self-conscious."

"Well, I'm sorry. You look good. Stop. Just leave the shirt alone. Besides, the little jacket works well with it. A lot of guys are going to be on you tonight. And your jeans are fine, too. They don't leave anything to the imagination." Tia stopped walking and ran her hands over her backside. Denise smiled, "I'm just kidding. Come on."

At the door, the security guard tried to give her a hard time because she had left her ID at home by mistake. She told him that she was related to the owner, but he still wouldn't let her in until Chauncey's younger brother, Greg, who was a bartender, walked in and said she was okay. Even though the guard was good-looking, she didn't like the looks that he was giving her or Denise for that matter. The nerve of some men. As if he had a chance of getting with either of them. That wasn't what she was there for anyway. A man was the last thing she needed right now. It was the last thing she wanted.

Walking through the front door, past a room usually reserved for coat checks but was presently being used as a photo room, Tia and Denise decided to have their picture taken in front of a backdrop of the city skyline. From there they walked down a hallway through the thongs of people until the hall opened up into a large open area. On each side, bars and lounges lined the outer walls. Small tables formed a inner circle the dance floor.

Looking up, they could see three crowded floors of people

already enjoying their evening. Beautiful lights blinked and swirled around creating rhythmic patterns on the dance floor. The floor was littered with people bumping and grinding, moving and grooving to the beat.

The club was very impressive. The size made it hardly possible to become overcrowded, which made you feel comfortable, not cramped. Everyone was having a good time. The atmosphere was relaxing, and the music was a mixture of R & B and hip-hop.

Every once and a while, a slow song or two was played. She glanced all around, but didn't see Chauncey anywhere.

Denise was her usual chatty self, but Tia was only half listening. Denise talked about her sister having to move in with her because her husband had caught her cheating and put her out.

The biggest complaint from Denise was her sister not being able to control her kids.

Tia was distracted. For some reason she kept getting this prickly feeling on the back of her neck, and the hairs were standing straight up. Chills actually went up and down her spine. Funny, that had only happened once before, and it was so long ago that it wasn't even worth thinking about. At least, she didn't want to think about it.

She and Denise danced a bit, ate a bit, and were about to dance again with two fine brothers—twin brothers. Tia was halfway out of her seat when the strange prickly sensation happened again. She turned to tell Denise about it and saw that her friend had stopped dead in her tracks. Denise's mouth was opened wide enough for an eighteen-wheeler to back right into it.

Then, all of the sudden, Denise's expression changed completely to one of absolute detestation. Tia wondered and followed her stare. She figured she should have known what would turn the usual good-natured Denise hard as stone.

Across the room from them was her cousin, Chauncey. He looked very attractive in his white linen pants and white short-sleeved shirt with a brown belt and brown Stacey Adams sandals to accent the set. On his arm was Keisha Talbert. Keisha Talbert was Denise's cousin, her first cousin, and they couldn't stand each other. Everybody knew this including Chauncey. Keisha saw Denise and made her way over toward her; the evil smile grew bigger with each step.

Chauncey was enjoying his success, greeting his patrons. He only wished that this darn girl would stop clinging to him like he was her lifeline. He didn't even really like her. She was a pest. After today, he would tell her straight out that he didn't want her as anything but a friend. He was sure he had already told her that before, but she was obviously hard of hearing. He would have to be a little tougher with his words.

She drug him across the dance floor, trying to show off as usual. To hear her tell it, she was the first lady of the night club, and she had a lot of others thinking so, too. He never understood why people were so gullible. But he had made the mistake of never setting the record straight. That was something that he would make sure he rectified, and quickly.

They finally stopped, and he came face to face with Denise Talbert, the only woman he had ever loved. He thought that with time he would get over her, but just looking into her eyes made him realize what a fool he had been to think so. It had only been three months since she had broken up with him, due to a misunderstanding, again caused by the crazy woman on his arm. It was just another reason for him to hate Keisha, and another reason to kick himself in the behind for not having straighten the whole mess out from the beginning.

If it were possible, he had to admit that Denise was more beautiful then the last time he had seen her. *God, how he had missed her.* He should have gone back to her on bended knee and begged for her forgiveness. But pride, male pride, had forced him to stand his ground.

Chauncey looked into Denise's eyes. He was so glad to see her that he almost missed that expression on her face. It took him a minute to realize that she was mad about something. When he realized Denise thought he was with Keisha, he unhooked his arm from hers so fast that Keisha took a step forward in order not to lose her balance. Unconsciously, he stepped to Denise.

"Don't you dare touch me," she drudged out through clenched teeth.

"It's good to see you again, Denise," Chauncey replied eagerly.

"I didn't think that you saw me at all, not with this trick hanging all over you." Denise was angry, and she was ready for whatever Keisha wanted to happen. One thing she knew how to do was fight. She wasn't scared to fight for what she considered hers, and she wouldn't be disrespected by anyone. Even though they hadn't spoken in three months, she wasn't done with Mr. Chauncey Avery, and he was definitely still hers.

Keisha looked at her. "I'm not going to be too many of those, but since you're family, I'll let that one slide."

"Whatever. Keisha, you're just as slimy as you've always been. I'm not at all surprised, but I thought that Chauncey had better taste."

"Denise, baby, it's not what you think. Keisha and I are just friends." Chauncey stepped between the two ladies and tried to explain.

"I can't tell," Denise said turning to him.

"Keisha, please go to the bar. I'd like to talk to Denise in private." Chauncey was suddenly exhausted. All of the work he did on a daily basis trying to run a successful, deceit, and legal establishment was nothing compared to refereeing two women about to go at it.

"You didn't want me to leave last night," Keisha replied in a desperate, last minute retaliation bid at being dismissed.

"What's that supposed to mean?" Denise asked her retreating back.

"Nothing, baby," Chauncey answered, turning her to face him.

"She's just trying to piss you off. Don't listen to that crazy girl."

Denise just snapped her eyes at him and stalked off toward the dance floor.

Tia finally got a chance to get her cousin's attention.

"Hey there, big guy," she said in reference to his 6'5" frame.

Chauncey followed her voice. "Oh, my God! Is that you, Tia Avery? Lord, you sure are a sight for sore eyes." He scooped her up from the floor and finished with a big bear hug. Tia felt like crying. She hadn't realized how much she had missed him.

The realization made her hold on a little longer than necessary.

"I see you're still getting yourself in the middle of things," she said laughingly as he placed her back on the floor.

"No, not this time. Keisha is trying really hard, but I still love Denise. She just isn't trying to hear me out."

"Well, I don't understand why you even let Keisha hang all over you like that. You know the type of person she is and what she's up to. It's as plain as day. Besides, you know Denise can't stand her. How can you say you love Denise then turn around and allow Keisha to act the way she does?"

Chauncey looked at her puzzled, unable to produce a valid answer to her question. Looking across the dance floor, he could see Denise dancing with one of the twins and hurt registered all over his face. Tia felt sorry for him.

"She wanted to come here tonight. I think she wanted to see you." Her hand fell on his arm.

"Well, Keisha messed that up, didn't she?" Chauncey sat down at their table defeated.

"Don't give up so fast. What happened to that fighter I used to look up to?"

"It just hurts, you know." He wiped his hand down his face and looked at her.

"You know I do. I'm so proud of you, though; look at this place." Using her hand, Tia gestured around her. "You fought so hard to get it together. Fight for Denise."

"Look. I have to get back upstairs for a minute. I need to take care of a couple of things, but don't leave before I return and don't let her leave either." Turning to his brother, he gave him the signal for all of their drinks to be on the house then walked upstairs.

Two and a half hours later, Tia was really enjoying herself.

She had seen a lot of people that she had grown up with and even a few family members. After she calmed Denise down, Denise began to relax again and socialize with some old friends, too. Around midnight, Tia's lack of sleep quickly caught up with her. She hoped that Chauncey would make his way back soon. She had already taken in her quota of drinks and was too tired to dance.

Even though they had taken a cab, she wanted to be in control of herself. She sat and watched Denise dance and occasionally chatted with a man who would come over to ask her about herself.

The tingling feeling came back, this time stronger than before. She felt hot air on her ear. Tia rubbed her neck.

"You are still the most beautiful woman in the world." The words were spoken into her ear on a whisper.

She froze. Tia would have known that voice anywhere, but she couldn't believe that he was there. Turning her widened eyes on Denise, who had just come back to sit down and was borderline drunk, she saw that her friend had a big goofy smile on her face.

And Tia knew that it was true. Jeffery Daniels. She couldn't believe it as he walked around and gave her a hug and kiss on the cheek. She stopped breathing. Her palms were wet. Her heart beat so fast in her chest that she was sure he could see it through her shirt.

She almost wanted to put her head down on the table, cover her face, and make herself disappear. How could her wildest dreams and worst nightmare be coming true? She pulled herself together and hugged him. Last thing she wanted was for him to see how much of an affect he still had on her. She was a little surprised herself.

"What…what are you doing here?" she asked.

"I've been in town for a couple of weeks now. Hi, Denise."

He watched her for a second. "Are you okay?" he asked, lifting an eyebrow.

"Yeah, no thanks to that best friend of yours."

He and Tia looked at each other. She couldn't take her eyes off him. "Well, when are you going back?" she asked suddenly wishing she had something to drink.

"I'm here for good. Chauncey asked me to come back and manage the place for him. I had nothing keeping me in Nevada, so here I am." Jeff moved the chairs and sat in the one closet to Tia. He put his elbows on the table, leaned on his hands and starred at her.

"What about your wife? That should have kept you there," she said with a little attitude.

"Whoa…let's not go there. I'm not married," he stated with his hands up as he leaned back in the chair. "Tia, I never got married. I couldn't go through with it, and luckily for me, I didn't. The baby wasn't even mine. She tried to trap me."

"And because it wasn't your child, everything's okay. You

should have never gone there in the first place."

"Tia, look, I've been watching you all night, afraid to come over here because this is what I thought I would have to go through. It's been five years. It's time to put it in the past.

I made a mistake. I apologize. I've grown up. I still think about you and what we had." Jeff watched her for some reaction, but got none.

"Hey, finally made your way over here. I was wondering how long it would take you," Chauncey said as he walked up and placed his hand on Jeff's shoulder. "Look, let's go up into the VIP section, things are slowing down here and Greg," he gestured to his brother, "can handle it."

"No. We're out of here. I don't want to spend any time alone with you, Chauncey Avery." Denise's words were slurred, and she got louder with each drunken syllable.

"Yeah, guys, sorry," Tia added. "We really should go. Could you get someone to call us a cab?"

"No," Jeff and Chauncey said together.

"We'll take you home," Jeff explained. "It's not safe."

"Besides," Chauncey finished, "I'll get you there faster."

"Well, if Denise doesn't mind…"

"Of course, I mind, but let's go," Denise agreed.

"All right, then, let's go."

2005 Publication Schedule

January

A Heart's Awakening Veronica Parker $9.95 1-58571-143-8	Falling Natalie Dunbar $9.95 1-58571-121-7

February

Echoes of Yesterday Beverly Clark $9.95 1-58571-131-4	A Love of Her Own Cheris F. Hodges $9.95 1-58571-136-5	Higher Ground Leah Latimer $19.95 1-58571-157-8

March

Misconceptions Pamela Leigh Starr $9.95 1-58571-117-9	I'll Paint a Sun A.J. Garrotto $9.95 1-58571-165-9	Peace Be Still Colette Haywood $12.95 1-58571-129-2

April

Intentional Mistakes Michele Sudler $9.95 1-58571-152-7	Conquering Dr. Wexler's Heart Kimberley White $9.95 1-58571-126-8	Song in the Park Martin Brant $15.95 1-58571-125-X

May

The Color Line Lizette Carter $9.95 1-58571-163-2	Unconditional A.C. Arthur $9.95 1-58571-142-X	Last Train to Memphis Elsa Cook $12.95 1-58571-146-2

June

Angel's Paradise Janice Angelique $9.95 1-58571-107-1	Suddenly You Crystal Hubbard $9.95 1-58571-158-6	Matters of Life and Death Lesego Malepe, Ph.D. $15.95 1-58571-124-1

2005 Publication Schedule (continued)

July

Pleasures All Mine
Belinda O. Steward
$9.95
1-58571-112-8

Wild Ravens
Altonya Washington
$9.95
1-58571-164-0

Class Reunion
Irma Jenkins/John Brown
$12.95
1-58571-123-3

August

Path of Thorns
Annetta P. Lee
$9.95
1-58571-145-4

Timeless Devotion
Bella McFarland
$9.95
1-58571-148-9

Life Is Never As It Seems
June Michael
$12.95
1-58571-153-5

September

Beyond the Rapture
Beverly Clark
$9.95
1-58571-131-4

Blood Lust
J. M. Jeffries
$9.95
1-58571-138-1

Rough on Rats and Tough on Cats
Chris Parker
$12.95
1-58571-154-3

October

A Will to Love
Angie Daniels
$9.95
1-58571-141-1

Taken by You
Dorothy Elizabeth Love
$9.95
1-58571-162-4

Soul Eyes
Wayne L. Wilson
$12.95
1-58571-147-0

November

A Drummer's Beat to Mend
Kay Swanson
$9.95

Sweet Reprecussions
Kimberley White
$9.95
1-58571-159-4

Red Polka Dot in a Worldof Plaid
Varian Johnson
$12.95
1-58571-140-3

December

Hand in Glove
Andrea Jackson
$9.95
1-58571-166-7

Blaze
Barbara Keaton
$9.95

Across
Carol Payne
$12.95
1-58571-149-7

Other Genesis Press, Inc. Titles

Acquisitions	Kimberley White	$8.95
A Dangerous Deception	J.M. Jeffries	$8.95
A Dangerous Love	J.M. Jeffries	$8.95
A Dangerous Obsession	J.M. Jeffries	$8.95
After the Vows (Summer Anthology)	Leslie Esdaile T.T. Henderson Jacqueline Thomas	$10.95
Again My Love	Kayla Perrin	$10.95
Against the Wind	Gwynne Forster	$8.95
A Lark on the Wing	Phyliss Hamilton	$8.95
A Lighter Shade of Brown	Vicki Andrews	$8.95
All I Ask	Barbara Keaton	$8.95
A Love to Cherish	Beverly Clark	$8.95
Ambrosia	T.T. Henderson	$8.95
And Then Came You	Dorothy Elizabeth Love	$8.95
Angel's Paradise	Janice Angelique	$8.95
A Risk of Rain	Dar Tomlinson	$8.95
At Last	Lisa G. Riley	$8.95
Best of Friends	Natalie Dunbar	$8.95
Bound by Love	Beverly Clark	$8.95
Breeze	Robin Hampton Allen	$10.95
Brown Sugar Diaries & Other Sexy Tales	Delores Bundy & Cole Riley	$10.95
By Design	Barbara Keaton	$8.95
Cajun Heat	Charlene Berry	$8.95
Careless Whispers	Rochelle Alers	$8.95
Caught in a Trap	Andre Michelle	$8.95
Chances	Pamela Leigh Starr	$8.95
Dark Embrace	Crystal Wilson Harris	$8.95
Dark Storm Rising	Chinelu Moore	$10.95
Designer Passion	Dar Tomlinson	$8.95
Ebony Butterfly II	Delilah Dawson	$14.95

Erotic Anthology	Assorted	$8.95
Eve's Prescription	Edwina Martin Arnold	$8.95
Everlastin' Love	Gay G. Gunn	$8.95
Fate	Pamela Leigh Starr	$8.95
Forbidden Quest	Dar Tomlinson	$10.95
Fragment in the Sand	Annetta P. Lee	$8.95
From the Ashes	Kathleen Suzanne Jeanne Sumerix	$8.95
Gentle Yearning	Rochelle Alers	$10.95
Glory of Love	Sinclair LeBeau	$10.95
Hart & Soul	Angie Daniels	$8.95
Heartbeat	Stephanie Bedwell-Grime	$8.95
I'll Be Your Shelter	Giselle Carmichael	$8.95
Illusions	Pamela Leigh Starr	$8.95
Indiscretions	Donna Hill	$8.95
Interlude	Donna Hill	$8.95
Intimate Intentions	Angie Daniels	$8.95
Just an Affair	Eugenia O'Neal	$8.95
Kiss or Keep	Debra Phillips	$8.95
Love Always	Mildred E. Riley	$10.95
Love Unveiled	Gloria Greene	$10.95
Love's Deception	Charlene Berry	$10.95
Mae's Promise	Melody Walcott	$8.95
Meant to Be	Jeanne Sumerix	$8.95
Midnight Clear (Anthology)	Leslie Esdaile Gwynne Forster Carmen Green Monica Jackson	$10.95
Midnight Magic	Gwynne Forster	$8.95
Midnight Peril	Vicki Andrews	$10.95
My Buffalo Soldier	Barbara B. K. Reeves	$8.95
Naked Soul	Gwynne Forster	$8.95
No Regrets	Mildred E. Riley	$8.95
Nowhere to Run	Gay G. Gunn	$10.95

Object of His Desire	A. C. Arthur	$8.95
One Day at a Time	Bella McFarland	$8.95
Passion	T.T. Henderson	$10.95
Past Promises	Jahmel West	$8.95
Path of Fire	T.T. Henderson	$8.95
Picture Perfect	Reon Carter	$8.95
Pride & Joi	Gay G. Gunn	$8.95
Quiet Storm	Donna Hill	$8.95
Reckless Surrender	Rochelle Alers	$8.95
Rendezvous with Fate	Jeanne Sumerix	$8.95
Revelations	Cheris F. Hodges	$8.95
Rivers of the Soul	Leslie Esdaile	$8.95
Rooms of the Heart	Donna Hill	$8.95
Shades of Brown	Denise Becker	$8.95
Shades of Desire	Monica White	$8.95
Sin	Crystal Rhodes	$8.95
So Amazing	Sinclair LeBeau	$8.95
Somebody's Someone	Sinclair LeBeau	$8.95
Someone to Love	Alicia Wiggins	$8.95
Soul to Soul	Donna Hill	$8.95
Still Waters Run Deep	Leslie Esdaile	$8.95
Subtle Secrets	Wanda Y. Thomas	$8.95
Sweet Tomorrows	Kimberly White	$8.95
The Color of Trouble	Dyanne Davis	$8.95
The Price of Love	Sinclair LeBeau	$8.95
The Reluctant Captive	Joyce Jackson	$8.95
The Missing Link	Charlyne Dickerson	$8.95
Three Wishes	Seressia Glass	$8.95
Tomorrow's Promise	Leslie Esdaile	$8.95
Truly Inseperable	Wanda Y. Thomas	$8.95
Twist of Fate	Beverly Clark	$8.95
Unbreak My Heart	Dar Tomlinson	$8.95
Unconditional Love	Alicia Wiggins	$8.95
When Dreams A Float	Dorothy Elizabeth Love	$8.95

Whispers in the Night	Dorothy Elizabeth Love	$8.95
Whispers in the Sand	LaFlorya Gauthier	$10.95
Yesterday is Gone	Beverly Clark	$8.95
Yesterday's Dreams, Tomorrow's Promises	Reon Laudat	$8.95
Your Precious Love	Sinclair LeBeau	$8.95

Order Form

Mail to: Genesis Press, Inc.

P.O. Box 101
Columbus, MS 39703

Name ____________________
Address ____________________
City/State ____________________ Zip ____________
Telephone ____________________

Ship to (if different from above)
Name ____________________
Address ____________________
City/State ____________________ Zip ____________
Telephone ____________________

Credit Card Information
Credit Card # ____________________ ☐ Visa ☐ Mastercard
Expiration Date (mm/yy) ____________ ☐ AmEx ☐ Discover

Qty.	Author	Title	Price	Total

Use this order form, or call 1-888-INDIGO-1

Total for books ____________
Shipping and handling:
$5 first two books,
$1 each additional book ____________
Total S & H ____________
Total amount enclosed ____________

Mississippi residents add 7% sales tax

Visit www.genesis-press.com for latest releases and excerpts.